APPLEGA

ROGER SHAW

ISBN: 9798650582045

Typesetting and cover design by Socciones Editoria Digitale
www.socciones.co.uk

Chapter One

He liked to approach the statue in the same way, a ritual that never varied. Pull the front door shut; turn left out of the cottage and stroll down the Avenue – his arrival at the hallowed place couldn't be rushed – then another left turn into the short tree-lined path leading to the Memorial Park. Approaching from this direction allowed the bronze statue to come slowly into view, and with every step, his sense of anticipation increased.

First, the man with his arms stretched upwards, his back arched in a perfect curve. The woman, her gown trailing graciously behind, her arm outstretched to meet his, her eyes gazing admiringly into his. The two figures caught in perfect harmony with the music, as they swept majestically across the imaginary dance floor. If there was perfection in this world, the statue of the Dancing Couple was surely it.

Reaching the end of the path, he paused to allow a brief smile of anticipation to flick across his lips. No matter how many times he stood on this spot, the prospect of gazing on the dancing couple, still made the hairs on the back of his neck stand up - still gave him a thrill.

As he cleared the hedge and caught sight of the statue, the figures appeared to be bathed in an unfamiliar pinkish hue. Was it a trick of the light, or something more serious? Hurrying to get closer, he realised with mounting horror it wasn't pink, but red. The statue was covered in bright red paint, flowing across the shoulders of the man, down his back and onto the woman's gown. Their legs and shoes glowed red as the paint continued its path across the base before morphing into the surrounding grass, leaving in its wake a repulsive red gash.

With his heart pounding and a cry of anguish, he raced to the statue and began scrubbing the surface frantically with his sleeve. Rubbing and scratching at the paint until his arms were sore with the effort and the realisation his efforts were having no effect. The paint was bone dry and it would take more than his feeble efforts.

Stepping back slowly and staring in horror at the desecration of his beloved statue, he slumped to his knees, with Bix his faithful border terrier resting on his lap.

For several moments, he was unable to move, overcome with anger, rage, and despair, but sanity gradually returned, as other feelings of revenge and retribution took their place. Dragging himself upright and feeling slightly embarrassed, he turned to see if there were any witnesses to his very public display of emotion. To his relief, the only other occupants in the Memorial Park on this bright sunny morning were a flock of starlings, more interested in the delicious morsels scattered by a kindly bird lover, than the antics of a semi-retired college lecturer.

Calling Bix his faithful companion, he set off for the High Street and the police station. This act of vandalism had to be reported and action taken immediately to apprehend the culprit. Police Constable Nigel Smith would have to be galvanised into greater activity than he normally displayed when serious crimes were reported to the local constabulary.

By the time he reached the High Street an action plan was beginning to formulate in his head. First and most importantly; a letter to the Stein Foundation to inform them of this act of vandalism. After that, he would alert the whole village with a strongly worded letter to the local paper. By some miracle, coming toward him was the very person he could call upon to investigate this terrible crime. 'Constable Smith, I would like to word,' he called out.

'Yes, Mr White, and what's troubling you on this beautiful summer's day,' the genial Nigel Smith, enquired as he ambled slowly toward him.

'I've just come from the Memorial Park when I arrived, it was to find the statue of the Dancing Couple covered in red paint from head to toe. I'd like to know what you're planning to do about it,' Jim demanded.

In other circumstances, PC Smith would have leapt at the opportunity to investigate a real crime. One that would require careful and thorough investigation. Sadly, today the village bobby had a more pressing matter on his mind. 'That's a shame, I'm quite fond of that statue,' he said pushing his helmet back on his head. 'It's just that I'm a bit busy now, but I'll try and get over there this afternoon,' he added amiably.

With as much force as he could muster, Jim roared in his face. 'What could possibly be more important at this precise moment than a major act of vandalism to *the* most outstanding treasure this village possess? Well!'

PC Smith leant toward Jim's ear and murmured. 'I would go now Jim, only I've got Mr Black on my back. There's been an accident just off the by-pass and the road into the village is completely blocked. Fortunately, nobody's been hurt, but Mr Black is worried, you see. He says if nothing is done some of the visitors might turn around and go somewhere else and that would never do. So, if you'll excuse me, I'd better sort it out.'

'Where is Jason Black?' Jim shouted angrily at the broad shoulders of PC Smith, fast disappearing down the High Street.

'Last time I saw him he was in the Pump Room,' came the reply.

'Right, I'll have a word with him. Anybody would think he owned the place.'

'I've heard that too,' opined Les Woods, who happened to be passing at that precise moment.

'Well he doesn't,' Jim shouted back, before realising his friend and fellow jazz enthusiast had disappeared into the chemist shop, leaving the few residents up and about to see who was disturbing the tranquillity of the High Street; in those few precious hours between dawn and BHA – or Before the Hordes Arrive, as it was more commonly known.

Chapter Two

Today, being a Saturday in July, with clear blue skies and a promise of temperatures in the upper twenties, the residents of Applegarth in the county of Gloucestershire, were preparing for the village to be filled with lines of visitors stretching from the Pump Room all the way up to the High Street. They came to this once peaceful village from near and far to partake of the spring waters, with their promise of a cure for all ailments and illnesses.

Opinions were sharply divided amongst the residents on the benefits of the spring, but even those who saw the Pump Room as a curse recognised the prosperity of the village now depended on it. With a fine day in prospect, the tills in the restaurants, cafes, souvenir shops and fancy gift stalls would be ringing throughout the day. Later, with the visitors gone, the celebrations in the Dog and Duck would stretch far into the night in praise of the Magical Waters of Applegarth and the riches they bestowed upon the village.

Not that it was always the case.

Only with the arrival of Jason Black and his wife, Katie, several years earlier, did the fortunes of the Pump Room and the village changed for the better. The couple appeared one autumn morning to announce they were purchasing the large derelict Victorian house on the edge of the village, with plans to turn into prestigious hotel and restaurant. For the next six months very, little was seen or heard of the pair as they devoted their time and energies to renovating the house, before launching it in a blaze of publicity as the *Magical Waters Hotel and Restaurant.*

With the hotel, up and running, in his wife's capable hands, Jason turned his attention to the spring and quickly concluded the committee of local worthies were not up to running a high-class visitor attraction.

The first thing was to get rid of Mr Horace Braithwaite, the old fuddy-duddy of a chairman. To his surprise and astonishment, the task was surprisingly easy. All it required, was few hints, dropped in conversation with a few of the more influential members of the Pump Room Association over a glass of wine in the hotel, about inefficiencies he had witnessed in the running of the Pump Room. A rumour about possible discrepancies in the accounts, a suggestion that maybe poor old Horace was past it and an honourable retirement with a suitable presentation might be the best way forward, and it was done.

With Horace gone the chair of the Parish Council was soon beating a path to his door. Would Mr Black do the village the honour of bringing his vast experience in business to the enterprise and take over the chairmanship of the Pump Room Committee? He would. How kind. How generous.

With his authority over the Pump Room firmly established, Jason set about cutting out the deadwood on the committee. It didn't require more than a push, here and a gently shove there, though the accident involving Colonel Blake was unfortunate. Loosening the wheel nuts on his car was only supposed to guarantee his non-appearance for a vital vote. Still, as Jason put it to Katie at the reception held at Wellbeck Hall after funeral service, it was a very tasteful affair and brought the village together in prayer.

Ousting Philippa Pearson proved to be a tougher nut to crack. Jason's eloquent speech to the Pump Room Committee on the excellent work done by the founding members, but it was time for the next new generation to take up the burden, appeared to go straight over her head. 'I am only thirty-six,' she complained, missing the point altogether.

Faced with Jason's determined opposition to her membership of the committee, Philippa rallied support within the village, and as Jason was the first to admit, her call struck a chord amongst many in the village. From several quarters came complaints about the Pump Room being taken over by grasping profiteers, who were intent of undermining the original purpose of providing access to the spring for the benefit of all. Worse, was talk in the Dog and Duck on raising a petition to demand a special meeting of the Pump Room Association, to vote out those responsible for this sorry state of affairs and replace them with members more sympathetic to the original aims.

Faced with this opposition, Jason decided an effective counterattack was called for, and his chosen weapon was in the form of an invitation for a quiet drink in the Dog and Duck to the man of the house. 'For a chat on a matter which must be deeply worrying to you,' was how he put it when he telephoned Bob Pearson one evening.

Settled at a quiet table, well away from the prying ears of the locals, he began his well-rehearsed speech in the sombre voice he reserved for these occasions. 'Now Bob,' he said planting his elbows firmly on the table. 'He was sure there was nothing in it, but he was concerned that this little difficulty in the village seemed to have brought young Philippa and the Vicar, Rev Alan Howard, together far more than was necessary for the smooth running of the church. He hadn't personally witnessed anything untoward, but some reliable witnesses swore they were seen together on Fullton Woods. He would be the last one to tell tales, live and let live that was his motto. Perhaps these little tete-á-tëtes were purely innocent, but no smoke without fire as they say, and after all, he didn't want people laughing behind his back, did he? Perhaps it might be better if Philippa were to use her undoubted energies and talents to take care of the needs of her husband and young family.'

Confident his little ruse had done the trick, he was rewarded a few days later with the arrival of a very short and curt letter of resignation.

With Philippa, out of the way, the rebellion quickly evaporated, and Jason was ready to begin the task of co-opting the right kind of people onto the committee. By which he meant, those members of the community who shared his vision for the future. As he put to so eloquently to anyone who was prepared to listen, 'one where the glorious benefits of the spring and the businesses in the village were harmoniously combined to provide a complete and satisfying experience for visitors.'

'A combination that could benefit the whole community,' he added before pausing and savouring the look of anticipation on the faces of the audience. 'After all,' he continued. 'If all went to plan, the local businesses might be persuaded to pay for a new computer for the local school, restore the Village Hall to its former glory. Or contribute toward providing facilities for the kids in the local park, swings, climbing frames, that sort of thing. No promises of course, but who knows what the future might bring.'

'In the meantime, as anybody with any sense could see, there was an urgent need for the Pump Room to be renovated and enlarged to cater for all the extra visitors who will be flocking to the village to enjoy its wonders and delights. A new car park was needed at the south end of the village to accommodate the extra cars. All this cost money and the Parish Council would need to think about how to raise extra revenue to pay for it. If the cost were shared between the businesses and residents, it wouldn't be too much of a burden on the village.'

Inevitably, a few narrow-minded fools felt compelled to pack the Annual Parish Council Meeting and condemn the tax-raising budget on the grounds, that if the local businesses wanted these extra facilities so desperately, they should pay for them. For a time, it seemed the protesters would carry the day.

Luckily, common sense prevailed in the end, but only after a lengthy and impassioned speech from Jason, during which he held out the possibility of free entry to the Pump Room for all residents.

Besides, as he said in his speech, 'this was only a phase one. Next year there were plans for a drive-thru facility to match the latest attractions in America. Admittedly, providing visitors with the opportunity to saviour the spring waters while sitting in their cars might prove to be difficult, but where there's a will, there's a way, as they say.'

Meanwhile, on this glorious Saturday in July preparations for welcoming the expected crowds were nearing completion. In the Pump Room, Jason was about to make his final tour of inspection. A slight shift in the pile of towels, a quick check to ensure the commemorative certificates were printed with the right date and from the fountain, a final sip of the spring water. Glancing toward his wife he asked pointedly, 'Katie does this taste a bit brackish to you.'

'How should I know? It tastes like rotten eggs to me. Give me a gin and tonic any day.'

'Katie, my love, we are talking about the elixir of life, the source of all our hopes and dreams. The future prosperity of this blessed jewel, this island, this... Oh, never mind, we mustn't get too poetic must we, time to move on, as they say, much to do, people to see etc. Now then Brenda, let's look at you and your little band of helpers.' Brenda and her two ladies were standing ready for inspection and as Jason walked slowly down the short line, he lingered in front of young Tracey. 'Hello, my dear, and how are you today.'

'Very well thank you, Mr Black,' she replied shyly.

'Are you going to ogle that young girl all-day Jason?' asked Katie. 'Or, are we going back to the restaurant to prepare lunch?'

Jason swivelled around to stare at his wife, his face contorted with rage. Then, with a cheery wave to all and sundry, he took a step back, and moved to the exit with as much dignity as he could muster, only to come face to face with Jim White, 'I want a word with you Mr Black,' Jim insisted, deliberately blocking his path.

Clearly irritated by this sudden and unexpected interruption to the proceedings, Jason managed an avuncular 'Ah, Jim, and how you are today. What a bright, sunny day it is, and what excellent prospects it offers to our visitors and local businesses.'

Unable to leave, Jason was forced to make a hasty retreat to the safety of the fountain and after a moment's hesitation, gestured toward Jim. 'You're an expert on the spring water, aren't you? Could you do these lovely ladies a huge favour and tell us whether the water tastes a bit brackish today?' He said handing him a plastic cup of spring water, 'It's all right going ahead, there's no charge.'

'Actually, Jason I didn't come here to talk about the state of the spring water. There are more important matters I'd like to discuss.'

'Jim, as much as I would love to spend the entire day putting the world to rights, duty calls as they say. We are expecting a full house for lunch and must crack on. Come, Katie,' he said, snapping his fingers. 'Incidentally, Jim if that's your bloody dog barking outside, I would be most grateful if you would shut it up before it frightens away the punters.'

With another cheery wave, he swept from the Pump Room, leaving Katie in the doorway face to face with Jim. 'Hi, nice to see you again,' she murmured, before dutifully following her husband.

Jim, left holding the cup of water, felt Brenda's hand on his arm, 'Shall I take that from you before you spill it,' she said kindly. 'And now, if you will excuse us, we must open up.'

Chapter Three

'Welcome ladies and gentlemen to Applegarth and the world-famous Magical Spring Waters and Kissing Stone.' Brenda liked to begin her introduction to the Pump Room this way. Having the attention of the visitors gathered around the fountain, she continued. 'As some of you may know, the spring water here in Applegarth was discovered purely by accident in 1994. A group of workmen from the Mid-Gloucester Water Company were digging in this area after complaints from several residents about water seeping up from underground. One of the workmen, a young man by the name of Graham Tucker, suffered from a skin problem covering his body in flaky scales. Over the years his doctor prescribed various creams and lotions to alleviate the condition, but nothing seemed to work.

On that fateful day in 1997, Graham stood just about where I am standing now and raised his pickaxe.' She paused for dramatic effect and pointed to the fountain. 'As the pickaxe struck the ground, a stream of water gushed high into the air, and in the process, poor Graham was soaked to the skin.'

'He dried out of course, but over the next few days, a miracle occurred, as the flaky scales began to disappear. Within a week, his skin was as clear and smooth as a young baby. So, convinced was Graham the water was responsible for the miracle cure, he insisted on telling everyone about its magical properties. After that, word quickly spread about the miracle cure and to celebrate the villagers banded together and constructed this little Pump Room to allow everybody to enjoy the benefits of the Magical Waters of Applegarth.'

'So, ladies and gentlemen please come forward and experience the Magical Waters for yourself. There're cups on the side here and towels if you need them. Incidentally,' she said holding up her hand as the crowd pressed forward, 'you might notice the water has a slightly metallic taste. This is nothing to worry about and is due entirely to the wonderful minerals and health-giving properties of the water. As you leave, please pick up a bottle of the spring water to take home with you, and don't forget to kiss the Wishing Stone for luck. One final word don't forget to pick up your commemorative certificate as you leave and the leaflet about all the other delights and attractions in the village. Are there any questions?'

'Can we purchase additional bottles of the spring water?' a middle-aged woman asked from the back of the group.

'Yes, madam, from the gift shop, located just beyond the Pump Room.'

**

On the other side of the village, Jim pressed the play button on his stereo system and waited for Bix Beiderbecke's, *The Four-Leaf Clover* to blare out. Having failed to make any progress with the local constabulary, he was left with the task of writing the necessary letters. The first, he decided, was to the Stein Foundation. Picking up his fountain pen he wrote:

The Stein Foundation
Russell Square
London WC2

Dear Sirs,

It is with great regret that I have to inform you of the considerable damage done to the statue erected by the Foundation in the village of Applegarth. The exact circumstances are not known, but sometime during last night, an unknown assailant cast a tin of red paint over the statue, which resulted in damage to the majority of the front elevation. I have reported the incident to PC Smith, the village constable and he is investigating the matter. At the moment, there does not appear to be any obvious clues as to the perpetrators, though the police have promised to thoroughly investigate the incident.
I will, of course, keep you informed of any developments, but in the meantime, I am sure the whole village would want me to express on their behalf, the sadness they feel at the damage done to this much-loved addition to our community.
Yours truly,
Jim White

Jim hoped it expressed the right tone of formality and concern.

Next, a strongly worded letter to the *Honiston Observer*.

To the Editor
Honiston Observer
Market Street
Honiston
Gloucester

Sir,

I am sure all right-minded people will share my sense of outrage at the recent desecration of the Dancing Couple statue in the Memorial Park, her in Applegarth. This gross act of vandalism must not go unpunished. I hope anyone with information about the perpetrators will immediately inform PC Smith, so that they may be apprehended and brought to justice.
The older members of the community will recall that Isaac Stein was born and spent his formative years in the village. In later years after graduating from the Slade School of Art, he went on to establish himself as a sculptor of national renown. Apart from our own beloved Dancing Couple, there are many other publicly displayed pieces, including the Man in Contemplation in High Park, London and the Women and Children on the quayside at Southampton.
I believe it was a great honour for the village when the Stein Foundation agreed to honour Isaac Stein's birthplace by erecting a replica of the statue commonly known as the Dancing Couple in the Memorial Park and an utter disgrace that someone from the village has chosen to desecrate it in this way.
In conclusion sir, I cannot help but think that this act of vandalism reflects the serious erosion in the traditional values of the village, which have become apparent in recent years with greater emphasis on commercialism and a loss of respect for the very architecture and artistic delights that drew many of us here in the first place.
I am sir, your obedient servant
Jim White

With the letters written and envelopes addressed, he decided to phone Philippa and put her in the picture about the damage to the statue and the letters he'd written. To his surprise, she answered on the first ring. 'After the matter of the Pump Room Committee and what that so-and-so Jason Black did, I have to be careful about getting too involved in village affairs. I love my husband to bits, but he can be jealous sometimes of my friendship with other men. There was nothing between me and Alan you know,' Philippa asserted when Jim had brought her up-to-date with the tragic news about the Dancing Couple, and the letters he had written.

'Well, he would have nothing to be jealous about from an old codger like me then, would he?'

With a mischievous laugh, Philippa replied, 'I think we'll skip over that. You're still a very attractive man Jim White and one day a very lucky lady is going to lead you down the aisle again.'

'I wish, but in the meantime, can we meet to talk about what we do next?'

There was a slight pause, during which Jim assumed Philippa was consulting the diary, he knew hung beside the telephone in her kitchen. After a moment, and with a slight hesitation in her voice, she said, 'Look, no promises, but I'm in town on Tuesday. I've got a couple of errands to do, so let's meet in the Cosy Café for a coffee at about 11.'

'Okay, and by then there might be a reply from the Stein Foundation,' Jim replied replacing the receiver.

Chapter Four

If there was one thing Stan Hawkins disliked about this job, it was being stuck with the Birmingham to Applegarth tour. Unlike the other coach tours offered by the company, this was little more than a straight run down the M5, a stop in the village car park for a few of hours and a race back up the motorway to reach the depot by five. He much preferred the tour that crossed into Wales and took in the Wye Valley, with a nice stop for lunch, and the opportunity to show off his detailed knowledge of the area. Today, he'd drawn the short straw with the run to Applegarth, which though profitable for the South Midland Bus Company, was utterly boring for him and his fellow drivers.

To make matters worse, he was currently sitting stationary in a line of traffic just outside the village. So far, the run had gone without incident. The motorway was unusually quiet, but the moment they left the by-pass they'd come to a complete halt.

'Ladies and gentlemen,' he announced over the loudspeaker system, 'unfortunately we've been held up on our way into Applegarth today. I'm not certain what the problem is exactly, but there's a constable directing traffic up ahead and hopefully, we'll have you safely in the car park within the next few minutes.'

'Let's hope it's soon. Some of this lot look in need of a miracle cure from the magical spring waters,' he murmured to himself as the coach slowly edged past the cause of the problem - a tractor and trailer had shed its load of manure on to the road - helped on its way with a cheery wave to PC Smith.

'Ladies and gentlemen, just to remind you, we have a two-and-a-half-hour stop here in Applegarth, which should give you plenty of time to visit the

Pump Room, wander around the shops and enjoy a spot of lunch. But, please be back here no later than 3.30. Thank you.'

Up ahead the village was already packed with visitors and the queue to the Pump Room stretched to the High Street. Inside, Brenda was launching into her sixth introductory speech of the morning. Everyone was in good spirits, and the movement of visitors through the Pump Room was as smooth and efficient as usual.

With the latest group moving toward the exit, clutching their bottles of water and certificates, Brenda called to her assistant, 'Janet, take over for a bit will you, and get young Tracey to man the cash desk. I need a break. It was Terry's birthday yesterday and we made a bit of a night of it.'

'Where did you go to then, the *Magical Waters Hotel and Restaurant?*'

'On the wages, they pay here, you're joking. No, we went to that Greek place in Honiston, one of their special nights. You know, all plate smashing and dancing like *Zorba the Greek* stuff. Anyway, what with the dancing and Terry feeling a bit frisky when we got home, I'm a bit fragile this morning.'

'Okay, we'll manage; you take a break, I'll see the next lot through.'

Emerging into the sunshine, Brenda stood for a moment surveying the queue and sighed, before sinking into one of the seats alongside the Gift Shop and lit a cigarette. Sitting in the sunshine, enjoying the warmth of the summer air, she thought life in Applegarth wasn't too bad. Though, if she was honest, she was past the age when the exertions of the previous evening could be repeated too often.

She couldn't deny she and Terry had made a life for themselves after the kids fled the nest. Terry had a decent job as a printer at Masons in Honiston, and the firm seemed to be doing well, while she had this job at the Pump Room. Okay, the wages weren't brilliant, but they were comfortable. They could afford the odd treat, like last night. Next year, maybe they could manage a trip to America. She fancied Florida and a couple of weeks relaxing in the sun. With that happy thought in mind, she lay back and pictured herself beside the pool, stretched out on a sunbed, Bacardi and Coke in hand and the promise of a huge lobster and salad for dinner.

'Brenda you'd better come, there's a problem in the Pump Room.' Jane said shaking her shoulder and bringing her dream to a sudden and violent end.

'What sort of problem,' Brenda murmured, assuming one of the elderly visitors had collapsed on the floor with a heart attack.

'You better see for yourself,' Jane replied hurrying into the Pump Room. Reluctantly Brenda rose from the seat and silently cursing Jane for disturbing her beautiful dream, made her way to the Pump Room. Inside, it was empty except for Jane and Tracey staring at the fountain. 'So, what's the problem then?'

'There's no water,' Tracey uttered innocently, her face a complete picture.

'What do you mean there's no water.'

'As Tracey so eloquently puts it, Brenda, there's no water. The spring has dried up. It happened as the last lot of visitors were leaving. It made a funny noise for several minutes and then began spurting and gurgling. It's done that before only to settle down again. This time a huge spray shot out almost to the ceiling and then it just died.'

'Did you check the spout? Sometimes it gets blocked. It happens when bits of plastic cup gets stuck in the hole.'

'That was the first thing I thought of. Even got a bit of wire and poked it down the hole, but it made no difference. Look for yourself, it is bone dry.'

The spring was indeed dry. Instead of the constant stream of water, Brenda was used to seeing, now not even a trickle spurted from the fountain. Sensing her companions looking at her expectantly, her brain went into overdrive. 'Stall everything. Tell the people waiting outside there's water some on the floor and we need to clean it up before allowing any more visitors in. If anybody questions it, tell them it's because of health and safety.'

'While you're doing that, I'll get on the phone and ring Mr Black. He'll want to know what's happened, and we'd better hope he comes up with a solution because I haven't a clue what to suggest.'

Chapter Five

'Good afternoon ladies and gentlemen. How are you today? My name is Gary, and I'm your server today. Here's the lunch menus if I may hand them around? Can I also draw your attention to our specials on the blackboard behind me? And, whilst you're contemplating the culinary delights, what can I get you to drink?'

'Whisky and soda for sir, sorry that's two whiskies and sodas. For the ladies: dry white wine and a gin and tonic. Right then, I'll be back with these in a few moments.'

In the *Magical Waters Hotel and Restaurant*, the restaurant was beginning to fill up with diners looking forward to a hearty lunch, washed down with an aperitif and a nice bottle of wine, having had their fill of the Pump Room and its magical waters.

With the restaurant fully booked, Jason was stationed in his normal position behind the reception desk, ready to greet diners as they arrived. On any normal day, they'd be met by a cheery, 'Hi folks and welcome to the *Magical Waters Hotel and Restaurant*,' but this was not a normal day. In place of the broad smile that usually played across his lips, a very pinched look sat upon the face of the master of this high-class establishment. Nor would the staff, have recognised the hesitant tone in his voice as he spoke into the telephone in response to Brenda's call. 'Slow down. What do you mean the spring has dried up? I have a restaurant full of diners and several people waiting for tables. I couldn't possibly come to the Pump Room at this precise moment. Can't you deal with it?'

Intrigued by this conversation, Gary paused on his journey to the bar and was rewarded with a loud snort from Jason and a blast down the end of the telephone. 'No, you can't close the Pump Room for the day, definitely, not, do you hear me?' In any other circumstances, this would have been followed by supine acceptance, but on this occasion, Brenda was determined to stand her ground and to force Jason to listen to her plea.

'All right, okay, okay.' Jason replied hurriedly. 'There's no need to go on. I'll come down as soon as I can. In the meantime, try and keep things under control as best you can,' he said replacing the receiver heavily on its rest and glancing across to Gary. 'What you staring at?

'Sorry, Mr Black, I was just on my way to the bar and... Is everything okay?'

'No, it's not and never you mind. Right then, what's the position with your tables?'

'Table 20 has arrived and I'm on my way to get the drinks. Fifteen and sixteen have their main course, the rest are on desserts and coffee.'

'Good, get the drinks to Table 20, then take over here. There's a crisis at the Pump Room, some cock and bull story about the spring drying up. It's probably nothing, but that fool Brenda is in a panic. It's damn nuisance but I have to go and sort it out. Okay.'

'Right will do, I'll get Belinda to cover for me until you get back. Don't worry we'll cope.'

At the Pump Room, Brenda replaced the receiver and turned to her two companions. 'Mr Black is on his way. He says we're to hold the fort 'til he gets here,' she paused tapping her thumbnail against her teeth. 'Right Belinda, go and apologise to the people outside. Tell them we hope to resume normal service very shortly, but don't say anything about the spring drying up.'

***

'How much longer are we going to have to wait for John?'

'I'm not sure Mildred, that lady came ten minutes ago, asking everyone to be patient. You'd have thought if the problem was just a bit of water on the floor, they'd have cleaned it up by now. How long does it take to mop up a few drops of water?'

John and Mildred Haines woke that morning, the day of their thirtieth wedding anniversary, undecided how to celebrate their nuptials.

Mildred rang the South Midland Bus Company after breakfast hoping to join the Black Hills of Wales and Wye Valley tour, but it was fully booked. Instead, they settled for a trip to Applegarth. So far, they were not very impressed with what it had to offer.

Joining the end of the queue, they planned to visit the Pump Room, followed by a nice lunch in one of the cafes on the High Street, before getting the coach home. Their daughter Gillian told them to be back by six as she had arranged a special treat for them in the evening. As Mildred said, after waiting another five minutes, 'at this rate we'd be lucky to get through the Pump Room by the time the coach leaves.'

'I don't know about you Mildred, but I have a good mind to abandon this for a spot of lunch. If I ran our hardware shop like this, we'd have gone bankrupt years ago, and certainly not enjoying a bit of retirement, that's for sure. Hey, up, some bloke has appeared, and it looks like he's got some info about what's going on. So, stop your jabbering and listen to what he's got say.'

'Ladies and gentlemen,' Jason announced in his most authoritative voice, 'I am sorry that you've been kept waiting. We're experiencing some problems in the Pump Room this morning. We've lost all the lights, and before anybody says it, yes, we have paid the bill, and yes, we have checked the fuse box. So, though we can accommodate visitors, I should warn you it's a bit gloomy in the Pump Room as we've only got a few candles to light the place. That being the case if you do decide to come back another day, we'll fully understand. On the other hand, if you are determined to taste the Magical Waters of Applegarth please come forward now.'

'What do you think Mildred doesn't exactly sound like a bundle of laughs does it?'

'No, come on John let's forget it,' and along with half the people in the queue, they turned away from the Pump Room and headed toward the High Street and lunch.

'I think that might have done the trick,' Jason said to Brenda inside the Pump Room. Remember, stick to the candles, and keep the lights off, and use the bottled water to fill the cups. When this lot have gone, put a notice up saying the Pump Room is closed for technical reasons. That should hold things for a bit. In the meantime, I need to the restaurant or the place will be in chaos. I'll bet a pound to a penny the booking form will be all over the place.'

'When you're finished here, get on to the members of the Pump Room Committee and tell them there's an emergency meeting tonight in the back room of the Dog and Duck, I'll fix it with Ted. You better say I'm sorry about the short notice but there's something important we need discuss, but not a word about the spring drying up, and let the people in before they kick the door down.'

Jason's move to the exit was brought to a halt by a loud buzzing noise emanating from inside his jacket. Pulling out a mobile, he stabbed the call answer button and listened for a moment. 'Yes, Kevin the garage doors *are* required to be repainted black. Why, because my dear wife doesn't like them red, that's why okay. End of story okay. So, just do it?' Finishing the call, he turned to Brenda. 'And remember, not a word to anyone. If it gets out the spring's dried up, we'll be dead, and you'll be out of job.'

Chapter Six

Before the discovery of the spring, the Dog and Duck was a typical English village pub, with a thatched roof, washed yellow walls and three bars, including a snug. In the summer, it offered a welcome haven from the heat of the sun, whilst in winter the roaring log fire gave life and warmth to many a weary traveller from the cruel winds that blew up the valley from the Seven River.

In those days, the landlord, Fred Grimes, took considerable pride intending his beers and was disappointed if the Dog and Duck didn't achieve a Highly Recommended Award in the Campaign for Real Ale's annual guide to the best pubs in Gloucestershire.

The quality of the beer and the darts team, with the occasional weekend trade, just about kept the pub afloat. With Fred's retirement, the brewery installed Ted and his wife Susan as managers, with the job of updating and upgrading the pub and its facilities.

Within days of their arrival, the public and saloon bars were knocked into one with an immediate hike in the price of all the beers. The new managers planned to turn the Snug into a private facilities room to serve their corporate clients from Honiston and surrounding towns, but this proved to be a step too far. After howls of protests from the pub regulars, Ted and Susan were forced to relent, but flatly refused to call it the Snug and insisted on referring to it as the Private Bar. To the locals, looking for a quiet drink, with a game of dominos and a chat with their mates, it became known simply as the Backroom.

Being a Saturday night, the pub was packed with locals and visitors tucking into the hearty meals cooked by Susan in the kitchen. In the bar, customers sat on the high stools or stood around chatting and supping their drinks.

One of the attractions introduced by Ted was live music on Friday and Saturday night. As he said to Susan, 'if the prospect of real ale, a good food, and some lively music didn't bring in the punters, then he didn't know what would.'

Drawing a pint of best bitter, Ted, looked up to see Jim waiting to be served. 'Hello, Mr White, we don't often see you in here on a Saturday night.'

'At these prices is it any wonder, but I hear you've got Jack Harley and the New Orleans Band in tonight.'

'With a line-up of trumpet, trombone, banjo, drums, and bass, I think you'll find it's your kind of music. What you'll have?'

'A pint of best please,' he replied. Leaving Ted to pull the beer, Jim turned to see who else was in tonight. He was hoping Les Woods and his wife Audrey had decided to venture out. They were a bit younger than him but discovered a common interest in jazz after they met at the Honiston Jazz Club and became firm friends. The place was packed but, he spotted them in the corner, with Les leaning against the fireplace. He signalled to them and Les raised a glass in recognition, with a gesture to come and join them. 'There you are Jim, that'll be £2.95,' Ted said placing the pint on the counter.

'You call it Applegarth Best Bitter, I call it daylight robbery,' said Jim smiling and handing him a £5 note.

Ted took the money, returning a few moments later with the change, 'Incidentally, I hope you and Les intend to keep out of trouble tonight.'

'We'll do our best,' Jim replied taking his beer, 'but it is difficult when you are pretty dam perfect to start with.' Still grinning from the exchange, Jim moved to the fireplace, 'What you are smiling at,' Les said raising his glass.

'The usual banter with Ted. 'You two here for the band, I suppose.'

'We thought we would give it a try,' replied Audrey, 'Otherwise it's a video and a Chinese takeaway.'

As Jim took a swig of beer, he noticed Jason Black striding toward the Backroom, with a cursory nod to Ted before disappearing. 'Now there's a strange sight,' Jim said turning to Les and Audrey.

'What business would Jason Black have in the Dog and Duck on a Saturday night. You would expect him to be lording over the diners at his fancy restaurant,' Les remarked.

'I heard there was a sign outside the Pump Room saying that *Due to Technical Reasons the Pump Room is closed today.* Perhaps they forgot to pay the electricity bill.'

'At least the village will be quiet for a few days and for that we should be grateful,' Audrey suggested, taking a swig of beer.

Unknown to Jim and his companions, Jason was the last member of the Pump Room Committee to arrive for the emergency meeting, the others having entered by the side entrance.

Taking the only vacant chair, Jason glanced around the table at the five members of the committee. The Rev Alan Howard could be a bit pious, but he represented the interest of the village and had to be tolerated, Tilly Swinburne, secretary to the Committee since time began was deaf but refused to wear a hearing aid. Jason politely informed her when he took over the chair, that her services were no longer required. Either she didn't hear or pretended not to because, at the next meeting, she arrived with a big smile and the Minute Book, and he didn't have the heart to throw her out, so she carried on.

The remaining members of the committee were carefully chosen and could be relied upon to take a business-friendly decision on any issue. Jack Thompson ran the Ye Olde Gift and Stationery shop on the High Street and was a bit of an old bluffer, but he meant well. Tony Bean was general manager of Masons the printers in Honiston and strong exponent of modern business practices. Lastly, Brian Thorpe, the owner and proprietor of the Cosy Café and Snackbar. Everybody in the village knew his wife Sheila was the brains behind the business, but she let him think he was the boss.

Jason launched straight in, 'Good evening lady and gentlemen. My apologies for calling this meeting at such short notice and on a Saturday night, but I have to report we have a real crisis on our hands.' He paused and waited for their reaction. With no immediate response, other than a look of expectation on their faces, he continued. 'Not wasting words, the spring has dried up. This means we have no water and therefore no business.' There was a long pause as he waited for the gravity of the situation to sink in.

The first to speak was the Rev Alan Howard, 'Lady and gentlemen,' he said in the loud booming voice he reserved for church services. 'I realise, of course, this must be a devastating blow for all of us around this table. As for myself, I can't help wondering whether it's a sign from above. God's way of expressing his disapproval for…'

'Excuse me vicar and I'm sorry to interrupt you, but I am trying to keep an accurate record of the meeting for the minutes. Could I clarify who has been tied up and left out in the snow…?'

'No Tilly I didn't say tied up, what I *actually* said was…'

'…cause it seems a bit strange to have snow in July. The snow usually comes in the winter. Do we know this person who was tied up? They must be very cold and uncomfortable by now.'

Jack, who found Tilley's refusal to wear a hearing aid very frustrating, shouted, 'Bloody hell, Tilly, when are you going to accept you are going deaf.'

'I'll have you know Jack Thompson I can hear as well as the next person. But I refuse to spend what little money I have from my widow's pension on buying a fancy hearing aid when I don't need it. So there.'

'Tilly you've been going deaf for the last couple of years and you know full well you don't have to buy a hearing aid. The NHS will provide you with one free of charge. All you have to do is apply.'

'As it happens, I do have one, thanks to my daughter. A right little madam she's turning to be I can tell you. One day I'll put her in her place. Anyway, where was I. Oh, yes, I remember. The reason I don't have it on all the time is because it wears out the batteries, okay.'

'I'm sorry to interrupt this fascinating discussion about hearing aids, but aren't we getting just a little away from the point. TILLY,' shouted Jason, waving his hands to attract her attention, 'PUT YOUR HEARING AID ON PLEASE.' In response, she fiddled about in her handbag and stuffed something in her ear as Jason continued, 'Good, now WHAT I SAID WAS THE SPRING HAS DRIED UP, THERE'S NO WATER.'

'There's no need to shout, I can hear perfectly well thank you,' Tilly replied with a look of pure innocence on her face.

'Right then, where were we.'

'Mr Chairman, if I may address you in that way. I know it is a bit non-PC these days, but chair or chairperson always appears slightly ridiculous when it's perfectly obvious you are a member of the… Well, if will excuse the phrase, the male gender. So, I prefer to address you…'

'Alan, if there is a point to all this, could you get to it, please. Otherwise, we'll be here all night.'

'Thank you chair, chairperson, dam it *Mr Chairman*. As I was saying, I can't help wondering whether the news you have imparted to us tonight is a message from above. A sign of how far we have travelled in the pursuit of the commercial interests and away from the original ideals of this magical gift from God. All of us sat around this table tonight should think very carefully about our moral responsibilities and consider the next step with great humility. In my view, there can only be one course of action and that is to close the Pump Room and put all it represents behind us for the well-being of the village. If you are prepared Chair, Chairperson, Oh, damn it, Mr Chairman to accept a proposal along those lines I will be honoured to….'

'It's all right for you vicar spouting all that nonsense,' Jack said, not waiting for him to finish. 'You don't have to rely on the spring to earn a living.'

'You should remember Alan, the businesses in this village puts money into the pockets of your parishioners, and a lot of that ends up in your collection plate. So, think on,' Brian from the Cosy Café, added rather pompously.

'Gentlemen, we'll get nowhere if all we are going to do is fight amongst ourselves,' Jason interjected.

'I agree Mr Chairman, what is required, in my humble opinion, is an objective analysis of the situation. At Masons, we find a brainstorming session using the Hummel Method developed by Professor Adolph Hummel at the University of Vienna, helps enormously.'

'With respect Tony, the bloody spring has dried up and without it, we'll be up shit creek. How's that for a detailed analysis of the situation.'

'Jack's analysis may have been, shall we say, a bit colourful,' Jason said to make progress, 'but I think we can agree it contains the essential elements of the situation.'

Steamboat down the Mississippi, Steamboat down the Mississippi, take me to the one I love, Steamboat down the Mississippi. Jack Harley and the New Orleans Band chose that precise moment to launch into their opening number with the sound reverberating throughout the pub. In the bar, Jim, Les and Audrey started to sway and tap their feet to the rhythm of the music.

In the Backroom, it was becoming obvious that any discussion about the spring was becoming impossible.

'WHAT WE HAVE TO DO IS DECIDE WHAT TO DO NEXT,' Jason shouted as the band went into a trumpet solo, with Jack Harley leading the way.

'Mr Chairman may I suggest one way to solve the problem…

'BRIAN. YOU SHOULD SPEAK UP WE CAN'T HEAR YOU.'

'MR CHAIRMAN ONE WAY TO SOLVE THE PROBLEM MIGHT BE TO EMPLOY OUT OF WORK SNOW CLEARERS.' With a big flourish, the band reached the end of *Mississippi Steamboat* and in the silence poor, Brian found himself shouting loud enough for everyone in the pub to hear.

'Sorry Mr Chairman,' he said lowering his voice. 'As I was saying, one way of solving the problem would be… *'Girl of New Orleans, you are my dreams, together we will make music,* Jack and the boys of the band launched into their second number, completely drowning out Brian's attempt to expound his idea for solving the problem of the dried-up spring. 'ONE WAY TO SOLVE THE PROBLEM,' he resumed shouting in a vain attempt to be heard above the band, 'WOULD BE TO EMPLOY OUT OF WORK SNOW CLEARERS TO BRING WATER FROM THE VILLAGE POND, IN A LONG CHAIN.'

'BRING WATER FROM WHERE? THIS IS HOPELESS, LET'S GO OUT INTO THE CAR PARK AND CONTINUE THERE.'

Not understanding, the members of the committee looked at each other and mouthed, "What did he say?" The problem only being resolved when Jason gestured to the rest of the committee to follow him to the car park.

With the band now coming to the end of *Girl of New Orleans*, Jim leant across to Les and whispered in his ear, 'Follow me to the gents, I think we might learn something interesting.' Not waiting for a reply, he fought his way across the bar to the toilets.

'You realise we're missing one of the best bands to appear around here for ages because you can't control your bladder,' Les said standing in the toilet.

'Don't say a word, just listen. I think there's a secret meeting of the Pump Room Committee taking place in the Backroom tonight, but the sweet notes coming from Jack Harley and the band have driven them out. If I heard right, they decided to adjourn to the car park.'

'So, what are we doing in here, or do you fancy me more than you've been letting on.'

'The point is the gent's backs onto the car park, and if we listen carefully, we should be able to hear what's going on.'

On any other day, the car park of the Dog and Duck would have offered a variety of places for the committee to gather on a warm July evening, but tonight packed with cars the only vacant space was indeed adjacent to the gentlemen's toilet.

The committee gathered around Jason like a group of furtive conspirators. 'We're not going to solve this tonight. The Pump Room will stay closed tomorrow and since it doesn't open on Mondays, we have until Tuesday to come up with a solution. I suggest we meet again tomorrow, any thoughts?'

'Well, the quietest place tomorrow is going to be the bloody Pump Room, so why don't we meet there at four,' Jack suggested. 'It's quite busy in the shop in the afternoon, but Jean can manage.'

'That sounds okay to me. Lunch will be over, and we don't open in the evening. What about everybody else?' With nods from the others, Jason assumed the arrangement was agreed. 'Right, then four o'clock in the Pump Room it is and remember, not a word to anyone. If you get any questions, say the closure is due to technical reasons.'

'I suggest we leave without delay before anyone notices otherwise tongues might start wagging,' Tony added, as they disappeared into the night, murmuring their goodbyes.

'Did you get that?' Jim asked as they look at each other in puzzlement.

'I think so. Being outside the Pump Room tomorrow at four will tell us more. In the meantime, my old mate we are missing some of the best blowing heard in this village for a long time, so let's get back to the bar'

Chapter Seven

Sunday dawned in Applegarth, and in place of the sun and clear blue skies of the previous day, it was cloudy and overcast. By mid-morning the rain was relentless, and the car park that would normally be full to overflowing was virtually empty.

The few brave souls who ventured outbattled their way up the High Street only to disappear into the shops and cafes for warming cups of coffee, or to simply seek shelter from the rain. If they noticed the hand-written signs carefully positioned at the entrance to the car parks, they chose to ignore the announcement of the temporary closure of the Pump Room.

In his office, Jason replaced the phone after taking another cancellation for lunch and silently swore. Bookings were down and were unlikely to improve while the Pump Room remained closed. If business was to return to normal the committee needed to reach the right decisions today, and they would if he gave them the right steer. Otherwise, that fool Alan Howard would try to sway them with, 'It's a sign from God,' rubbish.'

On the other side of the village, Jim was preparing a lunch for Les and Audrey. They often shared the burden of cooking Sunday lunch and this week it was his turn. Not that he minded, in fact, he loved cooking. It was an interest he shared with his dear departed wife, Nancy. They enjoyed entertaining friends and would happily spend the day in the kitchen preparing the meal, and then later join their friends as they sat, chatted, laughed, and tucked into the food and fine wines carefully chosen to accompany the meal.

Today, to the accompaniment of Louis Armstrong and the Hot Fives, Jim was preparing a roast leg of lamb with rosemary and garlic. Opening the oven and putting in the joint, he smiled as Satchmo and the boys launched into *Big Fat Mamie and Skinny Pa.* With an apple crumble to follow there weren't going to be any Skinny Pas today, he thought. 'Now where was that nice bottle of Argentinean Malbec on offer at the supermarket last week?'

In the Turner household, the atmosphere was subdued. Despite Jason's warning, Brenda felt she had to let Terry into the secret of the spring running dry. With the roast in the oven, the discussion inevitably centred on the impact it would have on their lives. Terry's job at Mason seemed secure. They recently won a large contract to print several magazines aimed at the hobbies market, and they had plans for other contracts. But there weren't many jobs in the village for Brenda if the Pump Room closed. 'We can only wait and see, and hope Jason comes up with a solution,' said Brenda, 'For the life of me I can't think what it might be.'

In the Memorial Park, PC Nigel Smith stood gazing up at the Dancing Couple. During his patrols through the park, he'd often stopped to admire the statue. Today, his scrutiny of the Dancing Couple was for a different purpose. Today, he searched for clues to identify the person responsible for splattering the lovely statue with red paint.

He would be the first to add admit he wasn't the brightest policeman in the Gloucestershire Constabulary. His posting to the village of Applegarth several years earlier reflected the chief constable's view of his abilities, after two unfortunate mishaps in the Stroud Division – or at least that is how they were referred to in the official reports following the board of inquiry.

Yet, PC Smith possessed one of the essential qualities required of any police officer, a hatred for unsolved mysteries. No matter how small or how trivial, he had a compulsive need to burrow away until a satisfactory explanation was achieved. Only last week, he'd discovered a small and mysterious blemish on the front door of his house. A careful examination of the offending mark failed to reveal the cause, but two days ago, standing quietly behind the door, the mystery was solved. It was simple. A new young lad had taken over the around, and instead of walking up the path and pushing the newspaper through the letterbox, he tossed it from the gate. If the aim and delivery were right, it landed squarely on the doorstep. On the other hand, if the wind was in the wrong direction, or the power applied to the throw was too great, it clipped the door causing a small scratch as it fell. So, pleased was he with his powers of deduction he decided not to complain to the newsagent. Later that day, having retrieved the tin of black paint from the garden shed, he carefully touched up the door, whistling quietly to himself as he painted.

Standing in the park, and studying the figures, there was something familiar about the colour of the paint. He couldn't put his finger on it, but sometime in the past few weeks, someone in the village was using a similar paint. All he had to do was let his brain mull it over for a few days, and the answer would come, and when it did the mystery would be solved.

On the other side of the village, the Pump Room was silent. The fountain, which normally spurted twenty gallons of water every hour, was bone dry. Sometime during the night, a small rumble from deep in the ground produced a huge jet of water hitting the ceiling, and then with one final gurgle it died. From that moment, not a drop of water issued from the fountain – it was dead.

As each member of the committee arrived, they made a beeline for the fountain and examined it carefully. Some tapped the spout, thinking they could jolt it back into life. Others peered down it, hoping a small blockage was the cause of the problem. But the spring was dry and would remain so.

'Right gentlemen,' said Jason when they were all gathered. 'We have apologies from Tilly, who has a migraine, so at least we won't have to shout today, so let's get straight down to the business in hand. As you can see there is no water gushing from the fountain and without the spring, the village is dead and our businesses with it. The question is what are we going to do about it?'

After a very satisfying lunch, Jim, Les and Audrey, despite the rain, were station outside the Pump Room and listening to every word. A minor panic was only narrowly avoided when Alan Howard, arriving late and strolling down the path from the High Street, nearly caught them crouching underneath the window. Only by Jim darting behind a convenient bush and Les and Audrey going into a clinch were they able to avoid being recognised.

'Was that okay,' Les said as the vicar disappeared into the Pump Room.

'From the smile on Audrey's face, I would say it was perfect,' Jim replied.

'What's going to save the village is a miracle, or failing that another source of water, but where the hell it's coming from, God only knows,' Jack said with his usual bluntness.

'If you may recall, I did put forward a suggestion on Saturday,' Brian replied.

'Yes, we know,' responded Jason, 'but with respect Brian, it wasn't very practical. We could hardly keep it a secret that the spring had dried up if fifty sweaty blokes are busily passing buckets of water from the village pond to the Pump Room. People might get suspicious don't you think.'

'Mr Chairman, I will not be a party to anything that involved a deception,' Alan interjected.

'I think we all know what you position is Alan, and if you'll forgive me on a Sunday, let's have no more of that, "it's a sign from God" stuff. Whatever the cause, the future of the village depends on what we decide today, so let's put our thinking caps on come up with a solution.'

'Mr Chairman, I resent the implication implicit in your last remarks that I represent a minority on this committee. If you recall, I was elected to represent the broad interest of the villages and will continue to do so, and I will not be intimidated by anyone.'

'Yes, vicar sorry' Jason muttered.

'May I also remind you Mr Chairman that this committee is only charged with managing the day-to-day affairs of the Pump Room. At some point, and I suggest sooner rather than later, the Association will need to be consulted and their approval sort for any solution we agree upon.'

'As chairman of this committee and the Association, I am perfectly aware of my responsibilities, thank you, Alan. At this precise moment, we need to find a solution to the problem, after that, I'll decide who should be consulted and when,' Jason responded angrily.

'Brian's idea of using a bucket chain, as you so rightly pointed out Jason, was rather impracticable,' said Tony, who was closely examining the fountain. 'Thinking about it, the pond could provide an alternative source of water. I would, therefore, propose a feasibility study to see how we can transfer water from the pond to the Pump Room.'

'And how long is a bloody feasibility study going to take. Bloody hell Tony, we don't have a couple of months for some poncy consultant to frat about and then charge more money than most of us earn in a year, only to tell us what we know already.' Tony didn't need to look to where the committee was gathered, to know Jack, with his usual finesse, had accurately expressed their views.

A smile suddenly crossed Jason's face. 'Hang on a bit Jack I think we may have a gem of an idea here. If we dig a trench from the pond to the Pump Room, lay a bit of piping and connect it to the fountain we'd have a spring again.'

Outside, Jim caught the eye of his two companions, 'Did you hear that the spring has dried up and they are going to pump water from the pond and pretend its spring water.'

'They can't do that,' Audrey replied, 'The village would never stand for it.'

"Heh up,' Les said pointing to the wall, 'Sounds like there's a row going on inside.'

'Mr Chairman, I must protest. What you are suggesting amounts to nothing more than the wholesale deception of the village and the paying visitors and I will not be a party to it.'

'Well before you stomp off in a huff vicar, let's put it this way,' Jason said looking straight at him. 'If you want the two thousand quid toward the Organ Restoration Fund my Katie promised, you'd better find a way of keeping your mouth shut otherwise you can kiss every penny goodbye. So, think on that.'

'That also applies to the five hundred quid you conned out of my Jean,' Jack chipped in.

'Mr Chairman, this is nothing short of blackmail and I protest in the strongest possible terms.'

'Blackmail is such an ugly word don't you think. I'd rather call it gentle persuasion, wouldn't you vicar?'

Alan was silent for a moment, as he saw the possibility of restoring the church organ to its former glory disappearing before his eyes. Accepting there was no alternative he stretched out his hands in a conciliatory gesture. 'It appears for the good of the church I have no option, but to bury my principles for this sordid little commercial enterprise to continue. Reluctantly and under protest, I agree.'

'Good. Then I propose we tell everyone we are closing the Pump Room to carry out major works designed to improve and enhance the experience of visitors.'

'How is it going to do that?' enquired Brian.

'Well, let's put it this way, since the spring is at this moment dry, pumping water from the pond will not only improve the experience for visitors but enhance them as well,' Jason said looking at his fellow conspirators as they all burst into spontaneous laughter. Apart from the Rev Alan Howard who looked decidedly unhappy.

'Would you credit it, the lying, scheming bastard,' Les said moving away from the wall and gesturing toward Jim and Audrey.

'How do we expose him?' Les asked. 'Unless we can rally the forces in the village who are opposed to the commercialism of the spring, we won't stand a chance.'

'Your right Jim, but we'd better leave before they come out and discover us.'

'Let's go back to our house. I'll make some tea and we can decide what to do next,' Audrey suggested, as they hurried up the path to the High Street.'

In the Pump Room, Jason was explaining how to deal with the immediate situation. 'What is needed is a notice on the path saying we are closed for renovations, coupled with some stuff about providing additional facilities to cope with the increasing numbers of visitors. Don't worry I'll take care of all that.'

'In the meantime, let's agree to meet tomorrow to decide how to get the work done. I'll let you know where and when.'

'Mr Chairman, you must excuse me I'm afraid, I have an important meeting with the bishop tomorrow. Regretfully, therefore, I will not be joining you.'

'Very well vicar, but remember mum's the word,' Jason says tapping a finger against the side of his nose. 'As for everybody else, I can only wish you good afternoon, until tomorrow then.'

As the group moved toward the door, Jason pulled Tony to one side, 'Hang on, I need a word.'

Chapter Eight

With the other members of the committee safely out the way, Jason and Tony quickly agreed on a plan of action. Number one priority was to phone the prominent members of the Association and inform them for health and safety reasons the Pump Room would have to be closed for a week. If pressed, they would say it was due to the unevenness of the floor, and emphasis Association would be responsible for the financial damages if any visitors fell and injured themselves. That should stop any probing questions, particularly if they hinted that members of the Association would collectively and individually be liable for any damages. This last bit came from Tony, who was lectured only last month by a lady health and safety consultant on the duty of care Mason's had to their staff and any visitors.

They had also agreed it would be prudent to pay the staff whilst the Pump Room was closed. That only left the question of who could be trusted to do the necessary building work. Tony suggested a builder who'd did some work for Masons in the past. If Jason agreed, he would ring Alex Potter, the manager, on Monday morning to sound him out. With a plan to deal with the emergency, Jason suggested another meeting wasn't necessary and agreed to contact the other members of the committee with a simple message. The condition of the Pump Room made it necessary to carry out urgent repairs and he was seeking quotes for the work. 'That's should do it,' he said, as they shook hands on a job well done before going their separate ways.

After drying off and enjoying a warming cup of tea, Audrey, Les and Jim spent the evening arguing what they should do to expose the committee's plans to pump water from the pond. Any number of suggestions were put forward and rejected before they eventually settled on telephoning the leading members of the Pump Room Association. The list of names was divided between them, but not wishing to disturb anybody on a Sunday night, Jim decided to leave his calls until the following day.

'Don't worry Jim,' Mrs Worthington replied when he rang the following day. 'Jason has explained it all. The Pump Room has been closed for essential repairs.' His attempts to tell her it wasn't true, only brought forth the reply, 'I'm sorry Jim, the village should be grateful to Mr Black, without his foresight the Association could face an enormous claim for damages.'

The message from the other members on the list was the same. Without the repairs, the spring and the future of the Pump Room would be jeopardised.

Audrey received the same reaction when she phoned later that day, except words like 'prejudice' 'spiteful' and 'malicious crusade against a respectful businessman' were thrown back at her.

'There's no point in ringing the names on my list. I'll get the same reaction,' Les bemoaned that evening. 'But, more worrying where does that leave us?'

'I don't know my old mate, but I'm meeting Philippa tomorrow to talk about the Dancing Couple. Hopefully, she will come up with something. I'll drop by in the evening and let you know what she suggests.'

Feeling dejected Jim trudged home unaware that a call the following day would bring an interesting and encouraging development into his life.

***

The call, when it came, was from Claire Steele, secretary to the Director of the Stein Foundation, calling to acknowledge Jim's letter. A representative from the Foundation would be visiting the village later in the week to examine the damage. If it was convenient, perhaps Jim and the assessor, Robin Caulfield, could view the statue together.

In answer to his question, she said it was impossible to say at this stage whether the Foundation would restore the statue as much depending on the assessor's report. Perhaps they could talk next week when the report was available.

At least they've responded to my letter, Jim thought as he replaced the receiver. Now he would have something to tell Philippa when they met later at the Cosy Café.

In Butler's Builders, Alex Potter was not having a good day. The phone call from Tony Bean asking the firm to undertake the urgent work in the Pump Room had seriously upset his plans for the week. They were fully booked already. July and the long warm summer days encouraged homeowners to order extensions, patios, and pathways. There were four crews out today and they were fully committed for the rest of the week.

The problem for a small builder like Butler's was big companies like Masons were more likely to require building work during the short days of autumn and winter when the firm was often scrabbling for work. The job Tony Bean was asking his firm to do was not to be sneezed at, but if they took on this extra work, it would mean disappointing an existing customer. Scanning the works schedule for the week ahead, he decided Mrs Graham in Radcliff Road (new chimney and replacement of broken tiles) would have to be that customer.

He would phone Jeff the foreman and explain the situation and tell him to make sure everything Mrs Graham's roof was secure. After lunch, he would also drive over to Applegarth and do a survey on the Pump Room.

Jim arrived early at the Cosy Café and Snackbar and with a few minutes to spare strolled down the path to Pump Room. As he approached, several people were reading a large notice displayed prominently in the middle of the path. The notice read:

We regret to announce the
Temporary Closure of the Pump Room
In order to carry out essential
Repairs and Renovations
We are sorry for any inconvenience
this may cause but we are confident that when reopened
the Pump Room will provide a
Enhanced and Satisfying Experience
for all our
Honoured Visitors

The carefully chosen words explained why and he and Audrey experienced problems convincing Mrs Worthington and her colleagues of the fraud being perpetrated on the village. On this occasion, he had to admit they'd been outmanoeuvred, but the fight wasn't over yet.

Making his way back to the High Street, Jim could hear several visitors loudly expressing their disappointment at the closure of the Pump Room. He was tempted to stop them and explain the whole thing was nothing more than a huge fraud but suspected his views on the benefits of the spring wouldn't be welcomed.

On the High Street and waiting for Philippa, Jim was relieved to see the village was virtually free of the usual hordes of people thronging the pavement.

'Hello Jim, what you are dreaming about?' He turned to see Philippa, looking radiant with her long auburn hair and wearing a white t-shirt and jeans.

'How peaceful it is with the Pump Room closed.'

Philippa looked at him intently. 'What do you mean, with the Pump Room closed?'

'Let's go inside and I'll tell you all about it. You'll be shocked when you hear about the scam Jason's trying to pull.' A few minutes later, seated at the back of the café, with a cup of coffee for Jim and a hot chocolate for Philippa, Jim told her about discovering red paint on the Dancing Couple and the response from the Stein Foundation.

'We'll have to see what this Robin Caulfield says when he gets here. I assume it is a he. Anyway, stop being a tease and tell me about the Pump Room.'

And he did, from the meeting at the Dog and Duck to the clandestine gathering of the committee on Sunday afternoon and their frustrating phone calls to the Association members.

'Is the Pump Room closed today?'

'Yes, sorry I forgot to tell you, there's a sign on the path.

'After the way, Jason Black trampled over everybody to gain control of the Pump Room, nothing surprises me about that man,' Philippa said firmly. 'I still find it difficult to believe he thinks he can get away with a stunt like this. What's happening at the Pump Room now?'

'Nothing, though presumably, the building work will start in the next few days.'

Gulping down the last of her hot chocolate, Philippa got up from the table. 'This is our best chance to expose Jason for the fraudster he really is. Keep a lookout and let me know if anything happens. In the meantime, I must dash,' kissing him quickly on the cheek, she picked up her shopping bags and headed toward the door. 'Bye Philippa' he called as she disappeared.

Looking around for Molly, to pay the bill, his gaze fell upon Katie Black at the counter with a fruitcake in her hand waiting to be served. Catching his eye, a broad smile filled her face. Jim hesitated for a moment, before offering a brief wave. Feeling guilty at being seen with Philippa, he put the money on the table and made for the exit.

Chapter Nine

By nine o'clock on Wednesday morning Jeff and the crew from Butler's Builders had erected the works hut and brewing the first mug of tea of the day.

To their obvious annoyance, Jason appeared soon after and begun supervising the erecting the screens around the site to keep out prying eyes. Standing at the entrance to the Pump Room surveying the unhappy scene, he remembered there was some good news. Alex Potter had uncovered a fast-flowing stream, during his survey of the site, that feeds into the pond. 'Taking water from the stream would enable the spring to be up and running again in a few days. Long before any of the village busybodies had time to make mischief,' Jason suggested on relaying the news to Tony. 'Once the visitors return, the village will be too preoccupied to worry about where the spring water comes from. They'll be happy just to hear the tills ringing again.'

'Now Jeff, are you and the lads clear about what must be done, we can't afford any mistakes.'

'Yes, Mr Black, Alex briefed us before leaving the yard this morning. The one problem is the pump. It was ordered yesterday, but the supplier can't deliver until tomorrow at the earliest.'

'Make sure you keep on top of them and let me know if there are any problems. I'll be back after lunch to see how you're getting on. You've got my mobile number if you need me? Well, I'll be off now. People to see, places to go you know.'

At that precise moment when Jason was leaving the site, a lady was dialling a local number from the office of the *Magical Waters Hotel and Restaurant*. If Jason knew who she was calling, he'd probably concluded he had a much bigger problem on his hands than getting the spring up and running again.

When the phone rang a few moments later in Jim's house, a voice said, 'Hi Jim, I'm sorry you rushed away yesterday. I was rather hoping we might have a chat.' It took him a moment to recognise the caller as Katie Black. They had met a few times before. In a village, the size of Applegarth, it was inevitable everyone knew you and your business.

'Hello Katie, sorry I couldn't stop. I had to get home to let Bix out, what do I owe the pleasure of this call today?'

'Does there have to be a reason?' Katie asked, hoping for an encouraging response, but getting none, she continued. 'I just wanted to say how sorry I was to hear about the damage to the statue in the park. I know you're very fond of it.' He wasn't certain whether her concern was genuine but felt there was no harm in telling her about the response from the Stein Foundation. 'Well that's good news,' she said, 'Tell you what, why don't you give me a ring after this Robin Caulfield has been – is that a man or women by the way.'

'I assume it's a man, but we won't know until he or she gets here, sometime in the next couple of days.'

'Promise me you will ring the moment they've gone. We may need to rally support in the village to raise money to help with the cost of repairing the damage.' He promised to call but was mystified by her sudden interest in the statue. The wife of Jason Black didn't make phone calls to relative strangers without a reason.

In another part of the village, Audrey was arriving at the village allotments from her part-time job at the Library. Before disappearing that morning to drive to the Honiston Building Society, where he was the manager, Les asked her to water his precious leeks. Apart from jazz, Les had one other consuming interest, growing prize-winning leeks. As Audrey told anyone who was prepared to listen, she was a poor third in her husband's affections, but with the Flower and Vegetable Show imminent, he would be keen to retain the first prize he'd achieved for the last three years.

Getting the watering can from the shed and filling it from the tap, her thoughts were more concerned about the Annual Water Festival. It's all very well her husband getting worried about his precious leeks, but the Flower and Vegetable Show was only a small part of the festival. As the secretary to the committee, there was still much to be done.

For the past seventy-odd years, since the end of the war, a Flower and Vegetable Show had been held in the village on the first Saturday in August. Everything went well until two years ago when Jason Black persuaded the committee to incorporate it into a larger festival to celebrate the gift of water.

The proposal came with a promise to underwrite any shortfall in the receipts should they make a loss. The Flower and Vegetable Show lost money every year, and the committee was naturally very keen to accept his generous offer. Audrey saw it as nothing more than a blatant attempt to take over a long-established village tradition and endeavoured to persuade the committee to reject the idea. Her plea to the committee was well received, with several nodding heads as she listed the reasons why the Flower and Vegetable Show should remain independent, but when it came to a decision, she was heavily outvoted.

Les said she should resign, but as with many voluntary organisations, there wasn't anyone to take over the job. Still smarting from her defeat at the hands of Jason Black, Audrey informed the chairperson, Annette Long, she would stand down as soon as a replacement was found. Her intention to resign was firm but as she quickly discovered, all the while she was prepared to carry on, the committee made little effort to find a replacement.

With the last meeting, of the committee before the festival on Friday, it would take her most of the afternoon to prepare the agenda and reports, but first, she had to water the leeks.

She was still working on the committee papers when Jim knocked on the backdoor at six o'clock, 'Bring out your dead,' he shouted walking into the kitchen.

'Hello Jim, put the kettle on will you, I'm parched,' Audrey called out.

'Where are you?'

'In the dining room, I'm working on the papers for the committee meeting.' Filling the kettle and flipping the switch on, Jim poked his head around the door of the dining room to see papers spread all over the table and Audrey tapping away on her computer. 'Where's the old man?'

Briefly looking up at him and then at her watch, she replied, 'I don't know, he is usually home by now, though that sounds like his car pulling into the drive now.'

'Hi, I'm home,' Les announced walking into the kitchen moments later. Seeing Jim, he called out, 'hello mate.' Audrey looked up from the keyboard. 'Where have you been; you're late?' Looking at Jim and smiling Les replied, 'I confess my love, I spent the afternoon in a strip club, drinking Whisky and gambling away our savings.'

Audrey responded with a well-rehearsed piece of banter. 'Don't lie to me. You've been up the allotment to check on your precious leeks.'

'There you are Jim, I'm ready to confess to a life of debauchery and my dear wife can do nothing more than accuse me of being a veggie anorak, which I suppose I am really.'

'As much as I would like to sit here exchanging banter with you, I have to get this finished. And, since my juvenile husband, bless him, can't boil an egg without burning the pan, Jim, be a love and search in the fridge for something for dinner.'

A few minutes later Jim passed a cup of tea through to Audrey and began gathering together the ingredients for a dish of chicken breasts poached in onion, pepper, and white wine sauce. 'Well come on mate, don't keep me in suspense, what happened this morning when you met Philippa?' Putting the chicken into brown and continuing the preparations for the meal, Jim told him about the phone call from the Stein Foundation, the meeting with Philippa in the Cosy Café and the mysterious phone call from Katie Black.

The two men were still pondering the events of the day when Audrey walked into the kitchen. 'That smells nice, Jim what is it.' In response to his description, she took a saucepan from the cupboard and put it on the hob. 'How about some rice, that'll go well with the chicken? Les open a bottle will you, the Australian Riesling we had last week will do nicely, there's a bottle in the fridge.' Whilst Les was opening the wine, Audrey took a spoon and helped herself to some of the sauce in the pan. 'This is really good. You'll make someone a very good wife one day.'

Thank you, kind lady, but did you hear what I was telling Les.'

Yes, through the hatch. I meant to tell you earlier, they've erected hoardings around the Pump Room.'

'When was this?'

'I noticed this afternoon when I was walking home from the allotments. There was also one of Butler's boards hanging from the screens, so presumably, they are doing the work.'

'You mean the builders in Honiston. That's no surprise, Jason couldn't risk getting anyone local doing his dirty work in case they let on the spring was dry.'

'There you are mate, try this.' Les said handing a glass of wine to Jim and then Audrey. 'Here's to our wives and lovers, may they never meet.'

'Les stop messing about and let's enjoy this wonderful meal Jim has prepared. Whilst we're eating, we can decide what to do about Jason Black and his cronies.'

A few minutes later with the three friends tucking into the meal, Jim suggested they should visit the Pump Room and see for themselves what was going on.

'Do they have security guards on the site?' Les asked.

Audrey replied. 'A Silver Knight Security Guards sign is hanging on the hoardings, so they probably have. Since Jason Black wouldn't want anybody knowing what he's up to, the place is bound to be guarded twenty-four hours a day.'

'I can just see it now. Dressed in black, we crawl down the path on all fours, then in complete silence, dig a tunnel and emerge like moles on the other side. It will be like a remake of the Great Escape, with us scattering dirt through a hole in our trouser pockets all the way home.'

Audrey sighed. 'Yes, Les we know you have this fantasy about playing the Steve McQueen role.'

'Being realistic, we need to dress in dark clothes, but I hope we can avoid the tunnelling bit,' Jim said, smiling at Les.

Chapter Ten

A few hours later, any late-night shoppers on the High Street would be surprised to see three furtive figures edging their way down the path leading to the Pump Room. Dressed in black from head to toe, with Les taking things one stage further by dabbing his face and hands with black shoe polish. On reaching the screens, Les pulled a torch from his pockets and shone the light at the Silver Knight Security Guards sign. 'For God's sake, Les turn that bloody thing off, or do want everyone to know we're here,' snapped Audrey.

'Sorry,' he whispered, switching it off.

'Right,' suggested Jim, eyeing the hoardings, 'I reckon if we pull these panels away from the frames, we'll be able to get through. Here, Les give me a hand. Using all their strength, they managed to open up a gap. 'That should be big enough,' Les suggested. Lifting his leg over the exposed steel frame, he gently placed a foot on the soft ground, only to pull it back. 'Bloody hell,' he called out.

A large Alsatian attracted by the noise of their forced entry, began snarling and barking in their direction. The only restraint stopping him sinking his teeth into the three friends being the strong, heavy metal chain in the hands of a large burly guard peering into the gloom.

'That's torn it,' Les said, stepping away from the fence. 'We'll never be able to see what's going on with that bloody dog barking its head off.'

Jim agreed. 'We need to distract the guard.'

In response to a, *what about it*, look from Les, Audrey responded angrily, 'don't look at me I'm not putting on some femme fatale act for the benefit of that big, ugly brute.'

'He's going to be suspicious if we approach him,' Les suggested. 'Come on

Aud do your weak and feeble female impersonation. You can do it.'

She looked hard at him for a moment, 'Okay, but this is going to cost you Mr Lesley Woods, and you know what that means?'

'Yes okay, my love, I promise,' Les said, avoiding Jim's intent gaze, who was intrigued as to the reward Audrey would be demanding from her husband.

'Right then you two stay here, where you can't be seen. As soon as the coast is clear slip in and find out what that Jason Black is up to, okay, but I warn you in ten minutes I'm out of here, so you'd better be on this side of the hoardings.' Without another word, she climbed through the gap and headed toward the hut.

Bill Thomas, the sole guard on duty at this lonely outpost of Silver Knight's vast security empire, was on the point of telling the dog to be quiet when a female figure appeared out of the gloom. When she was five yards away and beyond the reach of the dog, Audrey stopped and gave the guard her biggest smile.

'Attila, Sit, SIT boy,' Bill shouted at the dog as he stepped forward. 'Madam, can I help you,' he said holding back the dog and pointing his torch at Audrey.

'I hope so, young man' cos I am desperate.'

'Oh, right then you'd better come in. We can't talk out here.' Holding Attila tightly, he ushered Audrey into the hut.

Seizing their chance, Jim and Les slipped through the gap and headed for the Pump Room, ignoring the barking, and snarling from Attila.

With the door shut and the dog tethered outside, Audrey faced the guard and slowly eased down the zip on her fleece. She had only a bra underneath and hoped sufficient flesh was on display to ensure the security guard's undivided attention. 'I am so glad you are here. I was afraid there would be nobody about at this time of night.' Audrey spluttered in her best little girl lost voice.

'I'm here all night, we've got the job of guarding this place, though I can't think why there's nothing here of any value. Still, they know best I suppose. Anyway, what can I do for you lady?'

With Attila continuing to bark, Bill moved to the window to stare out into the darkness. 'The dog don't usually bark for no reason,' he exclaimed. 'Something must be up.'

'Perhaps it's the wind whistling through the trees that's disturbing him. Why not bring Attila inside, that way he can protect us from any intruders?' Bill, who had the company procedure on the location of dogs whilst employed on client's premises on the tip of his tongue, turned to see the zip on Audrey's fleece slip another few inches. 'Maybe that would be a clever idea,' he said swallowing hard and moving to the door.

With Attila safely tethered in one corner and commanded to be quiet, Bill turned his attention once again to this mysterious lady, who emerged out of the gloom to brighten his day. 'Now then miss, what can I do for you?' Bill enquired, staring at the ample cleavage on display.

At the Pump Room, Jim and Les were attacking the door. 'It's locked,' Les cried. 'So, what do we do now?'

'Let's look on the other side and see what's going on. Just be careful where you shine that torch.' Keeping close to the walls, the two men edged around to the far side of the Pump Room. 'This is must be how they intend to bring the water from the pond,' Jim suggested pointing to the trench, stretching out in front of them.

'The trouble is it doesn't prove a thing. Jason will say it's part of the improved drainage system they are installing.'

'Knowing what a slippery character he is, you're probably right. We'd had better get back before the guard gets suspicious and comes to investigate. Unless he's stupid, he must be wondering why an attractive woman turns up at this time of night and takes an interest in him.'

'I'm sorry miss you've lost a contact lens in the Pump Room, but it's all locked up and I don't have a key. So, I must ask you to leave.' Audrey glanced at her watch and deciding her time was up, edged toward the door. 'Is there nothing you can do? I am lost without my contact lenses. I can hardly see without them.'

Opening the door to check the coast was clear, she watched helplessly as Attila broke free of his leash roared passed her, barking and snarling.

'There *is* somebody out there,' the guard said moving past her.

The next few moments resembled the scene from a silent movie with Audrey in the role of the helpless spectator as Jim and Les scurried like mad to reach the gap in the hoarding with the dog in hot pursuit. Jim got to the gap first and squeezed through. Les a foot or so behind was within inches when the Attila made one a desperate lunge at his backside. The cry Les let out could be heard in the High Street, but despite the excruciating pain he struggled to squeeze through. With Jim urging him, Les managed to get halfway, but with Attila attached to his backside, something was bound to give. For brief a moment, it seemed Attila would win the tug of war. But, with one almighty heave, Les made his escape, leaving Attila chopping on the seat of a pair of black trousers.

'Heh, you come back here,' Bill called out, trundling toward the gap. He was rather overweight and not very fit, and Audrey was able to reach the hoarding well before him. 'Heh, take it easy,' she cried as he puffed and panted toward her. 'I have to go after those bloody hooligans,' he uttered gasping for breath.

'Take it easy, you'll have a heart attack if you carry on like that? Besides, there'll long gone by now.'

'You're right, they don't pay me enough to go chasing after hooligans at this time of night, but at least one of them got his arse chewed.'

'Yes, serves him right, now if you'll excuse me, I'll be off,' and before Bill could say a word, Audrey zipped up her fleece and disappeared through the hole, leaving Bill staring at the screens puzzled by the events of the last ten minutes.

Limping up the path, Les furiously rubbed his backside. 'That bloody dog got me,' he called out as Audrey joined them. 'We were doing okay until some bloody fool opened the door and let the dog out.'

'How was I to know you were going to choose that precise moment to make your escape? Serves you right, you should have been the other side of the hoarding.'

'Well that's all very well, but I'm standing here with my arse hanging out, I could die from exposure.'

'Ah, did your poor little botty get bitten, what a shame. You'd better cover it up before some nasty policeman comes along and arrests you for indecent exposure,' she added giving his backside a tap.

Reaching the High Street, Les turned to Audrey and in his most plaintive voice, asked, 'does this mean you won't be wanting, me to... I mean given my...'

'I don't see why not, after all, it's not as if the necessary appendage got damaged is it,' Audrey replied keeping a straight face.

Chapter Eleven

'Do I have the pleasure of addressing Mr James White?' a husky voice asked when Jim opened the front door on Friday morning. Standing on the doorstep waiting patiently for an answer was a tall, slim blonde with sparkling blue eyes, skin the colour of pale honey, and dressed in a yellow shirt and grey trousers. Faced with this beautiful creature, Jim was lost for words for a moment, before managing to blurt out. 'It's Jim actually. How can I help?'

'Okay, Jim. I wasn't sure whether I'd come to the right house.'

'You've reached the right house, but I don't understand,' he muttered struggling to regain his composure.

'Sorry, I'm forgetting my manners. My name is Robin Caulfield, from the Stein Foundation.'

'I was expecting, well actually I am not sure what to expect, but not…' was all he could manage before drying up.

'A man, yes I know. It happens all the time. People expect a great big strapping bloke and instead, they get little old me.'

'Well, I wasn't sure what to expect. They should make it clear.'

'You obviously spoke to my colleague Claire. She is always doing it to me. Never makes it clear its Ms Caulfield. I'm sure she does it to embarrass me. I'm sorry if you're disappointed.'

'No at all – far from it. Look, come in,' Jim said opening the door wide and walking into the living room. 'Let me turn this off,' he added moving to the CD player and cutting off Bix Beiderbecke in full flow.

'You're a jazz fan. My late husband was an admirer of Duke Ellington. We had all his recordings. And who's this,' she says stroking the black and white terrier, who on hearing voices, came through from the kitchen and was standing looking up and wagging his tail.'

'Oh him; his name is Bix – after Mr Beiderbecke of course – and he's as daft as a brush.'

'No, he's not, he's lovely aren't you,' she says stroking his head. 'I miss having a dog. We had a black labby, but he died shortly after my husband died and I didn't have the heart to get another one.'

'I know what you mean, but please take a seat. Can I get you coffee or tea?'

'Coffee, white with one sugar please.'

'Right, well I'll leave you two to get better acquainted whilst I put the kettle on,' he said going into the kitchen and opening the hatch. 'What's the plan for this morning, Robin, if I may call you that?'

Still stroking Bix, she replied, 'Yes, please do. I thought after we've finished our coffees, we might walk down to the Memorial Park and look at the statue. I need to examine the damage and take some pictures. After that, it's up to the Trustees.'

Jim appeared holding two cups of coffee. 'What are they likely to decide?'

'Hopefully, they'll agree to restore the statue. On the other hand, they might decide it's not worth restoring and ship it back to the warehouse. It could be down to what funds are available this year, for repairs and restorations.'

He handed her one of the cups. 'The statue means an awful lot to me and the rest of the village.'

Sipping his coffee, Jim sat in the armchair opposite and watched as Robin looked idly around the room. Pointing to a framed photograph on the mantelpiece she asked, 'Is that your wife, she is very beautiful?'

'Was I'm afraid, she died two years ago,'

'I'm sorry.' In the awkward pause that followed, Robin finished her coffee and returned her cup on the table. 'Right then, I'll leave you to lead the way. Is it far?' she asked.

'No, only five minutes away, I'll get my jacket. Do you mind if we take Bix, he likes a run in the Park?'

'No of course not, I'll get my things from the car and meet you outside.'

A few minutes later with Bix leading the way, they set off. To make conversation, Jim asked how long she has been with the Foundation. She told him she achieved a modest arts history degree from Bristol and then upped sticks to work for one of the large galleries in the capital. Her husband, who she met shortly after moving to London, was killed in an air crash eighteen months ago, she still missed him, but with the support of her family, it was time to move on and accepted an offer of work from the Foundation.

As they turned into the tree-lined path, Robin asked, 'What about you, are you retired?'

'Reluctantly yes, for twenty years I was a lecturer at Honiston Arts and Technical College, teaching on their graphic communication course. But with fewer students signing up and printing employers taking fewer apprentices, the college closed the department. They offered me a good pension and a generous redundancy package, and I took it. I still do the odd bit of lecturing on their graphic design course, but that's about all.'

'Any children, if you don't mind me asking?'

'No, of course not, I have a daughter. She married a guy from down under; they live in a beautiful house overlooking Sydney Harbour. I hope to go out and see them, and my grandson, next year. You?'

'No, we couldn't. Shame, because I would have liked kids: still there have been other compensations.'

They were on the hedge-lined path and the Dancing Couple was coming into view. Jim knew what to expect, but seeing the statue covered in red paint still brought feelings of anger and despair.

Jim released Bix, who scampered off his nose sniffing the air, as Robin began examining the statue inch by inch with a magnifying glass. After a few minutes, she stepped back, 'It's not too bad. I've taken a sample of the paint for analysis. I'd better take some shots from different angles,' she said pulling a small camera from her bag and taking pictures around the statue. Finishing with a close upshot of where the paint and bronze overlapped.

'It's a lovely piece: I've only ever seen a photograph. In the flesh, it's bigger than I had imagined. I can see why you're fond of it.'

'It's what my wife Nancy and I use to do, ballroom dancing that is. We took part in competitions all over the South West. We never won any big prizes but enjoyed the camaraderie and friendships.' Packing her things back in the bag, Robin asked, 'do you still do it, I mean the dancing?'

'Not anymore, it's not the same on your own. I kept in touch with a few of the guys after Nancy died, but it's a world of couples, a single man doesn't really fit in.'

'Right, I am finished here, let's get back shall we.' With one last look at the statue, Jim shouted to Bix and they headed out of the park.

Back at the cottage, Robin stopped with her hand on the car door. 'Jim, thanks for your help today. I can't promise anything, but I believe it can be restored. I'll certainly recommend it to the Trustees.' Getting in and starting the engine, she called out, 'I'll be in touch again when there is some news. Bye.'

'Goodbye. Safe journey,' Jim replied as he watched her car disappear out of view.

Later that day, he rang Philippa to bring her up to date, but she interrupted him before he could speak. 'I'm in the middle of lunch for some of Bob's clients, and I can't talk. I'm on flower duty this week. Meet me at the church tomorrow afternoon after three. We can talk for as long as you like.'

Jim felt thrilled and elated when he looked back on the day, though he couldn't explain why even to himself.

In the Pump Room, it was not the best of days for Jason. The pump needed to bring water from the stream hadn't arrived. Alex Potter rang in the afternoon to say they'd been let down by the supplier, but the pump would be on-site by Monday afternoon at the latest.

Chapter Twelve

A church, named after Saint Matthew, existed on the same site in Applegarth since the thirteenth century, though the Victorians managed to knock the tower about a bit and added chapel or two in honour of a couple of saints. Despite its lack of classical features, or maybe because of them, the magnificent stain glass windows, the five-foot-high gold cross above a simple slate altar, and high-back pews attracted a steady stream of visitors, seeking refuge from the blatant commercialism on the nearby High Street. In the summer, the blaze of colour created by the small band of devoted flower arrangers added to its attractions.

When Jim stepped into the church a little after three-thirty, the following Saturday, a change in light from the bright sunshine outside to the relative gloom of the interior forced him to stop for a moment to allow time for his eyesight to adjust.

His attendance at church had fallen away after Nancy died, though they were never regular churchgoers. Morning service once a month and the candlelight carol service on Christmas Eve was the limit of their participation.

As his eyes adjusted to the light, he could see Philippa standing below the pulpit and surveying the large box of flowers resting on the front pew. Hearing the sound of footsteps approaching, Philippa looked up.

'What's your knowledge of flowers like?'

'Are those the things with green stalks and white, yellow or red fluffy bits on the end.'

'Okay, so you're not going to be much help, are you?'

'Afraid not, but I did ask Les and Audrey to join us. Their house is always full of flowers, and I can't believe it's down to Les.'

'Excellent idea. Be a dear and fill this vase with water. The kitchen is through that door there,' she said pointing to the large oak door with black ironwork hinges.

Returning a few minutes later, Jim was pleased to see Les and Audrey sitting in the front pew admiring the stain glass window above the altar. 'Put it over there please,' Philippa said directing Jim to the wooden pedestal below the pulpit.

'Perhaps I can help,' Audrey said. 'I love arranging flowers. Our house is a bit small, so I don't get the chance to do big displays.'

'That's kind; perhaps you could make a start with the choir stalls. I thought the asters and marguerites would look nice together. You'll find a pair of scissors in the box.'

Philippa gathered up a bunch of gladioli and began arranging them in the vase. 'While I'm doing this, bring me up to date with what's been going on,'

And he did, though this version glossed over the incident involving Attila and Les losing the seat of his trousers; it played heavily on the courage of the two men in getting a good look at the Pump Room and concluded with the visit by the assessor from the Stein Foundation.

'Oh, so Robin was a woman, was she nice. I only ask because I detected a slightly more than professional interest when you talked about her.'

'That about sums it up,' said Les, who was passing on his way to the kitchen. 'Mind you she's out of his league. After all who would want a broken-down ex-college lecturer with a penchant for roasting dead animals and a passion for an alcoholic, jazz-playing American cornet player?'

'Les go and fill the vase,' Philippa said pointing toward the kitchen.

'Ask him about the phone call from Katie Black,' Les called out before disappearing.

'What about her,' Philippa said, pointing a large gladiolus at him. Sheepishly Jim described the encounter in the café and the phone call the following day. 'What did she want?'

'To get her hands on his body, though I can't for the life of me think why? Not when she could have mine free of charge,' Les said emerging from the kitchen with a vase filled with water.

'Les go and give Audrey a hand with the flowers. You're not helping.'

'I've no idea what she wanted. I was surprised as everyone else when she rang. She expressed an interest in the Dancing Couple, though whether it was genuine or not, I haven't the faintest idea' Satisfied with the arrangement of the gladioli, Philippa joined Jim on the front pew. 'I've only met her on a couple of occasions when the Pump Room Committee met at the hotel, but she struck me as someone on a different wavelength to her husband.'

'But what do I do. I promised to call her after Robin Caulfield left, but I am a bit reluctant. She is. after all, married to Jason Black.'

Having completed the choir stall flowers, Audrey stood listening to their conversation. 'On the other hand, Jim, she could prove to be the weak link in her husband's armour.'

'You mean like a Trojan Horse,' Les offered, as he moved to join them.

Philippa smiled. 'I wouldn't describe her in those terms, but I understand what Les and Audrey mean.'

'Take a look at my flower arrangement Philippa and tell me what you think, while I explain to Jim what he should do.' With a nod, Philippa wandered away, as Audrey took her place in the pew. 'It would be an enormous advantage if Katie was on our side. For a start, she could tell us what her conniving husband was up to.'

'Like a modern-day, Marta Hari,' Les said with a smile.

'Les, I don't know why every idea that comes into your head has to be viewed through the prism of your wartime fantasies, but in essence yes, you're right. And before you even think about it, spare us the scene where Marta Hari seduces the love-struck British Tommy.'

'That's beautiful, Audrey. You're very clever. I wish I could do them like that. I hesitate to ask, but there are some delphiniums and larkspur in the box. Could you do the other vase, the one below the organ?' Audrey nodded and wandered away to get the flowers, giving Les the vase to fill with water.

'From what you discovered at the Pump Room, it's going to be difficult to accuse Jason Black of anything,' Philippa said resuming the seat next to him. 'He would say the trench doesn't prove anything. It's part of a new drainage system they are installing.'

'Jim hesitated for a moment as a new thought filled his head. 'Have you considered the possibility it was just a ruse? The real purpose was to find out what we know.

'A fair point Jim, but it could still work to our advantage. For example, is if she can be persuaded, or cajoled into telling us what's going on at her end, we can feed her with misleading information about what we're planning to do. It's a win, win situation.

'Ladies and gentlemen how delightful to see you, and may I say how wonderful the floral displays are looking today,' Alan Howard offered, as he entered from the vestry and interrupted their conversation. 'Hello Alan,' Philippa said getting up to meet him. 'I've had the advantage of Audrey's help today. I tend to adopt the "chuck it into a vase and hope for the best" approach, but Audrey, as you can see, has real talent.'

Moving to below the organ, where Audrey was preparing the delphiniums and larkspur, he touched her arm, 'Thank you, my dear, your gallant efforts are much appreciated. Let's hope we see more of you in church. Now, if you will excuse me, I must dash to the stationers in the High Street before they close,' and with that, he strode down the aisle and disappeared.

'Do you think he heard anything?' Les asked.

'I doubt it, Alan is a good man, but he tends to be a bit preoccupied with his own thoughts. Now, about Jim. I say he should contact Katie. What about you?'

Audrey, arranging the delphiniums, looked toward Jim and Philippa, 'It could be the best chance we have of finding out what's going on. It's up to Jim, he's the one who's got to talk to the damn woman, not us.'

Jim looked around at the approving faces. 'If that's what everyone thinks I will, but the other thought I had was about the Pump Room Association AGM, when's that due.'

'You're not members, are you?' enquired Philippa. 'It normally takes place at the end of July, but the notices haven't gone out yet.'

'It will look a bit suspicious if Les, Audrey and I were to suddenly apply to join, but we have to find a way of creating a bit of a stink at the meeting,' Jim suggested.

'Right' Philippa responded, 'but let see what happens when you speak to Katie. Audrey that looks lovely,' she said getting up and admiring Audrey's handiwork. 'Now if you guys want to push off, I'll clear up here.'

'Are you sure Philippa?'

'Yes, of course, and thanks for your help: Jim, keep in touch, yes.'

'Yes, sure, take care,' Jim said as he joined Les and Audrey, walking down the aisle. 'What shall we have for lunch tomorrow then?' Audrey asked as Jim caught them up.

'Jim, I forgot.' Philippa called out. 'Did Robin Caulfield say how long before the Trust decided what to do about the Dancing Couple?'

Turning, Jim called back. 'No, but hopefully we'll know something next week.'

'Let me know the moment you hear from her,' Philippa called out, contemplating the mess left by the flower arranging party.

Chapter Thirteen

With the Pump Room closed, the approach roads to the village, normally filled with coaches was deserted, as the tour companies concentrated on selling tours to other attractions. Filling a forty-seat coach was challenging at the best of times and Applegarth with its Magical Spring Water was a money-spinner. It might be again, once the Pump Room re-opened. Until then, they would have to rely on the Black Hills of Wales and Wye Valley to bring in the punters.

Sitting in his office on Monday morning and totting up the takings for the weekend Jason Black was perplexed. The business had undoubtedly suffered from the closure of the Pump Room. For the first time in years, the restaurant wasn't fully booked for Sunday lunch, and the number of guests checking into the hotel was down.

Lying on his desk was a copy of the *Honiton Observer,* with a picture of the sign on the path to the Pump Room spread across three columns, with the headline, "Major Attraction Closed for Repairs.*"* He'd read the article the moment the paper arrived but didn't have worry. It was little more than a reprise of the basic facts, with a couple of quotes from local shopkeepers regretting the closure and hoping it would re-open soon. One of which he noted, with pleasure, was from Jack Thompson.

The closure of the Pump Room was under control, but it left a more immediate problem. Until the pump was installed, he couldn't begin to think about re-opening. The longer it remained closed, the more opportunities there would be for certain people in the village to cause mischief.

'I need to get behind Alex Potter at Butler's,' he muttered. 'Now where's his number, it was here on the desk yesterday.' Finding it buried under a pile of bills, he was on the point of picking up the phone, when it rang. 'Good morning, the *Magical Waters Hotel and Restaurant,*' he said into the mouthpiece.

'May I speak please to Mrs Black,' the voice at the other end asked.

'I'm afraid she is not here, can I help.'

'Never mind, I call back later,' the caller replied and with that, the phone went dead. Strange, Jason thought to himself, it must be one of those damn charities Katie was always going on about. They were forever ringing up asking for handouts of one sort or another. Did they think he was made of money?

Having put off making the phone call, Jim was taken back when Jason Black answered. What was he supposed to do now? Ring every ten minutes in the hope Katie would answer and slam the phone down if her husband picked it up?

As it turned out he didn't have to.

He was on the point of loading his mug and plate in the dishwasher after lunch when the phone rang, and a familiar voice said, 'Hi Jim it's me, Katie. I just ringing to check your in. I'm parked around the corner. I'll be with you in a couple of minutes.'

'Hang on Katie...,' Jim called out, but it was too late, she'd rung off. If he had a plan on what to say during the phone call, it went no further than a quick summary of the visit by Robin Caulfield and playing it by ear. The last thing he expected was for Katie to appear unexpectedly at his cottage. Now, he had only a couple of minutes to plan for this new situation. He was on the verge of deciding what to do when the front doorbell rang. With Bix barking and snapping at his heels he slowly opened the door and was met by, 'Hi, Jim, can I come in?'

'Eh, yes please do. For some reason, Bix has taken instant a dislike to you. He is not usually like this when people call. Look, why don't I close the door and put him in the kitchen.' When he returned Katie, was in the living room, holding the picture of Nancy he kept on the mantelpiece. 'She was very beautiful.'

Replacing the photograph, he said. 'Yes, she was, and I miss her still.'

'I'm sure you do, but perhaps you need to move on, you're still a relatively young man with a lot to offer.'

Ignoring the compliment, Jim invited her to sit in one of the armchairs. 'I tried to ring you this morning, but your husband answered.'

'Yes. I know. He told me there'd been a phone call from a strange man. He thought it was from one of my charities, but I guessed it was you. So, what did this chap from the Stein Foundation have to say?'

'Actually, it wasn't a man. Robin turned out to be a woman,' he replied

'Some old trout with twin set and pearls, I suppose.' He wanted to tell her about the gorgeous woman who appeared at his door, how cool she was, how professional she was, how concerned she was for the Dancing Couple, but merely mumbled, 'Something like that.'

'What happened then?' Katie enquired.

Composing himself, Jim described how they went to the Memorial Park to look at the statue. 'After studying the damage carefully, she took some photographs and a sample of the paint for analysis,' he added

'Did she say what happens next?'

'Yes, Ms Caulfield compiles a report to the Trustees, who decide whether to restore the statue or take it away.'

'Why wouldn't they restore it?'

'If the damage is too bad or if it proves too expensive to repair. She said something about it coming down to how much money was in the kitty.'

'I know how much it means to you. How much it means to all of us. Your letter in the *Observer* was heartfelt,' she said getting up and joining him on the sofa. 'I would really like to help restore that beautiful statue if you will let me,' she said looking straight into his eyes.

Jim hadn't been this close, this intimate with a woman for years. He had to admit Katie was an attractive woman, big hazel eyes, auburn hair wrapped neatly around her face, high cheekbones and full lips. Dressed in a white halter-top and tight red skirt that rode above her knees, she was also very desirable. This is madness he decided, getting up and sidling to the fireplace. This is the wife of that appalling man Jason Black, the lying cheating, conniving chairman of the Pump Room Committee, who was about to perpetrate an appalling deceit on the village and all the visitors to the spring. He couldn't be attracted to her; it didn't bear thinking about.

'That's very kind of you Katie,' he mumbled, as he sought to control the lustful thoughts circling his head. He was supposed to be using this opportunity to tease out information, not get emotionally involved.

'I thought we could work together,' Katie said getting up and taking a step toward him. 'Rally support; raise money for the restoration, that sort of thing. Would you like that,' she said reaching out and putting her full lips to his and pressing hard.

Jim's automatic reaction was to return the kiss. Her lips were soft and warm. Part of him longed to take her his arms and dam the consequences. But there was another voice inside his head, a more rational person. This one said: no. this is silly, this cannot be. 'Heh, what was that for,' he said pulling away and holding her at arm's length.

'You must know I like you. From the way you looked at me, I assumed the feeling was mutual.'

'Yes, but let's not rush things, let's get to know each other first,' he said letting go of her. 'There is also the small question of your husband.'

'Oh, Jason, he doesn't care about me. He's only interested in making money and touching up the waitresses in the restaurant. I'm sure something is going on with that Janie; she always strikes me as a bit too knowing. Now, where were we?'

He couldn't be explained afterwards what made Bix chose that precise moment to charge out of the kitchen, barking and jumping up at Katie, but he did. Faced with this attack Katie had no option but to defend herself. Surprised by this sudden turn of events, Jim was slow to react, but eventually, after a struggle, he managed to grab hold of Bix's collar and pull him away. 'I'm sorry about this,' he shouted above the noise. 'He's usually so friendly. You'd had better go. I'll ring in the next couple of days and we can arrange something.'

Katie, visibly shocked by the dog's reaction to her, stared at Jim with a, 'does it have to be like this,' look. Getting no response, she had no option but to give up and move to the hallway. 'Jason is out tomorrow, some meeting or other. Ring at about eleven and we can talk. Promise,' she said before disappearing.

With Bix sitting quietly at his feet, Jim stared at the door trying to make sense of the last few minutes. 'What earth came over me?' he muttered silently to himself. 'What made me think of Katie Black, the wife of Jason Black, my arch enemy in that way? More importantly, what the hell am I going to tell Philippa and the others.'

The answer came minutes later when Philippa rang, and without any preliminaries got straight to the point. 'What happened when you rang Katie Black?'

Putting aside his confused feelings and emotions, he recounted how Katie turned up out of blue and the reception she received from Bix.

Philippa enjoyed hearing about Katie being attacked and couldn't stop laughing. 'Serves her right the stupid bitch,' she finally managed. 'Is that all?'

'No, she promised to help in any way she could to restore the statue.'

'What about the Pump Room,' Philippa enquired, 'did you managed to get any information about what her husband's up to? Knowing he had failed. Jim changed the subject by recounting Bix's second attempt to scare her off. This set Philippa off on another round of giggles that continued until the phone finally went dead.

Later, he plucked up the courage and repeated Katie's offer to Les and her demand he should call her. 'What you going to do?' Les enquired.

'Keep my promise and ring again tomorrow,' Jim replied, without enthusiasm.

Chapter Fourteen

In the Pump Room, Jason watched with quiet satisfaction as the crew from Butler's began installing the heavy-duty pump needed to transfer the water from the underground stream. With the pump installed, he mused, it shouldn't take more than a couple of days to get the pipes laid and water gushing from the fountain. With a new floor laid and a lick of paint on the walls, they could be open by the weekend.

The brief smile flashed across Jason's face at the prospect, quickly vanished when he remembered the Annual General Meeting of the Pump Room Association still had to be organised. Strictly speaking, the notices should have gone out a week ago, but he'd held back. He didn't want to be censured for something as trivial as late notification of the meeting, nor did he want the meeting taking place while the Pump Room remained closed. If the notices were posted in two days, it would be okay. But it would mean keeping on top of the builders to make sure the job was not delayed.

The other problem occupying Jason's thoughts was the Honiston Business League. Today was the last meeting before the election for the new president and he was anxious to get to the pre-lunch meeting and canvass support for his candidacy. One of his ambitions since moving to Applegarth was to achieve the presidency of the League and this year he was determined the prize would be his. Once the gold-chained badge of office was adorning his chest, he'd show those snobby bankers and estate agents not to look down on him. Leading his pretty wife onto the floor for the first dance at the Annual Ladies' Night, as they stood, and watched would be his moment of crowning glory.

At that moment, Jason's pretty wife wasn't giving much thought to her husband's ambitions, or to the Honiston Business League Ladies' Night. She was, in fact, sitting in the car park at Fullton Woods. Her companion, Jim White, wasn't thinking about the Ladies' Night either. He was more worried about extracting himself from this delicate situation.

He kept his promise - albeit reluctantly – and rang Katie at eleven o'clock. She'd answered on the first ring, and before he could say anything, Katie announced she was on her way over and would be outside his cottage in five minutes. And she was, with a loud toot on the horn to announce her presence and with a throaty roar as they took off the moment Jim clambered in. Struggling to get his seat belt fastened, he asked where they were going. 'It's a surprise, just sit back and enjoy the ride,' she responded, with a knowing look.

Parked at Fullton Woods, Jim was not happy. He wasn't sure what sort car it was, he guessed a Range Rover or some such, though the size and make of car wasn't the problem. The problem was sitting opposite him in the form of a very attractive and desirable woman, who was making it perfectly clear what she wanted.

'We can't meet at your place,' she said. 'For some reason, your dog has taken an instant dislike to me though I can't think why. We can't meet at the hotel because my husband is usually around. So, I thought here would be nice and quiet and we wouldn't be disturbed,' Katie said moving across and putting her hand on his cheek.

Keep cool, don't get drawn, don't make any sudden moves, Jim decided. Don't let your emotions get the better of you, and bear in mind the only reason you are here is to find out what she knows about the Pump Room.

'How would we raise money to pay for the restoration - if we had to - that is,' he said conscious of a warm, soft hand on his cheek.

'We could always play a little game and the first one to come has to pay a forfeit,' Katie replied looking deep into his eyes.

'I'm serious,' Jim said removing her hand from his cheek and returning it to her lap.

Flopping back in her seat she said, 'you're no fun.'

Jim glanced across and the seductive look in her eyes overcame any ideas he had about staying in control. Without a word, he leaned across and kissed her hard on the mouth. She responded willingly and before long they were thrashing around kissing and touching. Several buttons of his shirt were ripped open, her green t-shirt was pulled up and bra unclipped, and his hand felt warm soft flesh.

Their passion might have reached a natural and satisfying conclusion were it not for an interruption in the shape of a motorised road sweeper, the property of Honiston District Council. According to the schedule stipulated by the Town Clerk, today was when the car park at Fullton Woods was due for its monthly clean-up.

By the time the lovers became aware of the sweeper, they were staring up at the cab and the driver, who indicated with very specific hand gestures how they and their car were hindering the execution of his civic duty. Hastily doing up buttons and bra straps, the frustrated pair flopped back in their respective seats and with a few deft movements, Katie backed the car onto the road and headed back to Applegarth.

Completely oblivious, Todd Brown continued his sweeping operations, up and down in neat rows unaware of the distress his action had inflicted on the newly paired lovers and the consummation of their passion.

Driving back to the village Jim and Katie didn't speak, their heads consumed by private thoughts and sheer frustration. Arriving at Jim's cottage, Katie put her hand on Jim's arm. 'I have to get back to the restaurant to oversee lunch, but we can't leave it like this. I'll ring you tomorrow.' Without replying Jim got out the car and putting the key in the door of his cottage, turned to see Katie's car disappearing in the direction of the village.

'That was a lucky escape,' he muttered to himself as Bix came bounding down the hallway to greet him.

Chapter Fifteen

The Rev. Alan Howard was also feeling frustrated, though not for the same reasons. His frustration was borne out of the advice, or lack of it, from the bishop on the question of the plan to pump water from the pond. Their meeting, the previous day, was a regular monthly get together to discuss parochial matters and the bishop's plans for an inter-denominational conference next year.

Inevitably, the subject of the Organ Restoration Fund reared up and the bishop enquired what progress the Parochial Church Council was making toward achieving their £50,000 target. He was particularly concerned about the promised donations from several local businesses leaders and asked pointedly whether they would be forthcoming.

Alan took a deep breath. He hadn't intended repeating the threats made by Jason Black and the members of the Pump Room Committee to withdraw their promised donations but felt he had no option. In many ways, he was relieved to share the burden and seek the bishop's advice on what his response should be. As the leader of the hundred or so souls who regularly worshipped at the church, life could be lonely at times. He missed his wife, Penny, nursing her sick father in Plymouth. Apart from the few days when she returned to pick up a change of clothes and cook dinners for the freezer, she'd been absent from the family household for over two months.

He didn't resent the attention she was giving her father; he was a sick man and not expected to last long, but it would be nice to share the burdens of his office with a sympathetic soul. There was Catherine Plimpton of course, a stalwart of the church who popped into the vicarage daily to check on whether was there was anything she could do to help, 'While the little woman was away,' she trilled.

An uncharitable person might suppose her visits were just an excuse to nose around the house. Her habit of picking up letters, opening drawers, cupboards and generally poking about was particularly irritating. 'Who is this from hen?' she would ask holding a letter sitting on the kitchen table waiting to be opened. He had no secrets from Penny, but he didn't see why busybodies like Mrs Plimpton felt they could invade his privacy.

If he was hoping for a few words of wisdom from the bishop, he was disappointed. 'I could not possibly advise you on such a delicate matter. It has to be for your conscience alone, dear boy,' was his only response.

Alan's attempt to pursue the subject was cut short by bishop launching into, 'now this conference, Alan. I very much hope I can count on the support of your flock in Applegarth. It will be so important to our success. Don't you agree?'

These thoughts were uppermost in his head as he strolled up the High Street to the Cosy Café and Snack-bar. He was hoping to catch Brian Thorpe and persuade him of the immorality of the proposal.

Opening the door to café, with its tinkle bell, he noticed Brian taking an order from a couple sitting in the window. Not wishing to disturb him, he sat at one of the side tables hoping to catch his eye on his way back to the kitchen. He didn't have long to wait, and as Brian passed, he touched his arm, 'Can we have a word.' Looking around the café and seeing only three tables occupied, 'Hang on a moment,' he replied, 'I'll pass this to through to Sheila. Do you want a coffee, vicar?

'Yes, that will be nice,' Alan replied as his host disappeared through the hanging curtain leading to the small kitchen at the back. Looking around at his surroundings, Alan took in the seven or eight tables in the café, each with a lace cloth and four chairs. He'd been in the cafe once or twice with Penny, but noticed for the first time, the flowered wallpaper and hunting prints on the walls and individual pots of sugar, salt and pepper set neatly on a paper doily on each table. 'We are not too busy today,' Brian said handing Alan a cup of coffee. 'Molly, our part-time waitress, can cope if anyone comes in.' Accepting the coffee and stirring in two sugars, Alan asked what happened at the meeting. 'Didn't happen,' was the reply. 'Jason rang on Monday to say

Butlers had agreed to do the work and he'd keep us informed of any developments. Oh, he also said he'd contacted a few of the members of the Association, including Mrs Worthington, and cleared it with them.'

'What is happening now, do you know?'

'I popped down to the Pump Room this morning and hoardings have been put up all around the place. There was a lot of activity, so I assume the work has begun. Given the drop in our takings, I'll be jolly glad when the spring opens again.

Alan was on the point of taking a sip of coffee but returned his to cup to the saucer. 'That can't be the only consideration, can it?'

'How do you mean?'

'There is a moral question surely. What's happening amounts to nothing more than a dreadful deceit on the village and the visitors who come to our community.'

'I respect your point of view Alan, but the way Sheila and I see it, the spring and all that stuff about curing ills and ailments is just a bit of fun. Nobody takes it, seriously do they?'

'Well, some do, I afraid. This gift from God is a lifeline to many poor souls and there are numerous tales of sick and distressed folk experiencing relief from their aliments after taking the water at the spring.'

'Do you intend to spend all morning gossiping with the vicar, sorry your Reverence, or are you going to help me prepare lunch?' The voice of authority was Sheila. Appearing from the kitchen and directing her remarks toward her husband. In her view, it was all very well for the likes of Alan Howard to adopt a moral tone, but his livelihood didn't depend on the spring. The sooner the Pump Room was up and running the quicker the village would get back to normal.

Brian edged back to the hanging curtains and the kitchen. 'Sorry vicar,' he said. Don't think I'm unsympathetic, but you know how it is. Why don't you have a word with Philippa Pearson, she was here the other day talking to Jim White, and I don't suppose it was about the skittles fixture list for next year.'

'Perhaps I will,' Alan replied, making for the exit. 'Yes, perhaps I will.'

Chapter Sixteen

Jason was beginning to believe this was going to be a red-letter day. Jeff and the crew from Butler's had dug a shaft to the underground stream, installed the pump and connected it to the pipes running to the Pump Room. As he looked on, they were boring a hole in the wall ready to lay the pipes across the floor to the fountain.

With one of the pipes in his hand, Jason tapped Jeff on the shoulder. 'Are those pipes new, they don't look at it?'

'They were left over from another job Mr Black. They are a bit mucky and covered in moss, or whatever that green stuff is, but to keep the cost down the boss thought you wouldn't mind if we used on this job.'

'Anything that keeps the cost down, but what's left to do?'

'Once the pipes are laid, it should be a simple matter to connect the supply to the fountain. Then, with the floor re-laid and a lick of paint slapped on the walls, the job should be finished.'

'Meaning we can re-open.'

'Not quite, it will depend on how long the water takes to clear. The building work stirred up the mud underground, and it'll take a while to settle, shouldn't be more than a couple of days.' Meaning the Pump Room could be open before the Annual General Meeting. Okay, so there might be a few awkward questions from a few stupid fools who wanted to nick-pick over the closure, but he could deal with that. A sharp reminder about what could have happened if the Committee ignored the safety problems would soon put a stop to any nonsense like that.

This was the second day when things had gone well for him. At the Honiston Business League, several members approached him to offer their support for his candidacy. After the drop-in takings at the hotel, getting the spring operating again and tying up the presidency would be the compensation enough.

In another part of town, his wife, Katie, was also looking forward to a red-letter day. With Jason, away for most of the day and the Pump Room closed, there were few guests booked into the hotel. With all those empty bedrooms going to waste it was an opportunity not to be missed. How to best engineer it though, that was the question?

She could ring Jim and tell him to book into the bridal suite, but that would be too obvious. On the other hand, her purchase at the Honiston Music Store during a recent shopping trip could be the answer.

At that moment, Jim would have settled for nothing more than control over a rather dirty and dishevelled looking terrier. Having spent the morning digging in the garden Bix was in urgent need of a bath. An undertaking that was bound to end with soapsuds and water all over him, the floor, and walls of the bathroom, but it had to be done.

The only problem was Bix had other ideas. With the first hint of water running in the bath, he shot through the dog-flap into the garden barking and squealing. Opening the kitchen door, Jim called out, 'Bix, it's time for your bath.' His favourite hiding place was underneath the shed at the bottom of the garden and Jim was on the point of charging across the lawn when the phone rang. 'Damn,' he muttered, but hoping it might be Robin, he changed directions and got to the phone just as it stopped ringing.

It took some persuading but eventually, he managed to grab Bix and dump him unceremoniously in the bath. After that, it was the usual story of fighting to wash him with Bix resisting every inch of the way. At the point when soapsuds covered most of the walls and he was soaked from head to waist, the phone rang again. On the sixth ring, the answering machine cut in and after the usual outgoing message, he heard Katie's voice through the speakers. 'Jim, I was in Honiston recently and picked up a recording of Bix Beiderbecke you might not have heard before. Ring me when you get this message.'

Jim was confident his collection included every recording ever made by the master, yet ten minutes later having washed and dried Bix he was dialling the number for the *Magical Waters Restaurant and Hotel*. 'Can I speak to Mrs Black please,' he asked when an unknown female voice answered the phone. He was put through almost immediately. 'Hello Jim, listen to this,' he heard Katie say before he could speak. After a few seconds, the familiar strains of one of Bix Beiderbecke's classic recordings came sweetly down the line. The music faded after a few bars and he heard Katie's say. 'Well?'

'It's *Ostrich Walk*, but when was it recorded,' he asked impatiently knowing his collection contained several versions.'

'Ninth of May 1927,' was the reply.

'Are you sure?'

'That's what it says on the sleeve notes. If you want it, you'll have to come and get it,' Katie replied with a throaty laugh. Rushing to his collection, he began searching frantically for any rendition of the *Ostrich Walk* to check the recording dates. He found two, but none from May 1927.

Hastily donning a clean shirt and leaving a very grumpy looking Bix hunched up on his bed and looking wet and forlorn, Jim was out the door and reaching into his pockets for the keys to the car.

'Mrs Black is expecting me,' he explained to the receptionist after arriving at the hotel out of breath and still a little damp.

'Just a moment sir,' she said picking up the phone and dialling an internal number. After a pause and looking at Jim with a wry smile, she said, 'Mrs Black is in Room 112 and she suggests that you join her there.' Jim nodded and headed in the direction indicated. Ahead were a pair of swing doors and once beyond them, the familiar strains of Bix leading the band into the *Ostrich Walk* filled the corridor.

Pushing open the door to Room 112, it wasn't only the sound of Bix Beiderbecke that greeted him. Standing at the bottom of the bed, wearing nothing more than a big smile and a pair of black stocking was the lady of the house. 'Come in and enjoy all the attractions on offer,' she whispered seductively raising her arms in the air and shaking her ample breasts at him.

Hastily closing the door, Jim pointed to the CD player and opened his mouth to ask about the *Ostrich Walk* recording. He got as far as, 'You said the sleeve notes...' before he was enveloped in the arms of the naked Katie and whisked away in perfect time to the music. With each movement, she swept him around the room, until with one last twist, Jim felt the back of his legs hard against the side of the bed. 'Mr Beiderbecke does provide such exceedingly beautiful music don't you think?' What's this pretty little tune called?' Katie asked as the music changed, and Bix and the boys launched into the next number.

Just an Hour of Love,' Jim muttered helplessly as the buttons of his shirt were slowly undone and the zip on his trousers pulled down.

'Well then, I'm ready if you are?' she whispered in his ear.

Any doubts he may have had melted away as Katie lay back and pulled him onto the bed and into her as their lovemaking became urgent and expressive. His climax when it came was quick and the sound of, *There Ain't No Land Like Dixieland To Me* bouncing from the speakers summed up his feelings perfectly.

Falling back on the pillow gasping for breath he let out a huge sigh as Katie rolled over on top, kissing and touching him, her voice whispering in his ear, urging him up and onwards again to another heaven in the sky.

At the precise moment when the two lovers were joined together in a glorious and wonderful climax, the fountain in the Pump Room gurgled for a second or two, when brown, brackish water spurted soared high into the air, before descending like gentle rain to the floor below. Watching this wondrous spectacle, Jason let out a huge cry of joy and danced a jig beneath the shower of water. Grinning, he turned to Jeff, who looked on with amusement at this unexpected display of emotion as Jason shouted, 'Yes, yes,' and punched the air.

At the hotel, the lovers were enjoying the soft, warm, satisfying sleep that comes with contentment and pleasure. Together they lay entwined, breathing in unison to the gentle accompaniment of *There's Cradle in Carolina* from the rosebud mouth of Mr Leon Bismark Bix Beiderbecke.

Much later Jim blinked a couple of times and slowly opened his eyes, struggling to make sense of his surroundings. This wasn't his familiar bedroom at the cottage, and this wasn't his warm, comfortable bed. As the fog in his brain gradually cleared and his eyes began to focus an arm fell across his chest. Reaching down, he found the fingers and gradually traced up the arm until the face of the owner came into view. 'Hello, was that nice?'

'Katie, yes it was, but...' he blurted out trying desperately to regain his senses.

'I thought it was wonderful too. In fact, if you're up for it, I'm ready for another round,' Katie said, looking at him expectantly.

'We need to talk. This is madness, Katie. It will never work.'

Flopping back on her pillow, Katie closed her eyes and muttered in a rather a resigned tone. 'Jim, dear, the last thing I'm looking for is a long-term relationship. To be honest, I have no intention of giving up the advantages and financial security that comes from being Mrs Jason Black. All I want is a bit of fun when the mood takes me. That's all.'

Looking down at her, he said with a slight hesitation in his voice, 'I suppose that means your support for repairing the Dancing Couple will depend on me satisfying as and when required?'

'I have some of my most charitable thoughts in bed' Katie replied reaching up to pull him down to her waiting lips. Jim pulled away after enjoying the sweet taste of her mouth for a moment and tracing his fingers around her face said, 'Talking of charities, what's happening at the Pump Room?'

Taking his hand away, Katie replied, 'What do you know about the spring?'

'Well, there is a rumour going around the village the spring has dried up and your husband is replacing it with water pumped from the pond.'

'All I know is what Jason told me? There was a problem with the floor of the Pump Room, and it needed attention. That's all,' she responded getting out of bed and going to the CD player in the room and pressing the play button. 'Now stop this inquisition Mr James White and let's play.' With that, she leapt on top of Jim and covered his face in kisses. Finding himself responding, Jim could hear Bix Beiderbecke and his cornet leading the band into *A Good Man Is Hard to Find*, as he rolled her over and pinning her arms down, kissing her face, neck, and shoulders. A small voice in his head whispered, 'What are you doing, this is wrong,' but it was shouted out by another more urgent voice, a stronger emotion that demanded to be satisfied.

Chapter Seventeen

'Katie knows nothing about what's going on at the Pump Room. Or, at least no more than the rest of the village,' Jim announced to the gang when they were gathered at his cottage a few days later.

'And you believe her?' Philippa asked.

'Jason tells her very little about what goes on there.'

Audrey looked around the group. 'If Katie Black has no idea what her lying, cheating husband is up to, is there any point in you having any further contact with the woman. Well, is there Jim?'

Jim shuffled in his seat, unwilling to respond to Audrey's pointed question. In the silence, that followed the other members of the group found an excuse to avoid eye contact, until Philippa reached into the pocket of her jacket and extracted a sheet of paper, 'The notice for the AGM of the Pump Room Association arrived today. There is no mention of any problems at the spring.'

'What is on the agenda?' Jim enquired, taking the notice from her. 'There is nothing here, only the usual bland stuff, Chairman's Report, Statement of Accounts etc.,' he added, passing the notice to Audrey. 'So, what are we going to do? Look, you guys carry on talking, whilst I put the kettle on. I rustled up a Victoria Sponge this afternoon thinking we might need some sustenance.'

'I can't stay long. I left the kids with Brian and promised I was only popping into town to get something for dinner,' Philippa called out as she joined him in the kitchen. Jim's hand was on the door of the hatch when Philippa caught hold of his arm. 'And what exactly did happen when you met Katie?' she said rather pointedly.

'Nothing, why?'

'I saw the sheepish look on your face when Audrey suggested there was no need for you to see her again.'

'We just met and talked. That's all,' Jim replied, opening the hatch door and passing the cups and saucers through.

'We should sneak into the meeting all dressed in drag,' Les suggested, taking the china and setting it down on the coffee table.

'Just be careful, you're playing a dangerous game,' Philippa whispered in his ear, as she flipped on the kettle. 'Now, where's the Victoria Sponge you were talking about?'

'Can I help,' Audrey asked looking through the hatch.

'No, I can manage. Why don't you all sit down,' he replied looking pointedly at Philippa. 'It's okay, I can manage,' he said firmly, ushering her out of the kitchen.

'As usual, my husband's come up with a sensible idea, albeit in a silly form. The only way we're going to make a fuss is to sneak into the Annual General Meeting and use the Chairman's Report to raise some awkward questions,' Audrey said sharing her thoughts between the living room and kitchen.

Philippa came into the living room and sat in the armchair. 'Jason Black will dismiss any criticisms as nothing more than a minor problem with the floor. If we're to expose his lies we have to find a way to pin him down.'

'You're the only one Philippa, of us four, who's a member and can officially attend the AGM,' Audrey pointed out.

'I know, but everyone will suspicious if I challenge him. The entire village knows there's no love lost between us after he forced me to resign from the committee. Talking of which, Alan Howard passed me a note after morning service saying wanted to see me.'

'What did he want?' Jim enquired from the kitchen.

'I don't know. It was such a surprise. I can't imagine what he wants.' There was a momentary silence as they all considered the question. The silence was eventually broken by Les, 'Actually, there's another problem.'

'What's that?' Audrey enquired.

Les took a copy of the *Honiston Observer* from the coffee table and flicked through the paper searching for an article. 'Ah, here it is,' he said folding back the page. The heading reads, "Applegarth Magical Spring Waters to Reopen," underneath it says, and I quote. "Jason Black, chair of the Applegarth Pump Room Committee, announced today that the Magical Spring Waters of Applegarth will re-open this coming weekend." End of quote.'

'We take all the local papers at the Society. It helps me keep in touch with the local property market. Before I left the office, the *Observer* landed on my desk and with a moment to spare, I scanned through and spotted that.'

'Here you are guys,' Jim said appearing from the kitchen carrying a tray with a pot of tea and the sponge cake. 'Clear a space on the table Les, will you? I'll leave you to pour your own tea and help yourself to cake.'

'This is really nice,' says Audrey wiping crumbs off her face. 'It's so moist and the filling is delicious.' They all murmur in agreement and the only sound for the next few minutes is tea being drunk and cake being nosily consumed. Finishing his slice of the cake, Jim picked up the paper, 'I haven't seen the *Observer* this week. It was only delivered this afternoon. Bix must have picked it up from the doormat and plonked it on the table. I was probably busy preparing the cake. But I guess, this changes everything.'

'How do mean?' Audrey asked, through a mouth full of cake.

'With the Pump Room closed, Jason was bound to face significant questions. Now it's open – or will be at the weekend - he can rely on the tills in the shops ringing to quash any questions or complaints.'

'So, at the AGM, Jason Black gets up and says, ladies and gentlemen, there was a slight problem with the floor, but it's been fixed, and it was business as usual,' Philippa said looking at the other members of the group. 'Unless we can prove the water is coming from the pond, our accusations will be dismissed as the usual anti-Jason Black prejudice.'

Jim looked around at his companions, 'Short of digging up the trench and letting everyone see the fountain is connected to the pond, nobody's going to believe us.'

'Look,' Philippa says getting up and gathering her things, 'the AGM is not for another week. Maybe we can come up with a way to expose this fraud. I'm sorry Jim, but I'd better go otherwise Brian and the kids won't get any dinner tonight. Walk me to the door. Bye Audrey, bye Les. Incidentally, Audrey, the flower displays drew lots of complimentary remarks last Sunday. I was tempted to take all the credit, but my conscience got the better of me and I had to admit to some outside help. I'm on flower duty again this week and wondered whether you would help me again?'

'Sure, be delighted,' Audrey said as Philippa and Jim disappeared down the hallway.

At the door, Philippa paused with her hand on the catch, 'Look me straight in the eye Jim White and tell me nothing occurred between you and Katie Black.'

'Like what?'

'Contact between body parts, say from the lips downwards.'

'Nothing happened,' Jim responded avoiding her gaze and reaching past to open the door. 'Besides, I can handle it.'

'I hope so for your sake,' Philippa replied sweeping out of the door with a curt goodbye over her shoulder. Closing the door, Jim muttered, 'So do I, so do I'

In the lounge, Audrey and Les were studying the newspaper. As Jim entered, Audrey looked up, 'In all the fuss about the Pump Room, we forgot to ask you about the Dancing Couple, any news from the Stein Foundation?'

'No, not yet,' Jim replied. 'Hopefully, there'll be a letter in the post tomorrow. Now, it just so happens that I picked up a new Bix CD at the Honiston Music Store yesterday. So just for tonight, let's stop worrying about the Pump Room and enjoy some good music.' Pressing the play button on the CD player the three companions sat back and let the artistry of the music carry them away as Bix and the band swung into the *Ostrich Walk*.

Chapter Eighteen

With the Pump Room due to re-open, Jason and Tony Bean agreed there was no need for another meeting of the committee. Besides, it would only allow Rev. Alan Howard to launch into another one of his sermons about the spring being God's gift to the world, and they didn't need that.

At Jim's cottage, Bix ears lifted-up at the sound of the letterbox flap opening and the mail flopping onto the mat. 'Okay, Bix get the post,' Jim said finishing the last of the two slices of toast he consumed for breakfast every morning. Moments later, Bix returned with two white envelopes and some leaflets. 'What have you got there,' Jim asked, gently.

Flipping through the post, Jim discarded the leaflets along with one of the white envelopes that looked suspiciously like a telephone bill. In the top left-hand corner of the second envelope in small type were the words: *If undelivered please return to the Stein Foundation,* followed by their London address. Unfolding the letter inside and scanning to the bottom saw it was from Robin Caulfield. Above her signature, she had written:

> *Dear Jim,*
>
> *I thought you might be interested in the current situation regarding the repairs to the Dancing Couple. The report and photographs taken at the scene were discussed with the Foundation's Director, Herbert Wise, and our recommendation to the Trustees is that the Foundation should go ahead and restore the statue. We came to this view after weighing up assorted options, with the deciding factor being the desire of the Foundation to maintain a continuing presence for Isaac Stein in his birthplace at Applegarth.*
> *However, we believe it is reasonable to ask the village to contribute toward the costs of the restoration. The Director is particularly anxious to have support from the village in the form of a monetary contribution. At this point, we don't know what the final cost of the*

*repairs will be, but the first estimates put the figure in the region
of £20,000.*

*It would therefore certainly help the submission to the Trustees if
there was some indication that the village was prepared to match
the Foundation's contribution.*

*I appreciate you're not able to make any commitment at this stage,
but it would be helpful if, having taken some soundings, you could
indicate what the likely reaction would be within the village to this
proposal.*

Kind regards

Robin Caulfield

Scrawled across the bottom of the letter was a hand-written note that read: Sorry. Jim. It was the best I could do. Ring me at home after 6 to discuss RC.

Jim read the letter again to make sure he understood it. To restore the statue, the village had to come up with £10,000. That's what the letter appeared to say, but where did it come from. What about the hand-written note at the bottom, what did that mean?

His felt an urge to ring Philippa and tell her about the letter but guessed she would want to talk about his relationship with Katie. He was fond of Philippa and it would never forget how she stepped in when Nancy died suddenly of a brain tumour. It was Philippa who helped organise the funeral and comfort, Jim, as he struggled to come to terms with the loss of his wife of twenty years. She was a good friend and he hated having to lie to her. To avoid any embarrassing questions from Philippa, he decided it would be better to reveal the contents of the letter when all the gang were together.

Robin's hand-written note was quite specific. Ring after six and with Audrey and Les not home until the evening, the only person he could ring to discuss the letter was Katie.

He got as far as picking up for the receiver dialling the first two numbers, but let it drop back into its cradle knowing what she would demand in return. Since Nancy death he had not looked at another woman, never mind enjoying intimate relations with one. Despite a wish to remain true to her, he had succumbed to the first temptation to come along. If that wasn't bad enough, Katie was the wife of his worst enemy. How could he have allowed himself to be seduced by a woman who wasn't even his type? They had no common interests, apart from the Dancing Couple. Even then he doubted whether she was sincere in her wish to see it restored. She was using him to gain information about what they were up to. Yes, that was it. Well, in that case, there would be no more physical contact between them, and certainly no more sex. The problem was at this precise moment he couldn't think of anyone else to turn to and he needed to talk to someone about raising the £10,000 demanded by the Stein Foundation.

His letter to the *Observer* generated a few responses, but most of the correspondents bemoaned the lack of traditional values and the rise in vandalism in the village. Nobody had offered any support.

After their last encounter at the hotel, Katie gave him her mobile telephone number and told him to use it if he wished to contact her. With decidedly mixed feelings Jim picked up the phone and dialled the number. After two rings, a voiced answered merely with, 'Hi.'

'Katie, it's Jim.'

'Hello, lover. Hang on a moment I'll just step outside onto the terrace.'

'Where are you?'

'At the hotel, we're meeting with the Executive Chef to plan the weekly menus. All boring stuff really, particularly as Jason insists on displaying his non-existent knowledge of food and what our customers like. Anyway, I am out on the terrace now, so tell me what I owe the pleasure of this delightful call today. Are you offering to whisk me away to some faraway shore for the sole purpose of making mad passionate love to me all day,' Katie said followed by her usually throaty laugh? Jim felt surprisingly excited by the invitation, but stopped short of an equally provocative response, 'Well actually I was ringing to say I've received a reply from the Stein Foundation and wondered whether you might be interested in hearing what they had to say.'

'Yes, of course.'

'I don't mean over the phone. I thought maybe we could meet somewhere.'

'Where do you suggest.'

'What about the Cosy Cafe in town?' That would be safe, he thought.

'No that's too public. Look, I'm busy this morning, but I'll pick you up at three. Lunch will be over by then, and Jason will have disappeared to the Pump Room.

'Right, I'll be waiting,' and before he could say another word the phone went dead.

'Bix,' he called out to his terrier, 'Get you lead, we are going out.' Katie would demand to see the letter and the stationers in the High Street offered copying facilities. It would be a simple matter to give her a copy with the hand-written note from Robin blotted out. Bix at his feet wagging his tail in anticipation, 'Oh, all right then, just this once we will go through the park,' he said heading toward the front door, with the Bix following excitedly behind.

It was dead on three when Jim heard the familiar toot of Katie's horn. 'Where we going? Jim asked as the car sped off with a throaty roar.

'You'll see,' Katie replied with a huge grin.

With each turn, Jim's foreboding about their destination increased until they finally pulled into the car park at Fullton Woods he felt compelled to ask. 'Why here? It's not very private if you remember.'

'It's a different time of day and they can't sweep the car park, every day, can they? Now, what's in this letter then?'

Jim didn't reply, but taking the photocopy from his pocket, he handed it over. Katie scanned the letter and then read it more carefully. When she was finished, she handed it back saying, 'I can't imagine how she thinks the village can come up with ten-grand. A few hundred perhaps, but that is about all.'

'That was my first reaction, but what about the Parish Council?'

'Well, Mr James White,' Katie said leaning over, 'I will only answer that question when you have given me a proper kiss.' She replied pressing her lips to his. Jim responded to her kiss and when they eventually parted, Katie sighed and looking into his eyes said, 'I suppose that will have to do.' Now, this statue of yours, the problem is the Parish Council's annual budget only amounts to ten grand. There are hardly likely to donate the whole lot to repairing the Dancing Couple, always supposing they wanted to. They might be good for a couple of hundred quid, at best.'

'What about the local businesses, would they help?'

'Some might. I could probably persuade my husband to cough up a thousand, maybe fifteen hundred. I would expect most of the other businesses in the village to chip in, and if they don't Jason will remind them of their civic responsibilities.'

'If we got two hundred from the Parish Council, fifteen hundred from you and your husband, and let's say another two thousand from the other shops and businesses, that still leaves nearly six thousand. I suppose we could have a collection in the High Street. You never know some visitors might want to contribute.'

'It's tall order to expect a bucket collection to come up with nearly six grand. Now, enough of this serious stuff,' replied Katie whispering in his ear exactly what she wanted him to do to her. Faced with such an intriguing invitation, Jim's resolve wilted like a drop of snow at the first sign of spring and their desires, and passions were well and truly consummated without any interruptions from the road sweeper from Honiston Borough Council.

Afterwards, the lovers dressed in silence, just smiling and grinning as they struggled within the narrow confines of the car to get limbs into armholes and trouser legs. Driving back to the village, Katie suggested Jim get in touch with the Stein Foundation and tell them they might raise a few thousand toward the cost of repairs, but not the ten thousand they were looking for. At the cottage, Jim jumped out called over his shoulder, 'Thanks for everything, I'll get in touch with the Foundation and let you know what they say.'

'You do that. Bye lover boy,' Katie said as she roared off down the road.

***

At six forty-five Jim decided it was okay to ring Robin. He was nervous as he picked up the phone and dialled the number. This was the first time they had spoken since her visit to inspect the statue and he wasn't sure what her reaction would be.

'Ah, well, here goes,' he said silently to himself as he finished dialling. The phone was picked after only three rings and a voice said, 'Hello, Robin Caulfield speaking.'

'Hello Robin, its Jim – Jim White from Applegarth.'

'Jim, how are you? I gather you got my letter today.'

'Yes, I and wondered whether we could talk.'

'Of course, the only trouble is I have guests arriving at any minute.'

'Sorry, is it an inconvenient.'

'A bit yes; look, tell you what, I am over your way on Saturday. Why don't we meet for lunch and I can tell you a bit more than in the letter?'

'That sounds fine. There's a decent pub in the village, why don't we meet there?

'Okay, see you there, shall we say twelve-thirty. By the way, what's the name of the pub?'

'The Dog and Duck.'

'Until Saturday then.' With that the phone went dead, leaving Jim wondering who Robin was entertaining for dinner.

Chapter Nineteen

It was the day of the grand re-opening of the Pump Room.

Arriving well before the doors were due to open, Jason fussed and fretted, to the obvious irritation of Brenda and the two ladies. Were the towels clean, dry, and neatly folded; were the plastic cups stacked in perfect columns; was the floor clean and dry; surely the bottles of spring water could be displayed to better effect. Everything had to be perfect, Jason explained, as he continued his inspection.

Jason's overbearing manner was beginning to irritate Brenda. I need this job, she kept repeating to herself as she responded to every question and query with a smile and a reassuring word. The Pump Room was ready to receive the first visitors of the day, and all she wanted was to get on with her job.

Processing visitors through the turnstiles was at the forefront of Jason's mind as well, but first, there was one more duty to perform. 'Now ladies, as you know this is a very important day for the Pump Room and it is essential everything goes smoothly.' He said as he wandered in front of Brenda and her two helpers, Jane, and Tracy standing in-line in their newly laundered uniforms ready for inspection. 'Being forced to close the spring for essential repairs was a major step,' he continued, standing in front of young Tracy staring at her chest, who responded by blushing with embarrassment.

'You were saying Mr Black,' Brenda said stepping forward in a vain attempt to divert his attention away from the young girl.

Jason spun around, glared at Brenda, before moving away and continuing his speech, 'If we are to regain the trust of our visitors, we will need to provide the best possible experience for their visit to the Magical Waters of Applegarth. So, I will expect a 100% effort from each of you today.'

Brenda listened to this speech with increasing irritation and decided she'd heard enough of this little homily. 'I think you can take it as read Mr Black that we're all conscious of how important today is.'

'I'm pleased to hear it, Brenda. Right then ladies, let battle commence. To the box office if you would Jane and let's get this show on the road.' Allowing a moment for the ladies to reach their respective positions, Jason took a deep breath, walked to the doors and with a flourish drew back the bolts and flung them open. 'Good morning ladies and gentlemen and a very warm welcome to you all. Please, step forward and enjoy the Magical Spring Waters of Applegarth and their amazing healing powers.'

The dozen or so visitors waiting outside surged forward and began thrusting money into the hands of Jane at the box office. Very soon the first group were assembled in the Pump Room and with her back to the fountain, Brenda launched into her standard speech of welcome. Jason would have been happier with a bigger queue waiting at the door but knew the crowds would return once the coach tours began running again.

As Brenda finished her speech Jason touched her arm. 'I have to get back to the restaurant to prepare for lunch but keep up the excellent work and ring me the moment anything untoward happens, okay.'

'Certainly Mr Black, you can be sure of it. Incidentally, is Mrs Black okay, only we were expecting her to join us, this being a bit of a special occasion.'

'Unfortunately, she was not able to be with us today. A crisis in the kitchen apparently, which was deemed more important than our grand re-opening. I wonder sometimes whether Katie shares our enthusiasm for this little enterprise. Still, I had better go, speak to you later,' Jason announced heading for the exit.

Brenda cast her eyes over to the first group, who were beginning to drift away, clutching their bottles of spring water and certificates. 'Oh well, it's back to the treadmill for you my girl,' she muttered as the next group of visitors began assembling around the fountain.

***

A few minutes before twelve-thirty, Jim cut an anxious figure as he stood on the High Street looking down the path leading to the Pump Room. Watching the queue of visitors edging toward the entrance, an idea suddenly jumped into his head on how to expose Jason Black and his lies. It might just do the trick, he mused. It was certainly worth sharing with Les and the girls later at the church.

Before that, there was a meeting with Robin, and he felt decidedly nervous at the prospect. He was looking forward to meeting her again but was fearful that any discussion on the subject of the Dancing Couple could sour their blossoming friendship. He had to find a way to convince her and the Stein Foundation to proceed with the restoration of the statue without a ten-thousand-pound contribution from the village and knew it would be easy.

Lost in thought, he was unaware of her approach until Robin tapped on the shoulder. 'Hi Jim, you looked like you were miles away.' He turned to see her smiling with her blonde hair tumbling down onto her shoulders and dressed in a blue and white-striped shirt, yellow jeans, and sneakers.

Taken back by her sudden appearance he only managed to say, 'Robin, how nice to...' before trailing off.

'You too Jim,' she responded. 'Right then, where's this pub of yours.'

'Just down here, he said pointing down the High Street. 'Let's see what they have for lunch.' As they strolled towards the Dog and Duck, Jim felt it polite to make conversation and asked about her journey to Applegarth. Their idle conversation continued during the time it took to locate a table and select from the menu.

As the waitress disappeared with their order, an awkward silence opened up, as they waited for the other to make the first move. Jim finally broke the silence. 'You said you'd tell me more than was in the letter when we met today.'

Pushing her sunglasses on top of her head, Robin replied, 'I'm sorry it was so formal, but my letter will be included with the report to the Trustees. You'll understand I had to appear professional and detached.'

'Two white wines,' said the waitress placing glasses of Chardonnay on the table. Picking up the wine, Jim and Robin touched glasses. 'Here's to the Dancing Couple,' they toasted in unison.

Playing for time, Jim took a sip of wine. 'Seems, a very popular spot,' Robin said. glancing around the patio, now fully occupied by couples and families.

'Yes, it usually is on a Saturday, though with the Pump Room re-opening there are more visitors to the village today' In response to her quizzical look Jim related the story of the closure of the spring and the attempts by the Pump Room Committee to find an alternative source of water.

'What are you going to do about it?' Robin enquired taking a sip of her wine. Casting aside any doubts, Jim relayed how the fraud might be exposed.

'Will it work?' she asked when he finished.

'Let's hope so, but I need to share it this with the guys. I'm meeting them later,' he added as an afterthought. There was another awkward pause as they studiously avoided the contents of the letter.

The lemon chicken, ordered by Robin and pork loin chop Jim chose, arrived at that moment. Providing another excuse to avoid the subject, while unwrapping knives and forks from the napkins and tucking into the food occupied them.

Taking a slurp of wine, Jim decided to confront a problem head-on. 'You were going to tell me what couldn't be said in the letter,' he said firmly.

Putting down her knife and fork and picking up the wine, Robin said most of the staff supported the restoring the Dancing Couple, but some of the Trustees questioned the wisdom of devoting the Foundation's limited resources to repairing a statue damaged by vandalism. They also questioned the commitment of the village to the memory of Isaac Stein, given what little money was set aside by the Parish Council each year to maintain the statue and surrounding area in the park. When she had finished, Robin put down her glass and resumed her meal. Jim, who had listened attentively asked, 'Is that why the Foundation is asking the village to pay half the cost of the repairs?'

'That's putting it a bit strong, but in essence yes. There is a view the village is more interested in promoting the spring than honouring the memory of Isaac Stein. That may not be fair, but several Trustees take that view and it has to be faced.' Jim, who had finished his meal, returned his cutlery to the plate, downed the last of his wine before looking pointedly at Robin, 'With the centenary of Isaac Stein's birth next year, the Trust surely can't leave the

Dancing Couple covered in red paint for all the world to see? The press will have a field day with pictures of the statue plastered all over the front pages and headlines calling it a disgrace and an insult to a well-loved national hero.

Robin, who had resumed eating, paused with her fork in mid-air, hesitated for a moment, 'That's a fair point and the staff would agree with you, but at as things stand, I wouldn't like to predict which way the Trustees will go. They could overcome the problem and any adverse press reaction by carting the statue away and focusing the celebrations on the London Gallery.' Putting the food in her mouth she added, 'so have you had the opportunity to make any soundings in the village.'

'Some, yes but with no firm commitments, we might come up with a four thousand.' Finishing her meal and laying the knife and fork on the plate, Robin asked, 'Where would it come from?'

'It's not confirmed, but the Parish Council might be persuaded to contribute. Then we'd be asking the local businesses to chip in. If there's still a shortfall, then a collection in the village. Do you want anything else, pudding, or coffee perhaps,' he asked?

'Coffee would be nice. Thanks.'

'I'll go and organise it,' Jim said getting up and heading for the bar. He was disappointed with the way the meeting was going. They seem to be sparring, hoping to detect what the other was thinking.

'What can I get for you,' a voice called from behind the serving counter.

'Sorry I was miles away.' Jim replied concentrating on the job in hand. 'Two coffees please, decaffeinated, we're on the patio.'

Walking back to the table, Jim was determined to turn the conversation away from the statue onto a more personal level. 'I ordered decaffeinated, hope that is all right?' he said resuming his seat.

Robin nodded in response and then looked up. I'm sorry it has to be so formal today. It's not how I planned it. I thought we could discuss it on a friendly basis. You know between friends. Why are you smiling Jim?'

'I believe how pleased I am to hear you say that. I felt quite miserable ordering the coffees. I felt we got on very well the last time you came and then the cold formal letter arrived. That seemed to change everything. And today we were more like sparring partners, trying to find a way through each other's defences.'

'I'm sorry. Ah, our coffee has arrived.' She replied, taking the two cups from the waitress, and putting them on the table. 'I'm sorry too,' Jim added, taking his coffee. 'I should have made allowances for the fact that you're an officer of the Foundation with a job to do. Let's agree that you've done your official duty and for the rest of the day you can relax.'

'I'll drink to that,' Robin replied learning back in her chair and sipping her coffee. For the next half hour, which included a refill of their coffee cups, they chatted away in that easy, lazy style friends have of finding out about the life and times of each other. Jim told her about his attempts to make a new life for himself since the death of Nancy and without prompting Robin recalled how her husband, David, was killed in an air crash. He'd been sent by his company to an international conference on pollution control in Vienna. On the return trip, the aircraft had wandered off course in thick fog and crashed in a field on the approach to the runway. She remembered vividly opening the door to two solemn-looking policemen.

One of the pilots misread one of the instruments according to enquiry report but dealing with it in the middle of intense media interest was very difficult. Seeking refuge at her parent's farm on the Yorkshire Moors and slowly coming to terms with her loss with their support and patience was her salvation. Afterwards, moving back to London, she had sold their flat and brought a small house in Wiltshire, preferring to avoid the capital. That was until the offer of a job came out-of-the-blue from the Stein Foundation.

When Robin had finished, there was a silence for a moment. Not an awkward silence but a more of a natural pause, broken by Jim saying, 'Unless you have experienced it, you can't begin to understand the emptiness in your life, when the person you expect to spend the rest of your life with, suddenly isn't there anymore.'

'Even at David's funeral I expected him to show up and give me a shoulder to lean on, an arm to guide me through the duties I had to perform, the words of thanks I needed to express to all those who came to the ceremony.'

Jim knew exactly what she meant.

'For month's afterwards, something would happen at college, or I would read a news item in the paper and rush home dying to tell Nancy all about it. It took a long time to get used to coming back to an empty house. Even now there is a bit of me that expects her to be there when I put the key in the door.' Robin didn't answer but looked away recalling similar feelings, even though David had never lived in the house in Wiltshire. Then looking at her watch, she rose and said, 'Jim, I am sorry to break up the party, but I have to be in Bristol by five. I am staying at with sister and promised to be there in time for her and her husband, Bob, to go to a concert this evening. I am supposed to be looking after their son, Toby. Walk me back to my car and we can carry on talking along the way.'

'Ok, I'll just settle the bill and be right with you.'

'How much do I owe you? I insist on paying my share.'

'If it won't offend you,' Jim replied, 'I am happy to treat you to lunch.'

'If you insist, but only on condition I can ask a little favour in return.'

'What's that?'

'I'll tell you when we are walking back to the car park. I need to use the facilities before starting my journey home. See you outside.'

A few minutes, having settled the bill, Robin appeared at his shoulder, 'That was a very nice lunch, Jim. Thank you.'

'My pleasure, but what's the favour you want to ask?'

'Well actually it's not a little favour, it's a big one,' Robin said as she strolled down the pavement to the car park at the south end of the village. 'Every year the Stein Foundation hosts a formal dinner as a way of saying thank you to those patrons who've been kind enough to make charitable donations to the Trust. So far, I've managed to get out of it, but this year Herbert Wise – the Director – is insistent I attend.'

'I sympathise with your plight,' Jim responded, 'but how can I help.'

'I need an escort and wondered whether you would help out?'

'What?'

Robin stopped walking and looking at him straight in the eye, 'Would you do me the honour of being my escort to the Benefactor's Annual Dinner. It's held at a posh hotel in London. If you would rather not, just say. It was only an idea.' Jim could hardly control his enthusiasm and simply replied, 'yes, of course, but why me?'

'Well you're reasonably presentable and I thought you might enjoy it. It's a black-tie job though. I hope that's okay.'

'Well, the old DJ hasn't been out for a while. I just hope it still fits. But yes, I would be delighted.'

'Good, I'll send you the details.' Robin said entering the car park, spotted her car several rows away. 'It will give you chance to meet Herbert, but I can't tell you how easier it will be to persuade the trustees to repair to the Dancing Couple if the village stumped up a contribution, no matter how small.'

'I'll see what I can do.'

'If you could firm up the four thousand,' Robin replied opening the car door and sliding into the driver's seat. 'I'll sound out Herbert and see if he's prepared to recommend it to the Trustees.'

'Okay.' Jim replied, pushing the door shut. Touching his arm briefly, Robin put the car into gear and through the car window, said softly. 'It was nice to see you today, and thanks for lunch. Speak to you soon, okay.'

'Bye,' he responded as he watched her car weave its way out of the crowded car park. Jim stood in the space left by Robin's car for a few moments, contemplating the lunch and what it meant for the statue and their relationship.

Checking his watch, he reckoned if he got a move on, he might make it to the church in time to catch Philippa, Audrey and Les.

***

Les was sitting in the front pew watching as Philippa and Audrey arranged the flowers in the church. 'Where's Jim today,' asked Philippa.

'I'm not sure.' Audrey replied. 'Les rang to suggest we meet here, but he only got the answering machine.'

Philippa placed the last of the asters in the vase. 'As you know I'm very fond of Jim, he's been a good friend, but I'm having doubts about where his loyalties lie.'

Audrey looked puzzled. 'How do you mean?'

92

'To put it bluntly, I think he's having a relationship with Katie Black.'

Les, whose attention had drifted away, leaned forward. 'You mean, like rumby pumby things?'

'Yes,' she replied. 'He looked decidedly shifty the other evening when he was talking about her. I tackled him in the hallway and asked him outright. 'Are you and Katie Black having an affair?' At first, he denied it, but then muttered he could deal with it.'

'The lucky bugger,' Les muttered. 'Sorry, Aud.'

'I should think so too,' Audrey said staring at him, before turning to Philippa. 'You mean Jim met Mrs Black, but it was only for sex.'

'That's my suspicion Audrey. So, I can't help wondering whether it's safe to discuss our plans with him.'

'He said that Katie didn't know what was going on at the Pump Room. No more than the rest of the village, were his exact words,' Les offered, thoughtfully.

'Yes, but she could be twisting him around her little finger to find out what we're up to,' retorted Audrey. 'With the AGM coming up, Jason will be keen to find out whether we're....' The rest of Audrey's observation was drowned out by the sound of the church door swinging open, causing a shaft of light to fill the knave. For a brief moment, the flower arrangers were blinded by the intensity of the light, but out of the shadows Jim appeared with a smile on his face, 'Hi guys, I was hoping to find you here.'

Without enthusiasm, they all responded, 'Hi Jim,'

'I rang earlier to suggest we met here, but all I got was your answer machine.'

'Sorry Les, I had an important lunch date and came straight here.'

'Who with,' Philippa asked, looking at him pointedly.

'Actually, it was Robin Caulfield. One of the reasons I came here today was to bring you up to date with the latest developments.

In response to Phillippa's invitation to join her on the front pew, Jim muttered 'Sure,' and when he was settled, elated the contents of the letter from the Stein Foundation, and the handwritten note from Robin. He was hoping for some reaction, questions even, but faced with nothing more than stony looks, he went to summarise the discussion over lunch, playing down the contribution from the village.

When he'd finished, Audrey glanced at the others. 'That's all very interesting Jim and we'd like to know more, but before that please answer one simple question. Are you having an affair with Mrs Black?'

Taken back by this outburst Jim looked at Philippa. 'What you been saying?'

'I only repeated our conversation in your hallway. Answer the lady, are you having sex with Katie or not? It's a simple question.'

'It's a ridiculous suggestion, what gave you that idea?'

'Your words, *I can handle it*. What exactly is *it* you can handle?'

'Well, Jim?' Audrey enquired, taking a seat next to him on the pew.

'This is just too silly for words.' Jim cried out, rising, and turning to face them. 'I came here today all excited after I met with Robin and eager to tell you about an idea, I've had to expose Jason Black, and all I get is this.'

'What idea?' Les asked.

Seizing the opening Jim dived in and laid out his plan to put dye in the pond.

Les looked at him quizzically. 'How exactly will that expose Jason and his lies?'

'Simple. When the water comes out red or blue, or whatever colour we decide, Jason won't be able to deny it's coming from the pond.' There was a momentary pause as the group pondered the practical implications before Les spoke, 'what sort of dye would we need and where do we get it from?'

'I was rather hoping one of you might come up with the answer,' Jim confessed.

'If we did it has to be before the AGM, and that's next week.'

'That's right Audrey. Has anyone got any idea, where we can get hold of a dye to colour the pond, without killing the wildlife? You know about these things Philippa.'

Philippa took a moment to throw him a, *don't think I didn't notice you dodging the question about Katie*, look, before saying: 'It would have to be food dye, that way we won't kill the fish. There would have to be enough to ensure the whole pond is coloured, otherwise, it won't show up at the fountain.'

'You can get food dye in that delicatessen in Honiston, but it only comes in small bottles. We might have to buy up all their supplies.'

'It is probably too late today,' offered Les. 'I'll go there on Monday and get what I can. But what colour?'

'The one they have the most of,' suggested Audrey

'Assuming Les gets the dye, I suggest we meet in the High Street on Monday at nine,' Jim suggested. They all murmured their agreement as Philippa and Audrey returned to arranging the flowers. 'What I want to know where's the contribution from the village coming from. You said that's what the Stein Foundation was looking for?'

Jim knew to choose his words carefully. 'Well, Philippa, I thought an application to the Parish Council might be worthwhile and we could tap the local businesses. Then there's always a collection in the village.'

'And how much has Jason Black promised, I assume you've asked Katie?'

'Not directly, but Jason will respond generously when the time comes.'

'Right, I've finished,' Audrey announced. 'Sorry to leave you with the clearing up again Philippa, but I need to get some stuff finished for the Festival Committee.'

'That's okay, Audrey. Thanks for your help. Jim, stay and talk to me.'

'I'd love to Philippa, but I have to get home and let Bix out,' Jim responded as he joined Audrey and Les, gathering their things together. 'If you're going to be busy this afternoon Audrey, how about I come over and cook a meal for us.'

'It's alright Jim, I think I can manage,' Audrey replied as they walked down the aisle toward the exit.

Philippa watched her three companions disappear and sighed. The problem with Jim and his involvement with Mrs Jason Black was still unresolved, she thought surveying the mess by the flower arranging.

Chapter Twenty

At some point during Sunday night, he couldn't be precise as to the exact hour, PC Nigel Smith sat bolt upright in bed and remembered when he'd last seen red paint being used. Not any red paint, but the exact shade of red that currently adorned the statue of the Dancing Couple in the Memorial Park.

A week earlier Jason Black had rung the station house just as he was preparing to begin his patrol around the village. One of the hotel's guests had made an official complaint about money missing from her room. The guest, an elderly lady, insisted on her room being searched by a member of the local constabulary, as she couldn't trust anyone from the hotel.

She fumed and fussed, as Nigel systematically searched the room and discovered fifty pounds hidden under the mattress. On being presented with her money, her only reaction was to mutter, 'Oh dear, I must have put it under there for safekeeping, you can never trust hotel staff can you, there'll rob you blind given half a chance.' Stuffing the money in her bag, he hurried off, leaving Nigel scratching his head and wondering at the vagaries of elderly ladies and their foibles about money and hotel staff.

Glancing out the window on his way downstairs, he noticed Kevin Jones, the handyman and gardener, painting the doors of the garages bright red. At the time, he thought the colour was out of keeping with the rest of the hotel, a tasteful green and grey. Down at the reception he stopped to have a sympathetic word with Jason Black about foolish old ladies who'd forget their heads if they weren't attached to their shoulders and went on his way. With the minor matter of the missing cash resolved, the garage doors and the red paint were dismissed - until last night.

Sitting at the breakfast table and finishing his second cup of coffee before facing the world, he decided a quiet word with Mr Kevin Jones was in order: nothing heavy, just a little chat about red paint and a certain statue. He recalled Kevin often spent his lunch hour in the Memorial Park. A haven of peace and quiet away from the busy hotel.

That would be his job at lunchtime, but before then there was a backlog of paperwork and statistics demanded by headquarters to be dealt with. That would keep him occupied for the rest of the morning, and afterwards, a stroll down to the park with his sandwiches with a flask of coffee, and a word to Mr Jones might solve the mystery.

At 12.45, Kevin Jones, handyman and gardener to the Magical Waters Hotel and Restaurant, stopped for a restful hour after three hours of trimming and preening the hotel flowerbeds.

The Memorial Park was as peaceful as ever, though PC Smith sitting on the bench opposite the statue of the man and woman dancing was a surprise.

'Hello, Constable, don't often see you in the park at lunchtime.'

'That's right, Kevin, but today I'm here for a purpose. You see there is a mystery and I thought you might help me clear it up.' Ignoring the question, Kevin opened his lunchbox and sat at the other end of the bench. 'I'm not sure what you mean,' he said through a mouthful of a cheese and cucumber sandwich.

'If you turn your head towards the beautiful statue to your left, you will see a masterpiece by the renowned local sculptor, Isaac Stein - commonly called the Dancing Couple. Being an observant sort of person, you will notice it's covered in red paint, which is a pity really, 'cos it rather spoils the look of it. Don't you agree?'

'What's that got to do with me?' Kevin replied defensively.

'I'm not sure, but I was rather hoping you might be able to throw some light on how it got there? The paint that is, not the statue.'

'Nothing to do with me,' Kevin replied continuing to chew on his sandwich. Nigel took a bite from his egg and tomato sandwich and carried on munching all the while watching the young man sitting at the other end of the bench. When Nigel finished his sandwich, he took the flask of coffee from the bag on the seat and poured into the cup. 'You work for Mr Jason Black as a general factotum, I believe. Do you want any of this coffee, by the way? I only made it this morning?'

'No thanks and my official title is, Handyman and Gardener if you don't mind.'

'Exactly, and it was in that capacity I observed you a few days ago, painting the garage doors bright red. Now, if my tired old eyes aren't deceiving me, that shade of red paint is not a million miles away from the colour currently disfiguring this lovely statue.

'So,' responded Kevin defiantly

'Well, it's like this Kevin. I'm a great believer in coincidences. You know how it goes, if it looks like a duck, swims duck and tastes like a duck, it probably is a duck. So, when I see someone dipping their paintbrush in a pot of red paint and then a few days later the same colour appears on a much-loved statue in the park, I can't help wondering about the coincidence. You see where I'm heading.'

'I have no idea what you are talking about Constable. Besides the garage doors at the hotel are green not red.' Kevin replied hastily closing his lunchbox. 'Excuse me, but I have to get back to work.'

'They're green now, on the orders of Mrs Black, to match the rest of the hotel. It was a bit garish that red wasn't it. Tell me Kevin, why this particular statue, why throw the paint at the statue?' This last accusation was aimed at Kevin's back as he turned to hurry across the park.

It appeared the question, was going to be ignored. But after a few yards, Kevin stopped and turned, 'I didn't throw the paint, it was an accident,' he muttered.

'How, come?'

'It's stupid and I am really sorry the statue got damaged, but it wasn't my fault,' Kevin paused before decided to go on. Pursing his lips, he walked back to the bench and stood in front of the police constable defiantly, 'It wasn't my fault. It was that bloody squirrel or whatever it was.'

'Do you want to tell me what happened?'

Kevin gave the briefest of nods and sat on the arm of the bench. He paused for a moment as if gathering his thoughts. Avoiding looking PC Smith in the eye, he recounted how after finishing painting the garage doors red there was half a tin of paint leftover.

When Mrs Black demanded that the doors be repainted green, he realised the red wouldn't be required any more. With the front door of his house needing a new coat of paint, he assumed no one would notice if he took what was left in the tin. He waited until it was time to go home on Friday night and popped the tin into the carrier on the front of his bike. He took, the same route he took every night, across the park, past the statue and into the Avenue.

The weather was dry during the day, but by late afternoon it was overcast and wet. To keep the rain out of his eyes he had kept his head well on down in his chest and didn't see the animal, a squirrel or some such thing until it was almost under his wheels. He should have ignored it. Instead, he did what most people would do in that situation and applied his brakes. With the grass, wet and sticky, the bike skidded, and the paint tin flew off the carrier. The encrusted paint on the lip prevented the lid from closing properly and when the tin hit the statue it burst open and ran down the man and woman.

'And that's how it happened?' asked PC Smith.

'Yes, I swear that's how it happened. I finished on the ground tangled in the bike with my trousers muddy and torn. I didn't know what to do, so I just panicked, grabbed the paint tin, picked up my bike and cycled home as fast as I could.'

'Why didn't you come and tell me about? You must have known questions would be asked.'

'Because I knew you wouldn't believe me. That's why.'

'It is a bit of a tall story you must admit, though why anyone would want to make up something like that I don't know?'

'What happens next?' Kevin asked, looking anxiously at Nigel.

'I don't know. I need to think about it and decide whether a criminal act has been committed. In the meantime, you'd had better get back to work. I'll be in touch when I've decided what to do, okay.'

'Thanks, Constable,' Kevin replied turning and walking away like a man with a great weight lifted from his shoulders.

Nigel continued drinking his coffee and watched Kevin until he disappeared out of the park.

Chapter Twenty-one

'Good evening Mr White can I have a word?'

'Certainly, Constable, come in,' Jim replied opening the door wide to allow PC Nigel Smith to enter. 'Go through to the lounge. Don't take any notice of Bix, he's harmless really.' When they were sat in the two armchairs with Nigel making a fuss of Bix, Jim enquired, 'what do I owe the pleasure of this call on a Monday evening: can I get you anything, tea, coffee?'

'Tea will be nice, thank you.'

'Whilst you amuse Bix, I'll go and put the kettle on,' Jim said moving to the kitchen and flipping on the switch. Getting the cups and saucers from the cupboard, his mind was working overtime. Had the plan to put dye in the village pond reached the ears of the local constabulary. Was that why he was here? How did he find out? Jim hadn't told anyone. Les and Audrey wouldn't have said a word. He doubted whether Philippa wouldn't have betrayed them. She may have misgivings about his affair with Katie but had no reason to talk to the police. Alternatively, she may have spoken to Alan Howard after the church service yesterday and mentioned it to him. He was on the Pump Room Committee and felt compelled to tell PC Smith to protect himself from any fallout.

Collecting the tea-things together Jim pondered the options. If Constable Smith was here to asked him about pollution to the pond, he'd better decide how to respond. He could make a clean break and say it was a foolish prank. That didn't sound very plausible and it risked betraying his friends. The alternative was to see what the police knew and to brazen it out. Picking up the cups of tea, he walked into the lounge. 'Here you are Constable, help yourself to sugar,' he said bringing the bowl from the hatch. When they were settled sipping their tea, Jim enquired, 'so, how can I help you?'

'I've come here tonight because I need your help on a matter of some delicacy.' Nigel hesitated for a moment and chose his words carefully. 'It's like this. Information about a criminal act has recently come to my attention and I'm uncertain how to proceed.

'Is it about the village pond,' Jim heard himself saying and cursing for having blurted it out.

'What about the pond?'

Jim reacted quickly. 'Nothing Constable, you were saying.'

PC Smith looked at him pointedly for a moment, but then dismissed the thought. 'Actually, it's about the statue in the Memorial Park.'

'Has it been damaged again?' Jim asked, fearing the worst.

'No, it hasn't Mr White, though I believe we know how it was damaged.'

Jim looked at him in disbelieve. 'You mean you've arrested the culprit.'

'No again, I'm afraid. Let me tell you what I've discovered and take it from there shall we.' Taking a drink of tea, Nigel related his suspicions about the red paint and visiting the hotel to investigate the alleged stolen money and Kevin Jones painting the garage doors.

'You mean the same colour as the paint thrown over the Dancing Couple?'

PC Smith nodded. 'Yes, only it wasn't exactly thrown.'

'If it wasn't thrown, how did it get there,' Jim demanded, putting his cup down.

'It wasn't thrown, because it wasn't an act of vandalism. It's an amazing story, but I believe the damage to the statue was a result of a freak accident.'

'I think you had better tell me the whole story, but finish your tea first, otherwise, it'll get cold.' Taking his cue from Jim, Nigel drank the tea and placed the cup on the table.

'Do you believe him?' Jim asked, after hearing about the meeting in the park with Kevin Jones.

'I'm not sure and that's my dilemma. Knowing who did it but proving it was a deliberate act of vandalism is another matter. If I am perfectly honest, I don't think there's a case. The lad's not a vandal and if he tells the magistrates his story about his bike skidding on the wet grass and the paint hurling off the carrier, they're likely to give him the benefit of the doubt. Besides, merely being charged will almost certainly cost him his job'

'The fact that he's subsequently found not guilty won't make the slightest difference because Jason will maintain he didn't have permission to take the paint in the first place.'

'Exactly, so I decided the best thing was to share the information with you and see if we can't arrive at a solution that satisfies all parties, so to speak.'

'I appreciate your dilemma, Constable, but you should read this,' Jim said, handing him the letter from the Stein Foundation. When Nigel had finished reading, Jim recounted the conversation with Robin and the contribution the village was expected to make toward the restoration. 'So, you will understand my first reaction would be to tell Mr Kevin Jones his actions caused serious damaged to a much-loved statue. It's no excuse to say it was an accident. He should have taken more care and should pay for the damage.'

'I can understand why you feel that way Mr White, but there's no way young Kevin can come up with the full cost, or even the four thousand. He has a wife and two kids and with what Jason Black pays him, I expect there're struggling to get by.'

'Okay,' Jim replied, 'but I would still like the Dancing Couple restored to its former glory. It would help if I could tell the Stein Foundation how the statue was damaged.'

Nigel hesitated for a moment, 'I'll tell you what I'm prepared to do. If the lady from the Stein Foundation were to ring me, I'll explain the circumstances, that it was an accident and not really the young man's fault.'

'Okay, let's leave it like that,' Jim said walking with him to the door, 'I appreciate you coming and telling me about the statue. I feel a lot easier now.'

'My pleasure Mr White, and thanks for being so understanding. I'll wish you goodnight then.' Jim closed the door and hurried back to the living room where the phone was ringing. It was Philippa, she was anxious to speak to him before he met Audrey and Les.

Jim inwardly groaned, knowing she'd want to talk about his relationship with Katie. He'd managed to avoid her questions on Saturday by sneaking off with Audrey and Les, but he knew it was only a temporary reprieve. Philippa was a terrier once she got her teeth into you and wouldn't let go until she got what she wanted. Despite all his misgiving, Jim heard himself saying, 'yes, of course. I'll expect you at 8.30.'

He didn't often feel the need to reach into the back of the sideboard and bring out the bottle of single malt whisky. Today though was going to be one of those days.

The whisky had lived in the cupboard for years, going back to the time when Nancy was alive, and they were in the habit of having a nightcap after a long journey home from a competition. 'Three fingers ought to do it,' he muttered pulling out the stopper and pouring the amber liquid into a glass. He would do his best to resist Phillippa's attempts to delve into his love life and the whisky would give him the courage. 'Cheers,' he called out, taking a large slug, and falling back onto the sofa.

On the stroke of eight-thirty Philippa knocked on the door and charged past him without saying a word. She was standing arms akimbo when he reached the living room. 'I've left Brian looking after the kids, so I can't stay long. I rang Audrey and she confirmed Les got the green dye in Honiston today and they'll meet you at the High Street at nine o'clock.'

'Hello, Philippa, how are you?' Jim said cheerfully, flopping into the armchair feeling relaxed and ever so slightly light-headed, the Whisky having worked its magic. 'Would you like to sit down? You look like a woman with something on your mind,' he said, making a determined effort to sound serious, but failing miserably.

Philippa studied him for a moment, sighed and pressed on determined to say what she'd come to say. 'No, I do not want to sit down, and yes I do have something on my mind. Quite simply, are you having an affair with Katie Black? Yes, or no.' When Jim didn't reply, she added, 'well are you?'

Jim sat up straight in the armchair. 'I see to remember the American military had a very sensible policy for dealing with gay men and women recruits. You will recall it was, if you won't tell, we won't ask. Could we have a similar arrangement on the subject of me and Katie Black?'

'Have you been drinking?' Not getting an answer, she continued. 'No, we can't, for the simple reason, we need to know where you stand on the question of Jason Black and the Pump Room. I don't see how you can expose him as a liar and cheat, while at the same time having an affair with his wife. Or maybe you can?'

'I thought you were keen on me getting close to Mrs Black,' he replied looking at her accusingly.

'Yes, to find out what was going on at the Pump Room. Not as an excuse for some sordid affair. For goodness sake, Jim, don't you have any sense of loyalty?' There was a long pause as they avoided eye contact, aware of the yawning gap opening up in their friendship. Eventually, the silence was broken by Philippa. 'How many times have you had sex with her?' she asked in a matter of fact way.

'Twice,' Jim replied not looking at her.

'Where do you do it, here?'

'Bix can't stand her. Once at the hotel, once up at Fullton Woods.'

Without a hint of sarcasm, Philippa replied. 'Well, at least someone in this house has good taste.'

Avoiding her gaze, Jim said, 'Katie wasn't looking for a long-term relationship, just a bit of fun when she felt like it.'

'What about Robin, I thought you had more than a professional interest in her?' Philippa said finally relenting and sitting on the sofa. Jim responded by recalling the invitation to escort Robin to the Stein Foundation's annual dinner. 'So, what you going to do, screw Katie in the afternoon and then trot up to London to be with Robin the evening, I suppose.'

'No, I am not that insensitive.'

"Which is why you must end this affair with Katie before it gets out of hand? I had better go. You know what you have to do Jim. For the sake of the friends, who love you, do the right thing.'

'I'll think about it,' Jim mumbled getting up and walking with her to the door. Outside, Philippa sliding into her car turned to him. 'I'll not to say anything for a few days to give you time to sort things out, but I'll not stay silent forever.' Not getting any response, she started the engine and drove away.

Watching the lights of her car until they disappeared, Jim called out, 'if only it were that easy.'

Audrey and Les were waiting on the High Street when time Jim arrived. He greeted them in the normal cheery way but received only a grunt in reply.

Les picked up the large carrier bag standing at his feet and joined Audrey as they walked down the path to the Pump Room, leaving a disconsolate Jim bringing up the rear. On reaching the pond, Audrey drew Jim to one side and told him his assistance was welcomed tonight, but it would be better if he stayed away from the Pump Room Association Annual General Meeting. And yes, they had decided what to do, but in the circumstances, it would be better if he didn't know. That way there was no likelihood of Jason Black finding out before the meeting.

Emptying the dye into the pond was accomplished without a hitch, apart from Les having trouble opening the dye. He'd brought a large pair of thick rubber gloves to avoid getting the colour on his hands, but that only made opening the small bottles more difficult. Most of the dye finished in the water, except for the contents of the last bottle, most of which ended up on the grass. But, as Les remarked, 'it's the same colour as the grass and it will grow out in time.'

With their mission successfully completed, the trio returned to the High Street in stony silence, with only a mumbled goodnight, as Audrey and Les headed homewards, leaving Jim to trudge back to his cottage alone.

Chapter Twenty-two

The Pump Room Association was the creation of the first chairman, Horace Braithwaite, who believed the involvement of the village in the affairs of the spring was essential for its success. Membership was open to any resident who had lived in the village for two years or more. The only condition was a nominal two pounds a year subscription, often wavered by a show of hands at the AGM.

With day-to-day business in the hands of the executive committee, the Annual General Meeting was a routine affair and normally over by 8.30. Having despatched the necessary business, it was customary for members and officers to retire to the Dog and Duck, and with the help of the pub's best bitter, give thanks for another successful year.

The AGM this year promised to be a livelier affair. The more vocal members of the Association eager to question Jason on why the Pump Room had been closed for a week. Alive to this mood, Jason knew his normal bland speech about the wonderful gift of the spring and the unstinting support of the members wouldn't do this year. If he was to enjoy the confidence of the Association and (more importantly) maintain his position as chair, his report needed to strike a very different tone. One that laid out the facts fairly and squarely and hammered home the decision to take to close the Pump Room was for the good of visitors and to protect the members of the Association.

With the election of the presidency of the Honiston Business League only days away his chances would be seriously jeopardised if he failed to retain his position of authority in the Association. Occupying the chair allowed him to keep a hand on the tiller and ensure the Pump Room was run to the benefit of the local businesses, including his own hotel and restaurant. He saw this as his civic duty, with the real honour - the one he set his heart on -

the presidency of the Business League. With that prize in his lap, he'd really be a man to be reckoned with.

But first, there was the small matter of the AGM. Every angle covered and no surprises. He had already spoken to Maurice Blake, the treasurer, and gone over the presentation of the accounts. The minutes of the last year's AGM were circulated with the notices, so they could be taken as read. Expecting Tilly, without a hearing aid, to read the minutes and take questions from the floor was a nightmare and not worth thinking about. That just left his report and the election of officers and executive committee to worry about.

Katie wasn't a member of the committee, nor for that matter, a member of the Association, though taking her seated prominently on the platform added a sense of glamour to the occasion. She was never enthusiastic about having to perform this duty, but as Jason reminded her that very morning, he didn't ask much of her. Tonight, was one of those occasions when supporting him on the platform and looking pretty was the least she could do to help him through this challenging time.

This casual statement – intending as a throwaway line - brought a demand to know what he meant by it. Was it anything to do with the closure of the Pump Room, Katie asked, pointedly? In response to his non-committal reply, she stormed away with an angry toss of the head. When he caught up with her in their bedroom, she told him bluntly that unless he told her the truth, she would refuse to attend the AGM, and certainly wouldn't be sitting on the platform.

Jason's further attempt to placate her only resulted in a more determined look on her face. Accepting there was no alternative, he gave her the full story. How he'd organised the fountain to be connected to an underground stream. Not the village pond, she demanded. No, not the village pond he assured her.

For the rest of the day Katie deliberately avoided him, but Jason was confident despite the petulant mood she wouldn't say or do anything to undermine him. She may be unhappy that he'd deliberately misled the likes of Mrs Worthington about the source of the spring water, but she wasn't about to jeopardise their business. The fortunes of the hotel and restaurant depended on a steady flow of visitors to the Pump Room. and she was too fond her creature comforts to give it all up on a silly whim.

Looking out from the platform at the members gathered in the Village Hall, Jason couldn't stop himself thinking how close the whole operation had come to collapsing around their ears. If it wasn't for people like him and Tony Mason, the village would be facing financial disaster. 'But that's all right,' he said to himself. 'That's why people like me were put on this earth, to save it from fools like you.'

The minutes of the last meeting were dealt with by a quick show of hands and then it was time to hand over to the treasurer. As Maurice began his report and a line by line explanation of each item in the accounts, Jason found himself drifting off into another world. A world bathed in a dazzling light: he was seated on a golden throne surrounded by beautiful women and adoring men. The saviour of our village from disaster they chanted and the threw flowers at his feet.

How this miracle was achieved had to remain a secret, at least not for now. In a year or so when the spring continued to cast its magic over countless visitors, a discrete announcement about a minor change in the source of the spring could be dropped into conversation. By then nobody would complain, not even Jim White and his gang of constant moaners. The whole village would give thanks to his foresight and ingenuity. As the glories and adulation continued to swirl around in his head, he felt a sharp nudge in the ribs and the treasurer whispering, 'Chairman's report, Jason, chairman's report,' brought him back to reality with a bump.

Pushing back his chair and rising to his feet, he noticed Philippa sitting prominently in the second row. For a moment, she caught his eye, he hesitated before turning away and transferring his attention to the friendly face of Gladys Bird, sitting three-quarters of the way down the hall. Coughing to clear his throat he began his speech. 'Ladies and gentlemen, I won't pretend this has been an easy year for the Association, though it began well with an increase in the number of visitors during the first ten months. The appreciation of many of those visitors for the glorious gift of the spring waters was expressed through the glowing letters, which – and please forgive the pun – flowed into the Pump Room. They were a joy to read. Each one telling a story of hope renewed and gratitude for the relief from pain and suffering after visiting the Magical Waters of Applegarth. Thank you, thank you they said....'

'Cut the waffle and tell us why the Pump Room was closed,' a male voice shouted from the back of the hall. Jason didn't see where the interruption had come from, nor did he recognise the voice. 'Bear with me friend, you will get your answer in a moment,' he exclaimed, hoping he didn't sound ruffled by the interruption.

'Answer the question,' this time woman's voice called out from another part of the hall. 'All in good time madam, I just ask you to be patient.' He turned to Katie, sitting a few places further along the top table and she smiled steely at him.

'What are you trying to hide,' the male voice called out, accompanied by a scattering of applause from several parts of the hall. Jason was beginning to get irritated by the interruptions and his most commanding voice replied. 'Now look sir, whoever you are, I am more than happy to give the members of the Association a full explanation for the closure of the Pump Room at the proper time, but I would be grateful if you would allow me to deal with it at the appropriate point in my report. Would you do that, please?' Turning his attention back to the main body of the hall, he glanced down to the notes scribbled on the back of the agenda, and looking up, said, 'Throughout the year, the staff of the Pump Room, consisting of Brenda and her team of ladies, have provided a professional and friendly service to all our visitors. It would, therefore, be remiss of me if I didn't take this opportunity to ask members to show their appreciation for their efforts in the usual way.' Pointing to Brenda sitting in the second row and beckoning her to stand up, Jason led the applause. When the applause died down and Brenda had resumed her seat, he continued, 'I should also like to thank....'

'What about the spring or is it just pond water' shouted the woman's voice over the top of him. 'I'm sure everybody here would like to...

'Enough, enough, I can see that common courtesy and respect for my position as chair of the Association is not going to prevail tonight. So, against my better judgement, I will deal with the question of the temporary closure of the Pump Room. A decision, I must say, that was taken by your committee with great reluctance and only after full and careful consideration of the facts. The situation we found ourselves a few weeks ago, with the floor of the Pump Room deteriorating to such an extent that it posed a serious health and safety hazard to staff and visitors alike. Having taken professional advice, your committee decided there was no option but to close the Pump Room to allow the essential repairs to be carried out. I should add that the advice we received was clear and precise. Expressed in simple terms, we were told if a visitor were to fall and injure themselves, then members of the Association would collectively *and* individually be responsible for any claim for damages awarded by the courts. In those circumstances, your committee felt they no option but to close the Pump Room immediately. You will understand that given the sensitive nature of the information, it was appropriate to issue only the briefest public statement. However, I did personally contact several members of the Association, including Mrs Worthington, who I see sitting in the body of the hall, to explain the situation and the decision taken by your committee.'

'Mr Chairman, if I may interrupt.' Jack Thompson, sitting at the front of the hall, rose, and addressed the body of the hall, in his usual booming voice. 'As a member of the committee I applaud your honesty in laying out the facts behind the closure of the Pump Room.' Jack paused for a moment to allow for a scattering of applause, before continuing. 'I wonder whether this would be an appropriate point, Mr Chairman, to scotch the ugly rumour circulating in the village that the closure was caused by the spring drying up. This is a nasty, pernicious allegation and deserves to be reputed in the strongest possible terms,' he concluded. Waving his arm in the direction of Jason on the platform, invited him to respond. Jack's intervention caused a stir in the hall since most of the audience were unaware of any such rumour. Now the cat was out the bag, they lent forward eager to hear what the chairman had to say.

Cursing under his breath Jason held up his up hands in a gesture of compassion. 'Thank you, Jack, for raising that question, which is probably behind the anonymous interruptions from the back of the hall. It is true ladies and gentlemen, the spring did dry up,' Jason paused to watch the horrified look on the faces of the audience, but having teased them, he continued, 'albeit temporarily. I have no wish to bore you with the technical details, but the problems with the spring and the deterioration in the floor were connected, I'm happy to report that everything in the Pump Room is back to normal. The spring continues to flow as it always has from an underground stream and to work its magic on the many visitors who are kind enough to grace the Magical Waters of Applegarth with their presence. And long may it continue to do so.' His rousing call was met by applause but as it died away, the male voice shouted from the back of the hall, 'What about the green water then,' Jason who by this time was feeling rather pleased with the way he had handled the question, decided it was time to silence this vile person for the last time. Pointing to Brenda, sitting in the front row, he said, 'We can get the answer, my friend, from the one person in this hall who should know. Brenda, who is our splendid supervisor, will be in a better position than most to tell us about the spring water. So, Brenda would you be kind enough give us the benefit of your experience and tell the meeting whether you noticed any change in the colour of water? Is it green, red or sky-blue?' To laughter and applause, he added, 'Maybe the water is pink and tastes like champagne, now that would really make our fortunes.'

Clearly embarrassed at being put on the spot, Brenda staggered to her feet, and in the voice, she used to make the presentations at the Pump Room, turned to face the audience. 'I can honestly say that the water from the spring is as clear and sparkling as it always has been. While it may not be champagne, it tastes as fresh and delicious as ever.'

'Thank you, Brenda,' Jason said over the applause and indicating she should resume her seat. When he had the attention of the meeting again, Jason continued, 'Ladies and gentlemen, I think that deals with the closure of the Pump Room comprehensively, so I would like to conclude my report by thanking the members of the committee for their hard work and to the members of the Association for their continued support. If I were fortunate enough to have a glass of bubbly in my hand at this moment, I would propose a toast to the Pump Room Association and to wish our endeavours every good fortune in the coming year. Who will join me in a toast!' he concluded to loud applause with smiles and shaking of hands amongst the officers? Even Katie joined him, smiling and waving, as the applause grew louder.

In the confusion, Audrey ducked out of the hall and seeing Philippa and Les joining her, shouted. 'The bastard got away with it again.'

'I don't understand,' Philippa said. 'I was certain he would be exposed. Well done by the way you two, your interruptions were first class.'

'I got some funny looks from the people around me, but I ignored them, particularly as he definitely looked rattled at one stage,' Les replied. 'As usual, he's managed to spin his way out of it.'

'After that performance, nobody is going to hear a word said against him. He's the hero of the hour,' Audrey said rather despondently. Looking at her companions rather pointedly, Philippa said, 'I think Jim has some explaining to do, don't you? It was his idea to put dye in the pond, and yet you heard Brenda, the water is clear. Why?'

'To be fair to Jim,' Les interjected, 'We both heard the committee discussing taking water from the pond.'

'So why didn't the water turn green? Unless of course there was a change of plan, which Jim conveniently forgot to tell us about?'

'I'm as disgusted as you over Jim's affair,' Audrey responded. 'But we mustn't overlook the possibility that Katie Black could have fed him false information knowing full well it would get back to us, and we like fools fell into the trap.'

'Jim better come up with an explanation, but for now, I suggest we leave before the meeting breaks up. We don't want anyone to see us huddled together like a group of conspirators,' Philippa suggested.

Back in his cottage, Jim was still feeling miserable and only an evening of Bix Beiderbecke accompanied by Frank Trumbauer and his Orchestra could lift his spirits. His mood was made worse by not being able to contact Robin. He'd rung earlier only to get her answer machine and had to leave a message asking her to call him, as he had some information about the Dancing Couple.

Little did he realise it, but his problems were about to get a whole lot worse.

Chapter Twenty-three

On most Saturday afternoons, Les could be found on his allotment tending the prize leeks on which he lavished much care and attention. The Building Society opened for business in the morning, but on the stroke of mid-day Les would scurry around, anxious to get the money in the safe and the doors locked and secured. Hazel, the cashier, would be out the door the moment the closed sign went up, but his assistant, Maureen had a habit of wanting to talk. 'I thought we had a very good morning Mr W. don't you,'

'Maureen, it's the weekend and the allotment calls,' Les would say, waiting at the back door, keys in hand, whilst she gathered together her things.

'Lots of people came and paid money into their accounts, and there were a couple of mortgages enquiries.' she said putting on the blue uniform jacket over the yellow blouse and tie provided for female staff

'Yes, Maureen it was a wonderful, fantastic, amazing morning. Now, grab your bag and let's go. That's better,' he said as she passed him in the doorway. 'Have a good weekend and see you on Monday.'

Arriving home, Les was pleased to see Audrey in the dining room staring at her computer. His pleasure increased when she announced her work on the Water Festival would take the rest of the day. Anticipating a whole afternoon tending his allotment with no arguments from Audrey, Les volunteered to prepare lunch. With ham, cheese and bread spread out on the kitchen table and Audrey happily tucking in, he planned the afternoon activities. There was a lot do and he was anxious to get on.

The Water Festival held no attraction for Les. For him, the Flower and Vegetable Show was one of the most notable events of the year. Not just for him, but for the whole village. There was keen competition amongst the gardeners for the top prizes. If he was to retain the coveted trophies for best leeks, his entries would have to be first-class. He'd won last year, but it was a close-run thing, and the other gardeners would be anxious to prise the trophy away from him. His leeks were coming along nicely, but with only a week or so to go he there was no room for complacency. Everything had to be perfect. When Audrey shooed him out of the house just after two, he didn't resist. Gathering his tools set off happily on the short walk to the allotments.

His biggest rival, Harry Travers, occupied the first plot inside the gate. Stopping for a chat, Les took the opportunity to cast an eye over on his rival's leeks: they were coming along nicely, too nicely for my peace of mind, Les thought.

'You've got a visitor,' Harry said nodding toward the small wooden shed that lay alongside the plot Les leased from the Parish Council. Following Harry's eye line, he saw Jim leaning against the shed door and looking anxiously in his direction.

'Don't often see you here on Saturday. Come to find out how to grow prize-winning leeks have you?'

'Why, do you know a man that does?' Jim replied with an attempt at a smile.

'I should be careful if I was you. I'm probably the only friend you've got at this precise moment,' Les said stooping down and gazing expertly at the row of leeks in front of him.

'I've tried talking to Audrey and Philippa, but they won't listen. I came here on the off chance you'd turn up.'

'With the show week or so away it was a safe bet,' Les said turning the lock on the shed door and returning with a watering can. Standing at the standpipe, conveniently placed alongside his plot, he began filling the can, adding feed from his pocket as the water reached the top. 'I'd lose all privileges for weeks if Audrey discovered me talking to you.'

'Yes, I know Les and I appreciate it. All I want is a way out of this mess, that's all.'

Les took the watering can and began walking along the row of leeks, pouring a dose of water on each plant. 'You could begin by explaining the cock-up over the dye.'

'Sorry, I don't know what you mean,' Jim replied. Les looked at him in disbelief for a second or two, before resuming the watering.

'I gather it didn't work?' Jim enquired.

'Not only didn't it work, and Jason Black is now in a far stronger position.' Pausing and putting the watering can down, he recounted how Jason had explained away the closure of the Pump Room, and how Brenda's declaration that the spring water was as clear and bright met with thunderous applause. 'At that moment, Jason Black could have the chairman's job for life if he wanted it.'

Returning to fill the watering can, Les stopped in front of Jim and looking him straight in the eye, said accusingly, 'Why did you allow us to put dye in the pond, when you knew perfectly well, we were wasting our time? That's what we don't understand.'

'I didn't know. There must have been a change of plan. Come on Les, you heard the committee discussing a plan to transfer water from the pond.'

'Exactly,' Les responded bitterly, continuing along the line of leeks. 'So, did the subject never come up during your pillow talk with Katie?'

'No, it didn't. She doesn't know any more than anybody else in the village,' Jim replied with as much sincerity he could muster.

Les turned to him and looked him straight in the eye. 'I don't believe you.'

'Why would I lie to you, it doesn't make sense.' Jim pleaded. Walking past him, Les disappeared into the shed and came out seconds later carrying a hoe. 'How about keeping your lover sweet so she continues to satisfy your carnal desires? That's two good reasons,' he said digging the hoe ferociously into the ground. 'You can't imagine how humiliating it was to be that close to bringing Jason Black down, and then see him triumph again. It was made worse knowing your best friend could have prevented it. You and Katie must have had a few laughs at our expense. Lying in bed together, you must have chuckled to yourselves. Knowing full well our plans would get back to her husband. I'm sorry but I don't want to talk about it, so bugger off and leave me to my leeks before I say something I might regret.'

Jim realised he'd underestimated the extent of his friend's anger. 'Les, I know you are hurt, but none of this is true. Katie said the problem was with the floor, and I believed her. We never discussed putting dye in the pond. You have to believe me?'

'No, actually I don't. Now, if you will excuse me, I've better things to do with my time,' and with a look of contempt, Les turned away and continued hoeing the ground around his leeks. Jim stared at him for a few minutes but realised it was futile to carry on, so he turned and walked out of the allotments and home.

Later that evening Robin returned his call. Still feeling bruised after his encounter with Les, he took a deep breath and recounted the conversation with PC Smith. Robin listened intently and promised to speak to PC Smith and pass on the information to Herbert Wise. There was no mention of the Stein Foundation's annual dinner and the phone call ended after the usual pleasantries about keeping in touch. Throughout the conversation, Jim had the distinct impression there was a man's voice in the background and wasn't particularly proud of his feelings towards whoever it was.

Chapter Twenty-four

'Hi Jim, its Katie, Feeling like a bit of fun? Good. I'll be over in ten minutes.'

Jim was seated at his dining table with several textbooks spread over the surface when the phone rang. He was due to deliver a lesson for the graphic communication course at Honiston Arts and Technical College the following Monday and was in the middle of preparing his lesson plan on the theory of colour and four-colour printing. The call from Katie came completely unexpectedly and before he could respond the phone went dead.

True to her word, ten minutes later Katie was sitting outside tooting her horn. This was the last time Jim resolved, and he was only going to quiz Katie on why the dye hadn't worked. Their affair had cost him too much in terms of his friendship with Philippa, Les and Audrey and it had to end.

'Hi, Jim you look sexy today. I love men in denim shirts. They always look rugged and delicious,' Katie said as Jim climbed in and they roared off. He started to say this was madness, their affair couldn't continue, but the car was travelling so fast, it was all he could do stop from falling out his seat. By the time, they reached Fullton Woods he was shaken up. With the car parked he managed to mutter, 'Katie we must talk,' before she pressed her lips to his and begun unbuttoning his shirt. 'Make it hard, make it quick,' she murmured demandingly in his ear.'

Afterwards, he slumped exhausted in his seat and turning to her said rather pointedly, 'What was that about.'

Smiling at him and buttoning her blouse, Katie looked at him. 'Didn't you enjoy it then?'

'Yes, of course,' Jim replied 'It's just that I have never seen you so aggressive before. Something must have happened today.'

Tucking the shirt into her short skirt she was wearing and turning the interior mirror to check her face, she said quite harshly, 'I was feeling randy and Jason was being boorish. The secretary of the Honiston Business thingy rang to say he'd won the election for the presidency or some such. After that he was like a dog with two tails, strutting around the place and getting ready for the meeting at lunchtime. You got the benefit – hope you don't mind.'

Jim smiled and watching her push her hair back in place. This might be the right moment to get some answers, he decided. 'Not at all. I guess Jason has good reason to feel pleased with himself after his triumph at the village hall.'

'You mean at the AGM. Yes, he was, gave me a right seeing too that night. There were a couple of hecklers, one of them sounded like your friend Les. They shouted some stupid stuff, but Jason talked his way out of it. What they didn't know was how close to the truth they really were.'

A voice inside Jim's head told him to play it cool, play it gently, so very tentatively he asked, 'Which is?'

Katie stopped patting her hair and looked at him, weighing up whether to say anything. 'It's no big deal. The spring dried up and they connected the fountain to an underground stream.'

'Not the pond then.'

'No, not the pond, what gave you that idea.'

'Just a rumour circulating in the village. It had nothing to do with repairing the floor then.' Again, she looked at him, deciding whether to go further. 'There were a few cracks in the floor, but that wasn't the reason. Look, Jim, I've told you all this confidence, you mustn't say a word to anyone. Not it would do any good, after the reception Jason got at the AGM no one would believe.'

'When I asked you before you laughed and said it was the floor.' Starting the engine, Katie reversed the car to the entrance. 'We had a row on the morning of the AGM. I said I wasn't going unless he told me the truth.'

Jim had what he came for and switched to the Dancing Couple, without mentioning young Kevin Jones and the damage to the statue.

Katie looked at him a couple of times as if she was about to make a comment but changed her mind. Back at his cottage, Jim jumped out of the car. 'When will I see you again.'

'I'll give you a ring, bye,' Katie replied revving up the engine and speeding away.

Walking up the path, Jim couldn't help letting the events of the last hour play out in his head. First, Katie calling unexpectedly, then their frantic lovemaking, and then the revelation about the fountain being connected to an underground stream: discovered while when the builders were digging out the trench. How to use the information? Particularly after his promise Katie.

These thoughts were only a distraction from the real question bothering him. Why didn't he end the affair? It's what he resolved to do, but - and it was a big but - he'd never known anyone so adventuress or demanding. She was unlike any other woman he had ever known, and he was drawn to her like a drug, and couldn't break the habit. Yet, she was still the wife of Jason Black, and no amount of fantasising was going to change that.

He might have continued to conjure up exotic thoughts about Katie's charms had his progress up the path not been halted by a sliver of an idea entering his head. Not yet fully formed, but the gem of an idea that it might help them discover what was really happening at the Pump Room. It was something Katie said when they were talking about the spring. It didn't register at the time, because conversation moved on to the Dancing Couple. He needed to develop it further and Philippa was the obvious person to talk to, even though she'd only want to discuss his relationship with Katie. With his key in the door, he decided to give her a call. It would involve a little white lie, and there were bound to be consequences, but he would live with them.

To his surprise the phone was picked up on the second ring and when he said, 'Hello,' a young girl's voice responded with, 'Do you want mummy or daddy?'

'Mummy please,' he replied gently. The phone went dead for a moment and then Phillippa's familiar voice came on, 'Hello, who's this?'

'It's Jim. Who was the young lady?'

'My daughter, Jermina, she gets to the phone first, and sometimes it can be a bit embarrassing. What can I do for you?'

'I wondered whether we could talk.'

'You know there's only one thing I want to hear from you,' she said rather sharply.

'In which case, you will be pleased to know I ended it today. More importantly, I also discovered the source of the water.' In response to her question, he told her about the underground steam. When he'd finished, there was a silent pause whilst Philippa considered this information. 'I'll speak to Audrey and Les and one of us will get back to you,' she said curtly as the phone went dead. Jim hoped by announcing his relationship with Katie was over things between him and the gang would return to normal, but apparently, he'd have to wait for one of them to call.

The next morning an envelope from the Stein Foundation popped through the letterbox and when he retrieved it from Bix, Jim was delighted to discover an official invitation to the Benefactor's Annual Dinner. Studying the gilt-edged card, he noted it was in two weeks at the Royal Knightsbridge Hotel, and the dress code was black tie.

Attached was a compliment slip with a hand-written note from Robin, which read:

'I've booked you in for the night at the hotel (the Foundation will pick up the tab) and I'll pick you up from your room at about seven."

That's more like it, he thought, taking his dinner jacket from the wardrobe. 'I'd better try this on to make sure it fits and get it to the dry cleaners,' he muttered, smiling into the mirror as he slipped on the jacket.

Chapter Twenty-five

'Welcome ladies and gentlemen to Applegarth and the world-famous Magical Spring Water and Kissing Stone.' Brenda announced as she began her fifth introduction of the day. The visitors were the usual mixture of the sick seeking relief from their illness or ailment, the curious and the downright sceptical. It wasn't the visitors who were the cause of her problem, it was young Tracey phoning in sick.

With Jane in the box office, Tracey and herself looking after the visitors, they could cope. With only two of them, it was left to Brenda to do the introduction, and shepherd the visitors through the gift shop Tracy wasn't the brightest star in the sky, but she managed to carry out that simple task well enough.

As the latest group began to leave, Brenda caught sight of Jason just inside the entrance. Acknowledging his presence by way of a brief nod, she deposited the last of the plastic cups in the bin. 'I just popped by to see how things were Brenda and to say thanks for your support at the AGM.'

'That's okay Mr Black,' she responded picking up towels from the floor. Taking a fuller look at him, she could see he had a more than a usual confident air about him, 'You look very pleased with yourself today if you don't mind me saying so, any particular reason.'

Jason was indeed feeling very pleased with himself, and he responded with a broad smile. 'I didn't realise it showed, but you are quite correct. I have received some good news in the last few days. Tiptop in fact. You now see standing before you the next President of the Honiston Business League, Brenda. The result of the election was announced two days ago. A great honour of course, but also a big responsibility.'

'Congratulations. After your performance at the AGM, I'm not surprised you're feeling pleased. Excuse me, but I need to let the next lot in,' Opening the doors and waving the next ten visitors in, she spent the next few minutes doing her standard introduction and helping to fill cups from the fountain, giving a helping hand to those who wished to kiss the Wishing Stone and distributing bottles of the spring water.

Jason stepped back to observe the process but found himself caught up in the throng and was forced to hand out copies of the commemorative certificates, and murmur suitable words of thanks and pointing to the Visitor's Book. When the last of the group had left, he came to stand behind the fountain, 'Where's young Tracey today?' he enquired pleasantly.

Brenda stopped picking up the discarded cups. 'She phoned in sick today Mr Black.'

'Nothing serious, I hope. She adds a youthful freshness to the place, don't you think?'

Brenda had no idea what that meant, but replied, 'Yes, Mr Black. A rash appeared on her hands overnight, and I told her to stay at home. It would upset the visitors if they saw her hands in that state. We are after all supposed to cure ailments, are we not?'

'Quite so Brenda. I presume you told her to see her doctor?'

Nodding Brenda continued, 'he'll prescribe some cream and it will clear up in a couple of days. You know these young girls they're always picking up things.'

'Exactly, but in the meantime, you and Jane can cope?' Jason enquired moving to the exit, but not waiting for a response. His inauguration as president was due next week and there was just enough time to drive into Honiston and pick up the new suit he had ordered. A nice grey wool worsted with a slight blue strip. He needed an outfit that would show off the gold chain of his office, to be presented by the outgoing president, that fool Stanley Bates at the next meeting. After that, the gold chain would be his to wear for an entire year and he intended to parade it with pride at every single meeting of the Business League. He almost tingled with excitement at the prospect of forcing all those stuck-up solicitors and estate agents to address him as Mr President and show the respect to he was entitled to.

After a successful year, his place as the natural leader of the local business community would be assured. What then? A seat on the National Council and the opportunity to share his thoughts with government ministers, and even an invitation to the garden party at Buckingham Palace would be in his grasp.

If there was a heaven, surely this was it.

Chapter Twenty-six

In one of those coincidences that never quite get explained, Jim's route to the dry cleaners in the High Street crossed the path of young Tracey, on her way to the local chemist. Brenda's prediction of her visit to the surgery was correct. After a cursory examination, a prescription of soothing cream was thrust into her hands with instructions to return in a few days if it didn't clear up.

Handing his dinner jacket and trousers into the dry cleaners, Jim remembered he required a supply of razor blades from the chemist next door. Waiting in the queue to be served, he spotted Tracey idly examining the displays of lipsticks. He didn't know her well; he'd seen her in and around the Pump Room a few times. 'Hi, Tracey,' he said as they queue shuffled forward, 'No work today?'

'Hello, Mr White,' she said picking up a deep red lipstick, 'I had to go to the doctors. I'm waiting for my prescription. They seem a bit busy today.'

'Nothing serious I hope,' he enquired, encouragingly.

Tracey held up her hands 'Just these blotches. Came on two days ago. It's so embarrassing having bright red hands.'

'About the same colour as that,' Jim said nodding towards the lipstick she was holding in her hand.

'Yes,' Tracey replied, returning the lipstick to the display case. 'I'm not allowed to work for now. I don't want to look for another job. I just hope it clears up soon,

Jim reached the counter and having paid for his razor blades, remarked to Tracey on the way out, 'Hope the hands clear up.'

The state of Tracey's hands continued to intrigue Jim, as he made his way home. Red blotchy skin was normally caused by contact with a harmful liquid. In the case of Tracey that was unlikely. Or was it? The liquid she was in regularly in contact with was spring water, and that was supposed to cure ailments, not cause them.

Could the water from the underground spring have been contaminated in some way?

Lost in thought he arrived at his cottage to be greeted by Bix bounding down the hallway. In the kitchen and flipping on the kettle for a cup of coffee, he wondered whether any of the staff had developed a similar rash.

Thinking back, he remembered one of the ladies worked at the cash desk, while Brenda and Tracey supervised the visitors. The other person most likely to be affected by contaminated spring water was Brenda. He poured hot water from the kettle into his mug and took a sip of coffee. The trouble was he couldn't march into the Pump Room and demand to inspect her hands. What about the visitors, had any of them developed a similar rash? They wouldn't necessarily blame the spring water, particularly if it developed a few days after they visited the Pump Room. He would like to chew this over with Les and Audrey or Philippa but wasn't sure if they were talking to him.

The answer was in a message left while he was out. Normally, he'd check it the moment he came in, but being pre-occupied with Tracey's skin problems, he'd hadn't noticed the flashing red light on the answering machine

It was Audrey welcoming him back into the fold. 'Jim, we'd be delighted to see you for lunch on Sunday. I need to work in the morning on stuff for the Flower and Vegetable Show. To stop Les poisoning us, could you pitch in and cook lunch. I'll get a joint of pork and the usual trimmings. You'll find an apple pie and fresh custard in the fridge, along with a bottle of Sancerre, so don't need to bring anything.'

Jim was delighted.

Arriving on Sunday, Audrey, greeted him warmly enough, though the look on her face betrayed a certain reserve. Jim wasn't complaining, he was glad to be back in favour, and just hoped he could maintain the lie about his relationship with Katie.

With Audrey working at the dining room table amidst piles of application forms, Jim set about preparing the pork joint. 'Where's Les,' he called through to Audrey.

'He announced a few minutes ago that he was popping down to the allotment to check on his leeks, which probably means he won't be back 'til lunchtime,' Audrey replied, not looking up from her computer screen. Finding a roasting pan tucked away in a cupboard, Jim began rubbing salt all over the joint and preparing the sage and onion stuffing. 'What's Les going for this year then?'

'There are two leek categories and Les has an entry in each. If you have a moment, put the kettle on, will you? A cup of coffee helps me concentrate when I am doing this detailed stuff.'

'What are you doing?' Jim asked, switching on the kettle. Audrey turned and seeing Jim peering through the hatch, explained she was typing up the entries for Flower and Vegetable Show. A few minutes later Jim joined her, with two cups of coffee, 'I'm so glad you saw sense over the thing with Katie Black, but you understand why we were upset?'

Jim reached and touched her arm. 'I'm sorry to have caused you so much distress.'

Audrey stopped typing and took the coffee Jim handed to her 'Forgotten, though I still don't understand what you saw in that woman.' To underline the subject was closed, she immediately changed the subject. 'When you rang, you said there was some news about the spring.' Jim put his cup down on the only space on the table and related his encounter with Tracey and his theory about the water from the underground stream. He also said he spoke to the manager at Mason's, the printers in Honiston, who was an ex-student of his. He'd made some excuse about being on the scrounge for paper for the college and used the opportunity to seek out Terry in the pressroom. Before steering the conversation around to Tracy and her rash, he asked his advice on a technical point Terry's response was to repeat the story about Tracy being off sick and Brenda having to cover for her.

'Did you ask whether Brenda had also developed a rash,' Audrey asked

'Yes, I did, though not as bluntly as that. I said, "Brenda's okay then," and

Terry replied, "she's fine, no trouble at all, just a bit tired,"

'Meaning she's hasn't been in contact with the spring water, or it hasn't affected her in the same way.'

'Either way, it doesn't help my theory,' Jim replied, picking up his cup and finishing his coffee.

'Look,' Audrey said picking up a pile of the entry forms lying on the table, 'I have to get this finished, otherwise, the catalogue won't be ready for the show. Let's talk more over lunch and see what we can come up with.'

'Yes, of course. I'll leave you in peace. I'll take this away if you've finished?' Jim replied picking up Audrey's cup and heading for the kitchen. For the next hour or so Jim and Audrey were busily engaged in their respective tasks and only stopped when Les' cheery 'Hi you two,' broke the silence.

Later, with the dining table cleared and prepared for lunch, they sat down to their meal. While Jim and Les tucked into the roast pork, Audrey recounted the story of Tracey's blotchy hands and Jim's attempts to discover whether Brenda was affected. When she'd finished, Les looked Jim straight in the eye. 'This is not one of your, put dye in the pond ideas, is it?'

Jim, taken back by the implied criticism, replied gently, 'If you mean another wild goose chase, then the answer is no. After talking to Terry and Brenda is okay, I'm inclined to dismiss it. The test will be if the rash comes back when Tracey's returns to work.'

Audrey, who sensed a circular argument developing, chipped in, 'nobody's going to believe you if it turns out Tracey is the only one affected. What would cause Jason Black real problems is if any visitors developed a blotchy rash. Then he'd have to admit the water was from an underground stream.'

'Well,' said Les, 'I can clear up one thing for you. I saw young Tracey on my way home from the allotment today and her hands looked perfectly normal.'

'You saw her?' asked Audrey incredulously.

'Yes, she was walking towards the High Street, arm in arm with some spotty youth. As they passed, Tracey said something I didn't catch and raised her hands in the air. They looked perfectly normal to me, no rash or blotches, nothing.'

Audrey looked at the two men despondingly, 'So, where does that leave us then?'

'The phrase up a creek without a paddle springs to mind,' Jim replied glumly.

Les, who refused to share their sense of gloom, lifted his glass and proposed a toast. 'Cheers. As it is Sunday and my leeks look like sure-fire winners again, I'm delighted to share with you my latest doctor joke.'

'If it's the one about the man who goes to the doctors and says, "Doctor, doctor I think I've turned into a dog" and the doctor looks at him and shouts, "nurse get this animal out of here," then don't bother because we've heard it many times.'

'Actually, the love this little humorous story has never seen the light of day before.'

'Go on then Les, get it out of your system,' Jim said taking a large swig of wine.

'Okay, since you insist: picture the scene if you will. A hospital late at night, and in the men's surgical ward all is quiet. The patients are sleeping, except for one bed with the light on and the curtains drawn. Suddenly from behind the curtains, a female voice is heard to say, 'Mr Jones, as your doctor I must ask you to stop trying to kiss me all the time. Come to think of it, I not sure it was such a good idea to get undressed and get into bed with you in the first place.'

The attempt by Les to introduce a lighter tone to the proceedings and lift the mood was met with stony silence, only broken by Audrey's monotone instruction, 'Les shut up and eat your lunch.'

Chapter Twenty-seven

Tracey's hands may have cleared up, but it didn't stop Jim brooding on what might have caused the infection, and why it cleared up so quickly. Only the brief hour or so during his presentation to the students at Honiston Tech did he experience any relief.

He wasn't questioning Les' powers of observation, he just needed to check for himself, which is why he was standing on the High Street on Tuesday morning awaiting the arrival of the Pump Room ladies. Brenda was the first to arrive a little after nine. He nodded as she hurried past, pulling a large set of keys from her pocket.

A few minutes later Brenda's assistant, Jane hurried past him. Twenty minutes went by and Jim was beginning to think Tracey was still off sick when she strolled towards him. 'Hello, Mr White,' she said, 'have you come to take the magical waters this morning?'

'I'm afraid my ailments are beyond the healing powers of the spring.' Jim replied anxiously looking at her hands. 'How's the rash, by the way?'

Sticking her hands up in a defiant gesture, Tracey said, 'All gone,' and continued down the path to the Pump Room. It was true her hands were pink and healthy. Whatever caused the problem had disappeared naturally or cleared up by the cream prescribed by her doctor.

Jim found it difficult to hide his frustration at the sight of her rash-free hands. Yet out of this turmoil came a gem of an idea. It would take some planning and a bit of organisation, but it might just work.

In the meantime, a visit to the supermarket was required. It wasn't a job he looked forward to. Nancy did the weekly trip to the supermarket in Honiston when she was alive or picked up any odd things they needed from the Spar in the village. Nowadays, it was a chore to be endured.

It was times like this he wished he'd kept their old car. Carrying the weekly shop home was a bind, but a car would just sit outside the cottage taxed and insured on most days.

Idly looking out of the window of the bus on route to the supermarket, he recalled the hilarious night they suffered a puncture on the way home from Exeter and walked miles to find a country pub and persuaded the landlord to let them have a room for the night. The landlord, a huge man with a barrel chest and thick bushy whiskers, assumed they were illicit lovers as they had no luggage and insisted on twin beds. 'You sleep in your own beds and stay there. I'm not having any hanky-panky under my roof,' he muttered, disappearing down the hallway as they pushed the two beds together.

His fond reminisces of happy days with Nancy were rudely interrupted by the sound of a familiar voice, 'Didn't realise you were into serious shopping, Jim. Always thought of you as a pop down to the village shop sort of guy, if you know what I mean.'

Without consciously being aware of it, he'd arrived at the supermarket and was idly pushing his trolley up and down the aisles, when he felt a sharp jolt at the front of the trolley. Jerked back to the present, he was faced with Katie dressed in a blue shirt and jeans, standing in front of him smiling in that open inviting way only she could manage. 'Sorry, Katie I was miles away,' he replied.

'Dreaming of fast cars and accommodating women, were you?'

Accepting he had been caught daydreaming, Jim replied flatly 'Actually, slow cars and unaccommodating landlords. It's a long story and I'll tell you about it one day.' Changing his tone and smiling at her, he continued, 'Anyway, what brings you here? I thought you got all your stuff from the cash and carry.'

Katie walked alongside him. 'Most stuff we do, but as you can see,' she said, pointing to the contents of her trolley, 'I still need to come here for cheese and things.' Stopping and looking at him, 'Do you want a ride home, or just a ride'? she said with a big smile.

Later, when Jim finished his shopping, he emerged into the car park and saw Katie loading groceries into the back of her car. As he approached, she looked up, 'If you want to dump your things in the back there, should be enough room.' With the shopping deposited in the boot, he slid into the passenger seat and buckled up, as Katie started the engine. 'Fancy a quickie,' she said, with a twinkle in her eye.

Taken back by the suggestion, Jim just managed to blurt out, 'What, here in the car park, you mean, where everybody can see us?'

'It could be exciting,' she said looking at him and laughing. When he didn't respond, she fastened her seat belt, shoved the car into gear and moved toward the exit, 'Suit yourself,' she added with an air of resignation.

The drive back to Applegarth was completed almost in silence, as Katie concentrated on manoeuvring the car through the traffic, only broken by Jim saying, 'I was sorry to hear about young Tracey's rash by the way.' Katie didn't reply, and Jim wasn't sure whether she hadn't heard, or considering how to reply. When she did, it was with a slight edge in her voice, 'How did you hear about that, you haven't been chatting up young Tracey as well have you?'

'As well?' Jim enquired.

'My husband's always ogling that little tart. As to your question,' she continued slowing for the traffic lights outside Applegarth, 'I understand she developed a bit of a rash on her hands, but the doctor prescribed some cream and it cleared up. End of story.'

'I thought the water from the underground stream might have affected her. You haven't had any complaints from visitors I suppose?' Jim asked.

Katie continued to concentrate on the road, but when she did reply there was a hard edge to it. 'Not as far as I am aware. Why do you ask?'

Deciding it was time to beat a retreat, Jim quickly added, 'I'm wondering whether the spring could be a possible cause and might be worth investigating that's all.'

'Mmm,' Katie murmured as she pulled up outside Jim's cottage, 'I'm not entirely sure I believe that, but listen Jason's got one of his Honiston Business lunches on Thursday, so why come to the hotel about three.'

As he gathered up his shopping bags, he looked across to her and said pointedly 'Sorry Katie, I have a meeting in London on Thursday. My professional association's annual conference but give me a ring next week if you are free.' Katie didn't reply, but accelerated away, leaving Jim to slam the door shut before the car moved off.

If Jim felt any sympathy for Katie's plight, he certainly didn't show it. He was due to meet Robin and that prospect was more appealing. Besides, there were things to do before he caught the train to London. A few minutes earlier as they drove through the village, he'd spotted Philippa coming out of the Spar. Waiting for Katie's to disappear, he dumped his shopping inside the cottage and headed for the High Street. Opposite the Cosy Café, he caught sight of her as she was about to cross the road. 'Philippa, Hi,' he called out as she approached. 'Got time for a coffee,'

Her attention was focused on crossing the busy road, and his welcome was greeted with a blank stare, quickly changing to a smile as recognition dawned. 'Not really Jim' but seeing the earnest look on his face changed her mind. 'Okay, but I can only spare ten minutes.'

Seated in one of the window seats, and having ordered their drinks, he told her about the rash on Tracey's hands and his theory that it was caused by the underground stream.

'It's a bit of a long shot,' Philippa replied when he'd finished. 'It could have nothing to do with the spring. You know teenagers, all those hormones buzzing about.' Putting her cup down, she thought for a moment, 'Having made ourselves look very silly over the dye we can't afford another mistake. You weren't at the AGM, but it was a masterstroke for Jason to get Brenda to stand up at the meeting and say the water was clear. If we're to nail him, it has to be over something he can't wriggle out of it.'

Jim listened and nodded as Philippa spoke, and took a sip of coffee before replying, 'There may be a way to get the evidence.'

'How's that?' Philippa asked eagerly, placing her empty cup in the saucer.

Looking around to make sure nobody could overhear, he whispered, 'Get hold of the Visitor's Book.'

'I don't see how that will help. People only write what a glorious and wonderful experience it was.'

'They do,' Jim said learning forward to command her attention. 'They also provide a name and address. In which case, we can ask if they've had any skin problems?'

'Okay, but how do we get Visitor's Book? You can't waltz into the Pump Room and demand it. Look, I have to go,' Philippa said gathering up her various bags. 'Maybe there is a gem of an idea there but discuss it with Audrey and Les and see what they think.' As she moved to the door, she turned and called back. 'I'll ring you tonight at Audrey's,' then seeing several customers staring at her, made a hurried exit.

Phillippa's mention of Audrey, made his face light up. Placing the money for the coffees on the table, he got up and left.

He needed to collect his dinner jacket from the cleaners, but first, a quick trip to the library was required. Audrey wasn't immediately insight when he walked in, but glancing around, he spotted her in one of the aisles holding an armful of books. 'Hi Audrey,' he said. 'I hoped I might find you here today.'

'Jim,' she replied returning the latest John Grisham novel to the shelf. 'We don't see you in here very often, so what do we owe the pleasure of this visit?'

Following her, as she walked down the aisle expertly placing the books in their rightful place on the shelves, he told her about his meeting with Philippa and the idea of getting their hand on the Visitor's Book. When he finished, Audrey straightened up from putting a book on the bottom shelf and enquired, 'Okay, but how?'

'I don't know. I was relying on to come up with an idea.'

Audrey continued replacing the books on the shelves. 'It would mean someone going in with the last group just before they close and hanging about on the pretence of waiting to sign the Visitor's Book, picking it up and walking out the door. But...,' she paused as a major problem occurred to her, 'how do we get it back in the morning? It might not be a problem at night. Brenda and the other women will be anxious to get off home. It must be a soulless job working in that place all day. Excuse me I have to get another pile of books,' Audrey said walking toward the counter at the front of the library.

When she returned a few moments later, Jim held up a finger. 'You're right. You could hardly walk into the Pump Room the following morning carrying the Visitor's Book and saying, "Sorry, I took this home by mistake last night," What about if you sneaked in the back door as the first group of visitors were leaving in the morning and slide it back on the little table just inside the exit, it's where it normally lives. That might work.'

Audrey looked at him searchingly as she continued to return the books to the shelves. 'It couldn't be me or you or Les even. Brenda or Tracey would immediately recognise us and get suspicious?'

'Who can we trust then?' Jim replied rubbing his finger up and down his nose in a thoughtful gesture.

With a large volume poised at exactly the right spot on the shelves, Audrey stared at Jim with a certain gleam in her eye, 'Come over tonight, and you may find the Visitor's Book in my eager hands,' she said pushing the book firmly into place.

When Jim tapped on their kitchen door and walked in with a brief 'Hello,' it was to find Audrey and Les sitting at the dining table studying the Visitor's Book. In answer to his unspoken question, Audrey replied, 'I got Joyce, the other librarian, to go to the Pump Room just before they closed and ask whether we could borrow it, saying the Parish Council asked the library to put together some figures on the visitors to the village. Not just numbers, but where they came from – UK, Europe, and America – that sort of thing. Anyway, Brenda was as good as gold. Said help yourself, keep for as long as you like.'

Looking at her with a sense of admiration, Jim enquired, 'What did you tell Joyce?'

'Nothing really, she looked quizzically at me when I asked, but she just nodded and said "okay." She's never voiced an opinion before, but she's heard me mutter about Jason Black and maybe agrees with us. Anyway, we've been able to identify about twenty-five names and addresses in this country. I was just in-putting the details into a little database I've created on my computer.'

Sitting down beside Les, 'What can I do to help?' Jim asked

In between tapping away on her computer, with Les reading the names and addresses from the Visitor's Book, Jim drafted the letter to send to the visitors. It took several drafts and one or two arguments, but the trio eventually agreed on what to say.

Friends of Applegarth
Cherry Cottage, Long Acre Road, Applegarth, Gloucestershire

Dear Visitor,

We very much hope you enjoyed your recent visit to our village and took the opportunity to see and experience the many delights on offer to visitors. From time to time we take the opportunity to contact those who have been kind enough to leave their address in one of the many Visitor's Books and bring their attention to the many attractions they may have missed, and to seek feedback on those they were able to visit.

For example, in the Memorial Park, there is a statue by the renowned twentieth-century sculptor, Isaac Stein, who was born and brought up in Applegarth. He didn't name the piece, but it is commonly known as the Dancing Couple. Next time you visit us why not take a stroll down to the park and see you for yourself how this delightful statue got its popular name?

Most of our visitors, of course, come for the spring and the magical waters and if you were amongst them, we hope your visit was satisfying. Indeed, the majority of visitors come away from the spring and can look back on the experience positively. If you have written or called to say how much you have enjoyed your visit, we thank you for your kind words.

For a few, and we do mean a very few, the waters of the spring do have an adverse reaction due to the high mineral content of the water, causing a slight reddish colouring of the hands. This usually disappears within a few days but if you are one of those, we would like to hear from you. Please write if you have experienced any adverse reaction within a day of visiting the spring to the address given above.

We thank you in advance and anticipate that in the light of the responses to this letter, there may be a need to post a warning in the Pump Room that the waters may harm those with sensitive skins.

Thank you for your cooperation.

With the letter, ready to be run-off, they filled the time until Philippa's call. When it came, she listened carefully as they read it back to her and when they had finished, she questioned the need for the third paragraph. Jim took the phone and said it was designed to make it appear like a general marketing letter, rather than a request for information about skin problems. In the end, with one or two changes, they agreed on the wording.

With the letters running out of the printer, Les appeared from the kitchen with glasses of chardonnay, which was drunk enthusiastically. Once the printing was completed, Jim offered to stuff the letters in the envelopes and post them the following day. Saying a cheery goodnight, he disappeared into the night.

The mood of the trio might have been more subdued had they been standing inside the hut on Les' allotment and watched as a hooded figure walked slowly down the row of leeks with large pair of shears. Standing above each plant, he, or she – it was difficult to tell from the hood covering their face – with a single quick swish of the shears cut through the leaves.

When all the plants were destroyed, the hooded figure surveyed with satisfaction the trail of destruction and walked over to the shed. Taking a note from their coat pocket, he (or she) carefully pinned it to the door, before hurrying away. The note consisted of five short lines.

> *This is what happens to those who*
> *Think they can destroy the*
> *Magical Waters of Applegarth*
> *With their malicious accusations*
> *Be warned!*

Chapter Twenty-eight

On Thursday morning, the weather was dull and overcast, with a hint of rain to come, but for Jim, it was of no consequence. Packing his suitcase to the upbeat accompaniment of Louis Armstrong's *On the Sunny Side of the Street*, perfectly matched his mood. He'd checked the timetables and identified a train from Honiston Junction, with a change at Swindon, would get him to Paddington by mid-afternoon.

His friendly neighbours, Bill and Joan, readily agreed to look after Bix overnight, and since he knew they would spoil him rotten, he had no hesitation in leaving the border terrier in their tender care. 'Have an enjoyable time, and don't worry about rushing back in the morning,' they called out as he closed the garden gate.

The journey to London went very smoothly and by four he was standing at the reception desk of the Royal Knightsbridge Hotel telling the young clerk, whose jacket badge announced her name as Sarah, a room was reserved for him. After completing the inevitable registration form, he was told Robin hadn't checked in and was told by Sarah for security reasons her room number couldn't be divulged. She did promise to inform Ms Caulfield of his enquiry when she arrived. Handing over the key card, she wished him a pleasant stay and directed his attention to the lifts on the far side of the lobby.

With a few hours to spare and the weather having cleared up, Jim was sat on a comfortable seat in the warm afternoon sunshine in the middle of Kensington Park. Watching the couples passing by hand in hand he recalled the times when he and Nancy came to London on their annual trip to the Ballroom Championships in nearby Olympia. They were fun and full of excitement. They couldn't afford to stay in posh hotels, their finances only ran to a cheap room somewhere out on the Bayswater Road. Maybe they didn't win any prizes but took great delight in cheering on their friends and if anyone won a prize, however minor, it was the cause for great celebration.

Jim was shocked out of his daydream by a large dog barking nearby and checking his watch, he realised it was time to return to the hotel and get ready for the evening's festivities. It was simple, all he needed to do was to retrace his steps. Somehow, he took a wrong turning and only found his way back to the hotel by hailing a taxi. By which time, there were only a few minutes to get showered and changed before a tap on the door revealed Robin holding two glasses of champagne, 'I thought you might like some bubbly before entering the fray,' she said walking into the room and putting the glasses down on the small table by the window. 'Now then, let's have a look at you.' She said smiling and eyeing him appreciatively. 'I must say for a country bumpkin; you scrub up quite well.'

'What about me, do I look like someone you might wish to escort to this esteemed event,' she asked coyly. Jim wasn't sure whether this was due to downing a couple of glasses of the champagne in her room, her shyness at being in his bedroom, or a genuine interest at seeing him. In truth, he didn't need to tell her how beautiful she looked, in a simple off-the-shoulder white dress that fitted tightly, before flowing outwards from the knee. A gold chain at her throat and the long blonde strands of her hair piled high on her head completed the stunning ensemble.

Gathering up the champagne and handing one to Robin, he raised his glass, 'You look absolutely stunning and I deem it a great honour to be your escort for tonight. Cheers.'

Pointing to the two club chairs and pulling one away from the table, he asked, 'Can you sit down in that dress by the way.'

'Just about,' she responded lightly. It's a question of approaching the chair at the right angle and slowly sliding into the seat. Once I'm there it's easy. There,' she said making herself comfortable.

To fill the silence, Jim asked about the arrangements for the evening. Placing her glass on the table, Robin launched into the history of the Benefactor's Dinner, as if she'd learnt it by heart that afternoon.

'To maintain the collection and cast new reproductions of Isaac Stein's work the Trustees relied on donations from wealthy men and woman. It's always a struggle and some years a fair bit of arm twisting is required to achieve the sum of money required', she added.

'By way of saying thank you, the Foundation hosts a dinner every year for the benefactors and their partners. As I explained when we met in Applegarth, I've never been to one of these dinners before. So far, I've managed to get out of it. Formal dinners are not my thing. I prefer small informal gatherings.'

'I gather this year, you're on a three-line whip.'

Robin took a sip of champagne, 'I pleaded with Herbert, to be excused but he was insistent. His exact words were, "I want you there because the dinner needs a touch of youthful glamour amongst us old fogies." I assume he was referring to the officers and trustees, not the benefactors.'

'I'll drink to that. By which I mean the bit about you lending a touch of glamour. Not the bit about old fogies,' Jim responded raising his glass. Robin looked away, slightly embarrassed at the compliment. 'Anyway,' she said before he could utter another word, 'we are supposed to be joining the other guests for a reception in a few moments, and dinner is scheduled for eight.'

'How many people are expected?' Jim asked putting his empty glass on the table.

'I haven't seen the full guest list, but when I spoke to Herbert a couple of days ago, he said there were expecting about a dozen benefactors and their partners. The six Trustees and their partners will be joining us, plus of course Herbert and his wife, and you and me. Is that ok?'

'I think I'll manage to talk high finance and the tax benefits of donating to worthy causes for an hour or so,' he said with a smile. 'Before we go, what about the Dancing Couple?'

'Whoops,' Robin said taking a last gulp of champagne, 'In the excitement of getting organised to arrive here appropriately dressed I forgot all about it.' Putting her glass down, she said. 'I rang PC Smith and he confirmed the damage was an accident and not malicious.'

'Did he tell you exactly what happened,' Jim asked.

'Only that was a tragic accident. Anyway, armed with the information I emailed Herbert and suggested he might want to share the news with the trustees. I haven't had the chance to speak to him since.'

'I promised PC Smith not to divulge what really happened to the statue, but I'll tell you in a quiet moment, but meanwhile have the trustees had another meeting?' Jim asked moving to the back of Robin's chair and helping her up. Robin took her handbag from the table and walked toward the door. 'Not that I'm aware, though I assume Herbert would have informed them.' Opening the door and taking his arm and heading for the lift. 'Don't be surprised if, when I introduce you, Herbert takes you aside to have a word. In the meantime,' she said pressing the lift button, 'put on your best smile and let's go and charm these lovely people.'

With Jim and Robin about to embark upon a night of wining and dining amongst the rich and glamorous people of the capital, in the Woods household it was doom and gloom. Les returned home in a state of deep depression. It took all of Audrey's persuasive powers to drag out of him that his precious leeks had been destroyed.

Over dinner, with Les hardly able to swallow a mouthful, they racked their brain to come up with who it was that hated them so much they would destroy the leeks. Jason was quickly dismissed as the culprit. 'Even he wouldn't stoop that low. If not Jason, then it had to be someone close to the Pump Room, but who?' Audrey asked.

'I can't see any of the committee doing that sort of thing,' Les replied, looking anxiously at Audrey. 'Besides most of them wouldn't have the energy to make it as far as the allotments late at night, never mind cutting down a row of leeks.'

'Why don't you give Harry a ring and ask whether he saw anything,' Audrey suggested taking away his half-eaten dinner.

***

At the Royal Knightsbridge Hotel, the Benefactor's dinner had reached the desert – an amazing concoction of meringue, strawberries, and ice cream. The whole meal, as Jim had to confess, was beautifully prepared and served.

He'd hoped to sit with Robin, but the seating plan placed them on different tables. Instead, he found himself sitting next to a lady who introduced herself as Mrs Irene Whiteman, sitting on the other side of him was Ms Jane Hulpin. During the reception, Robin had taken Jim to one side and said he needed to be particularly attentive to the two ladies. One was the wife of their most generous donator and the other a long-term contributor to the Foundation.

'That's quite a responsibility,' he'd replied. 'I just hope I don't make any social faux pas by using the wrong knife and fork. You start from the inside and work outwards, don't you?' he said teasing her.

Looking across to where Robin was sitting, her attention was focused on the two men seated either side of her. She was leaning on her right elbow and looking intently at the elderly gentleman on her left, who was in the middle of telling a long and convoluted story, about his efforts to overcome a bitter rival in the City. If she was bored, Robin had the grace not to show it. Instead, she followed every twist and turn with nods and gasps in the appropriate places. When he'd finished, she touched his arm gently and leant back to bring her companion on the right into the conversation. The perfect host, he thought. Looking in the direction of Herbert Wise, sitting at the top of the table, he noticed an approving glance at the ease in which she was handling the two men in the room with probably the biggest egos.

***

Les put down the phone and looked at Audrey. 'Harry says he was at the allotments until just before nine, in other words after I left. The last thing he did was to walk down to the tap fill up his can and my leeks were fine – not as good as his, but untouched.'

'So, whoever destroyed them, did it after that.' Audrey suggested.

'Yes, but that doesn't take us any further forward in identifying the culprit,' muttered Les, who was beginning to think they would never identify him.

***

'Tell me, what role do you play in the Foundation?' Jim turned to see Mrs Whiteman addressing him.

'None actually,' he replied. 'I'm a mere interloper I'm afraid.'

'Oh, how so?'

'My sole purpose this evening is to escort the lady in the white dress seated on the table opposite. She's the Foundation's Assessor.'

'That's why you have been looking at her all night, I detected a more than a passing interest, though I was beginning to suspect you were bored with our company,' she said.

Picking up the hint of disappointment in her voice, Jim, leaned toward her. 'Not at all, it's Irene is it not.' Getting an affirmative nod, he continued, 'I do have a personal interest in the sculptor, whose memory we are honouring tonight.' In response to her quizzical look, he launched into the story of Dancing Couple and the association between Isaac Stein and the village of Applegarth.

'It's interesting to hear you refer to the statue as the Dancing Couple,' Jane Hulpin interjected, who was listening with great interest, 'As far as I know Isaac never gave that particular piece any title. In one of the biographies, I believe it was Michael Yardley, he says Isaac only referred to the piece as his State of Grace. The statue was intended to depict the elegance, refinement and style he so much admired.'

'It certainly conveys that feeling for me,' Jim continued, but the sound of a spoon being rattled against the side of a glass brought an end to his eulogy, as Herbert Wise rose to his feet. 'Ladies and gentlemen, if I may have your attention please,' When the talk had died away, he continued, 'Forgive me for introducing a note of formality into these proceeding, particularly as we've all been enjoying the fine-food and wines provided by the hotel and the elegant conversation of your companions. It would, however, be remiss of me if I didn't take this opportunity to express the appreciation of the Trustees and staff for the generous donations made to the Foundation during the last year. I also have an announcement to make. What they call in the media, hot news, but more about that in a moment.'

'Our beloved Isaac Stein was one of this country's greatest artists and shortly after his death, the Foundation was established by a group of his admirers to keep alive his memory and promote to a wider audience the glorious works he created during his long and successful career. Yet, all that work would come to nothing but for the support and generosity of those in this room, and in particular, the benefactors, who have dug deep into their pockets again this year. We thank you most sincerely for your kind and generous support. Without you, there would be no Foundation. Thank you.'

Beaming, Herbert put his hands together and after a moment's hesitation led a hearty round of applause for the benefactors. With the applause beginning to wane, he held up a hand to indicate a wish to continue, 'A moment ago, I promised you some hot news, and I must ask you to keep this confidential for the time being, as discussions are at an early stage,' he said pausing to ensure he had everyone's attention, 'In the last few days we've been approached by an independent television company. I can't name the company, but I what I can tell you is they've been commissioned to make a programme to commemorate the centenary of Isaac Stein's birth. They can't. or won't tell me, which broadcaster has commissioned the programme, but my guess is BBC 2 – so watch this space. In the meantime, a big thank you to all our benefactors and please enjoy the rest of your evening.

Sitting down to a spontaneous round of applause, the room was immediately filled with voices speculating about the television programme and the impact it would have on the viewing public. At the top of the table, Herbert was besieged by all those around him. and attempted to respond patiently to all the questions hurled at him.

Glancing up, Jim caught Robin's eye, who turned away briefly from the conversation she was having with one of the men on her table, to indicate she was as surprised as everyone else by the news. For his part, Jim couldn't decide whether not revealing to the two ladies the true state of the Dancing Couple was a good thing or not. As it turned out, it didn't matter, because, with the announcement that coffee was being served in the lounge, the guests began moving in that direction. Having made a particular point of thanking his dinner guests for their company and conversation, Jim sidled over to where Robin was having a final word with one of her dinner companions. 'Well, that was a bit of surprise,' he said when they were alone.

'I was surprised when Herbert didn't say anything in his welcome during the reception. I realise now, of course, he wanted everyone to hear at the same time.'

Robin looked at him, and in a voice soft enough not to be heard by any passing guests said, 'I notice you were in deep conversation with the two ladies and heard mention of the Dancing Couple. I hope you didn't tell them about the damage to the statue.'

'No, I didn't, why?' he enquired slightly mystified by her concern.

Taking his arm and leading him in the direction of the lounge and coffee, 'Good. Did you enjoy the meal? You seem to have the ladies hanging on your every word.'

'Yes, I did,' he replied, as they helped themselves to coffee. For the next half hour, Jim watched and occasionally joined in as Robin worked the room, gently introducing herself to the various guests and their wives, listening intently to their views, shaking hands, and smiling. Standing behind Robin, Jim saw Herbert and his wife either side of the doorway saying goodnight to the guests who were slowly drifting away.

Then suddenly, there was just the four of them. 'Hello, you must be Jim White,' Herbert said striding across the room. 'This is my wife, Eileen,' he said pointing to a small, dark-haired lady by the door. 'We need to talk,' he said indicating a group of easy chairs. 'More coffee?'

'I'm okay,' he replied.

'What about you?' he asked and getting a shake of the head from Robin, turned to his wife. 'Eileen, be a dear and bring a coffee over for me will you, please.'

***

With no further clues, as to who might have destroyed the leeks, Les and Audrey pondered what to do next. Les' first thought was the programme and what to put in it. Having no entry in his name would be less embarrassing than being in the list of competitors and then not exhibiting. People would think he'd ducked out because his leeks weren't good enough.

Audrey checked the schedule and reported the programme was due the following day, so it was probably printed and packed waiting to be delivered.

'I am determined not to be cowed into submission,' Les had announced suddenly, 'Let's fight back, show them, whoever they are, that we're not frightened by their threats.'

'But since we have no idea who *they* are,' Audrey replied with conviction, 'how do we fight back.'

Les hesitated for a moment, as though seeking inspiration, 'By going public,' he said in a sudden outburst. 'Get the editor of the *Observer* onto to it. It's just the sort of thing he likes to splash across the front page. You could write the headline now, 'Prize-winning leeks destroyed in vendetta.''

'Except, Audrey replied with a note of caution, 'we can't reveal the contents of the note – otherwise, everyone in the village will know about our efforts to get at Jason Black.'

'You are right of course Aud, but a piece in the *Observer* with a picture will get us a lot of sympathy, and still send a message to whoever destroyed my leeks that we are not going to be intimated by them. I'll get on to the editor in the morning. The Society places a regular advert in the paper, so he'll at least to listen to me.'

***

'Right then Jim, this statue of yours, we'd better do something about it,' Herbert said, gesturing him to be seated. 'I got Robin's note after she talked to that village bobby of yours. What was this freak accident was by the way?'

Jim looked at Robin, as she took the chair next to him, getting only a non-committal smile, hesitated for a moment. 'I promised PC Smith not to reveal the details but, in the circumstances, I am sure it is safe to tell you.' With Herbert taking the coffee from his wife, who moved to join them, Jim recounted how the paint tin had flown off the front of the bicycle and poured its contents all over the statue.'

'Who was the young man responsible, do we know?' asked Herbert.

'Yes, we do,' replied Jim, 'But I'd be grateful to keep that part of my promise to PC Smith by preserving his anonymity.'

Herbert thought for a moment, before deciding not to press the question. 'Of course, but this interest from the film company puts some urgency behind the need to restore the statue. I haven't seen a script, though, given their intention to start filming in a couple of months, there must be one. In my discussions with their producer, I got the impression a substantial part of the filming will take place in Applegarth.'

'And that will include the Dancing Couple?' Jim asked.

'I got the impression the statue was at the heart of the film, though they didn't know the Dancing Couple is the name given to it by the village. Incidentally neither did we until I picked it up from Robin's report. Their working title is, *A State of Grace*, the unofficial name given to the piece by Isaac.'

'What's happening?' Robin asked, moving forward on her seat. 'I can see the whole project being jeopardised if the film company carry out a reconnaissance in the village and discover the statue covered in paint.'

'Which is why I have ordered the statue to be covered and removed from the site? The chair of the Trustees been away for the last couple of weeks and it's been impossible to speak to her. I did, however, manage to get hold of her yesterday and get her agreement to proceed. In the meantime, I've told the film company that as part of the centenary celebrations, the Foundation is planning to clean the statue, without letting on why it needs cleaning.'

Robin glancing quickly at Jim, jumped in before he could say anything, 'But, who's going to pay for the damage?' she asked nervously.

'Well,' came the reply, 'While you two were enjoying the champagne at the reception tonight, I was having a quiet word with Jane Hulpin. I thought she might be sympathetic to an approach.'

'That's the lady sitting next to me at dinner. What did she say?' Jim asked.

'It would have been a lot easier I'd known how the statue got damaged, but Jane, bless her, has been a long-term supporter of the Foundation, and when I told her about the film company's interest, she readily agreed to come up with the cash. I think we might be able to screw the film people for a facility fee for the use of our archives and that will offset some of the cost.'

'What about us,' Jim enquired. 'Will the village be expected to contribute?'

'Well, let's put it this way, if you came up with a couple of thousand, or even a couple of hundred, it would mean asking Jane for less. Since she contributes generously to the Foundation every year, I would rather not impose upon her generosity any more than I have to.'

Shortly afterwards the meeting broke up, Herbert and Eileen pleading a long journey home and an early start the next day. Robin offered to walk with them to their taxi, leaving Jim to ponder the events of the evening and the plans to clean the Dancing Couple. He was still deep in thought when Robin returned looking pensive, but non-committal in response to his enquiry.

'I don't know about you,' she said 'but I'm feeling like it has been a long day. I am off, are you coming up.'

Not sure what was supposed to happen next, and in the absence of any sign from Robin, they walked silently to the lift. Waiting for the lift, to arrive, Robin still had the same pensive look. Is she waiting for me to make a move he thought, as they entered the lift?

He noticed from the buttons she pressed her room was on the floor directly below his. As the doors closed and the lift started to ascend, he felt Robin pushing him firmly against the back wall and when their lips met it was in a long, passionate kiss.

Jim hardly had time to respond to her warm, soft mouth, when the lift came to a halt. As the doors swished silently open, Robin disengaged herself, and not looking back or saying a word, walked away. Jim stepped forward to reach for her but was confronted by the doors closing and the lift moving noisily upwards.

Back in his room, he was totally confused. Not sure what to make of Robin's unexpected display of passion, or what she wanted from him. Her room was on the floor below, but he could hardly go knocking on every door until she answered. On the other hand, if Robin wanted their relationship to develop further, she would have to make the next move.

Chapter Twenty-nine

The following morning, emerging from the shower, Jim noticed a piece of paper pushed under the door. Opening it, he saw it was a hand-written note from Robin on the hotel headed paper.

Jim, Thanks for your support yesterday evening. Sorry, but I have to dash away this morning. Last night Herbert asked me to take on a new job, and I need to be in Birmingham for an important meeting later this morning. Will be in touch shortly and explain everything – including the 'lift thing,' Robin

He understood now the reason for Robin's pensive look after seeing Herbert to his taxi. As for the rest of the note and what that meant, he could only wait for her to get in touch again, which was sooner than he expected.

***

The red light flashing on the answering machine when Jim returned to his cottage heralded a message from Robin, 'Jim, I owe you an explanation for last night and this morning. I don't know if it's convenient, but could we meet on Saturday at the Dog and Duck at about mid-day. Ring me if it's not okay.'

Jim was intrigued as to explanation she would offer for the fumbled kiss in the lift and her hasty disappearance in the morning. He entertained hopes of what it might mean, but he'd have to wait until the weekend to find out.

A second message was from Les. In a strained voice asked him to call urgently. Jim was at a loss to know what was troubling his friend. When he called the Building Society, his friend greeted him in his usual jovial way. When pressed, he related the news about his leeks being destroyed and the contents of threatening note.

'Who would do such a thing?' Jim enquired. 'We can rule out Jason Black.

After that, I'm at a loss to understand who could be responsible. What you going to do?' Jim asked.

Les summarized his conversation with the editor of the *Observer*. Jim thought for a moment and then suggested. 'A front-page story will send the right message but what it really needs is a picture of you standing over the leeks.'

'I mentioned that possibility to the editor,' Les replied, 'and he promised to send a photographer over this afternoon. I'm due to meet him at the allotments at five.'

'Les, I am very sorry to hear about your leeks. Look, we need to meet and decide what to do. On a brighter note, I've some good news about the Dancing Couple. How about we meet up tonight? How you fixed?'

'I should be back home by five-thirty. Why don't we meet at our house? I'll call to Aud see whether Philippa can join us.'

'Okay, see you then,' Jim replied putting the phone down.

***

The number of visitors passing through the turnstiles at the Pump Room had returned to normal. The coach parties, forced to go elsewhere while it closed, were back in greater numbers.

Inside, Brenda and her two helpers were moving groups through the spring with their usual efficiency. As a precaution, Tracy was wearing surgical gloves, and to those visitors who enquired, Brenda said they were to prevent any risk of cross-infection, which was good for visitors and staff alike.

In the Ye Olde Gift & Stationery Shop, Jack Thompson and his wife, Jean, were busy dealing with a constant flow of customers. The business had been in the family for two generations, beginning with Jack's father, who used his demob money from the army to buy the business at the end of the Second World War.

It had proved to be a sound investment, though in the early days there were few visitors to the village. Most of the customers were locals looking for basic stationery items – pens, pencils, writing paper.

Jack's childhood centred on the shop, as his parents were forced to put in long hours to support the family. When he grew older, he was expected to serve behind the counter evenings and weekends. When his father died, suddenly of a heart attack, Jack was left with no alternative but to give up any thought of going to university and take over the business.

Working until late and most weekends didn't leave much time to meet members of the opposite sex. Jack was a natural athlete and what spare time he had was spent at the local tennis club. The doubles – and in particular the mixed doubles – was the game he most enjoyed. Tennis was also responsible for bringing Jean into his life and together they had won through to the club finals six years in a row, winning the mixed doubles trophy on four occasions.

To Jean, turning their sporting association into a partnership for life seemed the next natural step. Getting Jack to pop the question was proving impossible and only a blatant attempt at seduction on his sofa one memorable Sunday afternoon persuaded him to utter the magic words.

Their married life together was very happy, and the two children that came along completed the family. Jack's only regret was neither of the two boys had expressed an interest in taking over the business. Having seen the burden, it imposed upon their parents, they decided – perhaps wisely – to pursue other careers. Both were doing well, Tim as a teacher and Keith the chartered surveyor. While the three grandchildren they produced, brought happiness and delight to Jack and Jean.

The discovery of the spring and the huge increase in the number of visitors transformed the fortunes of the shop. At about the same time the small hardware shop next door become vacant, which allowed them to expand with a range of souvenirs and gifts around the theme of the magical waters of Applegarth.

That side of the business was Jean's domain, leaving Jack in charge of the more traditional stationery side, and that's where he was today serving a steady stream of customers. Though the number of visitors who decided a trip to the village was the right time to buy basic stationery items like, sticky tape, envelopes and pens always surprised him.

It was part of Jack' routine to bank the cash at the same time every day. The bank manager, William Barlow, said you could set your watch by Jack's arrival at the bank with his little brown bag containing the day's takings. Putting up a sign asking customers to pay for their goods at the gift counter, Jack set off with the brown bag held firmly under one arm.

It wasn't far, just a matter of crossing the road and walking the fifty yards to the bank. Normally he didn't take much notice of other people on the pavement, besides swearing under his breath when his progress was blocked by a family idly strolling along, forcing him to step into the road.

To his surprise the journey today was achieved in double-quick time and completing the transaction, including obtaining a receipt from the bank teller, was achieved without a hitch. A few minutes later he was strolling back up the High Street, with the brown bag tucked under his arm. Up ahead he could see a commotion, as two young men appeared to be having an argument. With his mind on the two youths, who by now were exchanging blows his reaction was a bit slow at first when a hand reached out to snatch the bag. Whirling around to face his attacker, he felt a sharp blow to the side of his face and a screeched, 'Let go you bastard.' The effect of the blow was to release his grip on the bag, but the momentum carried him off the pavement and into the road. Any other time he would have regained his balance and seen his attacker running away and cursing his luck at being robbed in broad daylight – albeit of an empty bag.

On this particular day, Jack had the misfortune to step in the path of a large white van, which had just accelerated away from the crossing. Facing the wrong way, he didn't see the approaching van, as it struck and continued to drive over the top of him, before slithering to a stop a few yards further on, with the driver looking visibly shaken.

The bystanders, who a few moments earlier were distracted by the scuffle between the two youths, looked on in horror at the twisted body of Jack slumped lifeless on the ground. Their work done, the two youths turned and quickly disappeared through the crowd gathering around Jack and the ominous pool of blood seeping from the back of his head.

By the time, Jim reached the High Street on the way to Les and Audrey's house, the paramedics had rushed Jack away to the hospital in Honiston. The police were still there, and he could see PC Nigel Smith in the middle of a large group of people, with his notebook in hand, taking statements from witnesses. As he stood surveying the scene, Nigel left the group and approached him. 'Did you see what happened, Mr White?' he asked.

'I'm afraid I didn't. What's going on? Has there been an accident?' he replied looking curiously at the Constable.

'Ah, I assumed you knew. Mr Thompson was robbed this afternoon. In the confusion, he appears to have fallen into the path of that van.' He said pointing to the large white van parked a few yards down the road.

'How is he, do we know?'

'No, he was rushed off to the A&E at Honiston. According to the witnesses, he was unconscious and when the paramedics arrived, he was lying in a pool of blood.'

Jim thanked him and immediately set out for Jack and Jean's shop to offer what comfort he could but was met with hand-written notice stuck to the inside of the door, that read, 'Sorry we are closed until further notice,' Jean had gone to the hospital to be with Jack. Poor girl, she must be out of her mind with worry, he thought turning away and heading toward the Wood's household. Any joy he felt about the plans to make a film in the village on the life of Isaac Stein, were driven away by the news about Les' prize leeks and now the tragic accident to Jack Thompson.

It was a very sober-looking Jim that that greeted Audrey and Les when he pushed open their kitchen door. 'What's up?' Audrey asked as Jim slipped into the nearest chair in the kitchen table.

'I've got some very sad news. I think you'd better sit down.'

Audrey studied Jim's face for some hint as to what could be troubling him. 'There's a fresh brew in the pot, let's have a cup and you can tell us all about it. Les get another cup for Jim.'

Jim's report of the robbery and the accident to Jack Thompson was met in stunned silence. How a tragedy like this could happen in a small village like Applegarth was a shock. Robberies, in which people were attacked in broad daylight, happened in big cities, not in country villages in the heart of Gloucestershire.

Eventually, it was Jim who spoke, 'Is Philippa able to join us tonight?' he asked quietly.

'Brian arrived home yesterday and announced he had tickets for a concert in Bristol. She was delighted to have a night out with her husband, but it meant organising the kids and arranging a babysitter. She is helping out at the Townswoman's Guild Coffee Morning in the village hall tomorrow and said if anyone was free could they pop in and bring her up-to-date with any news,' Audrey replied still devastated by the news about Jack.

'You two will be working, and I have a lunch appointment, but I could drop by the village hall in the morning,' Jim offered.

'Another meeting with Robin?' Audrey asked with a knowing look on her face.

'I wasn't going to mention anything after the tragedy to Jack., but....'

Looking up, Les asked, 'What were you not going to tell us?'.

Jim hesitated, not sure whether this was the right moment to speak of the good news for the village. Having raised their expectations, he had no option but to tell them about the interest in the anniversary of Isaac Stein's birth and the plans to make a television programme in the village about the sculptor. As he continued with the story about his trip to London and the announcement by Herbert Wise at the dinner, his two companions, who were sitting slumped and their heads downcast, slowly came to life and by the time he finished, were almost smiling. When he had finished, Audrey was the first to speak. 'That is wonderful news, Jim, when does the film crew arrive?'

'I don't know,' he replied, 'It is one of the things I'm hoping to find out tomorrow from Robin.' The next few minutes were taken up with the trio eagerly discussing what impact it would have on the village and how the viewers might receive the programme. 'I know you're fond of the statue in the park, Jim, but I guess most people won't have heard of Isaac or know anything about the Dancing Couple?' Audrey suggested.

Jim looked across to Les 'You are probably right, but I thought the idea of us meeting tonight was to discuss what happened to your leeks and the threatening note.'

'To be honest Jim,' Les replied sitting back in his chair, 'after the news about poor old Jack my leeks being destroyed seems a bit trivial. There's going to be a piece in the paper next week, though probably not on the front page now. I'll probably go along to support the show. Harry will sweep the board this year. His leeks looked good enough to win.'

His attempt to put in a brave face couldn't hide the hurt he felt, and it would be a long time before the bitterness he disappeared.

When Jim arrived in the High Street, the following day there was barely any sign of the accident. Only a dark patch on the road gave any hint of the tragedy that struck the village the previous day. Otherwise, the village had returned to something approaching normality, except for a hand-written note in the window of the Ye Olde Gift Shop and Stationery Shop saying due to a family bereavement they would remain closed until further notice

In the village hall, small groups were clustered around the tables drinking coffee and talking in voices barely above a whisper. Philippa was seated with a group of ladies near the entrance and joined him as he gently closed the door.

'I suspect you don't have to be genius to guess the main topic of conversation this morning,' he whispered. Philippa didn't reply but pointed toward the kitchen. Once they were both inside, she closed the door, 'I only heard about poor old Jack this morning. Brian and I were in Bristol yesterday evening and didn't get back 'til late. Poor Jean she must be devastated. What else have you got to tell me?'

Jim would have liked to talk about the Jack and the impact his death would have on the village, but seeing the look of Phillippa's face, he had no option but to tell her about Les' leeks being destroyed and the publication of the story in the *Observer*.

'That's tragic. Poor Les, but is that all,' Philippa asked looking at him and raising one eyebrow. 'When I spoke to Audrey first thing this morning, she said to make sure he tells you about the film thing.' Jim laughed at the description, but still related the news about a television programme on the life of Isaac Stein.

'So, when are you seeing Robin again?' Philippa asked pointedly.

'Any minute now,' Jim replied looking at his watch and realising it was nearly mid-day. 'I'd better go, or the lady will think I've stood her up. Incidentally, the sad demise of Jack means there will be a vacancy on the committee. It's worth thinking about,' he said standing at the kitchen door.

'Ring me later after Robin's gone. And, let's wait until the poor fellow is buried before we start carving up the committee shall we,' Philippa responded as Jim disappeared.

Chapter Thirty

Jim's progress along the High Street was hampered by the throng of visitors crowding the pavement, and it was after midday by the time he reached the Dog and Duck. Robin wasn't to be seen anywhere. Anxiously searching in both directions, he spotted her heading for the car park. Putting on a sprint he managed to reach her as she reached the entrance, 'Robin, Hi,' he called out, catching his breath.

Turning, Robin saw Jim standing a few yards away, clearly out of breath. 'You're not as fit as you were,' she said gently as he stood taking deep breaths. 'I'd given you up.'

'Sorry,' he managed, taking a huge breath of air, 'I got held up this morning and had to fight my way up the High Street. There's a lot of people in the village today. Anyway, I'm here now, so let's go and eat.'

A few minutes later they were sat at one of the few remaining tables on the patio of the Dog and Duck, studying the menu. On the way, Jim had brought her up to date with the news of the tragic death of Jack Thompson. Having made her choice and put the menu down, Robin asked, 'Had he lived in the village long?'

Putting the menu aside, Jim briefly recounted the story of how Jack's family had arrived after the war. 'More recently he was a prominent member of the Pump Room Committee and his death creates a vacancy, but as I was reminded this morning, we have to wait until after the funeral before broaching the subject of his replacement.'

Picking up the menu and pretending to study the choices of offer, Jim took the opportunity to observe Robin, as her eyes moved around the patio, stopping briefly at each table in turn. She's pretending to take an interest in the families and couples enjoying their meals. It's her way of putting off having to explain the note pushed under the door of his hotel. Best leave her to work that out, he decided

Jim offered to order their meals, and when he returned with a bottle of wine and two glasses, she watched his every step as he weaved his way between the tables.

'You must have wondered why I suggested meeting today?' Robin suggested taking the glass of wine he offered, and when he murmured, 'Yes, he was,' she continued, 'Well, I suppose I better get it over with.'

'Before I do, I appreciate you telling me about poor old Jack Thompson, I need to know everything that goes on in the village. I'll explain why in a moment.' Taking a sip of wine, she put the glass down and looked him in the eye. 'When I left you to walk Herbert and his wife to their taxi, he said the Foundation was looking for someone to liaise with the film company whilst the programme was being made, and was I interested? When I asked him what it would involve, he said joining the director and crew while they were filming and providing whatever support they required.'

'And what did you say?' Jim asked tentatively.

'Since it would involve working with the director and crew, I'd like to meet them before saying yes.'

'Hence the trip to Birmingham, so what was he or they like?' Jim asked topping up their glasses.

Taking a sip of wine, Robin responded 'She actually - that's the film director - though the camera/lighting guy is a man. Suzanne and I got on straight away. She's about my age and we share lots in common. I didn't realise it until after, but we were both at Bristol at about the same time, though she was doing a film studies degree. Toby was a different kettle of fish. Comes across as a bit precious, but it's mainly Suzanne I will be dealing with so that's okay.'

The arrival of their meals forced a pause in Robin's account of meeting with the film company's key personnel. It wasn't until they were tucking into their food that she could continue. 'They're planning to visit the village in a couple of weeks to scout for locations and start filming shortly afterwards. It means I'll need to spend some time here and will rely on your help for introductions to the right people. How do you feel about that?' she asked taking another sip of wine and looking at him over the top of her glass.

'I'll give you all the help I can,' he replied quickly, 'but you also promised to explain, in your words, the "lift thing,"' he added cautiously.

'Ah, yes,' she said putting her glass down, 'I did, didn't I. Yes, I'm sorry if my kiss embarrassed you. It was an impulse. I don't usually act on impulse. Normally, I only do something after considering all the pros and cons. You looked so delicious in your dinner suit I couldn't help myself. I was totally bewildered by my feelings. All I could do was rush off without saying a word. Sorry.'

Pausing from eating and putting his knife and fork down, Jim asked gently 'What about now. What do you feel today?'

'Driving down here I was anxious to know how I would feel when I saw you. I tried to visualise standing in front of you but couldn't even remember what you looked like. When you weren't outside the pub, I decided to tell Herbert I wasn't interested in the job.'

'And now?'

Robin picked up her knife and fork and dug into her fish pie. While Jim eyed her expectantly. With no reply forthcoming, he took a sip of wine and waited.

Pausing with her fork in mid-air, Robin looked him in the eye. 'I thought I was ready to move on, but faced with the reality, I'm not sure. David dying affected me greatly. I still miss him, but when I met you, I thought perhaps I was ready to embark on a new relationship.' Putting her fork down, she continued, 'I am fond of you Jim - enjoy your company. There's clearly a part of me that finds you attractive, so please don't walk away.'

Jim, who had abandoned his meal, reached out and put his hand on her arm. 'I think it is pretty clear that I am attracted to you, but what do you want me to do.'

'Just be yourself, and let's take it a step at a time shall we and see what happens?'

'I'll drink to that,' Jim replied raising his glass.

Having successfully skirted around the "lift thing" they were relieved to move the conversation to the practicalities of the film company coming to the village.

After finishing their lunch, they took a stroll around the village, with Jim pointing out the Pump Room, Village Hall, and other attractions. With some hesitation, they took a walk down to the Memorial Park, but the statue of the Dancing Couple was gone, all that remained was the flattened earth where the base once stood.

Back at the car park, Jim stood waiting whilst Robin unlocked the car and when she turned, he bent forward to kiss her, but instead of proffering her cheek, as he expected, she twisted her head at the last moment, so their lips met and lingered. He wanted to envelop her in his arms, but she stepped back before he had a chance. 'Sorry, I wanted to know whether it would feel as good as last time.'

'Was it?' he asked looking deep into her eyes.

'Mmm I think so,' Robin replied with a hint of a smile dancing across her face. 'I'll be in touch as soon as I hear anything.' Without another word, she got in her car and drove out of the car park and away from the village.

Chapter Thirty-one

There were five replies to the questionnaire, and all arrived on the same day.

Eating his breakfast, Jim heard the letterbox flap open, and in answer to the excited look from Bix, called out, 'Off you go, then boy,' as his faithful border terrier scampered down the hall to snatch the mail from the letterbox.

All the questionnaire told the same story. After visiting the Pump Room, a blotchy rash developed on their hands. Three of the visitors were prescribed a soothing cream by their doctor, and the rash cleared up in a day or two. The others let the rash to clear up naturally, which it did in three or four days.

The responses appeared to confirm his suspicion. The new spring water was responsible for the blotchy rash, but the evidence was inconclusive. If challenged, Jason would brush it off, a small sample, compared to the thousands who visited the Pump Room every year. Their problems could have been caused by any number of things, unconnected to the Pump Room.

It was a powerful argument, as Jim would be the first to admit. Given the inconclusive evidence most of the village side with Jason side and dismiss the allegation as coming from the usual Pump Room detractors. Everybody knew their only purpose was to undermine the source of the village's fortunes and besmirch the name of the esteemed chair of the Association.

The phone ringing. interrupted his thoughts on the machinations within the Pump Room. It was Philippa to ask if he was going to Jack's funeral.

'If you are planning to go, perhaps we could meet beforehand for a coffee. You could tell me about the meeting with Robin.'

'Okay,' Jim replied, 'I'll also bring the five replies we've received.'

'Are they helpful?' Philippa enquired.

'They confirm our suspicions. In each case, a blotchy rash appeared within twenty fours of visiting the Pump Room. Like Tracey, the rash cleared up in a day or two with the help of a cream, or naturally within three or four days.'

***

There was no formal discussion, but by common consent, most of the businesses in the village were closed on Wednesday morning. Even the Pump Room, was closed, though it took calls from several prominent members of the Association before Jason finally agreed.

With the Cosy Café shut, Jim and Philippa were restricted to a stroll in the church graveyard. 'When's filming due to start,' Philippa asked as they stood gazing at the large and ornate headstone of the former Deputy Surgeon General for the Indian state of Punjab in the nineteenth century. 'Not for a few weeks, the director is coming in a week or so to scout for suitable locations. Filming is due to start shortly afterwards.'

Philippa didn't respond but wandered away. 'After the tragedy to Jack, the village is going to be in a state of shock. The Water Festival on Saturday is still going ahead, I assume. It's probably too late to cancel at this late stage.' Jim nodded in agreement and touched Philippa's arm. As she turned, he inclined his head toward the hearse and funeral cars rolling steadily toward the entrance of the church.

Using a side door, they slipped into the church and took two of the few remaining seats at the side, one row in front of Audrey and Les.

On the other side of the aisle Jean, dressed in black, occupied the front pew surrounded by her two sons and their families.

With everyone seated, the large doors at the back of the church opened and the funeral party entered carrying the coffin on their shoulders, placing it gently on wooden trestles below the altar. Rev. Alan Howard rose with a prayer book in hand, ready to address the congregation.

The service, as Jim expected, was simple, with a few traditional hymns, including, *Abide With Me* and a eulogy read by Jack's eldest son, Tim. In a loving and generous celebration of his father's life, he told of the family's struggle to make a new life in the village, his victories and disappointments on the tennis court and many run-ins with the bungling bureaucracy and red tape that was the blight of all small businesses.

At the end of the service, learning on the shoulders of her sons Jean, followed the pallbearers out of the church and across the churchyard to the newly dug grave. Jim, Philippa, Les and Audrey hung back to let the principal mourners join the procession. When they emerged into the bright sunlight, Jason and Katie were standing just off the path.

Katie took a step forward and smiled briefly before being pulled sharply back by her husband. 'Been up to your old tricks, I see then, Mr White.'

Jim, at first attempted to ignore the remark and carried on walking, but finding the path blocked, looked Jason in the eye. 'Excuse me.'

Jason didn't move. 'You've been telling lies about the spring and the wonderful benefits it brings to this village.'

'I'm sorry, I haven't the faintest idea what you're talking about,' Jim replied, stepping past to re-join his companions, a few yards ahead.

'You know perfectly well what I mean,' Jason said grabbing hold of his arm. 'With your address at the top, are telling me you know nothing about this,' he shouted pulling a piece of paper out of pocket and thrusting it in Jim's face. Les, who had moved to support his friend, didn't need to look closely to know it was a copy of the letter they sent to the visitors to the Pump Room.

Jim struggled free from Jason's grip. 'I'd be delighted to discuss the damage being done to the visitors by your spring water, but I don't really think this is the time or the place, do you?' he responded, angrily.

'Leave it, don't let him provoke you,' pleaded Philippa as Jim allowed himself to be pulled away, leaving Jason shaking the letter to his disappearing back, 'Go on run away, but you haven't heard the last of this. I am going to have you for this Mr James White, you'll see.'

At the graveside, Alan Howard was standing, prayer book in hand, waiting for the mourners to assemble around the grave.

Jim and his companions slipped into the crowd as the vicar began to commit Jack's body to the ground. Looking across the mourners gathered around the graveside, he could see Jason stopping every few yards to shake his fist at Jim. Katie following a few yards behind could only shrug her shoulder in despair.

Visibly shaken by the violent altercation, Jim found it difficult to concentrate as the Rev. Alan Howard intoned the sacred words for the burial of the dead. Only after the coffin was laid to rest and the Jean and the family members stood silently for a moment at the graveside before stepping away, was Jim able to express his thought to his three companions. 'I guess our confrontation with Jason Black has moved to another level,' he said as they walked reverently in line behind the mourners out of the churchyard.

***

The following morning as Jim was clearing away the breakfast things, two letters popped through the letterbox, and the phone rang. Urging Bix to collect them, Jim picked up the phone, wondering who could be ringing this early in the morning. 'Jim what on earth are you playing at, Jason was incandescent with rage yesterday. It was all I could do to stop him marching around to your house and beating you up.'

'Good morning Katie and how are you on this beautiful morning?

'I know you have misgivings about the whole Pump Room operation Jim, but I didn't think you'd stoop so low as to send out fake letters to....'

'Whether your husband likes or not,' Jim said interrupting her. 'Several people have developed blotchy rashes after visiting the Pump Room. I happen to believe the members of the Association are entitled to know what's going on. I'm sorry it took a subterfuge to discover the truth, but it had to come out.'

'Well, it's going to cause us a problem.'

'How so?' Jim asked

'When we got home after the funeral Jason went berserk, going on and on about how you'd stuck a knife into the Pump Room and the village. How you had undermined the staff and members of the Association. On and on it went. He was drinking heavily. I should have left him to carry on ranting until the whisky took over and he collapsed on the sofa, but stupidly I didn't. I started to defend you. I said I was sure it wasn't malicious. The letters had probably been sent out with the best of intentions. Well, that sent him off again. He accused me of being disloyal and betraying the Pump Room, whatever that means.

In the middle of this, he suddenly stopped and looked at me for a long time. Then he said, "are you screwing that bastard?'

'What did you say?'

'I denied it of course, but he kept on. In the end, to shut him up I grabbed a Gideon's bible from one of the guest's bedrooms and swore on my mother's life there was nothing going on. I'm not sure he believed me, but he'll be watching me like a hawk from now on, so we better cool it for a while. That means no contact whatsoever for the time being, okay. Look, I better go I think I can hear him calling. Bye,'

Jim held the phone in his hand, long after the line had gone dead, intrigued by the call and her decision to end the affair. He could now face Philippa and the Wood's with a clear conscience and say, quite truthfully the affair with Katie was over. They didn't need to know it was Katie who ended it.

Putting the phone down and wandering into the hallway he was confronted by Biz holding two letters in his mouth. When he'd wrested them away, they were two more replies to the questionnaire. In both cases, the visitors had developed blotchy rashes after visiting the Pump Room.

In one case, the rash had taken a week to clear up.

Chapter Thirty-two

On any other summer Saturday afternoon, the Memorial Park would be reverberating to the sound of willow on leather, and shouts of, 'well played, old chap,' as the Applegarth cricket eleven did battle with one of the many village cricket teams in South Gloucestershire, but not on this particular Saturday.

This being the first Saturday, in August, the park resounded not to leather on willow, but the sound and colour of the Annual Water Festival and accompanying Flower and Vegetable Show. With flags and bunting adorning the perimeter, and stalls from every organisation in the village ablaze with colour, the park took on a festive summer look.

Standing on the edge of the arena, Jason surveyed the scene with pride. It had taken a lot of challenging work to achieve, but they were ready to receive the visitors, who would soon be flocking into the Memorial Park in their hundreds. 'This is how the Water Festival should look,' he mouthed with pride.

In the Memorial Park, Les was wending his way to the marquee, where the Flower and Vegetable Show was being held. With his prize leeks destroyed, the chief judge, Bob Moon, had invited him to join the panel, and he was anxious to get started.

Pulling aside the flap in the marquee, Les caught sight of the other judges, with clipboards in hand, waiting to begin their task. The exhibitors had arrived earlier that morning, clutching their lovingly prepared flowers or prize vegetables. They were given an hour to arrange their produce on the allotted tables, before being shooed away and told to come back when the judging was over.

Seeing Les hesitating at the entrance, Bob strolled over to greet him.

'Welcome Les,' he said thrusting out a chubby hand. 'I'm thrilled you're joining our happy band.'

'Thanks, Bob. Though to be honest, I'd rather be waiting outside, fingers crossed with the other exhibitors.'

'Understandable Les, very understandable. Incidentally, while I have the opportunity, may I say on behalf of the whole village, how devastated we were to hear about the disaster to your leeks. A cruel blow, and who would blame you if you shunned this year's Show altogether. Being here today demonstrates what a fine fellow you are. Now, come and meet your fellow judges.' Feeling embarrassed by Bob's speech, Les dutifully followed, and shook hands with each of the judges, with murmurs of, 'Good on yer Les,' and 'Nice one.'

To Jason, the Flower and Vegetable Show was a distraction from the main event. He'd spent the previous weeks cajoling the clubs and societies in the village to design stalls with a water theme, and he was pleased with the result. The Scouts had come up with a neat variation on the Catch a Rat game, involving a plastic rat, and water poured down a pipe into a tub. The Townswomen's Guild had their usual hook a duck from a paddling pool. Even the Dog and Duck Skittles Team had devised a way to incorporate water into their Knock the Skittles Down game. It was all very satisfying, but the stalls and other attractions were only a prelude to the main event. It had taken some smooth talking, but he'd managed to persuade the Honiston Fire & Rescue Service to perform their water hose display as the highlight of the day.

Checking his watch, he knew from the strict timetable for the afternoon's events it was the time to invite the contestants for the Junior Water Queen competition to come forward. 'You would have thought a simple little event like choosing the most attractive young girl under ten to be crowned Water Queen of the Festival would be a straightforward matter,' he mused to himself. But, as he discovered last year, nothing was simple when ambitious mothers were involved. He would have preferred a contest for much older girls, but Katie had vetoed that as too sexist for this day and age.

Jim had little time for the Water Festival or the Flower and Vegetable

Show. As far as he was concerned, the festival was a just an extension of the commercialism of the Pump Room, and not being a gardener, the Flower and Vegetable Show held no great interest. Nancy looked after their garden and since her death, it had become overgrown and neglected. Yet despite his lack of enthusiasm for all things connected to gardening, he agreed to come along and support Audrey and Les. He also had another reason for being there, Robin had agreed to join him during the afternoon. A good opportunity to meet some of the locals, he suggested when he phoned a few days earlier.

At the rostrum on the edge of the arena, Jason was speaking earnestly to Fred Bloom. Unknown to him, the microphone was still on, allowing his words to be heard by everyone in the park. 'For Christ's sake, Fred, get a grip. The bloody Junior Water Queen is supposed to be on now. If we don't stick to the timetable the show will just descend into...'

Becoming aware his words were being broadcast, he pushed Fred away and hastily mouthed into the microphone. 'Sorry about that folks, just sharing a little joke here with our master of ceremonies and my good friend Fred Bloom. Now, without further ado, let me hand you over to our wonderful master of ceremonies for the afternoon. And to all the young ladies here today should pay attention, as Fred has an important message for you.'

Jim checked his watch and guessed Robin was due: the last thing he needed was another public row and a repeat of the scuffle with Jason. After his accusation over the letter, he knew another confrontation was inevitable. He was ready, but a public slanging match in front of an audience at the Water Festival was not something he relished. Besides, he had no wish to spoil the day for the many visitors who were here to enjoy themselves.

'Hello Jim, you look deep in thought,' Audrey asked, following his gaze to where Jason was standing beside the rostrum. 'Squaring up for row with Mr Blotchy-rash, were you?'

'Hello, Audrey' Jim responded cheerily. 'Actually, I'd decided to avoid any contact with that particular gentleman today. Not the time or place, I think you'll agree?'

'Yes, though it can't be avoided forever.' Audrey replied as Jason ducked under the ropes and begun welcoming the entrants for the Junior Water Queen competition. 'Anyway, Les is judging the entries in the Vegetable Show, so let's go and see what is happening over there. I've arranged a surprise for Les.'

Bob and the other judges were huddled below the rostrum studying a sheet of paper intently when Jim and Audrey entered the marquee a few minutes later. In most years the judges faced an arduous task in deciding the winning entries. Gaining one of the top three places was at the ambition of the many growers in the village. Achieving the first prize would provide the lucky few with plenty to talk about in the long dark days of winter.

Their decisions were never going to go down well with those who didn't achieve the reward their entry deserved. In past years, the judges were often accused of accepting bribes to favour one exhibitor. In one long-remembered instance, the feud between the judge and disgruntledly exhibitor went on for months. Only ending when the judge up sticks and left the village, protesting his innocence.

Looking over the crowd gathered in the marque, Les could see several anxious faces. The next few minutes would determine whether they went home happy or cheated of their rightful reward for all their hard work and dedication.

With a nod to Les and the other judges, Bob mounted the rostrum and moved to the microphone. 'Ladies and gentlemen may have your attention please.' There was a short pause, as he waited for the crowd to quieten down.

Having everyone's attention, Bob spoke into the microphone.

'The judges have completed their deliberations and I will announce the winners for the various categories in a few minutes. Before I do that, it is my great pleasure to announce we have new trophy this year,' he said holding up a large engraved silver plate, 'which will be presented to the winner of the competition for the best leeks. When I tell you, Mr Leslie Woods donated this handsome trophy, I think you'll agree it's a marvellous gesture from a great sport and a long-time supporter of the Show.' Bob's announcement was met by an enthusiastic round of applause, which grew louder when Les stepped forward to acknowledge the appreciation of the crowd.

Seeing the look on his face, Jim nudged Audrey. 'Is that what you meant by a surprise.'

Audrey turned and whispered in his ear. 'It's what he would have wanted if he'd thought about it.'

With the applause beginning to wane, Bob held up his hand for silence. 'A wonderful gesture, I think you'll agree, from a man whose leeks deservedly won first prize for the last two years, and who's chances of winning the prize again this year was destroyed by a wilful act of vandalism. So, without another word, let me hand you over to Les and ask him to present the Les Wood's Silver Plate to the winner of the Best Leeks Competition, Les.'

Les stepped forward and peered into the crowd. Spotting Audrey standing next to Jim. 'You're responsible for this, aren't you?' he mouthed pointing to the silver plate. Seeing a broad smile spread across her face, addressed the crowd. 'You're very kind ladies and gentlemen, but the person you should really thank for instituting this new award is my darling wife Audrey, who had the wisdom to know what I really needed to do to get over the tragedy of losing my crop of leeks.' This brought a fresh round of applause and putting his hand up to ask for silence, he continued. 'Let's not dwell on the past, but instead celebrate the future by welcoming the very worthy winner of this year's competition, Mr Harry Travers. Harry is here in the front, so I'd be grateful if you would step forward and accept this silver plate on behalf of myself and the committee. Ladies and gentlemen, please give a warm welcome to, winner of the Best Leeks Competition.'

Having performed his duty, Les stepped down from the rostrum and joined Audrey and Jim. Standing with his back to the platform, he whispered, 'I've seen enough, let's get out of here.' Not waiting for a reply, Les headed for the exit.

Outside, Les turned and waited until Audrey and Jim joined him. 'Thanks for arranging that Aud, it was a beautiful gesture and I'm so pleased you did it, but I'd rather not spend any more time in there if you don't mind.'

Audrey nodded and took his arm. 'I understand Les. Let's go and see if we can win any prizes on the stalls.' Turning to Jim, who was hanging back, not sure whether if he should be was intruding into a private moment, she caught his eye. 'Jim let's have a competition to see who can win the most prizes.'

'Okay, but I need to keep a lookout for Robin, she should be here shortly.'

In the car park, Jason watched as the Honiston Fire & Rescue Service brought their finest appliances to a halt alongside the conveniently placed hydrant. Moving to the cab Jason stretched out his hand ready to greet burly Chief Officer Rawlinson as he leapt out and took his hand. 'We'll use this hydrant and run our hoses to the showground and put on a good display for you Mr Black. Though I should warn you, if there's a shout and we're needed, we'll pull out, understood.'

'Of course,' Jason replied as he tried to restore some feeling into his hand after the big man squeezed the life out of it. 'The tower your guys erected two days ago has been moved to the arena. We have you down to start at four-thirty if that's still okay.'

Ignoring Jason, the Chief began barking orders to the fire crew who were un-reeling the fire hoses and connecting them to the hydrant. 'Right lads let's get started, these lovely people have paid good money to see you do your stuff, so we mustn't disappoint them.'

'Well, I'll take that as a yes shall we,' Jason muttered as turned and stepped gingerly over the hoses and headed toward the arena.

With all the car windows, open on a beautiful warm sunny day, Robin was happy to drift through the country lanes on her way to Applegarth. She was in a buoyant mood. Acting as the coordinator between the film company and the Foundation would be a new experience and she was looking forward to working with Suzanne, the director. It would also mean spending time in Applegarth and that inevitable meant in the company of Jim, whose contacts and local knowledge would be invaluable. He'd made it perfectly clear he was fond of her, and he was good company and there was a certain frisson when they kissed, but after David had died, she had assumed that aspect of her life was over. She would be a widow, dedicated to his memory for the rest of her life. Suddenly, this man came along, who was nothing like and David. Confused and bewildered, and with nobody to discuss it with she was unsure what to do. 'Damn that young man, his bicycle and the red paint,' she called out to the sky as the road into Applegarth loomed up and she was forced to concentrate on finding her way through the village to the Memorial Park.

At the arena, Jim, Audrey and Les were trying their hand on the Catch-A-Rat stall, run by the local Scouts. The game involved inserting a plastic rat in the top of a plastic tube, full of running water, and catching it before it fell into a large tub of water at the other end. Audrey had given up after one attempt, but the two men were determined to win a prize.

'Bloody stupid game,' Les announced after another unsuccessful attempt. 'Here give it to me, I'll show you how it's done,' Jim replied balancing the rat on the tube, and leaving it resting on the edge of the tube, half in and half out. He had worked that with his right hand supporting the rat and his body braced ready to make the dash to the bottom of the tube, he could catch the rat as it shot out the tube. The only problem, as he was about to discover, was water from the tub had spilt out, soaking the surrounding patch of grass.

'You watching?' he called, as Audrey looked on with half-concealed amusement.

Les, who had failed to catch the rat after three attempts, was getting bored with the game and was anxious to move on. 'The annual tug-of-war competition was due, and we don't want to miss it,' he added.

Jim took one last look at the rat and the end of the tube and calculated the distance. Slowly lifting his right-hand he tipped the rat into the tube and lunged forward. If the ground was dry, he would have stood a chance of catching the rat. But it wasn't and as he plunged forward, he slipped on the wet grass and fell flat on his face. Leaving the rat to sail gracefully out the tube and flop into the waiting tub of water. The sight of Jim floundering on the wet grass sent Les and Audrey into gales of laughter, as every attempt at getting to his feet only resulting in his feet slipping and sliding, leaving Jim face down in the wet grass.

Jim might have managed to get to his feet and recover his dignity if hadn't been for a female voice asking, 'What are you doing on the ground, Jim? Are you part of the Water Festival?'

Looking up he was horrified to see the smiling face of Robin. He was delighted she'd made it to the Festival, he just wished she hadn't arrived at the very moment when he was struck in this undignified position.

'Hello, Robin.' He finally managed to utter after struggling to his feet and making a feeble attempt to brush the water and mud from his shirt and trousers. 'I'm glad you could make it. Now, if you'll excuse me, I'd better go home and get cleaned up. In the meantime, let me leave you in the capable hands of my dear friends Les and Audrey who I trust will keep you entertained until I return.' Not waiting for a reply, he turned and hurried away, his trousers clinging to his legs and the water in his shoes sloshing and squelching as he walked.

'We'll be at the arena,' Les called out, as he turned to greet Robin. 'Hi, I'm Les and this is Audrey. It's a pleasure to meet.'

'You too' Audrey said, extending a welcoming hand. 'We've heard a lot about you, and it is so nice to be able to put a face to the name. As Les suggested, why don't we wander over to the arena and see what's going on there?"

When they arrived, the arena was occupied by the Applegarth tug-of-war team, who were straining every muscle, their heels dug into the turf, brows heavy with sweat, as they and their opponents from Westhamble took up the strain. For many of the spectators gathered around the perimeter, this was the highlight of the Festival. The annual grudge match between the two teams was fearlessly fought over. Westhamble had taken the trophy for the last three years, but the lads from Applegarth were confident of winning after their serious training sessions during the winter and spring. The whole of Applegarth was depending on the eight men of the tug-of-war team will bring the back the trophy and restore the pride of the village.

With their hands locked around the rope, their heels dug deep in the turf, and their coach urging them on, 'come on lads, heave, heave,' the eight Applegarth pullers focused on the red ribbon attached to the rope halfway along its length. To win they needed to pull the ribbon to beyond white line marked on the grass. The judge for this contest, a huge man, who in his day was the anchor for the Castlefield village team, was crouched, knees bent on the centre line, eyes glued to the red ribbon ready to track any movement in the rope.

For several minutes, the only sound was the team coaches, urging their teams on, but the ribbon refused to budge, apart from a slight quivering on the rope as the two teams dug in. The muscle in their arms and legs bulging from the effort.

'How we are doing?' Jim asked as he joined the trio.

Les glanced around as Jim returned, adorned in a blue blazer, cream-coloured trousers and deck shoes. Before Audrey or Les could speak, Robin turned and called out. "My goodness Jim, you scrub up well for a little old boy from the sticks.'

Seeing the huge smile on her face and her arms outstretched in welcome, Jim bowed graciously. 'Thank you, ma'am, you're most kind.' It seemed natural to accept the embrace, her arms in open invitation. Locked in her embrace he turned his face and kissed her firmly on the lips, much to the amusement of Audrey and Les. Did she respond, her arms remained wrapped around him, her eyes were closed. That's a good sign Jim thought releasing her looking into her eyes. 'I've wanted to do that ever since the lift thing and today seemed like the right time.'

Robin's cheeks had gone a slight shade of red. Gently pushing him away, but taking hold of his hand, she turned to Audrey. 'It's the blazer you know, it brings out the beast in him.'

Audrey nudged Les and inclined her head in Jim's direction. 'You considered getting a blazer? You must omit he does look very handsome.'

'You can put lipstick on a pig, but it's still a pig.'

Jim, still happily clutching Robin's hand looked at Les and pulling his best pig-like face, called Oink, Oink, Piggy, Piggy, Oink, Oink.'

Laughing, Les said: 'I rest my case.'

The banter between the two men - much to the amusement of Audrey and Robin - might have continued but for a sudden roar from the centre of the arena. Turning to look the foursome were thrilled to see the tug-of-war team from Applegarth had succeeded in dragging their opponents forward, with the red ribbon now only inches from the white line on the turf. From around the arena, the call from hometown supporters went up, 'Pull Applegarth, pull.'

The sweat was pouring down the faces the two teams, as they dug their heels into the soft turf. Both coaches worked alongside their teams urging them on. 'Heave, heave,' they roared. For a moment, it was stalemate as the red ribbon quivered under the strain from the two sets of pullers. Suddenly without warning the legs of the front puller in the Westhamble team buckled and he collapsed on the ground. With one man down the rest of the team quickly lost heart and released the rope. Applegarth had won and the pride of the village was restored.

From all sides of the arena, the crowd waved their arms in the air and cheered as the Applegarth team walked along the line and shook hands with their opponents, before turning to acknowledge the congratulations of the crowd.

Robin turned to her companions. 'I never thought I'd get so worked up about a tug-of-war match.'

Les turned to her, a huge smile on his face. 'That wasn't just any old victory Robin. 'That was like winning the World Cup, the Olympic hundred metres final and climbing Everest all in one. We haven't beaten Westhamble for years and that was sweet. There'll be many a pint raised in the Dog and Duck tonight in honour of the Applegarth pullers.'

Jim turned to Robin. 'He's right. Those eight guys won't be buying beer in the Dog and Duck anytime in the next year. Mind you, God help them if they lose next time.'

In the car park, Chief Officer Rawlinson was addressing the fire crew. 'Right lads, we're on. Now, remember we rehearsed this drill half-a-dozen times in the past week, so let's keep it tight and let's do it right, okay. Any questions? No, right. Then attention left turn and quick march.' On the command, the fire crew march smartly into the arena to take up their positions in front of the tower.

As the fire crew arrive in the arena, Fred addressed the crowd. 'Ladies and gentlemen, please give a warm Applegarth welcome to the gallant lads from Honiston Fire and Rescue Service under the command of Chief Officer Rawlinson.' He paused, as the crowd burst into spontaneous applause. With the applause fading away, he addressed the crowd again. 'The lads from Honiston are here today to demonstrate for your enlightenment and entertainment their fire-fighting and rescue skills. Before the first demonstration, Chief Officer Rawlinson has asked me to say if there's a young damsel in the audience who fancies being rescued from the tower by one these of these young hunks, sorry, valiant fire crew members, please come to the commentary box. Right, here we go.'

Right on cue flames appeared from the upper storey of the tower, and the fire crew immediately spring into action. In double-quick time, hoses are unfurled, and the extending ladder wheeled into position.

With the flames roaring away, Les pointed to the top of the tower.

'I hope the young damsel Fred was asking for isn't up there expecting to be rescued,' he said as the fire crew positioned the ladder alongside the tower.'

'Never mind what's happening up the tower, look who's just entered the arena,' Jim exclaimed, pointing to an area a few yards from the fire crews.'

'I'd bet any money he'd try and get in the act today' Les replied seeing Jason lurking just off to the left and waving to the crowd.

'Jason just likes to be the centre of attention and can't stand it when he's not. Look, one of the fire boys is climbing up the ladder to put out the fire.' Audrey pointed towards the tower, as a burly crew member climbed the ladder, hose in hand, ready to attack the fire. At the top of the ladder and with a shout to the crew below, a giant stream of water is directed at the flames. In a matter of moments, the fire is extinguished, producing a loud cheer and applause from the crowd.

Misunderstanding who the crowd were applauding, Jason shuffled into the centre of the arena and began waving to the crowd. Behind him, the firefighter descended the ladder, as the crowd continued to show their appreciation. Still mistaking the reason for the applause, Jason waved and pranced about, but in the process tripped over one of the hoses snaking across the grass. Pulling himself up and trying to make light of his encounter, he was met with hoots of laughter from the crowd, which grow louder as he attempted in vain to placate the crowd with an extravagant bow. From somewhere in the crowd a voice shouted, 'Get off you, stupid old fool,' a sentiment quickly echoed around the arena.

Being mocked by the crowd was not something Jason enjoyed. Sensing he had to bring the situation under control, he picked up the hose and pointed it at the crowd. Whether he was aware it was connected to the appliance was the subject of debate in the village for weeks after, but without warning a stream of water burst from the hose and as luck would have it, it was directed straight at Jim, Robin, Les and Audrey, soaking them to the skin in a matter of seconds.

It took a moment for Jim to recover and take stock of the look of the bewilderment on the faces of his companions, but seconds later he was leaping over the boundary rope and advancing on Jason, standing defiant in the middle of the arena.

It might have been an accident, but Jim didn't care. Jason was going to pay for this callous and hostile act. Moving swiftly across the arena, Jim grabbed the nearest hose, and the two men stood facing each other like gladiators, weapons at the ready.

'Right then Jason Black, are you going to apologise for drenching my three friends?'

'Apologise, your joking. After your treachery – never.' with a smirk spreading across his face, he sent a jet of water that hit Jim squarely in the chest and sent him sprawling.

Spreadeagled on the wet slippery grass, Jim struggled to get back on his feet. In the battle of the hoses, Jim was clearly losing, 'How do you like that Mr James White Eh. That'll teach you to spread lies about the spring.'

Les shook the water from his face and hair. 'Robin, Aud you okay.

'I'm soaked to the skin. I can't believe that was an accident,' Robin replied, wiping her face with a handkerchief

'No, it wasn't. That was deliberate. That bastard Jason…. Les, look what he's doing, you've got to help.'

Jim was sprawled on the ground with Jason sending a steady jet of water over him and shouting loud enough for everyone to hear. 'Take that you bastard.'

Leaping over the boundary rope, Les called out to Audrey, 'Look after of Robin, I have to help Jim, he's in trouble.'

Sensing Les approaching, Jason turned the hose in his direction, but he wasn't quick enough. Les dodged the stream of water and scooped up Jim's hose. 'Get on your feet mate and give this bastard, the soaking he deserves.

Turning on the hose, a solid torrent of water hit Jason squarely in the chest, sending him staggering back in a vain attempt to stay on his feet, until he fell, spread-eagled on the waterlogged and muddy grass.

Les' intervention enabled Jim to recover and he quickly joined Les as they sent a steady stream of water at Jason, who was floundering in the mud, unable to get to his feet. Their cry of triumph was brought to a sudden end by the arrival of Chief Rawlinson. 'Bloody hooligans,' he shouted snatching the hose and pushing them away.

Taken by surprise, the pair fall in the mud and roll around, much to the amusement of the crowd, who laughed and cheered at every attempt they took to get back on their feet. Laughing like a couple of kids they arrive with Audrey and Robin looking wet and dishevelled. 'That was fun,' Les says to his wife, who was delighted that Jason got a good soaking, but embarrassed by the spectacle of her husband performance in front of the whole village.

'We'd better get you two home before you make a complete spectacle of yourselves, Aye Robin?'

Robin smiled benignly. 'I hope you've got a change of clothes,' she Jim quips. 'You seem to be getting through quite a few today.'

At the top of the arena, Jason struggled to his feet. Wet and bedraggled, he called out to the departing backs of Jim and Les, 'That's right scuttle away, but don't think you've heard the last of it, I'll get you.' Taking a step forward to emphasis his point, he fell flat on his back and lay thrashing about in the wet grass, unable to get to his feet.

On the rostrum, Fred Bloom flicked on the microphone. 'Would all those stragglers currently occupying the arena please vacated it – yes Jason, that includes you – as we move on to the next event, a presentation by the splendid Applegarth Ladies Dance Troup, as they perform the finale from *The Lonely Water Fairy*. Thank you.'

Chapter Thirty-three

Back at the cottage, Jim quickly found towels. 'Here, take these and dry yourself,' he said, and then added rather plaintively, 'What else do you need?'

'I need a change of clothes and a hair-dryer.' Jim studied her, his mind racing on how he could provide the items she required.

Seeing the anxious look on his face, she replied, 'I can get a change from the car. I was planning to descend on my sister in Bristol tonight.'

Jim opened his mouth to say, 'Is she expecting you', but it wasn't necessary.

'It was a surprise visit. She's on her own this weekend – her husband's away on some training course; he's in the Territorial Army. Sorry, I'm babbling on. I was hoping you might have a hair-dryer hidden away somewhere.'

Jim turned away, deep in thought, then snapped his fingers. 'We do have one. It's tucked away in the back of the wardrobe in the spare bedroom. Belonged to Nancy, I kept it after she died, thought it might come in useful one day; though truth be told I could bear to throw it out. Don't ask me to explain why I kept the hairdryer and not all the other things of hers because I can't. Sorry, I'm going on a bit. I'll go and get it. I assume it still works after all these years. It is a bit ancient, but…. Sorry.'

Still apologising he disappeared up the stairs, muttering, 'I'll be as quick as I can.'

Robin pulled out her car keys and was on the point of opening the front door when Bix came scampering down the hallway to greet her. 'Hello, you,' she said bending to stroke him. 'I have to go to my car, but when I come back, we can say hello properly.'

When Jim came downstairs some forty minutes later, showered and dressed in an old pair of jeans and t-shirt, Robin was in a new outfit and sitting on the sofa, with Bix curled on her lap, and *Riverboat Shuffle* by Bix Beiderbecke playing softly in the background.

'Robin, I can only apologise for the unfortunate spectacle you were forced to watch this afternoon. I vowed not to get let Jason provoke me. I failed and I'm sorry.'

Stroking Bix, who was clearly enjoying the attention, Robin looked up and seeing his casual clothes and bare feet, let a brief smile pass across her face. 'I've seen a different side of you today, and I don't know whether I should be laughing at the sight of you floundering around in the mud or disgusted at your juvenile behaviour. What do you advise?'

Jim, on the point of making a flippant remark to lighten the mood, held back seeing the serious look on Robin's face. 'Mr White says he is very sorry and asks for your forgiveness. There will that do?'

'No, it won't. Jim. If you're going to win this battle with Jason Black, it won't be by silly, pointless displays like the one we saw today. You'll never win that way. Jason has the village in the palm of his hand. They are so beguiled; it doesn't matter what you say or do. His supporters will merely accuse you of being jealous of the spring's success and Jason's part in it.'

This straight-talking from Robin was something new. He'd never knew she felt so strongly about the struggle to expose Jason's lies and deceits. Reflecting her serious tone, he asked. 'What is then?'.

'Show the village an alternative. Show them a more honest way to prosper. One that will sustain the people and the business for years to come.'

'And that is?' Jim exclaimed, before adding. 'The Dancing Couple of course, and Applegarth as the birthplace of Isaac Stein.'

'Exactly,' Robin said and rising to her feet she planted a big, fat kiss on his lips. 'I knew you get there eventually.'

Taken back by this sudden display of emotion, Jim wasn't sure how to react. It was so unexpected; he didn't have time to respond. Moving to embrace her, Robin took two steps back out of his reach. 'When I was driving here today, I wasn't sure how I would react to seeing you. You've made it perfectly clear what your feelings are to me. There have been a few men since my husband died who assumed because I was a widow, I was fair game and having brought me dinner I'd be happy to jump into bed with them. You were not like that. You were, to use that old fashion phase, a perfect gentleman.'

Jim opened his mouth to speak, but Robin put a finger to his lips. 'Let me finish, otherwise, I'll never get it out. Today, in the arena I saw a different man, passionate, committed and something clicked, and I knew what I wanted. If you'll let me, I'd like to join you in your fight to promote the Dancing Couple as the future of the village.'

Jim hesitated for a moment. 'You mean as partners?'

'Yes, no I mean partners in the full sense. Christ, do I have to spell it out for you.'

Jim didn't need telling twice. 'Oh, my God Robin I'm so....' The rest of his expression of joy was lost as Robin's arms embraced him and their lips met in a long and passionate kiss. The next few minutes were lost in a haze as clothes were discarded and kisses exchanged. When they came together in a blissful coupling, their partnership was complete, and their passion satisfied.

Several hours later, finding themselves in the comfortable bed upstairs – though exactly how they got there neither could remember – Robin nudged Jim, who sighed, turned and with a big smile on his face, a condition that reflected his sense of contentment with the world, and whispered, 'Mmm, yes dear.'

'We have to make a plan, Jim. There's not a moment to waste.'

Reaching across to her with a glint in his eyes, Jim said. 'I agree, we've wasted too much time already, we've got a lot to make up for. What do you say?' he added reaching to embrace her.

'I don't mean that. Listen to me. Suzanne and the camera/lighting guy will be here shortly to scout out locations for the TV programme, we should use their time in the village for our advantage. Jim what are doing, no I am not ticklish. Will you stop that. No, Jim stop. Unable to stop herself, Robin descends in ticklish laughter as Jim's hands explore the sensitive parts of her body. Okay, I give in, but promise we'll talk...' The rest was blotted out as Jim covered her mouth in passionate kisses.

***

'You can't come into the house looking like that Jason, you're soaking wet and covered in mud from head to toe.'

'Well, I don't intend to stand outside all night. Bloody Jim White's responsible for this. That bastard will pay for it. He's not going to get away it this time, you'll see.'

Kate threw a towel and it on the floor. 'Stand on this and get out of those clothes.'

Struggling out of his wet, soggy clothes, Jason continued his tirade. 'Unbelievable, Jim and that mate of his, blasted me with a hose. Hit me with the force of a train, sent me sprawling on the ground. Every time I tried to get up, they hit me with it again. All the time laughing their heads off. Bloody hooligans, that's what Chief Rawlinson called them, quite right too.' Standing in his underpants, Jason looked wearily at his wife. 'I think you better go in the shower. I'll fix you a Whisky and soda, you'll feel better then.'

'Yes, dear.' Jason muttered.

***

The following morning, Jim stumbled down the stairs clutching his dressing gown, while making a feeble attempt to knot the belt. He'd been woken out of his slumbers by the sound of the telephone ringing and Bix making that mixture of barking and whining denoting he wanted to go out. Carefully, so as not to disturb her, Jim extracted himself from Robin's embrace. When he reached to the phone it was Philippa. 'Jim, you okay,' she asked in response to his gruff, 'Hello'.

'I was still in bed. It is Sunday morning, and I usually lie in.'

'With two young kids, Sunday morning lie-ins are a distant memory. I'm sorry to wake you, but what's this I hear about you and Jason at the Festival yesterday?'

Jim groaned again, only this time silently. 'You heard about our set to with the fire hoses then.'

'It was the talk of the congregation at Holy Communion this morning. What were you thinking?'

'I allowed Jason to provoke me. It was stupid. I only went to the damn Festival to support Les. I'd invited Robin, thinking it would be a good excuse for her to get a feel of the village, and maybe meet a few people. I'd made a pact with myself not....'

Philippa interrupted him. 'Robin was there?'

'I snapped, okay! Jason was playing with a fire hose, pretending to be part of the display by the Fire guys. He deliberately turned it on us. We all got soaked, Robin included. It was too much. I just charged into the arena.'

'It Robin with you there now?' Philippa asked.

'Yes, she stayed the night. Her clothes were soaking wet she and couldn't drive home like that.'

The sound of footsteps caused Jim to turn and see Robin coming down the stairs dressed in one of his old coats she must have found in the wardrobe. Signalling she'd make the coffee Robin disappeared into the kitchen.

Wanting to get away from the subject of the debacle at the Festival, Jim mentioned Robin would be staying for a couple of days. 'With the film crew, due, she needs to get to know the layout of the village and meet the people who might be included in the film. Folk who could talk about what it was like when Isaac was growing up as a young man in the village.'

'I could suggest a few names. What was that?' Philippa exclaimed, hearing, a large crash on the other end of the phone.

'Look, I'd better go. Robin appears to be having a smashing time in the kitchen. I'll talk to you later.' Replacing the phone, Jim made for the kitchen to find Robin surveying several china mugs in pieces scattered across the floor.

Robin looked up from the smashed crockery, and with a crestfallen grin on her face, said, 'Whoops.'

***

'What's the name of the film lady, the one who's supposed to be directing the TV programme?'

Suzanne Spencer. The lighting/camera guy is a rather precious individual by the name of Toby Henshaw, why do you ask?'

'Suzanne, or at least the production company, have asked to come and see me next week. When asked what it was about, they said it was just background, part of their research into Isaac and the role of the Foundation.'

'Do you want me to sit in, Herbert.'

'If your free Tim, Tuesday at eleven. Now, where are we with this blessed statue? The one, Jim whatsit calls the Dancing Couple.'

'Thanks to the kind and generous donation from Jane Hulpin, I was able to persuade Wheelers to take it into their workshop and start removing the paint. When I spoke to Bill Briggs, he's the manager of their Restoration Department, he said it could take several weeks, as the painstakingly scraped the paint back to the bronze. Apparently, they won't know whether there's any permanent damage until they clean it and examine the surface.'

'Okay, but keep on them, Tim. It has to be back on its plinth by the time Suzanne turns up in the village.'

'At the moment, I don't think we have an exact date for Suzanne to scout for locations, I believe is the technical term. I'll get onto Robin and see whether she's got any more info.'

'God keep me in the loop. Now, where are we with the exhibition here...'

***

Jim and Robin spent a lazy, hazy, relaxed day on Sunday, with much lovemaking, delicious food and copious amount of fine wine. By Monday morning, their appetites having been satisfied, they were ready to face the world. 'I think it would be a clever idea for you to meet Philippa, 'Jim suggested as they finished a meal of smoked salmon and scrambled eggs and downed the last of the coffee in the pot. 'As soon as we've cleared these things away, I give her a call and see if she can meet us in town, how does that sound?'

'I'll clear these things away, and I promise not to break anything.'

Philippa, he announced, was looking forward to meeting Robin and suggested they meet at the Cosy Café at eleven.

'Okay, good. Jim, I have a few phone calls to make, who don't you take Bix out for a walk. When you get back, I'll be done. I'd like to visit the Pump Room, see for myself what all the fuss is about. Do you mind?'

Jim shrugged his shoulders and replied, 'No, of course not. It only right you have an insight into everything going on in the village.' With a brief wave, he took the dog lead off the hook on the back door and calling Bix set off, leaving Robin, unsure whether he was upset or not at her suggestion.

When Jim returned thirty minutes later, Robin was waiting for him. 'I won't go if you'd rather I didn't,' she said taking his arm as they walked towards the High Street. 'Only you seemed troubled by the mere thought.'

'Of course, you must go,' Jim replied. 'As I said everybody will expect you to experience village life in all its various aspects, including visiting the Pump Room.' Robin wasn't sure if that amounted to a ringing endorsement but decided to let it go. Instead, she changed the subject. 'Can we keep our relationship just between ourselves for now. I'd like to get used to it before we tell the world.'

Jim stopped and held her hand. 'If that's what you want, of course. You'll just have to kick me if I start walking about with a stupid grin all over my face.'

When they reached the High Street, they paused at the top of the path leading to the Pump Room, 'Go on then, there's just time before we're due to meet Philippa. Don't expect me to join you though. I'll be here when you come out.'

'Okay, please yourself.' Robin replied striding down the path. 'Perhaps the magical waters will cure all my ills and maladies.'

'Don't bet on it, 'he called out. 'You'll just as likely to end up with a rash.'

He may have reservations about Robin visiting the Pump Room, but Jim was a very happy man. As his eyes focused on the door to the entrance, he visualised Robin inside listening to Brenda's introduction and couldn't help but recall the words she whispered his ear as she lay in his arms that morning. "I love you, Jim White. I think I loved you from the first moment we met, on the doorstep of your cottage. It just took a while to accept it."

'Hi Jim, Jim it's me, Philippa.'

Shaken of his trance, Jim turned to see his friend looking at him with obvious concern. 'You were miles away, weren't you? Somewhere nice?'

'Good morning Philippa. A very happy, glorious place, which must remain a secret for now, even from you. Sorry.'

'Okay, but where's Robin?'

'She insisted on experiencing the Magical Waters of Applegarth for herself. She went in a few minutes ago, so she shouldn't be too long.'

Philippa pulled him away. 'I know you don't want to think about it, but it is the talk of the village. You undoubtedly have some support, while others think you attacked a well-respected and leading figure in the community. They will be very vocal in expressing their feelings, so be prepared. The other thought I had was there was bound to be a reporter and photographer from the *Observer* covering the Festival. So, don't be surprised if the paper carries a front-page story, with a damming picture of you and Jason hard at it. If the gossip in the village doesn't stir things up, a story in the paper will.'

Philippa's description stunned Jim. It never occurred to him that a harmless water fight might cause such consternation in the village. With Philippa's words echoing in his head, he took a quick look around, expecting to see several men, or even women, advancing towards him, their fists raised ready to strike him. 'It can't come to that surely. The crowd seemed to enjoy it.'

'You might like to think that Jim, but from the comments I heard, some see it, not as a bit of fun, but a nasty, vicious fight between two bitter rivals. They say, and I'm only reporting what I heard, but for the intervention of the Fire Chief one of you could have been seriously hurt.'

Jim wasn't certain how to respond but saved by Robin arriving at his shoulder. 'That was interesting,' she said sidling up and indicating she should like to be introduced.

Snapping out of his stupor, Jim said, 'Philippa, I would like you to meet Robin.'

Philippa held out her hand, 'Robin, delightful to meet you at last. Jim talks about you all the time. It's nice to be able to put a face to the name.'

When the introductions were over, Philippa suggested they retired to the Cosy Café for coffee. Once sat around the table, away from any prying eyes on the High Street, Philippa asked the question she'd been dying to ask from the moment Jim suggested they meet. 'Robin,' she said directing the question directly at her. 'What do you make of Jim's little escapade at the Memorial Park on Saturday? Foolish, or a justified attack on one the village's bad guys.'

Robin looked at Jim and getting the merest nod, replied. I believe it was wrong-headed because it didn't achieve anything. I told him he needs a plan, properly thought out,' Philippa nodded in agreement, as Robin continued.

'Jim has told me about the deception over the source of the spring and about the rash on the hands of visitors.'

Philippa interrupted her. 'You went to the Pump Room. Wasn't that a bit of a risk?'

'Yes, I suppose. But I felt I had to test the spring water for myself. So far Jason Black is concerned I'm an ordinary member of the public; Let's see what happens. What I was about to say before was that the centenary of Isaac's birth allows the village to change direction.'

'What Robin means is that the long-term prosperity of the village should be based on a celebration of the great sculpture's contribution to twenty-century art, and not some mystical con-trick with dubious spring water.'

'This is getting a bit serious,' Jim said before Robin could respond. 'It was only meant to be a happy social occasion, mainly for you Philippa to meet Robin and get to know her.'

Philippa was in the middle of finishing her coffee, and having done so, addressed Robin. 'Jim is quite right, let's put aside any discussion about the Pump Room and talk about more pleasant things. How long you going to be in town Robin? There are lots of people who would like to meet you. Despite what you have heard, some of us revere Isaac and want to help in any way they can to make a success of the film.'

'That sounds like a good idea,' Jim said jumping in.

***

In the offices of the *Honiston Observer*, the editor, Pete Marshall, was reviewing the images from the Applegarth Water Festival and Flower and Vegetable Show, with the reporter, Brigit May. 'There are some great shots here Brigit. Was there really a water fight between these three guys?'

'You bet and would have gone on if the Fire Chief hadn't stepped in. Is it a front-page story?'

'We should definitely make a splash of it if you'll excuse the pun. I can see the headline now. "Local hotelier and community leader get a soaking." You had better get onto Jason Black. Tell him we are running the story and get a quote. No need to tell him we're running it on the front page.'

'Okay, boss, anything else.'

'Let me have five hundred words to accompany the pic. I think we'll use that one.' Pete said pointing to an image Jason Black flat on his back and getting soaked. Do we know who the two guys doing the soaking were?'

'People I spoke to in the crowd, who by the way loved it and were egging them, said they were Jim White and Les Woods.'

'That could make it a much bigger story. Les is the manager at the Honiston Building Society. We ran a story a few weeks ago, about his leeks being destroyed. The other guy, Jim White, you need to check out. I'm sure we published a letter from him a month or so ago. Something about paint on a statue in the local park. I can't help wondering whether there's a connection between the stories involving Les and the other guy and the water fight? Do a bit of digging and see what you come up with.'

'You mean it wasn't just three guys playing about for a bit of fun?'

***

Pouring over the sales figures for the weekend, Jason was oblivious to the front-page story in the local paper. A story that could have lasting consequences for his standing in the local community, and more devastating, his leadership of the Honiston Business League. This morning he could bask in the knowledge that the hotel and restaurant had performed well over the weekend, thanks, in part, to the Water Festival. Not that the events in the arena had been dismissed from his mind altogether. Those two renegades would pay for the humiliation they made him suffer at their hands. His revenge when it came would be very public, and very sweet. A plan was forming in his head and when it was fully formed, he would unleash it with all the force at his command.

Meanwhile, the new season at the Business League would be upon him next month. Working with the secretary, it was his job to organise speakers for the monthly meetings. Under the previous President, they were mind-boggling boring. He would introduce a programme of bright, scintillating speakers, tasked with the role of inspiring members to achieve their personal and business goals. No more lectures on taxation and stock control. Not on his watch.

Then, there was Ladies Night, the highlight of the winter season. This year it would be spectacular, far above the rather dowdy, dreary affairs of previous years. The thought of the glory that would be heaped upon him when the members realised what marvellous decision it was to appoint him President, almost banished any negative thoughts he might have had the humiliation he suffered at the hands of Messrs White and Woods.

Except, it was just about to get worse, much worse.

At the point of his elation and the prospect of future glory, the phone on his desk rang. The voice on the other end said that she was calling from the *Honiston Observer* and her name was Brigit May.

***

Later that day, Les came home from work to find Audrey busy in the kitchen preparing their evening meal. 'Hi Aud, what's for dinner?' he enquired standing over her as she stirred a pot on the hob. 'Pork chops with apple sauce,'

'Sounds good. I'll just go and wash my hands and I'll be down.' None of this sounded right to Audrey. Normally, when Les came home he gave a quick peck on the cheek, before making some quip, or some odd or funny thing that happened during the day. Usually, involving a customer. Something happened to disturb him, and she was determined to track it down. Audrey was sat at the table with their meal laid out when Les appeared. Waiting until he had served himself from the vegetable dish, she looked across to him. 'What happened today to upset you?'

'What makes you say that my dear' Les replied cutting into his pork chop.'

'Because my dear, you don't usually ask me what's for dinner in that earnest enquiring way the moment you walk through the door. Something, or more likely someone upset or disturb today, and you've spent the journey home worrying about it.'

Les stopped eating and laid his knife and fork on the plate. 'I knew I'd never be able to keep it from you. You know me too well. I had a phone call from a reporter, she works for the *Observer*.'

'And,' Audrey enquired, sensing she might be necessary to drag it out of him.

'She said they were running a story in this week's paper about what happened on Saturday. She asked me to confirm I was one of the people involved.'

There was a pause before Les continues. 'I had no choice; besides I couldn't lie. She probably knew already.'

'What else did she say?'

'She asked me who the other two men were, and I said I wasn't prepared to say. Then she asked me what the water fight was about? Was there an argument between the three of you? When I said no comment, she then said was it something to do with the fact Jason was chair of the Pump Room Association.'

'She was obviously guessing, but it wouldn't take much digging. All she needs to do is talk to anyone in the village and they would tell her about the feud with Jason. Anyway, what did you say?'

I said I wasn't prepared to comment and put the phone down. I phoned Jim straight away to warn him that she'd probably be in touch. Jim said he was ex-directory. He wasn't on Facebook or Twitter, so that wouldn't help. Then he told me some really disturbing.'

'Well, don't keep it to yourself,' Audrey said, the anxiety she felt coming through in the tone of her voice.

'When I was speaking to Jim, I thought I could hear Robin's voice in the background. She was talking on her mobile.' He paused for a moment to let that sink in. 'I thought she was only going back to Jim's to dry out. If I'm right about hearing her voice, it means she stayed there for the weekend. Intriguing don't you think. Anyway, Jim said Robin insisted on visiting the Pump Room. Said she ought to experience it for herself. That was on Monday, and today – wait for it – she's got a blotchy rash on her hands.'

'Just like Tracey and all those visitors to the Pump Room.'

***

Robin put down the phone after calling Claire Steele at the Stein Foundation to let her know she was staying in Applegarth to do some background research, before the visit of the film crew. Entering the hallway, and seeing the anxious look on Jim's face, she asked. 'Something wrong?'

'I've just had a call from Les. Apparently, a reporter from the local paper rang yesterday to get his comments on what happened last Saturday at the Water festival.'

'Will they be calling you to ask for your version?'

'I'm ex-directory, so they can't just look me up in the telephone book, and I don't have a Facebook or Twitter account. Given their resources, I don't suppose it will take them long to track it down. I'm more concerned with the rash on your hands.'

'It's not very nice, and they itch like made. I'll go to the chemist in the village and get some cream. I've phoned the office and told them I'll be staying here for a couple of days.' Seeing his face light up, she jumped in, 'Before you get too excited, it's obvious I can't go into the office or meet anybody outside the Foundation with my hands looking like this.'

'Jim took her hands in his. 'If it's any consolation the visitors who replied to our questionnaire said the rash disappeared after a few days.'

'Let's hope so because I have more on my plate than Applegarth and your Dancing Couple. There are other statues by Isaac scattered around the country that need checking over before the anniversary.'

Jim refrained from pointing out he did warn her that a visit to the Pump Room might result in a rash on her hands. 'Look, I've just had an idea and please don't take this wrong way. But, this rash, - he was still holding her hands – could work to our advantage.'

Pulling her hands away, Robin enquired, 'How?'

Jim leaned forward and kissed her gently. 'By demonstrating to the village what the spring water is doing to visitors.'

This did not re-assure Robin. 'You mean parade me around the village with my hands stretched out in front of me, like some circus freak.'

'Yes, no my love. I'm sure the rash will have disappeared in a day or so – it has with everybody else. What we need to do is,' he said thinking frantically, is take a photograph of your hands, and use the pictures. With the evidence of the pictures, Jason won't be able to deny the spring water is the cause of the rash.'

Robin was only partly satisfied with Jim's plan. 'Okay, but what happens next?'

'Thanks, my love,' he said all excited. 'There's a professional photographer in town. His main trade is weddings, baptisms, and souvenir photos for the visitors. I'll give a ring and see if he can fit us today.'

'Why not just use the camera on my phone?'

'Because,' Jim replied, his hand on the handle of the front door, 'we need the image to be authenticated by the photographer.' Seeing the quizzical look on her face, he added, 'his signature says the picture is an accurate representation of your hands. Otherwise, Jason will say it could be anybody's' hands or an image downloaded from the Internet.'

'Oh, right. I understand, or I think I do.'

The next hour was a whirlwind of activity, as they made hasty arrangements to arrive at the photographers, wait impatiently while he finished a mother and baby session and get Robin's blotchy hands committed to print.

'I'll ring Les and Audrey and see if we can meet up tonight,' Jim exclaimed as they came out of the photographers, clutching several 10x8 prints.

'I never thought my hands would be the subject of much interest,' Robin muttered and then under her breath, 'Having a relationship with this man is going to be interesting.'

Chapter Thirty-four

Jim and Robin arrived at Audrey and Les' house that evening clutching the 10x8 prints. Standing at the front door, Jim looked at Robin. 'Do we tell them?'

'About us or the state of my hands.'

'About us my darling. About us. I'm not sure I can keep it a secret for much longer.'

Giving the knocker a firm slap against the brass plate, Robin replied. 'Well, try your best then, my love,' giving him a quick kiss on the cheek.

Moments later sat around the dining table, Audrey examined Robin's hand. 'They look better than in the photos.'

'As soon as we left the photographers, I went to the chemist and brought the cream the pharmacist recommended. It's good stuff. I'll be okay in a couple of days,' she said pulling her hand away and placing it on her lap underneath the table.

Les, was holding one of the 10x8s up to the light to get a better view. 'These certainly show the rash up well. Jason Black will have a job explaining these away.'

'Your right Les, but we need to think carefully about how we use them. Robin, for understandable reasons, is not keen to be thrust into the limelight. Her position at the Stein Foundation would be compromised if they got wind that she was involved in the campaign to discredit a leading member of the community when they need all the co-operation they can get from the whole village.'

Audrey gave Robin a comforting smile.

"The problem is how can we use these pictures without letting on who they belong to?'

'Thank you, Audrey, but I would go further than Jim. My job at the Stein would be at risk if I got embroiled in a local row involving the spring. With a big celebration coming up next year, the trustees won't allow anything to distract from the centenary of Isaac Stein's birth, particularly in the place where he was born. I want to help you, but I hope you understand the position I'm in.'

Les looked at the others gathered around the table. 'I think I can speak for everyone when I say we understand your position entirely. I can promise you there's nothing we will do put your job with the Stein Foundation in jeopardy.'

'Thank you, Les, we appreciate it,' Jim replied and paused for a moment to gather his thoughts. 'The problem is, if we only have the photos, I know exactly what Jason's reaction will be. Standing at the entrance of the Pump Room he will proclaim to the world "The spring water here at the Pump Room is perfectly safe. Whereas these,' he will say, holding up the 10x8s, 'are lies, fakes, and bogus. When I asked for proof, they won't say who they belong to. They can't even provide evidence that they ever visited the Magical Waters of Applegarth." With that, the crowds will stream forward and probably give him a pat on the back on their way in, and cheery, "Well said."'

The group sat in silence staring at the table, conscious that every word of Jim's imitation of Jason's speech was exactly how it would sound.

Robin glanced around the table.

'I know what high hopes you pinned on something like this,' she said picking up the photos and letting them spill across the table. 'And I'm really am sorry to disappoint you.'

'Wait a minute,' Les said his face alight with excitement. 'Everything is not lost. You can't tell from the photos who the hands belong to. They could be anyone's hands. Why don't we produce them and say they belong…'?

'To somebody else. No, Les,' Audrey interjected. 'That would make us no better than Jason Black. They would be fakes, bogus. The end doesn't justify the means.'

Audrey's abrupt dismissal of the idea forced the group into silence.

Robin had an idea and pulled a bottle of water from her bag.

'Have you had the water tested. They hand out one of these to every visitor.'

'They are required by law to have it analysed, the results are posted on the entrance to the Pump Room,' Audrey replied. 'Whether the analysis is up to date, I have no idea.'

Looking around the table and seeing their glum faces, Audrey nudged Les. 'Get that bottle of white wine out the fridge and some gasses, I think we're going to need it.'

With the glasses filled and the obligatory "Cheers" echoing around the room, Les felt it was a good moment to change the subject. 'Robin, we're delighted to see you here tonight, honoured in fact, because we assumed you were only here for the Festival on Saturday.'

Robin shot a glance in the direction of Jim that said, "have you said anything?" Receiving a blank stare in response, she turned to Les. 'With my hands in this state, I couldn't really do my job, especially as so much of it involves meeting and dealing with people. Mayors, local dignitaries and company executives.'

Les opened his mouth to say, 'that was only after you visited the Pump Room, what about the weekend,' when he was cut off by Audrey, 'Les stop hounding the woman, she suffered enough.'

Jim sensed the conversation was drifting into an area he was uncomfortable with. He was dying to share with them that his relationship with Robin had developed into a full-blown love affair, but her insistence on keeping it, to themselves for the time being left him with no option but to hold his tongue. Rising from the table, he said, 'I don't think we are going to come up with a workable to solution tonight. I suggest we all put our thinking caps on and meet again in a couple of days, perhaps at a time when Philippa can join us.'

Taking her cue from Jim, Robin rose and said, 'That sounds like a sensible idea. So, we'll say goodnight and thanks for your hospitality.'

Jim and Robin were back on the High Street before either spoke. 'You heard Les, he was definitely fishing. You haven't said anything, have you?' Robin asked.

'He had no hint from me. How much longer we can keep it a secret, I'm not sure.'

'For now, let it be just between us.'

On the High Street, a lone figure, watched from the doorway of the chemist as Jim and Robin passed. Katie had left the restaurant a few minutes earlier to pick up her hay fever pills from the chemist. Grateful for any excuse to get away from the hustle and bustle of the busy restaurant, and for the chemist for having a late-night opening.

Standing in the doorway of the chemist, she watched as Jim and Robin strolled arm in arm down the pavement until they turned the corner and disappeared. Seeing Jim with someone else, someone he was clearly on intimate terms with, left her with mixed feelings. Was she jealous, or indifferent? Their affair was only ever meant to be a bit of fun, a distraction when she needed some relief from Jason. She made it clear from the start that's all it was ever going to be. Jealousy shouldn't enter her head, but she was still determined to find out who this woman was who had wormed her way into his heart.

By the next morning, the cream has worked its magic and Robin's hands were restored to their normal colour. She announced over breakfast it was time to return to work and meet up with Suzanne. Getting in her car, she turned to Jim, I promise to be back at the weekend, but mum's the word, okay.'

'Okay,' Jim replied. 'Drive safely and I'll see you on Friday,' he added, pushing her car door shut and waving until she disappeared.

Chapter Thirty-five

Publication day for the *Honiston Observer* was on Friday. In anticipation that the latest edition might contain some sensational news, the appearance of the paper was awaited with eager anticipation. There were no queues outside the various shops that stocked the paper, but by mid-morning many had sold out.

The paper was delivered to Jim's cottage and appeared on the breakfast table courtesy of Bix, who snatched it the moment the paperboy pushed it through the letterbox. Not knowing quite to expect, he unfolded his copy to be presented with a photograph of himself, Les and Jason battling out under the caption, "Local hotelier gets a soaking at Water Festival." At the foot of the page, a story under the by-line of Brigit May laid out in detail the build-up and battle of the fire hoses between the three men. The story spread over onto page two, and included a quote from Chief Officer Rawlinson, who managed to avoid the description, "bloody hooligans", but made clear his displeasure at the use of Honiston Fire and Rescue hoses by unauthorised persons.

Towards the end of the piece, a quote from Jason made no attempt to temper his anger. "I was attacked and humiliated, without any provocation, by those two vandals. I can only assume it was part of their continued effort to wage war against the wonderful and successful Magical Waters of Applegarth, and my role in bringing prosperity to the businesses and folk of the village." That quote was carefully prepared, Jim thought as he continued to read the rest of the story. Unlike Les, who was probably caught on the hop and could be quoted as saying, "It was only a bit of fun, and the crowd seem to enjoy it."

Casting the paper aside, Jim thought the general tone of the report made them look like over-grown juvenile delinquents, providing amusement for the village.

In his office at the Honiston Building Society, the paper having been delivered to his desk, as usual on a Friday, Les quickly scanned the story and groaned. He shouldn't have responded with a comment over the phone. It was clear Jason had taken time to put together the quote he wanted the paper to use and probably phoned it in later. While Jim had escaped altogether, because at it said at the end of the piece, "we were unable to contact Mr White to get his reaction." Lucky him, he thought, at least he won't have to face the wroth of Audrey and explain why he'd be allowed that Brigit May to pressurize him into making a flippant comment.

Jason didn't see the story in the paper until Katie came barging into the office brandishing a copy, as he was in the middle of talking to Mrs Worthington. She had rung to ask how he proposed to deal with the situation, given the adverse impact it could have on the Pump Room. Waving Katie in and taking the paper, he quickly scanned the picture and article. 'My dear Mrs Worthington,' he purred into the phone, 'if you study the piece by Ms May, you will see it says quite clearly that I was the innocent party and suffered an unprovoked attack by those two thugs. I have remained silent so far Mrs Worthington because I was forced to spend to the last few days recovering from my terrible ordeal. Now I am recovered, it is my firm intention to report the matter to the local constabulary. I expect those two thugs to pay dearly for the pain and humiliation they inflicted upon me.' Jason paused to let that sink in before continuing in a quieter, softer tone. You know, Mrs Worthington in one way, I'm glad this has happened because it will bring an end to the unfounded and vicious lies, they insist on spreading about the spring and the Pump Room.'

'Are you seriously intending to go to the police?' Katie asked as Jason replaced the receiver. 'Of course, my darling, I was subjected to a prolonged and unprovoked attack by those two thugs Jim White and Leslie Woods, and they are going to pay for it. As I said to Mrs Worthington, this little episode will finally bring an end to their dishonest allegations against the spring. And, thank goodness for that.'

Katie snatched the paper from his grasp. 'Are sure about that, because the way I hear it, this little episode, as you call it, was started by you. So, how do you propose explaining that to the police.'

Jason leant back in his chair. 'I may have accidentally pointed my hose in their general direction as part of the display by our wonderful Honiston Fire and Rescue Service, but that doesn't excuse their attack on me. No way.'

'And you think PC Smith is going to buy that, do you.'

'Nigel will do as he is told, Katie. That is if he wants to continue to enjoy a nice, secure, leisurely job in this village.'

***

Robin's arrival later that day lifted Jim's spirits from the depths of gloom he'd fallen into over the article in the paper. The moment she was in the hallway and the door closed, they were in each other's embrace, kissing and murmuring affection and desire. When they finally, broke away, it was to see Bix panting and eagerly waiting for attention. Robin bent down and lifted him into arms. 'Hello, you,' she said stroking his nose and picking him up. 'have you missed me?' Bix replied by reaching up and licking her cheek. 'I've prepared a special meal,' Jim said pointing to the kitchen, 'Come through.'

As they sat around the table Robin asked, 'Was there anything in the paper about the Water Festival?'

'Lots of pictures, with the centre spread, was devoted to shots of the tug-of-war, the Junior Festival, Oh and the winners of prizes from the Flower and Vegetable Show. Though, I suspect you don't mean that.'

Robin took a mouthful of the meat sauce and pasta dish Jim had prepared. 'Was it that bad?'

'Yes, it was. Splashed all over the front page. I'll show you after we have finished our meal. Now, eat up, and tell me how you got on with the director lady.'

Robin put down her knife and fork and took a sip of red wine. 'We get on really well, though I not so sure about Toby, the camera guy. I believe I mentioned it before, but he never looks you in the eye: there's something creepy about him that made me uncomfortable. I can't explain, there just was.'

'Why does she work with him then? As a top director, she can surely choose her camera/lighting guy.'

Robin took another sip of wine. 'He comes as part of the package the producer put together for the programme. He's probably cheap, who knows?'

For the next few minutes, they concentrate on finishing their meal in silence. As they lay down their cutlery neatly on empty plates, Robin sat back in her chair. 'What I didn't tell you is Suzanne talked again about scouting out locations for the film. And, here's where I need help. She wants me to line up interviews. With local people, who might have a story to tell about Isaac, when he was young before, he went off to Art School.'

'There's a couple of men, both in their later eighties, or one of them might even be ninety plus. I talked to Philippa during the week and she suggested them. They both live in the village, have done all their lives. Bert Smallwood resides at the Hillside Retirement Home on the Bristol Road. The other, Ted – sorry I've forgotten his surname. Philippa did tell me, and I should have written it down. He lives in one of those cottages just off the High Street in Rose Lane.'

'That's helpful. Perhaps we could give them a call and arrange to go and see them over the weekend. Maybe I could talk to them first. It will make things easier for Suzanne if she has some idea of what they can tell us about Isaac.'

Before Jim could respond, Robin cut him off. 'Now, let's have a look at what the paper had to say about your little escapade last Saturday, you've put it off long enough.'

'I was only going to say I have the number for the Retirement Home, and for Ted, whose surname is Smith - there you see I remembered.' Seeing Robin rising from her chair, he quickly added,' Okay then let's get it over with.'

'Here, see for yourself,' Jim said taking the paper from the newspaper rack and handing it to her. They had finished their meal and were sitting on the sofa in the living room, with Bix curled up on Robin's lap and *Blue Rover,* with Bix the trumpeter serenading them in the background. Jim hoped the mellow sounds of a second-generation German immigrant would create the right mood for what he guessed might be rather disturbing images for Robin.

'Well, aren't you going to say something?' he asked looking at her anxiously.

Robin continued to study the front page of the paper, turning upside down at one point. 'It's not good, is it.'

'Is that all you have to say.'

'There's not a lot you can say is there? You'll have to hope it will be quickly forgotten and something else comes along to take people's minds off a stupid, mindless prank carried out by a bunch of overgrown schoolboys who should have known better.'

Chapter Thirty-six

'This is it,' Jim said, pointing to a white-walled cottage in Rose Lane. 'When I rang Ted yesterday, he said it would be all right to call around today at about this time. Not any earlier as Mavis his carer comes in first thing and gets him, as he put it, ready for the day.'

'I'll knock on the door, and hope he hears me. I've not idea what he can tell us about Isaac. According, to Philippa he was at school with Isaac and likes to tell anybody who will listen, his stories about the great man.'

Robin pulled a notebook and pen out of her handbag. 'I'll jot down a few keys words to help Suzanne, in case Ted gets a bit tongue-tied by the camera and crew.'

'Let's hope it's not necessary. Hang on, I think I can hear someone coming to the door.'

'Who is it,' a voice called out. 'If your selling anything I don't want it.'

'Ted, it's Jim, Jim White. We spoke on the phone yesterday, remember. I said we wanted to come and talk to you. You know about Isaac Stein.'

The sound of keys being turned, bolts withdrawn heralded the door opening and an elderly gentleman holding the door in one hand and a silver-handled cane in the other. 'You can't be too careful these days, can you? Who's this then?' Ted asked looking at Robin.

'This is my friend Robin; she works for the Stein Foundation.'

Ted continues to stare at Robin. 'When you said, you'd be bringing along someone called Robin, I assumed it was another man.'

'Let me assure you this Robin is all woman. Now, can we come in.'

Ted stepped back to let them in, and as Jim passed, he whispered 'She reminds me of my Maisie, she had the same colour hair. A lovely girl she was.'

Closing the door, Ted pointed to the living room and invited them to take a seat. 'My chair is the one nearest the fire,' he said. 'I had specially made to fit my bum. Now then, what's this all about?'

Jim sat on the sofa opposite, but Robin remained in the doorway. 'I'll let Jim do the introductions Ted, and why he's doing that, why don't I make us a cup of tea. The kitchen is through, here, is it?' she said pointing down the hallway to the back of the cottage.

'That's very kind of you my dear, I have mine with milk and two sugars.'

'Ted, we really appreciate you agreeing to see us today. What it is, let me put it this way. I'm told that you knew Isaac Stein as a young boy. Do you remember?

Ted leant back in his chair and smiled, as the memories came flooding back. 'You called him Isaac, that's not what we called him. To us he was Jessie, and always will be. Jessie was a bit older than me. I'm ninety-six you know?' Ted paused, waiting for the usual reaction to the announcement of his great age, but Jim just looked at him expectantly. 'Who was the us, Ted. You said, he was Jessie to us.'

'The Scouts of course. You could join when you were eleven. Some of the girls wanted to, but they weren't allowed. Later, they had their own, called the Guides. My Maisie was a Guide you know, though I didn't know her in those days.'

Robin, who had been watching this from the doorway waiting, for the kettle to boil, chipped in. 'Why was he called Jessie?'

Ted glanced across to her. 'You can't have a prissy name like Isaac if you're a Scout dear. Besides, Jessie thought he was better than us town boys. Just because he lived in the big house. I believe nowadays it's a hotel run by that: I was just about to use a swear word, but with a lady present I won't. Let's just say, and using an old fashion word, that bounder Jason Black.'

Robin and Jim looked at each other and grimaced at the irony of Isaac Stein living in the same house as what was now the *Magical Waters Hotel and Restaurant.* It also crossed Robin's mind that getting permission to film in Isaac's birthplace was going to require all her powers of persuasion.

'I'll tell you one thing though. Jessie was a big lad, strong. We'd play this game. In the Scout's hut. You had to get this round, flat thing – made of wood.'

'Puck,' Jim suggested.

'Well, the point of the game was getting the thing, okay puck, in the other team's bin but you could only carry it in your hand. As you can imagine it involved a rough and tumble, pushing and shoving as you fought to get the puck thing in the team's bin, and they tried to stop you.' An effective way to work off surplus energy amongst a group of small boys, Jim thought.

'The thing was Jessie loved this game. He loved being in the middle of all pushing and shoving. He took the knocks, but he gave as good as he got.'

At that point in Ted's story, Robin walked in with a tray containing three cups of tea. 'Here Ted,' she said handing him a cup. 'Milk and two sugars.' Ted took the cup and cradled it with both hands. 'One day he didn't come any more. We didn't know what happened, it was only years later we found out he'd gone to study at some special school in London. Arts School, I believe. We had no idea he was like that. Bit of a shock for us boys.'

'Yes, Ted he did. He studied at the Slade School of Art, where his talent as a sculptor was first recognised.'

Chapter Thirty-seven

'What did you make of that?' Jim asked when they were back on Rose Lane having left Ted in his chair complaining he needed to rest.

Robin took his arm as they headed for the High Street. 'Certainly, revealed a side of Isaac we have never heard before. Jessie indeed. I'll be interested to see if Suzanne decides to include it in the programme.' Arriving on the High Street, Jim suggested they wander down to the Dog and Duck for a spot of lunch. 'We can't see Bert Smallwood at the Hillside Retirement Home until two-thirty. The manager says they have their lunch just after mid-day and they insist the residents have a rest after.'

'Sounds good,' Robin replied, 'but I insist it is my treat.' They hadn't gone ten yards when a man appeared from nowhere. The pinched-up angry look on his face and the clenched fists suggested he was clearly bent on a mission. Looking Jim straight in the eye, he exclaimed, 'You're one of them, aren't you?'

Jim attempted to step back, as the man was right up in his face, and his breath smelled of alcohol, but it was in vain. He was intent on a confrontation. From the look in his eyes, it was going to get physical. Out the corner of his eye, Jim could see several passers-by had stopped to watch. 'I'm sorry, what do you mean?'

'One of these,' he replied brandishing a copy of the *Observer* and sticking it in Jim's face. 'The yobs who attacked and humiliated one of the finest and honourable men who has brought jobs and prosperity to this village, which you want to destroy with your petty, vindictive and spiteful accusations against the spring and Pump Room.' Turning to the crowd that had gathered around them, 'I say the only decent thing for this creature to do is make a public apology. What about it,' he says by way of encouragement to the crowd, and several voices are heard to shout out, 'Yeh, apologise you bastard.'

The situation was beginning to turn ugly, and likely to get worse unless Jim could placate this man. He shot a glance across to Robin, who in the melee had become separated from him, and was now surrounded by the crowd. She attempted to reach for his hand but was pushed and manhandled to the back of the crowd.

With Jim hemmed in, the call for him to apologise was taken up the crowd. Sensing he had the approval of the crowd, he thrust his fists in Jim's face. You heard them,' he shouted, 'apologise, you bastard.'

Jim attempted to barge past him, but his accuser held his ground. Suddenly, a small section of the crowd began to disperse, their attention drawn to the imminent arrival of the local constabulary. 'Stand clear, let me through.' Arriving at Jim's shoulder, PC Smith spoke directly to the man. 'Stand back Maurice or I'll have to arrest you for disturbing the peace.' Maurice stared at Jim, his eyes blazing. Seeing the determined look on PC Smith's face, he let his fist fall to his side and shuffled back a few steps.

PC Smith turned and addressed the crowd. 'There's nothing for you to see here, so move along now. I said NOW.' Slowly in ones and twos and they drifted away until there was only the four of them, Jim, Robin, PC Smith, and Maurice. 'So, what was that all about, Heh Maurice.'

Staring straight at Jim, he replied. 'This lying bastard needs to apologies for the lies and slanders he makes against the Pump Room and our benefactor, Jason. I was suggesting this was as good for him to do just that, officer.'

'It looked to me 'like you were threatening this gentleman with physical violence egged on no doubt by the crowd. You've been drinking, and I've warned you several times about causing a disturbance whilst under the influence, and I am arresting...'

Jim quickly butted in and said he wouldn't be pressing charges. It was just a little misunderstanding that got out of hand. PC Smith took a breath. 'Since this gentleman is not prepared to press charges, I'm prepared to overlook it on this occasion, but in future just behave yourself. Now, be on your way.

Maurice muttered under breath, but turned away and swaying slightly, staggered down the High Street. When he was safely out of sight, PC Smith turned to Jim. 'A word to the wise, be careful about what you say and do. I won't always be on hand to step in and protect you from idiots like Maurice Henderson. Many people in this village think like him. They might not express themselves in the same violent manner, but they will get their point of view across in more subtle ways.'

'We will be careful Constable and there will be no more accusations against Mr Black or the Pump Room, I can assure you,' Robin said having returned to Jim's side.'

'Glad to hear it miss,' Nigel replied. 'Now, if you'll excuse me, I'll be on my way.'

Robin waited until PC Smith was out of earshot, 'You okay Jim, you look a bit shaken up. Would you prefer it if we went straight home?'

'I never dreamt our opposition to the Pump Room would produce such hostility. But, in answer to your question, my darling, I may have been shaken up by that horrible man, but I'll be damned if I am going to let him intimidate me. Let's go and have lunch.'

***

'What the hell happened? People were coming into the library saying there'd been a fight between you and another bloke. I was so shocked when I heard you were involved, I could believe.' Audrey said after she and Les had hurried over to Jim's cottage the moment Les got home from work.

Robin answered before he could speak. 'Jim will say it was nothing, just a misunderstanding. But, if that Constable hadn't turned up when he did, it could have gotten nasty.'

'What was it about Jim. The story in the village is the guy threatened you.'

I appreciate your concern Les, and Audrey, I really do. He was called Maurice Henderson and wanted me to apologise for the accusations - false accusations he says, I've made against Jason and the Pump Room.'

'You've got nothing to apologise for,' Les jumped in before the others could speak, confident he was speaking for them all. 'So, what are we going to do about it?'

Robin, sensing where this might be going, decided she had to put a damper on it. 'I, or more accurately, we gave our word to PC Smith there would be no more accusations against the Pump Room or Jason.'

'What,' Audrey exclaimed. 'You had no right to say that. You've seen what he's done to this village. We can't let Jason get away with all his lies and deceits.'

'I'm sorry Audrey, but you weren't there. It was a very ugly scene. Not just the guy threatening Jim, but the crowd who gathered and egged him on. Jim, or any one of us, could easily get hurt if it happened again.' She paused and held their attention before adding. 'Since Jim and I have only just got together, I would rather….'

She was unable to finish her surprise announcement before Audrey and Les cried out in unison, 'You mean you two are an item?' Receiving a shrug and nod, Audrey replied, 'That's wonderful news, congratulations.'

Jim was all smiles and glancing in Robin's direction, mouthed, 'You told them.' And to Les and Audrey, 'We wanted to keep it to ourselves for a bit until we got used to the idea. Addressing Robin, he said, 'Since Audrey and Les know, can we tell Philippa?'

Robin nodded, then added, 'You mean right now?'

'Next time we see her, which is likely to be in the next few days. We were going to make an announcement, not about us but about…. No, I'll let Robin tell you.'

Les and Audrey turned to Robin, their faces alight with expectation. 'I had a phone call from the production company today to say that Suzanne, the director wants to come to the village in a couple of days to scout for suitable locations and set up interviews for the people who will appear in the programme.'

'That's marvellous,' Les replied. 'What about the interviews, do you have anyone in mind? And, before Audrey says anything. I don't mean me.'

'Jim and I talked to Ted Smith. It was after we left Ted and were on our way to the Dog and Duck we were attacked. Anyway, Ted will be okay. Suzanne needs to meet him: he has a couple of interesting stories to tell about Isaac. We also saw Bert Smallwood at the Hillside Retirement Home. He was a lovely old chap, but he couldn't tell us anything about Isaac. All he wanted to talk about was when he served in the Eighth Army. According to Bert he and his mate, Chalky White, were responsible for kicking Rommel out of North Africa and Montgomery had very little to do with it.'

'If the director is coming in a couple of days, what about the statue, the one in the Park.' Les, who had only visited the Park a couple of times in the last year – his allotment proving more attractive – was concerned the Dancing Couple would not be in pride of place. 'The phone call I mentioned earlier was also to tell me the statue has been cleaned and due to be restored to the Park tomorrow. Isn't that wonderful news.'

Jim looked as surprised as the others. 'You've kept it a secret all day, Robin....'

'I wanted it to be a surprise my darling when we took Bix for a walk tomorrow, and to see your face when you set eyes on the statue in place on its plinth in the Park.'

Jim couldn't resist the temptation to lean across and kiss her, cheered on by Audrey and Les.

Chapter Thirty-eight

'Did they say what time the truck would arrive?' Jim asked over the top of his newspaper.

Robin put down the coffee cup she was cradling in both hands. 'I was told the statue was due to leave the Warner's in London first thing and be here by mid-day. That's at least a couple of hours away, so why don't you eat your breakfast and finish reading the paper.'

Jim put the paper down. 'I'm sorry my love, but there's a piece about funding for FE colleges. I was interested to see what impact it might have on our college in Honiston. It's not clear whether they will get any more money or not.'

Robin swallowed the last of her coffee. 'I have to make some phone calls, so I'll catch you later,' she said rising from the table.

'You'll come and see the Dancing Couple restored to its rightful place, won't you?'

Robin leant down kissed him gently on the check. 'Wouldn't miss it for the world. Now, if you'll excuse me, I have work to do.

Unknown to either of them, the truck carrying Jim's beloved statue was pulling into the Memorial Park at that very moment. The Dancing Couple wasn't their only delivery, a second – a huge piece of granite in the shape of a ship's anchor – was due to be installed on the Hoe at Plymouth. To complete the two deliveries, the truck left the depot the previous afternoon and stopped overnight at a service station on M4. 'This is it,' Steve the driver said, pulling the truck to a halt alongside the plinth. 'Let's get these beautiful people back in the place where they can dance to their heart's content.'

Back the cottage, Jim read the newspaper from cover to cover, drank several cups of coffee, checked his watch, and when Bix came scampering into the kitchen demanding this morning walk, Jim shooed him away. 'Later Bix.'

The minutes dragged by until eventually, the two hands of the clock met at the top of the dial, and with Bix in tow, Jim was at the front door calling out, 'Robin, it's mid-day, we have to go.'

'I'm coming,' Robin answered descending the stairs dressed in a jacket and sensible shoes. 'I've just had a call from Warner's – the company doing restoration work. They say the statue was returned to the Memorial Park at eleven o'clock this morning.'

'You mean my gorgeous Dancing Couple was restored to its rightful place an hour ago, while we've been stuck indoors all morning? Why didn't you say something?'

Hustling him and Bix out the door, Robin replied, 'Because, as I just said, I only got the message a few minutes ago. They might have rung earlier but couldn't get through because my phone was engaged.' Closing off any further discussion, she added,' Anyway, whatever time it arrived, it doesn't matter because it's there now, so let's go and see what sort of job they've made of cleaning it up.'

Leaving the Avenue and entering the tree-lined path, Jim experienced the same of anticipation, the hairs on the back of his neck tingled as each step took him nearer.

And, there it was in all its glory. The man with his arms stretched upwards, his back arched in a perfect curve. The woman, her gown trailing graciously behind, her arm outstretched to meet his, her eyes gazing admiringly into his. The two figures caught in perfect harmony with the music as they swept majestically across an imaginary dance floor. Running forward, he fell on his knees. Without Robin, he would have given the bronze statue a hug.

Robin came up behind him, 'At first glance, it's looking good.'

Conscious of his position on the ground, and feeling slightly embarrassed, Jim took a step back. 'It certainly does. You're the professional Robin, but I would say it looks better than ever.' Jim said as he walked slowly around the statue, admiring the grace of the figures and the beautiful craftsmanship by the master sculptor.

Robin was taking shots with her camera from every angle. 'Herbert asked me to email back photographs to show Jane Hulpin, so she could see what an amazing change had been brought about as a result of her generous donation.'

Returning to the stare at the statue from the front, Robin remarked how much bigger it looks in real life. 'Much bigger than I had imagined. I could seriously stand here for the next hour wondering at the beauty of it, but I need to get these pictures off to the Foundation. With Suzanne, due in the next few days, there will be keen to know the Dancing Couple is back where it belongs, and ready to impress the world.'

'Yes, of course, and I must call Les, Audrey and Philippa. They'll be amazed by how wonderful it looks. Cleaned and shiny in the sun. Brilliant!'

Chapter Thirty-nine

Robin took a deep breath and approached the reception desk. 'Mr Jason Black, please.'

The receptionist, whose badge on her left lapel announced her name as, Marcella, looked up from the computer screen below the counter, and asked, 'Do you have an appointment. Mr Black doesn't see and reps without an appointment?'

Robin looked the woman in the eye, 'He is expecting me and no, I'm not a rep.'

With an expression that said she was only doing her job, Marcella picked up the phone from the desk in front of her. 'Who shall I say is here to meet with him?'

'Robin Caulfield from the Stein Foundation.' The receptionist dialled a number and spoke briefly into the handset, and in answer to a question posed to her, cast a critical eye over Robin before speaking again into the phone. Replacing the receiver, she addressed Robin. 'Mr Black will join you. Please take a seat, he will be out shortly.'

Robin nodded in acknowledgement and wandered away and took a seat on one of the leather sofas scattered around the reception area. She was here on behalf of the production company, and much would depend on the outcome.

According to Ted, the Isaac family once owned the house that was transformed into the hotel by Jason Black and his wife. She was hoping to persuade Jason to allow the production company to film in a couple of the reception rooms largely unchanged from the original house. This snippet came from Jim, who offered to accompany her, an offer she resolutely refused. 'If Jason discovers any connection to you in this enterprise, he will turn us down flat. 'I have to do on my own,' she said pecking him on the cheek as she waltzed out the door. 'Wish me luck.'

She used the time walking from the cottage to the hotel to consider how to phrase the question. There seemed little point in coming straight out with it. Jason Black might be a liar and cheat, but he was no fool. She had to convince him there was something in it for him. Promoting his hotel and restaurant on national television would appeal to his ego, but the production company would never agree to something so blatant. But what? She had come up with several ideas, 'Let's hope one of them works,' she said to herself.

'Ms. Caulfield, or may I call you Robin. Thank you for coming, and I'm sorry for keeping you waiting.' Robin rose and took the hand outstretched in greeting. 'You can be a real charmer when you want to,' she thought giving his hand a firm shake.

'Let's adjourn to the terrace, a shame to stay indoors on such a lovely day. I've ordered some tea to be served, hope that's okay?' Robin smiled in acknowledgement and followed Jason out of the reception onto the terrace, where tea and a plate of cakes were set out on a table discreetly positioned away from the other guests. When they were seated, and Jason had poured the tea and offered cake, which Robin politely declined, he sat back in his chair. 'You said you were from the Stein Foundation. It's not an organisation I'm familiar with.'

Now we get to the serious bit, Robin thought. 'The Stein Foundation is a charity devoted to preserving the memory and artistic works of Isaac Stein.'

'Okay, but what's the connection between your esteemed organisation and this wonderful hotel and restaurant?' Jason asked, stirring two sugars into his tea.

Robin brought the cup to her lips and took a sip of tea. This is starting to resemble an interrogation, I need to bring it back to a more even keel she decided, carefully placing her cup on the saucer. 'Isaac Stein was one of this country's greatest artists, his figures were extremely popular in his lifetime, there are numerous examples of his work in towns and cities across the UK. Following his death, a group of his friends got together to preserve his legacy. That's why the Foundation was created. In turn, it is supported by the many men and women, who hope his works will continue to be enjoyed for years to come.'

'A fine speech Robin, but what's got to do with our hotel and restaurant?' Robin took another sip of tea and let the liquid swirl around her mouth, using the excuse to gather her thoughts 'Quite a lot actually. What I didn't say was that Isaac was born and raised in Applegarth. One of his creations is in the local park. Isaac referred to it as the *State of Grace*, though to the locals it is more commonly known as the Dancing Couple.'

Jason looked thoughtful, 'Mmm. I have heard my wife mention it. Wasn't it damaged in some way?'

'Yes, it was, but now it's been restored and back on its plinth in the park. You should go and see for yourself, it's beautiful.' Robin paused hoping for a reaction. 'I mentioned that Isaac was born and raised here in Applegarth, what I omitted to say was, he was born and raised in this building. This was his parent's house until they died, in the fifties.'

'Well I'll be damned, a real live artist actually lived in my hotel,' Jason exclaimed.

His attention had been focused entirely on Robin up to that moment, but without an explanation, he suddenly stood up. 'Will you excuse me my wife is trying to gain my attention. There must a problem in the hotel I need to deal with. I'm fascinated to hear more about this sculptor of yours. Please, finish your tea and I'll be back.'

Katie had arrived on the terrace a few moments earlier, looking for Jason. Seeing him in earnest conversation with Robin, she immediately beckoned to him over. 'Who's that woman?' she demanded when he was in earshot

'She's from the Stein Foundation,' Jason replied casually. 'She came to talk to me about some guy, a sculptor I believe, who lived in this house. Why?'

'Because, my darling, the last time I saw the lady in question she was on the High Street walking arm in arm with Jim White.'

'Was she by damned, she never mentioned him.' Turning to observe Robin sipping her tea, he continued. 'She's hasn't let on what exactly she wants, but knowing she's in league with that viper Jim White, you can rest can be assured she'll get no help or co-operation from us for this little project of hers, famous artist or not.'

Robin turned her head and watch as he approached and opened her mouth to say, 'That was quick, everything okay.' Before she could get the words out, Jason stood in front of her. 'I have to curtail this meeting. Ms Caulfield. You can see yourself put. Now, if you'll excuse me, I'd have get on.'

***

'What happened then?'

'Well, nothing. He disappeared into the hotel and left me to gather myself together and leave. It was frustrating because I never got around to asking him about filming in the hotel.'

Robin and Jim were seated around the dining room table at Audrey and Les' house relating to Philippa and the Woods her meeting with Jason.

Jim picked up the narrative. 'One minute she and Jason were happily chatting away, with Robin working up to asking him for permission for the crew to film a couple of scenes in the hotel, and the next he virtually throws her out.'

'Something happened or was said when he talked to his wife Katie – she appeared on the terrace for a moment then disappeared After that his manner was completely different. Cold, dismissive. even' Audrey had provided wine and nibbles for her guests and told them to help themselves. Philippa took a swig from her glass. 'Where does that leave the film crew?' she asked addressing Robin.

'I don't know. I was expecting him to say let's arrange another meeting, but he doesn't have my mobile number or contact details. So that's probably not going to happen.'

Jim had a shrewd idea why the meeting had come to a sudden end, but he wasn't willing to share it with his companions. He guessed Katie had made a connection between Robin and him. Armed with that information, Jason was never going to allow the film crew anywhere near the hotel.

As much as he loathed the idea, he had to persuade Katie to change his mind, to put aside their differences for the sake of the village. It wouldn't be easy, and she would demand a heavy price in return, but he had to try.

Les decided this was the right moment to take the conversation in another direction. 'Since we are all together for a change, has anyone got any thoughts on where go from here? According to Robin, the director will be in the village in a couple of days, and that's bound to generate a lot of interest in the film. We can also assume the spring will continue to work its blotchy-hand magic on the visitors silly enough to patronise the Pump Room. The question is, how do we turn these events to our advantage? Any ideas?'

Silence descended on the room as they turned their thoughts to finding an answer to the question. Eventually, Audrey broke the silence. 'Could we use the local press in some way to promote the film and close the Pump Room.'

The answer came from Philippa. 'Tell them the visitors are getting blotchy hands.'

'They would certainly be interested in that story, but if it comes from Jim or me, it will be dismissed by Jason as another example of our feud against the spring.'

'Les is right. The story will quickly turn into another example of our unfounded allegations against the Pump Room and Jason Black.'

Audrey chipped in. 'But we can't stand by and do nothing.'

'I'm not saying we do nothing. All I'm saying is if the press gets involved it could backfire and hand another victory to Jason. That's all.'

'All we're hearing from you is negative thoughts. Why not come up with something positive for a change Jim? And not another bloody dye in the pond for God's sake.'

'That's not fair Audrey, you know as well as I do none of us knew about the underground stream.'

Philippa had heard enough. 'Guys, bickering amongst ourselves isn't going to get us anywhere. I believe the problem at the Pump Room will solve itself. I don't how or when, but it will. Jason will not be able to hide or dismiss forever the damage the spring is doing to visitors. It'll come out and the Pump Room will be forced to close. I'm convinced of it. In the meantime, I suggest we concentrate on promoting the centenary of Isaac, the restored Dancing Couple, and the upcoming film'

'I agree,' Robin replied, deciding this was the right moment for her contribution to the discussion. 'When, and not if, the Pump Room is forced to close for health and safety reasons, it will send shock waves through the village. The number of visitors will dry up and the local businesses will suffer, with the inevitable loss of jobs and income.'

The rest of the group listened intently to this analysis. It was Les who asked the obvious question. 'So, Robin, what should we be doing?'

'Preparing for the day when the Pump Room is no more. If you haven't already done so, go along to the Memorial Park, and see the Dancing Couple, or State of Grace as Isaac called it. The restoration has not only removed the paint but all the dirt and grime of the last half-century. It looks glorious.'

'It certainly does. In the afternoon sunshine, it did look glorious.'

'Okay Audrey the statue looks glorious – I could add so did my leeks – but that still doesn't tell us what we should be doing.'

'Les, your leeks are glorious and for us non-gardeners, a wonder to behold,' Philippa replied picking up the theme. 'What we should be doing is encouraging visitors to stroll down to Park to see the Dancing Couple. In other words, give visitors two attractions – the Dancing Couple and the Pump Room.'

'Create an alternative revenue stream. Sorry, that's the manager of Honiston Building Society talking. But you see what I mean.'

'Okay, your right. But first, we need, what's that phrase the whizz-kids of the financial world use – Ah, yes, to raise the profile, that means making sure visitors knows about the Dancing Couple and its association to the village.'

'Exactly Audrey,' Jim was listening to the discussion with great interest. 'We need posters and leaflets to put up in the car parks and leaflets to hand out telling the story of the statue and what it means the village. I'm happy to get my graphic design students to create some drafts for us to have a look at it will help. It'll be a good project for them.'

'An excellent suggestion Jim. I think that's as far as we're going to get tonight. So, let's drink a toast to the Dancing Couple, the saviour of the village,' Philippa proposed, and they all raised their glasses and sang out, 'to the Dancing Couple.'

Chapter Forty

'I watched you when Robin talked about the meeting with Jason. You guessed Katie had found out about you and Robin, and that's why Jason crashed out?'

'I don't see how she could, but I suspect you're right.' Jim and Philippa were meeting at her request in the Cosy Café a few days later. It was the day of the visit by Suzanne and Toby. Jim had offered to join them on their scouting for locations, but Robin had insisted, firmly but politely, this was her job and she should be allowed to get on with it. If they wanted help or information, she would call him.

'So, what are you going to do?' Philippa asked. 'You know how important it is for Suzanne and the crew to film in the place where Isaac was born and grew up.'

'I have to try and reason with Katie. Make her understand this is not about our relationship, but it's for the good of the village.'

'When will you speak to her?'

Jim's reply was interrupted by the appearance of Brian at their table. 'Hi Jim, I heard about your - what's the word - argument shall we say with Maurice Henderson. I just wanted to say, well me and Sheila are sorry, it was wrong of him. We may have our differences over, you know the Pump Room, but there's no reason for that sort of behaviour. That's all I wanted to say. Coffees are on the house, by the way.' Taking their bill from the table, he tore into two and drifted away to take the order for a couple sitting at the adjacent table.'

'That was a turn up for books.' Jim observed when Brian was out of earshot. 'I must admit I was a bit wary about coming into town today, but I refuse to be intimidated by Mr Henderson or anybody else

'Good for you, but you were about to tell me about speaking to Katie?'

Jim took a drink of the coffee and let the liquid swirl around his mouth. Until Philippa posed the question, he hadn't given the matter any serious thought. It was something he said he'd do but it was nebulous, something for the future, as yet undefined. Faced with the question and knowing Philippa would demand an answer - and keep him to it - he replied. 'I'll have to pick my moment. A time when Robin's out – away working perhaps – but before the crew arrives to start the filming.'

Philippa got up from the table. 'I have to go, my husband will be expecting lunch, but let me know how you get on. And, be careful. By which I mean, don't get yourself trapped into something you'll regret.'

Jim didn't reply, but merely nodded as Philippa gathered her things together, and with a friendly wave to Sheila behind the counter, made her way out the café.

***

'Gentlemen settle down, please. Let's come to order. I appreciate meeting at this late hour it is not ideal, and I thank you for your indulgence. 'We have a fair bit to get through and I'm sure we all want to get home at a reasonable hour.' Jason pleaded as he strove to get the monthly Pump Room Executive Committee underway. 'Alan,' he said addressing the Rev Alan Howard, 'Please take a seat, I'd like to open the meeting.'

'The vicar, in deep conversation with Brian Thorpe, muttered his apologies and shuffled into one of the two vacant seats around the table. 'I'll talk to Sheila and get back to you Alan,' Brian promised sitting in the last remaining seat.

'We're all here, and Tilly's got her hearing aid in so let's make a start.'

'Mr Chairman forgive me if I butt in, but I can't stay as I'm expecting a call from my dear wife Penny and hoping for some good news. My father-in-law, that's dear Penny's pater was rushed into hospital today and we are anxiously awaiting the diagnosis from the hospital. It's a worrying time for all the family as dear Ernest was....'

'Alan, if you must interrupt our business before we've even got started, can you at least get to the point. Turning to the minute taker he covered her writing hand, 'None of this is for the minutes, Tilly.'

Getting the nod from the chair, Alan continued. 'I was merely attempting to explain Mr Chairman why it becomes necessary for me to take my absence from the committee due to…'

'Forget the bloody explanation, Vic just get to the point.' This was Ed Martin, who joined the committee following the death of Jack Thompson. He managed the Applegarth Junior Football team, and possessed the same gruff, down-to-earth personality as Jack 'Some of us would like to get home to our beds and cuddled up to the misses before mid-night if it's all the same to you.'

'I'm sorry Mr Martin if my wish to extend a simple courtesy to the committee disturbs your nocturnal ambitions. All I was trying to say was…'

'Alan!'

'Sorry, Mr Chairman. I was merely alluding to our lovely service on Sunday when the church was again filled with a wonderful floral display by the estimable body of ladies who every… Sorry, Mr Chairman. Anyway, after the service during our very friendly and sociable coffee hour, I got talking to Mrs Hanley. She's the widow of the brave and heroic Alfred Hanley, who you will recall… Sorry, Mr Chairman. Anyway, Mrs Hanley's daughter Tracey is, one the gallant band of ladies who cater …'

'I have a horrible suspicion where this is going,' Jason muttered under his breath.

…. to the needs of visitors to the Pump Room. And it appears young Tracey has been provided with a pair of plastic gloves when carrying out her duties, by order of the venerable Brenda. The said plastic gloves are uncomfortable and cause her hands to perspire. This calamitous situation being caused by, what dear Mrs Hanley described, as…'

'A rash on her hands, that cleared up in a couple of days.' Jason said interrupting his flow.

'A deep red blotchy rash that required medical intervention and took several days before the young lass was able to return to her duties,' Alan responded, determined to complete his narrative.

The other members of the committee remained silent, apart from Brian. 'We all feel sympathy for young Tracey, Alan of course we do but I'm not sure what you want the committee to do. We could, I suppose supply her with a pair of more comfortable gloves.'

'I appreciate your concern Brian, but this is not about her gloves, comfortable or otherwise.'

'So, what is it about then?' Ed asked rather pointedly. 'You had better have a good reason for wasting our time and preventing our honourable chairman from getting down to the business we're here for.'

'Mr Chairman, I appeal to you. I am attempting to make a serious point here, one which I believe is vital to the continuing success of this enterprise. I may have doubts about the morality of the operation, but as the representative of the…'

'Alan, we've sat here for the last ten minutes waiting for you to get to the point, whatever it is, so please…'

'The point, gentlemen, according to Mrs Hanley, the rash on her daughter's hands was caused by working in the Pump Room, and specifically by the spring water.'

Jason was onto it like a shot. 'That's a very serious accusation to make Alan. So, I bound ask whether you or Tracey's mother have any evidence to back it up? Nothing I've heard tells me that other members of staff or visitors have experienced a rash on their hands. Can you back up this wild accusation, because if not you will need to think very seriously about whether you can continue to serve on this committee.' Jason paused to let the seriousness of his words sink in, before continuing. 'I have to warn if you were to repeat these wild accusations outside this room, there will be very dire consequences.'

Alan was not the brightest button in the mending basket, but even he could recognise blackmail when it reared its ugly head. Swallowing hard he pressed on. 'Mr Chairman, at the funeral of Jack Thompson, you were heard by several mourners making an accusation against Mr White for spreading false rumours about the operation of the Pump Room. Would you care to explain to the committee what rumours you were referring to?'

'Jack's funeral was a higher charged occasion as you well know. After what happened to poor old Jack, emotions were bound to be running high. Things were said in the heat of the moment that were not meant to be taken literally. You can't expect any of us who were there to pay our respects to Jack and his family to be held accountable for what might have been said in that atmosphere.'

Alan was not about to let go. 'I appreciate you rushing to the defence of our chairman, Tony, but Mr Black never says anything without considering the consequences, do you, Jason?'

Jason looked around the committee, from the lack of eye contact, it was obvious they suspected there might be some truth in it. Okay, if that's how it's going to be, I guess it's down to me then. 'Alan, I think we can all agree, Tony Bean was right when he suggested the atmosphere at Jack's funeral was highly charged. Given the tragic circumstances of his death, and the charged atmosphere, we ought to forgive anything said in, - to borrow Tony's phrase – the heat of the moment.' Jason's plea was met with nods of approval by Tony and Brian.

In his most solemn tone, Jason continued. 'For many years Jack was a highly-valued member of this committee and his support and friendship was something that I valued and trusted through our first difficult and testing years. I only allude to Jack's departure from this world because Alan referred to something I am reported to have said to Jim White. I admit we did exchange a few words. It was a mistake; I'll own up to that. In my defence, I would only say Mr White has been a thorn in the side of the Association from the beginning. The committee will be aware of the number of false allegations and lies Mr White and his associates have made despite the enormous pleasure we have given to the thousands of visitors who come to the Pump Room every year. You will be also aware of the completely unwarranted attack on me by Mr White at the recent Water Festival. An attack, I have to say, that left me bruised and humiliated. What else can I say, gentlemen, here is a man who will use any excuse to besmirch the good name of the Magical Waters of Applegarth?' Jason paused and looked around the room gauging the effect his little speech was having on the committee. Here it comes, he thought, the bit that will win the committee over and silence Alan and all the critics. 'I have to say I was shocked to see Mr White at Jack's funeral. Given his feud against the Association and members of this committee, including dear Jack, I would have thought he'd do the decent thing and leave us to bury our colleague in peace. Seeing him with his friends amongst all the other mourners laughing and joking as if it was some happy occasion and not the solemn burial of a dear friend and colleague, was too much. I snapped and yes, it was a mistake, I admit it, but I felt compelled to challenge him about his latest lie, to provide evidence that the spring water was harming our visitors, but of course, he couldn't because there is none. I can say with a clear conscious that the Magical Waters of Applegarth are as fresh and clean and wonderful as ever, and if you have any doubts try them for yourselves. I promise you will come to no harm and leave refreshed and invigorated by the experience.'

'I believe colleagues the explanation offered by Jason clears up the matter pretty convincedly, don't you Alan,' the last three words given special emphasis and intended by Tony to put an end to any further argument. Alan bowed to the inevitable but resolved to take the chairman's invitation at his word and test the Magical Waters of Applegarth for himself.

Chapter Forty-one

Jim returned from walking Bix in the Memorial Park to see Robin coming from the High Street looking decidedly weary. 'Hi Jim,' she called outputting on a brave face. 'And hello to you too,' she added, bending down to beckon Bix to join her. Bix needed no further encouragement. He scampered forward and was soon jumping up to be stroked and patted.

Joining them, Jim asked. 'You finished for the day? How did it go?'

'I'm parched. A cup of tea and a chance to put my feet up would be lovely. I don't know how far we've walked today, but it seems miles.'

A few minutes later, with Bix lapping up water from his bow, they were sat around the kitchen table with tea and blueberry muffins. Robin lent back in her chair and put her feet on the chair opposite. 'That's better,' she sighed. 'One thing I must tell you; I hadn't realised until Suzanne told me. I've always assumed the programme was a documentary. You know the sort of thing – few pictures of Isaac, shots of his well-known pieces, plus the usual talking heads. In fact, it's going to be a drama-documentary. There'll be professional actors – she even let it slip that the guy who was in that thing on BBC1 on Sunday night, the one about murders in Northumberland, has been signed up to play Isaac. Anyway - these blueberry muffins are very good by the way, you make them?' Getting an affirmative nod, she continued. 'Suzanne said they will be casting local people as extras and the casting director is holding auditions in the village hall later in the week.'

'What about filming at Jason's hotel?'

Robin held up her hand to indicate her mouth was full of muffin couldn't speak. With one last swallow and a gulp of tea, she said. 'Suzanne is still keen to film the interior scenes in the hotel. I told her about my attempt to persuade Jason to let the film crew in, and how I was virtually kicked off the premises. Suzanne said not to worry, she would talk to Jason, she's a formidable woman – as she would be to get to where she is – and not used to taking no for answer.'

'Good luck with that; more tea, or perhaps another muffin.' Jim asked as the thought crossed his mind that if Suzanne were successful in persuading Jason to allow filming at the hotel, he wouldn't need to talk to Katie, and what a relief that would be.

***

'Good morning Brenda, and how are you today. Well, I hope?'

'I'm fine Rev. Howard,' Brenda replied taken back by the unexcepted appearance of the local vicar and member of the committee amongst the group of visitors to the Pump Room. She had finished her standard introduction and along with young Tracey begun shepherding the group through spring. 'Is there anything, in particular, I can help you with?' she asked her mind racing and eyes darting around the Pump Room, checking everything was in order. 'Only we don't often have the pleasure of welcoming members of the committee to the Pump Room. Mr Black pops in, of course, just to make sure everything is running smoothly but we don't often....'

Alan pulled back from the group to observe the group, as they slowly completed the rituals all visitors went through, before heading for the gift shop. 'How's young Tracey by the way? I'm sorry the gloves she's forced to wear all day are so uncomfortable.'

'Mr Black did say the committee had expressed concern for Tracey's well-being, that was the word he used.' He actually said a great deal more. Most of it interspersed with swear words she'd never heard before, but in essence, it amounted to whatever happened to Tracey and her hands were not be discussed with anyone, and he meant anyone.

'Forgive for asking Brenda, but I don't see you wearing gloves? Is there any particular reason for you not wearing protection on your extremities?'

Brenda, sensing one of the visitors was attempting to attract her attention looked across the room to see an elderly gentleman waving a bottle of spring water in the air. 'If you want more of our wonderful spring water sir, additional bottles can be purchased from the gift shop.' Signalling with his free hand he understood, the gentlemen shuffled off taking the arm of his companion and muttering about why he couldn't just take two bottles from the selection on the table.

When the last visitor had disappeared into the gift shop, and Tracey was busy tiding-up the discarded plastic cups from around the fountain, Brenda turned to Alan. 'Sorry, you were saying?'

Alan ignored her and walked over to the fountain and began rubbing his hands together in the water, making sure every inched was covered by the water. When he was convinced his hands were thoroughly soaked, he took one of the towels provided for visitors and gently patted his hands. Living them still slightly damp, he tossed the towel to Tracey, and declared, 'Mr Black says that these magical waters cure all ailments and conditions, so, my dear Brenda and lovely Tracey any disorders on these hands will surely be swept away by after that glorious wetting, what do you say?'

Brenda didn't answer but knew she'd be ringing Jason the moment the Rev. Alan Howard left. He'd want to know about the strange behaviour of one of his committee members and be able to tell her what was about.

Chapter Forty-two

Jim was feeling happy and content with the world. Even Robin announcing she was going away for a couple of days to check on a few sites and make sure everything was ready for the film crew, didn't dampen his spirits. What caused a change in his otherwise cheerful disposition was the sight of the car parked outside his cottage. It wasn't the car's fault, but knowing who was inside, reduced his progress to a saunter - anything to delay his arrival and the inevitable confrontation that would follow.

But he did eventually arrive at the cottage gate and immediately the car window was wound down and a familiar voice called out. 'Where have you been, I've sat here for twenty minutes waiting for you. Get in, we need to talk.'

'Hallo Katie, this is a surprise.' Jim replied nervously. 'Me and Bix have been to the Park, glorious day isn't it.'

Katie leant across and opened the passenger door. 'Never mind all that, get in.'

'As you can see, I have Bix in tow and can hardly just abandon him on the pavement.'

'Take the dog inside then, but be quick about it, okay.'

Giving a tug on Bix's lead he, very reluctantly headed indoors. 'Why did she have to turn up,' he muttered to himself, putting the lead on the hook near the front door where it belonged. With his hand on the door handle, Jim looked at Bix, sitting on the doormat with his head cocked to one side, the look he adopted when he sensed something was not quite right with his master. 'I don't know where this is going Bix, but there will be no sex.'

'No sex, definitely no sex,' he muttered striding across the pavement and thrusting his head through the open car window. 'The last time we spoke, you said we had to stop seeing each other. So, what's changed, Katie?'

'I know what I said, but…. Do you want to tell me about the statue in the park, the, what do you call it – Dancing Couple, or don't you.'

'It's back on its plinth and looking better than ever. What else is there to talk about?'

'Are you going to get in the car or do I have blast my horn so everybody in the street can hear and come out to investigate. Well!'

'Okay, I'm coming' Jim replied hastily climbing into the passenger seat and fastening his seat belt. 'Where are we going, anyway?'

'You know damn well where, and that bloody road sweeper better not be there.' Katie replied, putting the car in gear as they bounded forward with a roar from the exhaust.

'This is madness Katie,' Jim called out as they shot around first one bend and then another at high speed. 'You said Jason was getting suspicious, so where does he think you are?'

'At the hairdressers, but then I could have my hair shaved off and I doubt he'd notice.'

A few terrifying moments later they pulled into the car park at Fullton Woods. 'Right then Mr White, you know what we're here for, so get your kit off.' Seeing the horrified look on his face. Katie gave a loud throaty laugh. 'The look on your face Jim, it was a picture.'

Jim could have quite easily strangled her at that precise moment, but he didn't. 'If you haven't brought me here for, you know what, why are we here?'

'The you-know-what comes later, but first…'

'First, what? No, let me guess. Filming at the hotel, it was you who vetoed the idea?'

Katie shifted in her seat. 'All I did was mention to Jason that the very attractive Ms Caulfield – the lady from the Stein Foundation, you called on old biddy with a pearl necklace – was seen walking arm-in-arm with you through the town.'

'Actually, the old biddy was your description. I just didn't contradict you.'

Katie didn't reply and they both remained silent, staring out the front window at the rows of trees beyond the car park. 'I know I said we shouldn't meet, but I didn't mean forever. I know I said I wasn't looking for a relationship, it was just a bit of fun, but... Anyway, what's Ms Caulfield to you, is it serious, or just a fling while this film thing is going on.'

'This is wrong Katie; we shouldn't be sitting here like this. Whatever we had, is over. We can still be friends, though your husband might not be too happy about it.'

The look on Katie's face changed, became hard and fixed. She turned and looked at him and waited until they met eye to eye. 'It's not over. It's only over when I say it's over. Is that clear.'

'It is over Katie, I'm in love with Robin. From now on we can only see each other with other people around. Now, please drive me back to town.'

Katie was not about to be dismissed in such an abrupt way. 'My guess is you haven't told her about us, have you? Well, have you?'

'Meaning?' Jim replied fearing the worst.

'If you don't want her to find out, then you'd better find a way of keeping me happy.'

'You wouldn't dare?'

'Try me.'

Chapter Forty-three

Jim held the phone to his ear and waited for the call to be picked up. It rang three times before he heard a familiar voice said, 'Honiston Building Society, Les Woods speaking, how can I help you.'

'Les, its Jim.'

'Hi, Jim. I wondered who was calling on my private number. What's up?'

'Is there any chance we can grab a bit to eat at lunchtime today?'

'I'm not sure. You're lucky to catch me, I was on just about to go into a meeting to discuss a couple of large mortgage applications with two of our directors. They like to satisfy themselves they are a sound investment for the Society.'

'I appreciate I'm intruding into your working day, but it's important.'

'Mmm. Okay, look I should be free by about one-thirty, why don't I join you at the King's Head. You know the place, in the High Street, opposite the Post Office.'

'I appreciate it, Les, I'll see you at one-thirty.' Jim replied ending the call.

Jim checked his watch and reckoned there was enough time to catch the bus into Honiston, pick up the toiletries he needed from the chemist and still have two beers on the counter by the time Les arrived.

'I got you a pint of best,' Jim said, handing Les a straight glass, knowing he never drank out of a tankard.

'Shouldn't really drink at lunchtime and breath my fumes over the customers all afternoon,' Les replied downing most of the pint in one gulp. 'but since you're paying.'

'Cheers,' Jim said raising his glass. 'How did it go this morning?'

Les put the glass down on the counter and took a quick look around the bar, packed with lunchtime drinkers, checking there was nobody from the

Building Society. 'We decided we couldn't lend one couple all the money they wanted. They will probably have to get the seller to reduce the price or come up with a bigger deposit. They are not going to be happy when I break the news to them. Anyway, what's this about? You said it was important.'

Jim picked up the lunchtime menu from the counter and handed it to Les. 'I didn't want to order any food 'til you got here, so, what can I get for you?

Les, glanced down the menu and said he'd have a chicken salad. 'There's a table just come free over there, why don't you grab it, while I order the food. Do you want another one of those?' Jim asked pointing to his half-empty glass.

'No, this will do. I take it with me,' Les replied.

When Jim returned, having ordered the food, and settled in the seat opposite, Les asked rather pointedly. 'You still haven't told me why it was so important to meet up?'

'They said the food could take fifteen minutes; the kitchen is quite busy today. Is that okay?'

Les inwardly groaned, knowing he would be late back for the scheduled meeting with a young couple looking for their first mortgage. 'Something's happened that you don't want to talk about, right?'

Jim took a draft of beer and set the glass down on the table. 'It's Katie, she...'

'Oh no, you bloody fool. You said that was all over.'

Jim took another draft of beer, hoping it would give him the courage to tell Les the full story. 'After Jason turned Robin down, I felt I had to try and persuade Katie to change his mind. Then when Robin said Suzanne would approach Jason, I assumed it wouldn't be necessary. But then...'

Les was beginning to get frustrated by Jim's determination to avoid the real story. 'And, then?'

'Katie turned up outside my house yesterday and forced me to drive in her car to Fullton Woods.'

'And what happened. Don't tell me you succumbed to her obvious charms and...

Yes. No. She said if I didn't find a way to keep her happy, she'd tell Robin about us. So, we did it – or at least got started on the preliminaries – but when it came to the main event - I couldn't. Never happened before, but I couldn't. At which point she started shouting and calling me names. I said I was sorry and maybe next time, but she kicked me out of the car and drove off in a huff. I was left stumbling around the car park doing up my clothes, and when I finally got myself together, I had to walk home. I don't know what to do. Or, more importantly, I don't know what Katie will do, she doesn't like to be rejected.'

'Jim, you have been such a bloody fool. You'd better hope Katie doesn't carry out her threat. One thing you can be sure of if Robin finds out your dead mate.'

'I know, but you mustn't tell anyone, not even Audrey.'

***

The Rev Alan Howard was also not a happy man. After his flamboyant visit to the Pump Room, he was hoping, or more accurately expecting his hands to become red and blotchy. The problem was they hadn't. No matter how hard he rubbed them, his hands remained the same slightly sun-burned browny-pink they always were.

It was so frustrating. He was looking forward with eager anticipation to confronting Jason Black and offering red blotchy hands as evidence of the damage caused by the spring water. This display would be accompanied by a lecture – a very stern lecture – on the evils of the Pump Room and the harm it had inflicted on the village. In triumph, he would demand the immediate closure of the Pump Room, and a public apology for the damage to staff and visitors alike.

Sadly, it wasn't to be. His unexpected appearance in the Pump Room would have been reported to Jason, of that he had no doubt. He was also under no allusion that Jason would lampoon him mercilessly at the next committee meeting and use his clean hands to proclaim once again that the spring water was clean and clear as ever.

Jason would enjoy his moment of glory, but his nemesis when it came, would come from an entirely unexpected source.

Chapter Forty-four

'Jim, this is Suzanne, she plans to start filming tomorrow and reckons they will be here for two, or three days.'

Jim held out his hand in greeting. 'Pleased to meet you. If there is anything, I can do to help you during your stay in our village, don't hesitate to ask.'

'Thank you, I'll probably take you up on that. Robin says you have lived in the village for many years, and a huge fan of The State of Grace.'

'Yes, I am, though we tend to call it, The Dancing Couple.'

'Yes, of course, I forgot. Sensing Jim's interest in the man standing to her left, she introduced him. 'This is my lighting/cameraman, Toby.'

Jim stretched his hand out, but Toby who was more interested in observing the crowds, strolling up and down the High Street, offered a limp hand and muttered, 'Yeh.'

'Nice to meet you, Toby.' Turning to Suzanne, he asked. 'How did the auditions go; I believe there was quite a good response?'

'Yes, there was. We've managed to recruit some...' Her response was interrupted by a jangling noise from the back pocket of her jeans, 'Excuse me, I have to take this,' she says pulling her phone out and walking away to answer the call

Jim turned to Robin and asked when the actor playing Isaac was arriving. 'He is due to film a couple of scenes, along with other members of the cast tomorrow.'

'Where are the film crew staying?

'The production company have taken over a complete floor of the Magical Waters Hotel. And before you say anything, I didn't know until Suzanne called me this afternoon and asked me to meet her in the hotel lobby.'

Suzanne finished her call and re-joined them. 'Sorry about that, my Production Director had a query about tomorrow's schedule.' Not expecting a reply or needing one, she addressed Jim. 'Where's the Pump Room? Several of the guys, by which I mean Toby, in particular, want to test the water and its supposedly magical properties. He believes in all that mumbo-jumbo stuff and convinced it will cure the ugly rash on his legs. We've all told him he needs to go to a chemist and get some cream, but he won't hear of it.'

'It's at the other end of the High Street,' Jim replied. Receiving a quizzical look from Suzanne, he said he was surprised anybody could be taken in by the claims put out by the Pump Room about the properties the spring water

Robin, who had heard it before took up the story. 'A soon as Toby knew they would be filming in the village, he scoured the internet for any information he could find about the supposed magical properties of the spring water. He knows about Graham Tucker. He was convinced his problem would be cured by the spring water, just like Graham Tucker.'

Jim became conscious of someone standing behind him. Turning, he was shocked to see Katie, smiling her eyes alight with anticipation. 'Jim Hi, Nice to see again. Aren't you going to introduce me? I've met Suzanne, of course, she's a guest at the hotel. But your friend, I don't believe we've met before.' Seeing Jim staring at her accusingly, she walked past him and holding her hand out in greeting, 'Hi, I'm Katie Black, delighted to meet you. Jim and I are old friends and I believe you are....?'

'Robin Caulfield, I'm the...'

'The lady from the Stein Foundation. Jim's told me such much about you. You must be really pleased to see that lovely statue in the park restored. Such a shame to see it damaged, but then as Jim says, it's a treasure the whole village, isn't that right?'

Jim wasn't capable of agreeing or denying anything, as all the possible explanations he could offer to explain his apparent friendship with this woman – the wife of his worst enemy – spun around his head.

'Actually Jim, what *do* you say?' Robin asked pointedly. 'Since it appears you have enjoyed lengthy discussions with Mrs Black on the restoration of the treasure in the park.'

'Come on Jim,' Katie said by way of encouragement, 'you must recall our very intimate conversations on whether man and woman in the statue were more than just dancing partners. Whether his right hand was exactly where it should be. I remember you insisted on showing me exactly where it should be placed. We parked at the time at - where was that exactly, can you remember?'

Seeing the horrified look on Jim's face, Katie began backing away. 'I've probably said too much, maybe I should....' Still in earshot called out over her shoulder, 'It was Fullton Woods, by the way.'

Suzanne announced to no-one in particular. 'What was that about, or am I missing something here?'

With the question hanging in the air, Jim chipped in, 'I'm sure you two ladies have a great deal to be getting on with, why don't we meet for lunch at the Dog and Duck?'

'That's a kind offer, Jim, but I'm going to be tied up all day with production meetings of one thing or another. What about you Robin.'

Robin smiled sweetly. 'That's a lovely idea, Jim,' and then added while looking at him pointedly, 'I believe there are a few things we need to discuss, don't you?'

Jim could only nod in agreement. 'See you at twelve-thirty then my love.'

***

A very nervous Jim sat on the patio of the Dog and Duck just after mid-day, tucked away in a quiet corner well away from the other tables. He had no wish for the conversation Robin would insist on having, being overheard by any of the other diners.

He'd spent the hour or so, since leaving Robin and Suzanne, racking his brain for a plausible explanation as to why he was seated in Katie's car at Fullton Woods discussing the Dancing Couple. Ideas flew around his head like a swarm of bees, only to be rejected as impracticable or unbelievable. With only minutes before she was due to arrive, he still hadn't decided what to say to her. And, now it was too late, she was here.

Robin stood at the entrance to the patio, scanning the various tables for any sign of Jim. She was a few minutes early, but she assumed he arrived in time to get a table. On the point of giving up, he spotted him tucked away discreetly on the far edge of the patio.

The friendly and relaxed atmosphere that normally prevailed when they met to share a meal, was absent as they took their places at the table. Studiously avoiding eye contact, they grabbed a copy of the menu and began studying the choices available.

To brighten up the atmosphere Jim asked, 'I've got a beer, but what can I get you?'

Robin, without looking up, replied, 'I'm fine at the moment, maybe later.'

'That Katie, she's a real comedian. She certainly can tell a delightful story. She's well-known in the….'.

Robin looked up. 'So, it's Katie and not Mrs Black then?'

'Well, yes. In a small village when everybody knows everyone, using first names becomes natural, I mean…'

Robin decided the moment had come to confront the issue head-on. 'From the way she was speaking, it seemed a bit more than friendship between you two. Is there something you haven't told me about you and Mrs Black? For example, what were you doing sitting in her car – I assume that's what it was – what was that place?'

'Fullton Woods,' Jim replied sheepishly, taking a long draft of beer.

'You were having a conversation with the wife of your sworn enemy in a secluded spot and I'm supposed to believe it was for the sole purpose of discussing the restoration of the statue in the Memorial Park.'

'Yes.' Jim paused, forming the words in his head. 'We obviously couldn't meet in public… We, that is Philippa, Les Audrey and I decided it would be a good idea for me to cultivate Mrs Black. After all, she had expressed a wish to help with the restoration of the Dancing Couple, and we thought it might lead to information about what her husband was up to in the Pump Room.'

'And that was the only reason. How often did these private meetings take place?'

'They ended when it became obvious Mrs Black knew nothing more than the rest of us. Whatever Jason was up to, he wasn't telling his wife.'

Robin was non-committal, 'Mmm,' she said picking up the menu and studying the wine list. 'I'll have a glass of dry white wine if you're still offering.'

'Of course,' Jim replied hastily heading inside to the bar.

Robin leant back in her chair and let the sunbathe her face and neck. She was confused. One minute the Blacks were the sworn enemy, and the next Mrs Black was being cultivated to provide information about her husband's nefarious activities. – or was it a cover for a full-blown affair between the two of them. Jim's explanation that Philippa, Audrey and Les encouraged his liaison with Mrs Black, sort of rang true. She let that thought to circulate around her head for a few moments, before deciding it could be easily be confirmed by Philippa.

'A glass of Sancerre, I hope that's acceptable,' Jim said placing a large glass of white wine on the table.

'Perfect,' Robin replied taking the glass and enjoying a generous swig of the wine. '

'Excellent choice,' she confirmed. 'It brings back memories of a long, leisurely lunch David and I enjoyed in the village square at Sancerre. Afterwards, we strolled down to the battlements on the edge of the village and feasted our eyes on the beautiful valley and rows of vines. We brought a case of the wine we had with our lunch from the local Wine Shop, but it never tasted quite the same back home. That was the last holiday we spent together; he was killed in the air crash six months later.'

'I'm sorry about David, but it's good for you to talk about happy times together. Occasionally, something happens, and a moment Nancy and I shared leaps into my head, and I smile remembering how happy we were on that day in that place.'

Robin knew what he meant but didn't think it was necessary to say so. Instead, she picked up the menu. 'I'm hungry, I don't know about you. Let's order.'

'Okay, what would you like?'

Chapter Forty-five

'What about my performance, pretty convincing don't you think?'

Listening to Katie boasting about her performance, as she called it, made his blood boil. Taking a deep breath and telling himself to stay calm, Jim replied. 'What do you want?'

'Nothing, but let's just say it was a taster of what could happen unless you're prepared to keep me happy. It's only over when I say it's over, is that understood,'

Katie, this is ridiculous. We had fun, of course, we but it's over, why not accept it and let's be friends, what do you say?'

'It's not over until I say it is.' Having delivered her ultimatum, Katie finished the call, leaving Jim feeling decided uneasy about what she might do next.

'Who was that on the phone?' Robin enquired as she descended the stairs into the hallway. 'I thought I heard the name Katie mentioned.

Startled by her sudden appearance, Jim quickly improvised. 'Her real name is Kathleen, she's the Administrator of the Graphic Arts Department at Honiston Arts and Technical College.' Receiving a quizzical look, he added, 'She was checking on the date for my next session and saying a couple more of students had signed up for the course.'

'Oh right. I'm on my way to meet Suzanne. She managed to sweet talk Jason into letting the film crew shoot a couple of scenes in the hotel.'

'Really, how did she manage that?'

'Suzanne is a formidable a lady, if she wants something, then God help anyone, man or woman who stands in her way. Incidentally, she's asked to meet up with Philippa, do you have a number for her?'

'Why?' he replied, the anxiety he felt reflected in his face.

'She didn't say, but since she's lived in the village most of her life, she might be able to help with a couple of scenes in the film.' It sounded a bit contrived, but it was the best she could come up with. It sounded contrived to Jim as well, but since he had no reason to withhold the number, he reeled it off. It was one of the numbers he knew off by heart, along with that for Audrey and Les,

'Thanks, I'll see you later.' Robin said giving him a quick peck on the cheek, as she waltzed out the door.

***

It had been a busy morning for the film crew. Technical problems with the generator powering the lights put them behind schedule, and Suzanne was beginning to show her frustration with the lack of progress. The latest problem was a blind spot on the set. 'For God sake, Toby can't you at least put some bloody illumination on the cast when they move to the back of the set?'

Toby mumbled under his breath, 'I'll fix it, damn it.'

'And what's with the gloves. Something wrong with your hands?' she asked referring to the bright yellow plastic gloves adorning the lighting cameraman's hands. Toby, conscious of the fact that he was wearing gloves at all, would appear out of place to the rest of the crew, thrust his hands out of sight behind his back. 'It's nothing,' he said in response to Suzanne's question and shuffled off, 'Colin, we need to change the angle on stand five.'

Suzanne dismissed the incident and turned to address her leading actor. 'Darling when we do the scene again, can you give me something a bit more muscular? You are supposed to be at the height of your powers, not some haggard old drama queen.'

Robin, loitering behind the camera, sensed they were about to shoot another scene, stepped forward. 'Suzanne, 'You'll be okay won't you. I need to speak to someone, it's really important and could decide what I do for the rest of my life.'

She tempted to ask the obvious question, but with the crew were waiting to shoot the next scene, Suzanne replied. 'Go ahead, I'll be fine.' And then to the crew. 'Positions please guys for….' The rest was lost as Robin hurried away. She had arranged to meet Audrey at the library. Philippa was evasive when she phoned and suggested it might be better if she talked to Audrey.

When Robin walked into the library a few minutes later, Audrey was behind the counter date stamping a pile of books. 'Hope you enjoy those,' she said passing the books across the counter to a middle-aged woman, who eagerly thrust them into her bag and departed with a contented smile on her face.

On the point of moving away from the counter, Audrey noticed Robin approaching. 'Hi Robin, have you come to join the library.'

'Hi, Audrey. Have you got a minute?'

'I don't get off until…' Seeing the anxious look in Robin's eyes, added, 'I'm due for a break, give me a moment, while I get my colleague to take over here.'

'I spoke to Philippa earlier, but she was busy today, something about providing lunch for her husband's clients. She said you might be able to help. It's about Jim…'

Audrey returned, to the counter, and pointing to the Reference Section, suggested it would be quiet over there and they could talk without being disturbed.

'What about Jim?' Audrey asked when they were sat down. 'Has something happen?'

'No, nothing like that, Jim is fine.' Robin paused, not sure how to broach the subject. 'You've probably heard – nothing happens in this village without everybody knowing about it – but we were confronted by Mrs Black alleging - how shall I describe it- alleging an intimate relationship with Jim.'

'Actually no, I hadn't heard that. When was it?'

'In the High Street, I was there with Suzanne and Jim, when Mrs Black appeared and started hinting about things between her and Jim. I mean she didn't actually come out and say they had an affair, just broad hints and a reference to Fullton Woods.'

Audrey, who had an inkling where this was going, decided to play the innocent. 'What did Jim say, I assume you asked him.'

'This is where it gets difficult and why I wanted to talk to you. According to Jim, he met Mrs Black in Fullton Woods for the sole purpose of persuading her to reveal what her husband was up to.'

'Did you believe him?' Audrey asked, putting off answering the question again.

'I wanted to of course. I love Jim and hope we'll spend the rest of our lives together, but I have to know if what he says is the truth.'

'Did he also tell you we encouraged his friendship, for want of a better word, with Mrs Black?'

'Yes, he did. By we, I assume that refers to you, Philippa and Les. What I'm struggling with is how did this friendship start. Jim and Mr Black are supposed to be sworn enemies, so how come he strikes up a friendship with Mrs Black.

'She expressed an interest in restoring the Dancing Couple. Robin, I can see my colleague has a queue of people waiting to check books out, you will have to excuse me.'

'I'm sorry to have taken up so much of your time, but before you go, could I ask you a straightforward question. Did the friendship go any further?'

Later that day as Audrey and Les were sitting down to eat their dinner, Les posed the obvious question. 'What did you say.'

Audrey finished chewing the food, in her mouth. 'I was dreading the question even though I knew it was coming. As far as we know the affair with Katie was over before Jim and Robin got together. So, I lied and said there was nothing of that kind. I was right, to say that wasn't I?'

Les didn't reply. Forking a large piece of beef into his mouth he began chewing furiously. 'Les say something, was I right to lie to Robin?' Not getting any response and with Les avoiding eye contact she guessed why. 'You're not telling me something aren't you.' And then after a pause. 'I don't believe it, the affair has started up again, hasn't it!'

Les swallowed the beef and returned his knife and fork to the plate. 'Sort of.'

'What does that mean. Either it has or hasn't, which is it?'

Accepting he had no option, despite his promise, Les recounted the meeting in the pub and Jim's confession that the affair had resumed.'

'Oh no.' Audrey cried. 'What on earth was he thinking?'

242

'According to Jim, Katie made it plain if he didn't continue to satisfy her, she'd make sure Robin got to know he had cheated on her. Again, according to Jim, when it came to it, he couldn't do it.'

'Did you believe him?'

'Yes, no – I don't know, it sounded plausible.'

Chapter Forty-six

In the Pump Room, things were winding down at the end of the day. The last group of visitors were wending their way through the spring. As the last of them made their way to the gift shop and home, Brenda let out a sigh and stretched to ease her aching back. It had been a long day and she was looking forward to home and a long, hot soak in the bath.

Before that pleasurable experience, there was the slight problem of Jason, who arrived ten minutes ago and lent against the back wall studying the last group as they completed their tour of the spring.

Leaving Tracy to clear up and Janet to calculate the takings for the day, Jason drew Brenda aside. 'There have been some complaints – no let's say observations – from several visitors that things have gotten a bit slack in the Pump Room of late Brenda

'What do you mean Mr Black, slack?'

'Perhaps slack is not the right word, in fact, I know it isn't. The right word is hasty, the truth is our visitors have the impression our sole aim is to get them through the experience of the Magical Waters of Applegarth, as quickly as possible. Whereas, I like to think our visitors should be encouraged to linger, soak up the atmosphere, and absorb the magic that flows through this wonderful and glorious place.'

Brenda was beginning to wonder whether Jason had been at the happy juice again but restrained herself. 'Everybody gets the same treatment, Mr Black.'

'And that's the problem, Brenda...' Jason's oratory on the deficiencies in the Pump Room was interrupted by loud hammering on the door. Turning abruptly to Tracy, he barked out, 'Tell whoever that is we are closed for the day. Now, Brenda where was I. Ah, yes. The problem is everybody does get the same treatment...'

The hammering continued accompanied by someone shouting. 'Let me in you bastards, let me in. I know you're in there.'

Jason's lecture on the visitor experience was clearly doomed. 'Okay, before they wake the whole neighbourhood, you'd better let them in.' Tracy moved gingerly to the door and carefully lifted the latch. The moment the door fell open, Toby stormed in. 'Look what you've done to me,' he cried, waving in the air a pair of bright red blotchy hands, the colour spreading across his fingers and palms before disappearing up the sleeve of his jacket.

Jason moved to quash any attempt to blame the spring. 'My dear chap that looks really nasty, but you have no cause the blame the Pump Room for your unfortunate predicament.'

'Oh, yes I have, Toby cried. These horrible red blotchy spots came up a few hours after I was here, washing my hands under that spring.'

Jason was determined to stand his ground, but under Toby's menacing gaze he retreated to the fountain. 'I'm very sorry for you, but I can assure you the spring water is pure and clear as a mountain stream. We have thousands of visitors who come to…'

Standing over him, Toby blasted in his ear. 'I don't care about your bloody visitors, all I care about is what you are going to do about these?' he enquired, thrusting two hands into Jason face, and wiping them across his cheeks.

The three women had never seen their boss the subject of such aggressive behaviour before - and if truth be told, we're quite enjoying it. Janet and Tracy's view of Jason was partly obscured, but Brenda standing to the side had a perfect view and could see the anguished look on his face, a plea to be released from the grip of this mad man.

Taking a step forward, she attempted to gain Toby's attention. 'Sir, if you would care to discuss your concerns calmly and sensibly, I'm sure we can satisfy you that your fears about the spring water are unfounded.'

Toby peered over his shoulder, his eyes flashing. Releasing Jason, he moved to stand immediately in front of Brenda, his face so close she could smell the alcohol on his breath. 'And how exactly are you going do that?'

Standing her ground, Brenda said defiantly. 'The water comes from an underground spring and is pure and clean as a mountain stream.'

'So, how come I've got these.' Toby said thrusting his hands into her face and rubbing his fingers across her cheeks. Brenda flinched from the smell and roughness of his fingers on her skin.

Recovered from his ordeal, Jason thrust himself between Toby and Brenda in a vain attempt to regain control of the situation. 'Sir, you are clearly very distressed by whatever has infected your hands. We are naturally very sorry, but you can't barge in here and start making completely unjustified accusations against our glorious, spring water.'

Toby pushed him away and stuck a finger in his face. 'I reckon this village depends quite a lot on this place. Well, let's see how they feel when I tell 'em what your magical waters are doing to visitors,' he said sliding his hand across Jason's face and moving quickly to the exit. Jason attempted to cut him off. 'Sir let's discuss this calmly and sensibly.' But Toby had vanished into the night.

Returning to the distressed and shocked three women, Jason asked. 'Who the hell was that? Have you seen him before?'

Janet was the first to speak. 'I believe he is connected to the film crew. The one filming in the village about that sculpture guy. And, yes. I have seen him before Mr Black.'

'When?' he asked. 'You mean here, in the Pump Room?'

Janet glanced across to Brenda for guidance, who silent mouthed, 'you better tell him.' 'It was yesterday. He was here. I remember him, we all do because he seemed so happy. He kept on saying what an honour it was to be in this special place. To partake, that was the actual word he used, of the wonderful Waters of Applegarth with all its healing powers. It was all like that. He insisted on telling the group about how many people had been cured of complaints and illnesses after taking the waters. We all thought he was mad, but he didn't sound mad, it was as if he was a disciple for the spring. I know that sounds daft, but was like a religious thing, with his as a place of worship.'

'Well, one thing is for sure, that film crew can pack their bags and get out of my hotel tonight. They are no longer welcome. Not after this.'

***

246

Jason burst into the restaurant and stormed across to the table where Suzanne and the film crew were sitting, having a quiet dinner after a busy day of filming. 'You lot can pack your bags and get out; you are no longer welcome here.'

Suzanne looked up at the angry and distraught figure standing over them. 'I beg your pardon?'

'You heard, pack your bags and get out. Now!'

Placing her knife and fork neatly on the plate, Suzanne asked, 'Is there a problem, Mr Black, you seem distressed.' The red face and breathlessness, she assumed were not the only cause of his distress.

'You bet there is. One of your lot burst into the Pump Room and physically assaulted me and a member of my staff while making malicious and unfounded accusations.'

This didn't make any sense to Suzanne, 'When you say it was one of us, who are you referring to because we're all here eating our dinner?'

'The big guy, beard and heavy glasses.'

'You mean Toby.'

'If that's his name, then yes, Toby. Where is he, by the way?'

'We haven't seen him since we broke for the day,' one of the film crew replied, looking up briefly from his dinner.

'Toby and you lot are not welcome here, so you can clear out tonight.'

Determined to stand her ground, Suzanne eyed him defiantly. 'We're not going anywhere.' Turning to the rest of the crew, she picked up her knife and fork. 'Finish your meal guys, and if anyone wants a dessert, you can have that as well.' Looking Jason straight in the eye, she hoisted food onto her fork and began eating. Her look said quite plainly she wasn't going anywhere, and there was nothing he could do about it.

Raising his voice, Jason shouted, 'I said you are not welcome here, so get out.' The encounter with the film crew had largely gone unnoticed up to that point, but with Jason raising his voice, the rest of the dining room suddenly became aware of the confrontation

'Is there a problem here Mr Black?' Gary asked sidling over, concerned at the impact the disturbance was having on the other diners.

'Get back to your duties Gary, I can deal with this.'

Trying another tack, Gary said, 'There's a problem with table 12.'

'You deal with it,' Jason snapped. Having been summarily dismissed, Gary shrugged his shoulders and set off in search of Mrs Black.

Closeted in the kitchen with the Executive Chef, Katie became aware of Jason shouting at the guests in the dining-room. Pushing through the swing doors, she immediately spied Jason towering over the film crew. 'Can I have a word?' she said dragging him into the kitchen. 'What's going on? Why are you shouting at the guests?'

Jason pulled his arm free. 'I was ordering them to leave. One of them, a guy called Toby, burst into the Pump Room and threatened me and Brenda.'

'He did what? Why?'

Jason edged towards the kitchen swing doors. 'Wild, unfounded accusations about the spring water.' With Katie still looking puzzled, he added, 'His hands were red and blotchy, said it was caused by the spring.'

Katie struggled to understand what this had to do with the crew eating their dinner in the restaurant. 'Okay, one of the crew, Toby, I think you said, behaved badly and I can see why you're upset – understandably I suppose – but what has that got to do with Suzanne and the other guys out in the restaurant?'

'They are no different. If he goes, they go. Watch me.' Before she could stop him, Jason pushed through the kitchen swing doors and marched across the floor to confront the film crew. 'I told you lot to get out.'

Katie arrived at the table seconds later. 'Suzanne, I apologise for any distress my husband may have caused you and your colleagues. I can only offer as an excuse a rather unsettling incident earlier this evening, which he took too much to heart. Enjoy the rest of your dinner, which will be on the house, of course.' Having said her piece, she took Jason firmly by the arm and led him away, as he continued to shout insults at the group. Tucked away in the office away from all the hotel guest, Jason slunk in the office chair. Katie stood over him. 'You can't behave like that to our guests, Suzanne and the crew have paid top prices for their stay and we can't afford to upset them. You understand that. Well!'

'If you say so. But Toby goes.'

'What's this about the red blotchy hands.'

Jason struggled to his feet. 'He stuck his spotty, blistering hands in my face and ran his fingers up and down my cheek, it was horrible.'

Katie could see the potential problem it posed for their business. 'We have a crisis Jason and need to act quickly, otherwise, we'll be ruined.'

'What crisis. You mean the whole thing about blotchy red hands.' Jason was determined not to concede the point. 'He can't prove it was anything to do with the spring, water, and in any case, nobody will believe him.'

'You're forgetting young Tracy. She had the same symptoms, as did the people who replied to Jim's questionnaire.' Jason opened his mouth to protest, but Katie cut him off. 'Before you say anything, I know it was politically motivated, but with this latest case we need to show the spring water poses no threat to our visitors, and we need to do fast. I suggest we begin by....' Katie's suggestion for overcoming the problem was interrupted by the phone demanding to be answered. Jason studiously ignored it, leaving Katie to answer. She picked up the receiver and placed it against her ear. She listened and could be heard to say, 'Yes,' 'Okay,' 'Oh, right', in response to the caller. And then. 'Thank you, PC Smith, we will deal with it right away.'

She returned to the phone to its cradle and leant against the desk. 'That was Nigel, he thought we should know someone has pinned a large poster at the top of the path. Written in big capital letters it accuses the spring of being a health hazard. They're not the exact words – he did tell me, but I was so shocked didn't take them in.'

'It's that bloody Toby again. I'll get down there and remove it. We can't afford to have that sort of thing on display when the visitors arrive in the morning.'

A sizable crowd had gathered around the poster when Jason arrived a few minutes later. 'What you been putting in the water Mr, Black?' one of them commented as he burst through their ranks to stare at the offending artwork. In large capital letters, it read:

THE SPRING WATER IS BAD
IT MAKES YOU SICK
FIGHT BACK

Tearing at the poster, Jason announced to the crowd with as much jollity as he could muster. 'It's as safe and pure as always, you know that. This,' he said pointing to the poster is just a silly prank by some spotty teenager, you know what they are like.' Tearing the poster into strips, he crunched them up into a ball and marched off, throwing the ball into the nearest wastepaper bin. 'Don't believe a word of it,' he shouted over his shoulder as a parting word to the crowd.

Out of sight and hidden in the shop doorway, Toby waited until Jason had disappeared. Stepping out with a roll of paper under his arm, he approached the post and pinned up a new poster, that read:

WASH YOUR HANDS WITH SPRING WATER
AND THIS IS WHAT YOU GET

Underneath a crude drawing a pair of red blotchy hands. 'That's the truth, 'he announced to the crowd, 'And, here's the evidence,' he said holding up his hands.

Arriving at the hotel, Jason sought out Katie in the kitchen. 'It was gone. A few people were hanging around, but I think I managed to convince them it was just a silly prank.'

'Well, you'd better get down there again, there's another poster and this one is worse.'

Turning smartly around, Jason headed out, calling over his shoulder, 'I'll have him, I will. I'll have him.'

Chapter Forty-seven

If Jason assumed his only problem was the Pump Room path poster, he was mistaken. When dawn broke the following day, and the first locals and visitors began filling up the High Street, they were assailed with posters proclaiming the spring water as the cause of visitors getting red blotchy hands.

On the point of finishing her breakfast, with Jim stuck in the bathroom, Robin got a call from Suzanne requesting an urgent meeting at the hotel. She refused to say what it as about, only that Robin should come at once. Intrigued, Robin downed the last dregs of coffee, grabbed her bag, and at the bottom of the stairs shouted up to Jim, 'I have to go and meet Suzanne, I'll see you later, bye.' Not waiting for an answer, she set off for the hotel.

On most mornings Audrey's route to the library took her along the normally near-deserted High Street, with only a few souls about to disturb the peace and quiet. Today when she entered the High Street, she was surprised to see groups of people clustered around every tree, telegraph pole, lamp post or shop window.

Curious as to what was engaging all these people at this hour of the morning, she wandered over to the nearest group. Peering through the crowd at the object of their interest, she couldn't quite believe what she was seeing, Audrey pulled out her mobile phone and dialled the number for the Honiston Building Society. When it was answered, she could hardly contain her excitement, 'Les, you'll never believe it, but someone has stuck posters all over the High Street accusing the spring water of causing the red blotchy hands.' Les, who was only a few minutes into his working day, took a few moments to take it in. 'That's amazing, have you rung Jim and Philippa?' he asked.

'I was just about to, but Robin's coming up the High Street, I'll see what she knows. I talk to you later Les, bye.' Cutting off the call, she wavered. 'Robin over here.'

'What's going on?' Robin enquired. 'What are all these people looking at?'

'A poster accusing the spring water of causing red blotchy hands.'

'You mean hands like mine.'

'And many other visitors to that wretched place.'

'Who's responsible for the posters, do we know.'

'At the moment, it's unclear. Does Jim know?'

'He was still titivating himself in the bathroom when I left. I've never known a man who could spend so much time getting ready in the morning. And they talk about woman hogging the bathroom. Sorry, Audrey, I'm talking out of turn.' Getting a sympathetic look from Audrey, she continued. 'I am on my way to meet Suzanne at the hotel, but I'll ring Jim and see what he knows.'

At the hotel, Suzanne was in the lobby surrounded by the rest of the crew, apart from Toby, their bags and equipment loaded in the van awaiting the arrival of Robin. 'I'm sorry guys, I know you want to get on to the next location, but I need to explain to Robin why we are leaving a day earlier than planned.' Suzanne's apology was met with murmurs from several members of the crew, accompanied by much shuffling of feet.

'Ah, here she is,' Suzanne announced. 'Robin, thanks for coming and I'm sorry for all the mystery.'

'What's going on? I thought you were doing the interviews today; I've got Ted Smith all lined up and ready to go.'

Pointing to a group of club chairs away from the main area of the lobby, Suzanne suggested they talk there. 'I'll come straight to the point. We've been kicked out of the hotel.' Robin was dying to cut in, but Suzanne wasn't to be deterred. 'Apparently, a confrontation occurred between Mr Black and Toby. According to Mr Black, Toby attacked him and threatened one of his staff.'

'What was it about?' Robin asked, finally got a word in.

'I haven't spoken to Toby. In fact, we haven't seen or heard from him since we broke for the day yesterday.'

'I think I might be able to help you there,' Robin suggested, relating the scene in the High Street and contents of the posters.

'You think Toby was responsible?' Suzanne replied.

'I can't be certain, but it would make sense. I know from my brief conversations he was very keen on visiting the Pump Room. I got the impression he was into all that magical waters mumbo-jumbo in a big way.'

Their discussion on the beliefs, or otherwise of the unit's lighting/cameraman was cut short by the sudden appearance of Jason and Katie in the lobby. Causing the film crew and their bags to scatter as the pair forced their way to the exit. 'I thought I told you lot to clear out,' Jason spat out as the Blacks burst through the exit and beyond.

'I think I can guess where those two are going,' Robin suggested.

By the time, Jim arrived on the High Street, prompted by Robin, most of the crowd had

disbursed, leaving the posters displayed for the world to see. Jim was studying the example at the top of the pathway leading to the Pump Room when a familiar voice boomed out of the still air, 'You're responsible for this aren't you. I might have known you and the other haters of the spring would stop at nothing.'

Jim turned to see a rather red-faced Jason bearing down on him, with Katie struggling a few yards behind. 'Actually, Jason I can honestly say on this occasion, I'm not responsible. Whilst I can applaud the sentiment, they are nothing to do with me or my friends. You'll have to look elsewhere for the culprit, I'm afraid.'

'Yes, maybe, but I wouldn't put it past your lot to have a hand in spreading vicious lies about a major asset to this village.'

Jim, who had every intention of exploiting the situation for that it was worth, turned to Katie. 'They are very artistic don't you think. I particularly like the way he's drawn the fingers. Long and slender and such a delicate shade of red,'

'She thinks the same as me, they are disgusting.' Jason lunged forward and tore the poster down, ripped to shred, tossed the pieces onto the path. 'That's what we think.'

Jason watched amused. 'You're in for a busy day if you're planning on tearing down all the posters. Though if I was you, I'd make sure someone wasn't walking behind putting new ones up.'

'Ignore him, Katie, we have work to do before the coach parties arrive.' Pushing her ahead of him, the pair set off down the High Street. 'There's one there, and another over there...'

Jim turned his attention away from the Blacks to greet Robin. 'You've just missed Jason and Katie on a poster hunt.

'You're enjoying all this, aren't you?'

'Just a bit.'

Robin waited for the smug smile on Jim's face to fade. 'I came to tell you that Jason has thrown Suzanne and the crew out the hotel. When I arrived, the crew were in the lobby, their bags packed ready to leave.'

In answer to Jim's obvious question, she recounted the incident in the Pump Room and Jason yelling at the crew in the restaurant.

'Toby's responsible for the posters then?'

'It seems that way, though nobody has seen him since yesterday.'

'What's the crew doing now?'

'Moving onto the next location, they don't have any option. It means I'll have to go with them, sorry.'

Jim's response was cut short by the appearance of Mrs Worthington hurrying down the street. 'Have either of you seen Mr Black,' she exclaimed. 'I went to the hotel and was told he'd just left.'

'Good morning Hazel,' Jim replied. 'Jason was last seen running down the High Street tearing down every poster he came across. Can't think why. Has something terrible happened in the Pump Room?'

'You know damn well what's happened, and I wouldn't be surprised if you were responsible.'

'Me?' Jim called out to Mrs Worthington's disappearing back. 'Sorry. No. Nothing to do with me,' Before adding, 'More's the pity.'

'Who was that,' Robin asked.

'Mrs Worthington, a leading member of the Pump Room Association. She'll be expecting Jason come up with an explanation for the posters.'

'I have to go and talk to Ted Smith. Tell him they won't be filming his interview today. I'll leave you savouring your triumph.'

'Okay, I'll see you before you go. Hello, everybody's on the High Street today,' he said as Philippa appeared out of nowhere. 'Good morning, and what brings you to our poster gallery on this bright, sunny morning. Or, let me guess.'

'Is it true somebody's stuck up posters accusing the spring water….'

'Of being responsible for the red blotchy hands. Just like our survey revealed.' Jim said interrupting her.

'Morning Robin. Who's responsible, do we know.'

'One of the film crew,' Robin replied. Camera guy called Toby. I'll talk to you before I leave Jim.'

'Okay, bye love. Much as I'm enjoying this, the real question is what are we going to do about it? We can't let Jason's silver tongue talk himself out of this one.'

'I think the answer might be heading in our direction,' Philippa inclined her head in the direction of the Blacks and Mrs Worthington.

'Jason, you can't dismiss this as just another vicious lie. The whole village knows about the posters and they will almost certainly demand an explanation.'

'I'm sorry Mrs Worthington, I disagree. The posters have gone, and by this evening the whole thing will have blown over.'

As the trio drew level Jim decided to offer some advice of his own. 'Another extraordinary general meeting is called for, don't you think?'

'It's got nothing to do with you.' Jason spat out as they hurried past.

Jim watched them go by, but as they did, Katie glared at him and mouthed 'You'll pay for this.'

Shocked by her hostile reaction, Jim could only hold up his hands in a gesture that said. 'Nothing to do with me.'

Philippa watched this exchange with interest. 'What was that about.'

Jim took a moment to reply, his head reeling from Katie's implied threat. 'She's threatening to tell Robin about us unless I keep her satisfied – that's the word she used.'

'And are you keeping her satisfied?' Philippa asked, a slight edge to her voice.

'No, since you ask. I was persuaded against my better judgement to go with her to… But, when it came to it, I couldn't. She wasn't very pleased. As you saw, she's blaming me for the posters and… I tried to persuade her it's over, but she refuses to accept it.'

'You know what you have to do. Confess to Robin and hope she loves you enough to forgive and forget. Once it's out in the open, Mrs Black won't be able to threaten you.'

'Robin will be away for the next few days with the film crew, I'll tell when she gets back.'

'Good, make sure you do.'

Chapter Forty-eight

The following morning Jim, having finished breakfast and loading the dirty cutlery and china into the dishwasher, was surprised by a knock at the door. When he chose to ignore it and carried on setting up the machine, the knocking became more urgent. 'Okay, Okay, he called out, 'I'm coming, I'm coming,' When he opened the door it was to reveal Katie in an agitated state. 'Where's Robin,' she demanded.

'Good morning Katie how are you this morning.'

'Where's Robin, I demand to speak to her.'

'You can demand all you like, but Robin is not here.'

'Yes, she is, you just don't want her to hear the truth about us,' Katie said bursting into the hallway. 'Robin, where are you. I know you're here. I have some news; I think you will find interesting. It's about me and...' The rest of her announcement was cut short by the arrival of Bix's. He was quietly resting on his bed in the kitchen, on hearing her voice, came scampering down the hallway, barking and snapping at her legs.

Katie tried her best to defend herself, but it was hopeless, and she was forced to retreat. If she was wound up before, she was now fuming. Unable to get her words, she edged past Jim, who made no attempt to grab hold of Bix or to stop him barking. When Katie reached the relative safety of the doorstep, Jim turned to her. 'Robin left with the film crew yesterday. Since your husband kicked them out of the hotel, but then you knew that.'

Finally, able to speak, Katie blurted out, 'You haven't heard the last of this, I promise you.' And with a toss of her head, she turned and strode up the path. 'I had nothing to do with the posters, I promise you,' Jim called out, but Katie chose to ignore his protest and drove off at high speed.

That evening Jim, Audrey, Les and Philippa were gathered around the dining table at the Wood's house intent on planning their next move. 'This is what we know,' Les said when everyone had their fill of the wine and cheese laid out on the table. 'This guy Toby, a member of the film crew, goes to the Pump Room and alleges the skin complaint on his hands was caused by the spring water. Not getting a satisfactory response, he attacks Jason and insults Brenda. Jason aggrieved by the assault decides to kick the film crew out the hotel.

Later, a poster appears on the High Street, which Jason tears down, but the following morning more posters appear all over the village repeating the accusation. Jason tears of those down too, but is confronted by Mrs Worthington, who says the Association will demand an explanation. Does that sound, about right?' The nodding heads around the table confirmed it was.

'What's Jason's next move going to be? You probably know him better than us.'

'I know he is a lying, conniving bastard,' Philippa replied. 'Seriously, Jim and I overheard him tell Mrs W it was nothing more than storm in a teacup, or words to that effect, and would blow over and be forgotten within twenty-four hours.'

'Perhaps our plan should be to make sure it doesn't, by which I mean blow over,' Jim suggested.

'The question then is how do we keep it going?'

'I suggested he should call an extraordinary meeting of the Association. It was only intended as a wind-up, but in answer to your question Les, if he did, or more likely if he was forced to, he would have to answer the question the whole village is asking.'

'And what's that?' Audrey asked.

'Is it true,' they all replied in unison.

***

In the hotel Jason and Tony Bean were cossetted in the office, discussing the very question being raised in the Wood's house. Though not whether the accusation was true – they knew it wasn't, and therefore there was no point in even discussing it. 'We have to avoid another damn general meeting,' Jason pleaded. 'I managed to pull it around at the AGM, but it was a close-run thing. I'd rather not go through that again.'

'How about we put up our own poster – positive advertising – there was an article in last month's *Modern Advertising* that put forward a very convincing case for it. You know promoting the benefits of the spring to the village.'

'Much as I agree with promoting the benefits of the spring, it would only draw attention in the current climate to the other posters. Besides which, I have said it will blow over – a five-minute wonder and forgotten in a couple of days.'

'So, why are we meeting like this, your phone call this afternoon made it sound urgent.

'Well, yes. Sorry about that. I may have panicked a bit. Still, maybe it's a clever idea to have a plan, in case we need it.' Their conversation might have continued in a similar vein, helped by an expensive bottle of wine from hotel's wine cellar – the one they kept for those special guests, had the phone not rang to interrupt their discourse. 'Hello,' Jason said picking up the phone, 'Magical Waters Hotel and Restaurant, how can I help.'

The phone was on speaker, allowing Tony to hear both sides of the conversation.

'Ah, Mrs Worthington, good evening.'

'I'm glad I caught you, I was afraid you might be engaged this evening in the restaurant.'

'No, Mrs Worthington, it's a bit quiet tonight and in any case, my dear wife is looking after the few guests dining with us.'

'Oh right. Well, I'll come straight to the point. It's about the posters plastered all over the village. I've been speaking to…'

'As I said to you this morning Mrs Worthington,' Jason said interrupting her. 'all the posters have gone and the whole thing will be forgotten in a couple of days.'

'That's as maybe Jason, but I've been in touch with several members of the Association. In at least two instances, they took the trouble to ring me, and we are concerned about the accusation contained in the posters…'

'I can assure you and your colleagues, Mrs Worthington you need have no fears about the spring. It is as clear and pure as ever.'

'Mr Black will you kindly stop interrupting me. Thank you. We would like a meeting, tomorrow evening, to discuss the situation. And before you tell me again how pure and whatever it was, the spring water is, we're aware this is not the first time an allegation has been made about the spring water.'

'Mrs Worthington, I'm not sure I know what you're referring to.' Jason replied, his brain working overtime.

'What I'm referring to is a survey by Mr White. If you will recall, you made an oblique reference to it at Jack's funeral service. I think we can all agree Jim White is no friend of the Association, but if his survey demonstrated other people have been affected by the spring water, it must, therefore, be a cause for concern.' Fearing she would be drawn into the merits or otherwise of the survey, she quickly added. 'Before you say anymore, we'll be at the hotel at eight o'clock and expect you to be prepared to discuss our concerns.'

'Do you really think that is necessary, Mrs…, but the line was dead.

Jason replaced the receiver and glanced across the room to Tony. 'You heard that. She and other members of the Association are demanding a meeting tomorrow for God's sake. What am I supposed to say to them when all they want to talk about is the posters and that bloody survey by that bastard Jim White? Hell's bells.'

***

At the Wood's house, three bottles of wine later the Philippa decided the discussion was beginning to go around in circles. 'Sorry, guys I must love you and leave you. With Brian away, I had to get a babysitter and I promised Kirsten I'd be home ten minutes ago. Let me know if anything happens, I rely on you to…'

'Keep you satisfied,' Les stood and saluted, only to be pulled back in his seat by Audrey, 'Sit down for goodness sake and stop making a fool of yourself.'

'It no matters Audrey, but I am away. Night guys.' Philippa said sweeping up her bag and heading for the door.

With Philippa gone the room descended into silence, broken by Les pointing a finger at Jim. 'I know what we should do. Make a huge hand out of paper mâche and parade it through the village. Painted bright red, with finger pointing up, as in up yours.'

'You've had too much vino, my friend,' Jim suggested, 'I should be getting home. Bix will be at the front door with his legs crossed waiting to go out.'

'No, listen my dear friend James, my very good friend, have I told you my latest story about many hands,' Les blurted out, still pointing his finger, now was wavering uncontrollably as if having a mind of its own.

Jim sighed but hung back at the door. 'No, but I expect you're going to.'

'Well, Mmm, how's does it begin? Ah, yes. There was an Englishman, Irishman and a… No, that's another story. Whoops. Concentrate Mr Leslie Woods, concentrate Now where was I.'

'For goodness sake, Les, tell the bloody story, or shut up and go to bed.' Audrey said.

'Excuse me, the love of my life, my wife. Right, tell the story, Les, well, my darling here is the story. In this story, there was this group of people. Yes, many people, lots of people and suddenly the lights go out Boom, and the room is plunged into darkness. Black as the ace of… I've forgotten. But then…'

'The leader tells everybody to put their hands up because many hands make light work,' Jim said finishing the story for him.

'Aud, he finished my story, Aud, he finished my story.'

'I think we are done here for tonight,' Audrey suggested. 'I better get his one off to bed before he falls asleep at the table.'

'Sweet dreams then. Night.' Jim waved and swaying slightly made for the street and the chilly night air. Outside, he was beginning to wish he'd worn a coat, and as the wind whipped around his head and shoulders, he felt quite dizzy and realised he'd drunk more wine than he should have. 'Best foot forward,' he muttered to himself and headed home. With his chin, down on his chest and his eyes firmly fixed on the pavement, he missed the first poster attached to the telegraph pole, but he could hardly miss the next, lying on the pavement, having been blown down by the wind whipping along the High Street, signalling the first taste of autumn.

It one was hand-drawn, not as artistic as the others, but the message was clear enough. "Old Applegarth saying: Spring Water Makes Hands Go Red." Checking no-one was watching, he scooped up the poster, quickly folded and stuffed in his trousers pocket. The other posters were likely to disappear once Jason found out, and he wanted a souvenir to share with the others.

Back home, the light on the answering machine told him there was a message awaiting his attention. Pressing the replay button, he was delighted to hear Robin announcing she would be back in Applegarth at the weekend. The crew have completed the filming and were moving into post-production.

Delighted as he was at the thought of Robin's return, he was also painfully aware of his promise to Philippa, to tell Robin the truth about his relationship with Katie.

Chapter Forty-nine

'Katie, stop fussing, they will be here any minute.'

Katie ignored him and continued to move around the table checking the water glasses and drinks were properly positioned.

'Is my tie straight?' Jason asked. 'I should have worn my blue one, the one with the little flower motif.'

'Your tie is fine darling and sit up straight. You don't want them to see you slumped in the chair.'

'I should have never agreed to this meeting. After the second lot of posters, the police should be investigating it. Sheer vandalism. Why isn't PC Smith out there arresting the culprit? Mrs Worthington ought to be insisting Nigel does his job, not setting up a posse to hound me and the beautiful spring water.' He paused and fiddled with his tie for the umpteenth time. 'What am I going to say to them?'

'Calm down Jason, you'll be fine. You've always confounded your critics before, and this will be no different.'

'After all, there's no proof the spring water is contaminated, is there?' Jason jumped up, startled by the sound of the telephone ringing on the side table. Katie moved quickly to pick up the receiver. She listened for a few moments, spoke briefly in the mouthpiece, and replaced the receiver. 'They are here. I told Alison on reception to ask them to wait. Since you are up, I suggest you greet them when they come in and invite them to take a seat around the table. I will offer water or soft drinks, and you should take your place at the head of the table. Remember Jason, a lot depends on you convincing them there's nothing wrong with the spring water. Our business is based on lots of visitors coming to the village and spending their money.'

'Right Katie, I can do this.'

'Good, I'll go and collect them.' With an encouraging nod in Jason's direction, Katie left the room.

In reception, Mrs Worthington and the three other members of the Association were beginning to get anxious. They arrived in time for the meeting and couldn't understand why they were being kept waiting. Mrs Worthington was beginning to hear murmurs from the other members of the group when Katie appeared at her shoulder. 'Mrs Worthington, or may I call you Hazel, welcome to you and your colleagues. We've set aside our conference room, so let's go through and we can complete the introductions.'

Mrs Worthington bristled. 'I'm sorry, Mrs Black this is not some social occasion, we have important business to discuss.'

'Yes, of course, Hazel. Right, here we are, please go through.' Pushing back the door, Katie stood aside to let the group pass.

With the appearance of Mrs Worthington, Jason reached out to greet her. 'Good to see you Hazel, and Jonathan, Adele, and not forgetting Jeff. Welcome, let's make ourselves comfortable.'

'Actually, Mr Black, it's Jeffrey, not Jeff if you don't mind.'

'Yes, of course, my apologies Jeff. Now, if I sit here,' Jason said indicating the chair at the head of the table, you can tell me what's worrying you. I should say before we begin, Katie's set out some drinks and some nibbles, so do help yourself.'

When they were settled, Jason took his seat and threw out a big beaming smile to everyone in the room, it was intended to disarm, but was met with a stony stare. 'Before we begin, could I just say this. Knowing all the wonderful members of the Association - including the four stalwarts sitting around this table - are happy to lend their support to the wonderful work we do in helping the many visitors who come to us with their ailments and serious conditions and seeing their lives transformed by the magical spring waters, is a source of great comfort to me and our loyal, hard-working staff. Without your support, it would be….'

'Excuse me for butting in Mr Black, I've heard that speech, or variations, at every AGM for the last… I don't know how many years. What you have to understand is – if you'll excuse the pun - it no longer washes. Serious allegations have been made about the spring…'

'Mrs Worthington, I aware of the specious and false allegations that have made, but there is no truth in them, trust me.'

Jeffrey decided this was the moment to have his say. 'Until we can clear up this matter, Mr Black. By which I mean at a point where we can reassure local residents and visitors that the spring water is safe and doesn't – and I'm going to say it – leave you with red blotchy hands, then we should close the Pump Room.'

'No, no Jeff that is not the answer. We shouldn't even be thinking about closing the… That will only present our detractors with ammunition. They will say because we have closed the Pump Room, there must be something in the rumours, don't you see?'

'So, what's your answer, Mr Black.' This was Adele, who didn't feel strongly about the whole issue but had been dragged along as part of the delegation by Mrs Worthington. She was prepared to be open-minded, allow Jason to put forward a feasible explanation, but all she'd heard so far was making her feel uneasy. 'Brazen it out, tell the world there's nothing wrong. Is that what you're suggesting?'

'That's not the word I would use Adele. I believe the Pump Room and the spring enjoy a great deal trust within the village and given the number of visitors who come to sample the Magical Waters of Applegarth and come back again and again, tells me they have faith in the purity of the spring water.'

'That still sounds like brazing it out.'

'If you let me finish, what I was going to say, or more accurately suggest, is we invite a few volunteers from the village.' He paused as an idea circled around his head. 'No, let's ask a hundred people from the village to sign up to test the spring waters for themselves. We publicise scheme throughout the village and wait, wait, we'll hold it this Saturday and close the Pump Room to visitors. I'll have let the coach companies know. What do you think Mrs Worthington?'

Mrs Worthington glanced around the room, hoping for some guidance from the others. 'If I understand it correctly, your idea Mr Black is that if a hundred villagers test the spring waters and if none of them suffer any after ill effects, then the spring water must be safe.'

'Exactly, Mrs Henderson and I am confident the spring water will come through with flying colours.' Looking around the room and getting nods of approval, he added, 'That concludes our meeting, I think you will agree?'

Mrs Worthington and the rest of her group trouped out, and when they were gone, Jason looked up at Katie, 'I think I pulled that off, don't you?'

'You're taking a huge risk, Jason, I just hope you are right.'

'About the spring? 'Of course, I am just you wait and see.'

Away from the reception desk and hearing of the hotel staff, the group gathered around Mrs Worthington. 'He's done it again,' Jonathan suggested, getting in before anyone else could speak. 'We arrive expecting to confront him and pulls that rabbit out of the hat.'

'It's a high-risk strategy. If he pulls it off, he's home and dry. If not, the impact on the village doesn't bear thinking about.'

'You are right Jeffrey. I suggest we spread the word amongst the members of the Association and encourage them to sign up for the testing.

***

By noon the following day, the High Street was once again festooned with posters. Unlike the previous day, these advertised an "A Grand Testing by the 100". Underneath the headline, a hundred villagers were invited to register as volunteers to test the purity of the spring water on the following Saturday. There was no mention of why it had become necessary, but it didn't need to, most of the villagers knew perfectly why, and those that didn't were quickly put in the picture.

Audrey caught sight of the posters on her way home from the library. She rang Les to tell him and then called Jim. Their reaction was the same when she called Philippa's. This is it; this is what will bring Jason Black down. Amongst the hundred testers, there was bound to be a dozen or more who develop red, blotchy hands. When they displayed their infected hands around the village, the spring will be exposed for the fraud it always was, Jason will be disgraced and driven from the village for good.

In the Pump Room, Jason was in engaged in conversation with Brenda. 'Remember, when you sign up the volunteers, preference must be given to members of the Association. We need names, addresses and a contact number. Perhaps you could draw up a little form.'

'This is on Saturday? And there's going to be a hundred?'

'Yes, Saturday. By then this place should be clean from top to bottom, we can't take any chances that some speck of dirt causes any of the testers to finish-up with... Well, we can't, can we?'

'No, Mr Black, your right, we can't.' Brenda hummed.

Chapter Fifty

In the Cosy Café and Snackbar, Brian and Sheila were working in the kitchen preparing the cakes, scones, and fancies in anticipation of the rush later that morning. 'I was thinking this testing thing on Saturday and whether we should sign up for it? I mean we depend on the Pump Room for our business don't we.'

'I don't know Sheila. If the spring water is bad as they are saying, we don't want to catch anything, do we? It won't look good if we've got red hands, will it?'

'Do you think the water is safe? Here take these through to the counter.' Sheila said, handing him a plate of scones.

'Oh right. I'm sure it is. Well, put this way, if Jason says it is, then I for one are prepared to believe him. I'll just take these through.'

Jim and Philippa were occupying a table at the back of the cafe. 'The first I knew about it was when Audrey rang. I was struggling to get Bix into the bath - he hates it - when the phone rang. Then I had to juggle Bix in one hand and the receiver in the other. I was so shocked, I loosen my grip on Bix, who shot out of my arms and disappeared into the garden.'

'What brought it about, do we know?'

'According to the gossip in the village, Jason had no choice. A delegation led by Mrs Worthington demanded answers and Jason pulled the testing thing out of the bag. That's according to Jeffrey Tidy, who insisted on broadcasting this titbit onto anyone who was prepared to listen, as he stood outside the Pump Room this morning.'

'They are giving preference to members of the Association, apparently. I've already had a phone call from – I think it was Mrs Worthington – urging me to sign up.'

'Here's someone we can ask.' Approaching their table Brian was ready with pen and pad to take their order. 'Hot chocolate for Philippa and a coffee for me please.' Jim waited a moment while Brian made a note of their order and leant back in his chair. 'So, Brian you going to be one of the hundred then.'

Brian slumped into a vacant chair. 'Funny you should ask because me and Sheila was just talking about it. We're not sure. I mean, you can't risk getting it, can you?'

'Scared of getting red blotchy hands, are you Brian?'

'Yes, no. Look, if Jason says the water is safe that should be good enough for anyone.'

With Philippa looking on, Jim was determined to enjoy the moment. 'If the water is safe Brian, why is Jason asking a hundred people to test it, doesn't make sense?'

Sheila appeared from the kitchen with a plate of pear and chocolate muffins. Seeing her husband engaged in conversation with Jim and Philippa, she moved closer and didn't like what she was hearing. 'Brian don't answer, he's just trying to wind you up.'

'What about you Sheila, you going to be one of the hundred?'

'No, I'm not. Just serve them what they've ordered Brian and then help me in the kitchen, we've still got a lot to do.' Turning to Jim, she added, 'We all know your views on the spring, and I'd appreciated if you didn't come in her stirring up trouble and goading my husband.'

The Thorpe's disappeared into the kitchen, leaving Jim and Philippa smiling at their small victory. 'That was fun,' Jim said.

'Let's hope the entertainment continues on Saturday. Now, Jim, you said Robin would be back in the village on Saturday. In all the excitement about the spring water, remember you have to tell her about...'

'Me and Katie, Yes, Philippa, I haven't forgotten.'

Chapter Fifty-one

Jim spent the day, preparing and cooking dinner. It was to be a special occasion, Robin was coming home, and he wanted to welcome her with a really delicious meal. He planned a romantic dinner, with soft jazz playing in the background, all done to create the right atmosphere.

There was cause for celebration, of course. The anticipated exposure of the Pump Room and all its works on Saturday was reason enough to raise a glass. A victory over Jason Black was bound to be an important feature of the meal, but there was another more pressing purpose. The tricky subject of Katie had to be raised and dealt with. Getting the timing right was essential when they were both relaxed and the wine and music had worked their magic.

He was still busy in the kitchen when he heard the front door shut with a firm clunk, and Bix scampering down the hallway to greet the new arrival. 'Hi, Jim, it's only me,' Robin called dumping her bag at the bottom of the stairs and heading for the kitchen with Bix following excited behind. 'Something smells good, what are you cooking?'

Jim turned away from the stove. 'Hi, I wasn't expecting you for a couple of hours.' Robin ignored the implied question and came over and kissed him. 'I made better time than I thought. The traffic was light. Anyway, I wanted to get home to my two lovely, gorgeous men,' she purred, giving Bix a hug.

'To celebrate your return, I'm cooking a special meal. It's all been happening while you were away. We, my darling, have cause to rejoice and give thanks.'

'What's happened. Tell me.'

'While I finish preparing dinner, why don't you freshen up. When you come down, I'll have a nice glass of bubble ready and I tell you all about it.'

Robin started to protest, but faced with the stern look from Jim, she relented in and headed for the bathroom.

When Robin returned half-an-hour later bathed and wearing the blue dress she knew Jim liked, she was led into the dining room. 'I must go away more often if this is what greets my return,' she muttered to herself, surveying perfectly laid out table.

'Here,' Jim said, handing her a glass of champagne. 'Welcome home. Cheers.' They clinked glasses and kissed. 'You smell nice,' Jim said as they sipped their wine. 'Have a seat, while I bring in the starter. Just a simple salad, but I hope you like it?'

Robin surveyed the immaculately arranged table: the napkins folded into shells, the cutlery for each course perfectly aligned, the glasses set in exactly the correct position, the polished wood table mats, the flowers beautifully-arranged in the middle of the table, and the soft jazz burbling away in the background. 'Has Jim gone to all this trouble to celebrate some village event?' she wondered.

'Here we are, a tomato, avocado and gorgonzola salad, hope you like it?' Jim said appearing from the kitchen and placing a plate in front of her.

'Looks delicious, you have been busy today. All this to celebrate…?

'Let me pour the wine, a cheeky little number, I think you'll agree.' Jim poured the wine and raising his glass in a toast, added, 'To us.'

Robin joined in the toast. 'You still haven't answered my question?'

Jim put a fork full of the salad into his mouth. 'What question, my love.'

Robin demanded an answer. 'What exactly are we celebrating? You've gone to a lot of trouble with this meal, so it must be something important.'

'The demise of the Pump Room and the exposure of Mr Jason Black, no less.'

'How so?' she asked, forking up the salad.

As they continued eating, Jim narrated the events of the week and Jason's decision to ask a hundred volunteers to test the spring water. 'He's obviously relying on none of them being infected.'

'A bit of a risk, I would have thought.' Robin replied, recalling her own experience at the hands of the spring water.

'Exactly. He may be able to brush it aside if a visitor finishes up with red blotchy hands, but he won't be able to if it's someone local. The evidence's will be there for the whole village to see, and Jason will be exposed for the liar and cheat he is.'

Their conversation continued amiably through the main course of beef medallion, and another bottle of wine. Jim speculated on the likely outcome of the testing of the spring water and how Jason would try to wiggle out of it if any of the tester's hands became infected. In turn, Robin recounted her time spent with the film crew and how different new camera/lighting guy was compared to Toby.

After clearing away the plates and serving dish for the main course, Jim was in the kitchen putting together the desert, a raspberry pavlova. The meal had gone very well, and Robin seemed to be in a good mood, happy and relaxed. Was this the moment to confess his affair with Katie? he wondered. Would she forgive and forget that he'd lied to her? 'Right, better get it over with then,' he murmured, picking up the dessert plates and heading for the dining room.

'Here you are, my darling. A little pavlova to finish with. I have some dessert wine if you wish?'

'No, I'm fine thanks. A glass of water would be nice.' Jim returned a few moments later with the water. 'Here,' he said placing the glass on the table.

Robin picked up her spoon but hesitated. 'You okay Jim, you've been on edge all evening. Is something bothering you? Has something happened while I've been away?'

Jim plunged his spoon into the pavlova and was on the point of swallowing a generous portion of the desert. 'No, nothing's happened, but I do have a confession to make.'

'Don't tell me. You didn't cook this lovely meal; it came from the supermarket and all you did was take it out the packet.'

'Actual, I made everything from scratch.' Jim finished swallowing the pavlova and loaded another spoonful. 'What I have to say is more serious than that, I'm afraid.'

Robin stopped eating and put down her spoon. 'Now, I really am worried.'

'Robin, my dear, you know I love you dearly and would never do anything to hurt you or jeopardize our relationship. You have to believe that. What I have to say grieves me. I sincerely regret what I have done and can't believe I could have been so stupid. All I can do is hope you will find a way to forgive me. That somehow our love will be strong enough to overcome this indiscretion. That we can put it behind us and move on. If you do forgive me, I promise I will never, never do anything like it again.'

'That's a beautiful speech, but I'm not sure what I'm supposed to be forgiving you for.'

Jim leant across the table and took her hand in his. He opened his mouth to speak, but nothing came out. 'Jim, just tell me. Oh, my God. Are the police involved, is that what you're trying to say?'

Jim finally managed to speak. 'No, my love, nothing like that.' He took both her hands in his. 'You recall our conversation about Mrs Black?'

Robin stiffened. 'Yes, what about her?'

'I might not have been entirely honest with you. It might have gone further than I admitted.'

Robin was beginning to understand where this was going and why Jim was reluctant to talk about it. 'You mean you didn't just meet to discuss the Dancing Couple?' she asked pulling her hands free.

Jim hesitated for a moment. 'No, we didn't.'

Robin stared at him; part of her brain was urging her to close this conversation down. Change the subject, talk about something else, because she didn't want to hear the answer to the next question, but she had to know, even though it would hurt. 'So, what exactly was the nature of your relationship?'

'We had an affair.' At that moment, the look on Robin's face changed. Anxious, understanding, sympathetic, became steely-hard, displaying no emotion 'You're now telling me you had a full-blown affair with the wife of your sworn enemy. Did you have her here in this cottage, upstairs in the bed we've shared? Did you?'

'No never, Bix didn't like her. He took a huge dislike to her.'

'So, you would have done, but for Bix.'

'Yes, no. It was over before we got together. Long before. It meant nothing; I promise you. You must believe me, Robin. You're the only one I love.'

Robin stood up. 'I'm shocked, stunned, not sure what to say.

'Sit down, please Robin. Let's just talk, see how we can find a way forward.'

'You were very careful to say this affair was over by the time we got together. Does that mean it was still going on when we first met?' Not receiving an answer, she took that to mean it was. 'What about the Benefactor's dinner?' Jim's gave a brief nod of the head.

'Robin, it doesn't have to be like this. All you really need to know is I love you and want to spend the rest of my life with you. Surely, nothing else matters.'

'Yes, it does. I don't believe it. While I'm wrestling with my feelings, unsure whether to tell you how I felt, and yet all the time you were screwing that woman. How could you be so - excuse my language - so bloody heartless? I'm sorry Jim, I can't forgive you. You've humiliated me, and I can never forgive you.' Jim started to speak, but she cut him off. 'My bag's still packed upstairs. Don't try to contact me, because we're finished. Goodbye.'

Jim sat staring into the space Robin occupied until a few minutes ago. His hands dropped to his side and he felt his finger being licked by Bix, who had wandered in from the kitchen. He turned and look down at his friend. 'She's gone Bix, and I don't know what I'm going to do.

Chapter Fifty-two

Early on Saturday morning, the queue of volunteers stretched all the way up to the High Street. At the entrance to the Pump Room, Janet was checking the names off the list and marshalling them into groups of ten.

As each group entered Jason carefully observed each member, paying particular attention to their hands. Anyone displaying discoloured fingers and palms was rejected.

Ignoring Jason's presence, the three women went about guiding the volunteers through the visitor experience. Jason had insisted there was to be no variation, it had to be exactly the same as when the spring first opened. 'How many is that?' he asked as the latest group moved through to the gift shop and the exit.

'Forty,' Brenda replied. 'Did we get the hundred volunteers?'

'Could have had been hundred and fifty. The Association members have rallied around and supported us. They know the spring water is clear and pure, and happy to help us prove it'

'There's a lot of local businesses who depend on us to bring in the visitors.'

'Exactly, and after today all the doubters will be silenced. Look sharp, here's your next group.' Jason resumed his position against the back wall. Amongst the next group, he noticed several familiar faces, including Mrs Worthington. Offering a brief nod in acknowledgement, his gaze continued down the line. A quick mental calculation suggested there were only nine. Where was the tenth volunteer in this group? Had Janet miscounted? Ah, there she is. 'Philippa, what you doing here?' he asked, surprised to see her amongst the volunteers, and concerned about her appearance as one of the testers.

Philippa looked around to see where the voice was coming from. 'Jason, hello,' she replied, seeing him leaning against the back wall. 'I signed up for this – what's the word – little PR exercise as an interested, but impartial observer. To ensure fair play. You can't object that can you.'

'Unlike some of your companions, we always play fair. We have no need to be anything other than upfront and honest. This test by the locals will shut the cynics and disbelievers up and prove finally that our magical spring water is clear and pure.'

Philippa smiled. 'Let's wait to see how it turns out before we start crowing from the rooftops, shall we?'

'Have a good day, Philippa.' Jason replied, cheerfully as the group headed for the gift shop. 'Halfway, Brenda,' he called out as the next group began to file in.

***

'You've reached the number of Robin Caulfield; she is unable to take your call at this time. Please leave a message after the tone.' After a loud bleep, Jim took a deep breath. 'Robin, darling it's me again. We can't leave like that. I love you and will do anything to make it up to you. Please, please call.'

He had made numerous calls to her mobile since she walked out, but they all went straight through to her voicemail. There was one occasion when it rang and rang, and he was hopeful she would answer his call, but the line went dead. She recognised the caller and cut him off. He tried ringing the Stein Foundation, but it being the weekend, there was nobody there to take his call.

Jim slumped back on the sofa and pulled Bix onto his lap and began gently stroking his head. He hadn't slept a wink last night and could only manage a lukewarm cup of coffee at breakfast. He was at his wit's end as to what to do.

He might have stayed in that stupefied position for hours, had the phone not rung and jolted him back to reality. Hoping it was Robin, he rushed to pick it up. 'Thank goodness you've rung my darling, I've been so...'

'Jim, it's Philippa. What's happened?'

Realising he'd spoken out of turn; he took a deep breath. 'Hi, Philippa. Sorry, I was expecting a call from Robin. What do you want?' The last four words came out sharply and were intended to get her off the line.

'Jim, what's wrong?'

'Nothing. What do you want?'

Try another tack, she said, 'I was ringing to tell you I was one of the testers. At the Pump Room. You know, one of Jason's hundred.'

'Why did you do that?'

'To check on how it was being done. Make sure there were no tricks involved. You know Jason. Has something happened between you and Robin?'

There was a long pause before he replied. 'She's gone. Left yesterday.'

'Why, what happened?'

Another long pause. 'I confessed to my relationship with Katie. I said I was sorry, that I loved her. I pleaded with her to forgive me.'

'But she wouldn't and walked out.'

'I've rung her half-a-dozen times or more, but she won't take my calls.'

'I'm sorry Jim, I don't know what to say. I pushed you into this and assumed it would clear the air, not that it would end like this.'

'Neither did I, Philippa. Neither did I.'

***

On the following day with the village bathed in warm sunshine, and with the businesses expecting a busy day, even though the Pump Room remained closed. Jason's plea for the spring to remain open was overruled by the committee, led by the Rev Alan Howard. 'At this time of turmoil in the Pump Room, I urge all – particularly on the Lord's Day – to pause and let nature take its course. Today in church, I will be leading prayers for all those poor souls who were forced to take part in this ill-conceived ordeal, and pray, with God's help, they come through it unharmed.'

In the Dog and Duck, a few of regulars –after a downing, several pints of the best bitter served up by the landlord, Ted – declared in more salty language 'that Rev. will be on his knees Sunday praying no bugger gets blotchy red hands.' With hilarious laughter and much waving of hands in the air, with cries of 'Piggy pink, piggy pink.' The same irrelevant attitude prevailed amongst the villagers as friends and neighbours waved their pink hands in the air at every passer-by, 'Piggy pink, piggy pink,' they sang.

Inevitable. it fell to a few younger members to make light of the situation by smothering their hands in red paint and parading their trophies around the village. Faced with this onslaught, the locals fled in panic. Fearing the disease - because surely that's what it was – could be contracted by being in the presence of the victim, they reeled away, covering their mouths and noses so as it to inhale the same breath. Whereupon the perpetrator called out, 'got yer,' and with a merry laugh moved onto the next victim.

In his office, Jason faced the day with mixed emotions. The testing of the spring water by the hundred volunteers had gone without a hitch and he was confident the spring would be cleared of any accusation of causing harm. But the Pump Room was closed, much to his dismay, and the taking at the hotel and restaurant would inevitably suffer as a result.

In Wood's household, the mood swung from exhilaration to depression and back again. Jason's decision to allow an official testing of the spring water, was, in the words of Les as he punched the air, 'a spectacular own goal.' There was no way he'd be able to wriggle out of this one if any of the testers developed an infection in their hands.

Their exhilaration at the prospect of bringing Jason Black down, quickly turned to gloom and depression, at the prospect of the tests being inconclusive.

'It's a bit weird Aud, I mean, here we are wanting several of our neighbours get infected by the spring water, so we can bring Jason Black down.'

'I know what you mean. Part of you hopes nobody gets infected, and yet there's another part that prays they do.'

'All we can do is wait and see.' He paused as another thought struck him. 'I meant to ask earlier, is Jim coming to lunch?'

'It's my turn to cook, so I'd better get cracking.' Audrey moved to the kitchen and paused in the doorway. 'You haven't spoken to him, have you? When I phoned to remind him, it was our turn to do lunch, he sounded really down, quite short with me, hope there's nothing wrong.'

Lunch at the Wood's house was a destined to be more dramatic affair than they could have anticipated. Not that any confession from Jim would have disturbed the visitors and locals occupying the High Street and enjoying the afternoon sunshine. The earlier pranks had ceased, as most people got tired of the jokes about red hands. It might have been funny the first time, maybe even humorous third and fourth time, but not anymore. By late afternoon the village had settled into its normal semi-sedentary mood, looking forward to a delicious cream tea and the prospect of a quiet evening in front of the telly.

By the time the sunset over the distant hills, none of the testers were showing signs of developing red, blotchy hands, though all of the hundred spent most of that Sunday examining their hands at regular intervals for any tell-tale signs.

Chapter Fifty-three

Still, in his PJs and with nothing on his feet, Jim stumbled down the stairs, 'I'm coming, I'm coming,' he called out to the phone ringing incessantly in the hallway. At the bottom of the stairs, Bix ran around in circles and barked.

He had been woken from his slumbers by the phone, and with the fog of sleep still filling his head, he missed the third step, caught off balance, he tumbled down the remaining stairs, landing heavily on his back. With the breath knocked out of him, he was hardly in a position to get up, never mind answer the phone.

Struggling to his feet and with his chest heaving, the phone switched to answerphone and the caller was instructed to leave a message. A loud beep and Philippa's voice burst from the machine. 'Jim, help. My hands have turned red, with dark blotches on my fingers and palms. It's horrible. I'm not sure what to do? Give me a ring please when you pick-up this message.'

Jim stood staring at the phone, struggling to take in the implications of Philippa's message. He knew her number by heart, and his call was picked up immediately. 'You got my message. Sorry, to have called so early on Monday morning.'

'Let me get this straight. You were one of the testers and your hands have been infected with whatever it is that causes the spring water to give people red blotchy hands, right?'

'Yes, but who is going to believe it's not fixed. Everybody in the village knows my views about Jason and the whole Pump Room thing.'

By now Jim was fully awake.

'They might not believe you, but you still have to let Jason see your hands. Let's meet at the Pump Room and confront him.'

'Okay, I can be there in half-an-hour, no make it three-quarters.'

That suited Jim, who still needed to get dressed and down some breakfast.

When he arrived at the High Street the path leading to the Pump Room, a dozen or so men and women were queuing up at the entrance, animatedly displaying their hands to each other – their bright red hands. Jim recognised several of them, including of all people, Mrs Worthington, who was at the head of the queue and hammering on the door.

'What's going on?' Philippa asked, appearing at his side.

'The blotchy-hand brigade is demanding entry to the citadel, and I imagine the head of Mr Jason Black. Let's join them and enjoy the entertainment.' As they reached the back of the queue, the door opened and needing no invitation, the crowd surged forward. By the time, Jim and Philippa were inside, the crowd were shouting in unison, 'GET JASON BLACK DOWN HERE, NOW.'

Brenda arrived that morning to check on the supplies and ensure they were ready when the Pump Room re-opened to visitors. Faced with the chanting crows, she had no answer to their demands. One of the loudest voices in the crowd began chanting, 'WHAT DO WE WANT,' 'JASON BLACK DOWN HERE' the crowd responded in unison. 'WHEN DO WE WANT IT?' 'NOW, NOW, they replied.

This was too much for Brenda. 'Okay, she called out, 'I'll ring Mr Black and ask him to come and meet you, but he won't be happy.' Not waiting for an answer, she fought her way through the throng to the pay booth. Firmly shutting the door, so no one could disturb her, she reached for the phone and dialled Jason's office number.

It rang four times before Jason answered. 'Magical Waters Hotel and Restaurant, how can I help you?'

'Mr Black, you need to get down here. There's a crowd of people. They burst in. They are demanding you to meet them.'

'Hang on, is that Brenda?' Getting confirmation, he continued. 'Who are these people? You told them the Pump Room is closed. What the hell is that noise in the background?'

'It's all the people shouting and waving their hands in the air. Their red, blotchy hands, Mr Black. I really do think you should come, otherwise, they'll wreck the place.'

Jason had no intention of facing an angry crowd, demanding his blood. 'I'm a bit tied up at the moment and can't possibly leave the hotel. Look, here's what you do. Take their details and tell them we will look into their complaint and get back in a couple of days.'

'Sorry, Mr Black. They are getting pretty ugly. I'm scared at what they might do, I've locked myself in the...'

Her plea was shattered by Mrs Worthington banging on the glass. 'If that's Mr Black on the phone, let me speak to him.' Not waiting for an answer, she burst in and snatched the phone from Brenda's hand. 'Jason, this is Hazel Worthington here. There are a group of very angry people in the Pump Room. I urge you to come and explain why they have developed red blotchy hands after taking part in your testing of the spring water. If you don't, there won't be much of this place left by the time they finish with it.'

'Mrs Worthington, I'm suspect there's a simple explanation for this outbreak of...bad hands. Look, here's what you should do. Keep it simple but tell them the spring water is clean and pure, and if for some reason they have contracted some sort of infection, they should look elsewhere for an explanation. Would you do that please.'

'No, Jason I won't, because I'm one of them, and I too would like an explanation. So, are you coming or not?'

There was silence on the line as Mrs Worthington waited for an answer. After several moments, Jason replied. 'Put Brenda back on the line, please.'

'Here, he wants to speak to you.' Mrs Worthington said, handing over the phone.

Brenda put the phone to her ear and listened as Jason issued his instructions. 'Brenda, there are two things I want you to do: first check everybody is on the master list of volunteers. Okay. When you've done that, tell them I will be along shortly to reassure them that there is nothing to worry about as far as the spring water is concerned. Is that clear?'

The next few minutes were a bit chaotic, as Brenda attempted to move amongst the crowd, checking the names on her list. She was halfway through the list when Jason appeared. Immediately, the crowd surged forward him, thrusting their hands in his face.

'Please give me some space. I can only listen to your concerns and give you the reassurance if you allow me to address everyone.' The crowd reluctantly moved back, out of the corner of his eye; Jason spotted Jim over by the fountain. Pushing his way through the crowd, he confronted him. 'What you doing here? Come to gloat have you.'

'Actually, I'm here to support Philippa, whose hands have been infected along with all these other volunteers. Like me, she is looking forward to hearing your explanation for this disaster.'

'You're enjoying this, well stick around I'll have this lot eating out of the palm of my hand in no time, you'll see.' Jason moved to the front of the fountain and held his arms as he wanted to speak. 'Ladies and gentlemen, if I may have your attention for a moment, please.' There were cries of 'What about these,' as the crowd waved of hands in the air.

'I can see you are angry and upset, and you have every right to be. I haven't studied your hands, but I can see they have been infected and causing a lot of discomfort.'

'So, what you going to do about it?' a voice in the crowd shouted out.

'Simple sir. You are members of the Association – honest and loyal members – and entitled to the full support of the Association. Clearly, there is a need for a full and thorough investigation into how this happened and who was responsible. Let no stone be unturned in the search for the culprit. I am prepared to donate one hundred pounds out of my own pocket to the fighting fund, now who will join me? How about you sir?'

Jim turned to Philippa. 'He's trying to brazen it out, just like every other time.'

'What about the spring water,' another voice in the crowd shouted.

'The spring waters. The waters that have brought an end to the suffering of thousands of visitors, who came to the Magical Waters of Applegarth seeking relief from the misery of their ailments and illnesses. Let me tell you about the spring water, which is as clean and pure as it's always been and always will.

'Are you saying the spring water isn't responsible for this?' A woman at the front of the crowd held her hands high in this air.

I'm saying the clean and pure Magical Waters of Applegarth are not responsible and we should look elsewhere for the cause. I have already offered one hundred pounds of my own money towards the fighting fund. If this investigation is to identify the culprit, we need to get it underway as soon as possible. What do you say?'

This was too much for a burly fellow at the back, who shouldered his way to the front and took up a position alongside Jason at the fountain. 'I say that won't do. We all took part in the testing of the spring water in good faith, and now look at the result.' Turning to address Jason, he continued. 'We have the greatest respect for all you have done for the Association and the village, but we don't need to look for the culprit because it's right here in this room and coming out of this fountain.'

Cries of 'Hear, hear,' and a loud round of applause greeted this suggestion.

'Len, may I call you that. That was a fine speech, but you will excuse me if I point out the testing took place on Saturday, and today is Monday. If - and it is a big if - the spring water was responsible, surely the infection would have flared up with a couple of hours at most, not two whole days later. No, I'm sorry the cause is to be found elsewhere, and we need to put all our energies into investigating other probable causes. I urge you not to jump to the conclusion and try to put the blame on the spring water when there are clearly other reasons for this unfortunate outbreak of... red... hands.'

Jason's abrupt dismissal was greeted with groans and loud cries of, 'It's the spring water, it's the spring water.'

Mrs Worthington stepped forward and joined the two men at the fountain. She held up her hand to ask the crowd to be quiet. 'I'm afraid Mr Black we're not prepared to accept your dismissal of the spring water as the cause. It is too much of a coincidence that all the people in this room took part in the test on Saturday and now have infected hands, you must see that' This was greeted with loud applause, and when it had died down, Mrs Worthington continued. 'I propose that the Pump Room remains closed until a thorough inspection and testing of the water has been made by the appropriate authorities. In the meantime, everybody infected should be compensated for any treatment they may require and any loss they have incurred.'

'Here, here,' came the response from a voice at the back, accompanied by thunderous applause.

Jason stepped forward. 'I'm sorry ladies and gentlemen this is not a properly constituted meeting and therefore cannot make decisions binding on the Association.'

'In which case,' the burly man standing next to him said, 'we'll stay put until we get what we want. And, since we'll be occupying this place, you won't be able to open it, will you?'

The cry began in one small section but quickly spread to the whole group. 'We shall not, we shall not be moved,' they chanted. Waving his fist, Jason elbowed his way through the throng of people. 'You'll get nothing, you do hear, nothing,' he shouted defiantly before disappearing.

Philippa nudged Jim. 'I'd liked to stay and support the protest, but I'd better pop into the chemist and see what they've got,' she said waving her hands in the air.

'Robin got some cream, that seemed to help.'

With Jason gone, some of the group started to move towards the exit realising there was nothing to be gained by staying, but a small, hardcore were determined to sit it out and squatted on the floor around the fountain. They were defiant and prepared to occupy the Pump Room until Jason apologised and offered them compensation, no matter how long it took.

Jim joined Philippa as they shuffled behind the people leaving. 'Will they stick it out?' he asked.

Philippa glanced back. 'They look pretty determined.'

'I'll go tell Audrey the good news, she's usually at the library on a Monday.'

'Let me know if there are any developments. I'm off to the chemist. Bye Jim.'

By mid-afternoon, a reporter and photographer from the *Honiston Observer* had arrived on the scene. Brenda made a brief show of barring them entering the Pump Room, but she was brushed aside. Very soon several pictures of the sit-in were safely stored in the photographer's camera, as the squatters waved their blotchy hands in the air. Moments later the reporter joined the squatters on the ground and began scribbling down their horror stories in his notebook. This was a big story and would be the lead on the front page of this week's paper.

In the library, Audrey was behind the counter stamping a pile of books and handing them over two elderly ladies. When she was free, Jim approached her. 'What brings you into our little cultural haven this morning,' she asked.

'Apart from the pleasure of seeing and conversing with you dear Audrey, I thought you might be interested in joining the protest after you've finished work today.'

'What protest would that be?' she enquired. 'The jungle drums, or more accurately, the two old ladies you saw taking out books, told me something was happening at the Pump Room. What can you tell me?'

Jim related how Philippa hands had developed an infection and how they were joined by a crowd of testers with the same condition. Her eyes lit up when Jim got to the part of Jason's intervention and the decision of the crowd to stage a sit-in. 'Will it last?' she asked when Jim had finished. 'They seem pretty determined to sit it out. The question is, what will Jason do next?'

The answer would come in the form of a complete surprise to Jim and the rest of the village.

Chapter Fifty-four

By the following day, the sit-in was firmly established, with family and friends laying in blankets and pillows, along with food and wine – this was not to be a protest lacking in the essential creature comforts of life. Outside the Pump Room, banners spelt out in big bold letters, "Justice for the Scarred Eleven", fluttered in the breeze.

Jason made a return visit to the Pump Room on the second day in an attempt to persuade the protesters of the futility of their demands. Only to be told their sit-in would continue until he apologised and offered them compensation. Shaking his head in despair at their refusal to accept the inevitable, he retreated to the hotel.

Supporters of the sit-in were milling around when Jim approached the Pump Room, the following day. Taking a two-pound coin from his pocket, he happily tossed it into the nearest bucket, raised his arm high in the air and shouted, 'Justice for the Scarred Eleven.'

He was on his way to the Magical Waters Restaurant and Hotel after receiving a mysterious call from Jason that morning. He had just returned from walking Bix in the park when the phone rang. Hoping it was Robin, he was surprised to hear a male voice say. 'Good morning Jim, it's Jason here.'

'Oh, it's you. What do you want?'

Jason ignored the hostile tone in his voice. 'I wondered whether it would be convenient for you to drop by the hotel sometime today. There's something Katie and I would like to discuss with you. We've had our differences in the past. I'd be the first to admit it, but we both wanted what was best for the village. At this challenging time, we need to find a way forward that works for everybody. What do you say?'

'I'm not sure there's anything we have to say to each other, is there?'

Jason had anticipated a refusal and was prepared. 'If I said it involved the statue in the Memorial Park, would that be enough to change your mind?'

At the hotel reception desk, he was directed to the terrace, where Mr and Mrs Black were waiting to receive him. They had taken a table in a quiet corner - tucked discreetly away from the hotel guests enjoying their morning coffee in the warm autumn sunshine.

Spying Jim arriving on the terrace, they stood and waved, Katie came forward and gave him a quick peck on the check. 'Nice to see you, Jim, again, and thanks for coming. We're over here,' she said leading the way. Jason held out his hand, as Jim approached and insisted on giving his hand a firm shake. 'Have a seat Jim, can we get you anything. Tea, coffee or something a bit stronger perhaps.'

'I'm fine thanks,' Jim replied taking the seat opposite. A pot of coffee sat on the table and Jason made a point of pouring a cup and holding it to his lips. He used the time to gather his thoughts, knowing the next few minutes could decide the whole future of the hotel and the village.

Placing his cup carefully on the table, he looked Jim in the eye. 'Since Katie and I invited you here today, I guess it is incumbent upon us to spell out what we had in mind.' Jim held back from answering, offering only a brief nod of the head.

'The events of the last few days have been unfortunate. The action taken by a few misguided individuals has not been good for the local businesses or indeed the village.'

'If you've invited me here to deliver a lecture on the protest at the Pump Room, thinking I might have some influence over them, you sadly mistaken.'

'No, Jim. It's not like that,' Katie interjected. 'Please, hear us out before you rush to judge.'

'Okay, so why don't you tell me what this is really about. You mentioned something about the Dancing Couple.'

'It plays a part yes. But, first let me paint you a picture of how I see the situation before us, by which I mean the whole village - the people and the businesses. You might not agree – indeed you and your friends have made it perfectly clear you don't – that the spring and all its associations have been good for the village. Bringing jobs and prosperity to the whole village.' Seeing Jim was on the point of raising another objection, he held up his hand. 'I know this is difficult but bear with me. All will become clear if you let me finish.'

'As I said, the spring has been good for the village, but – and it is a big but – it is now tainted, perhaps permanently.'

Katie unable to contain herself burst in. 'The publicity generated by the protest can't be contained within the village or even the county. It will be picked up by the nationals and all the television news channels. In the last twenty-four hour's we've had a call asking for comment from the *Bristol Evening Post*. Naturally, we refused to respond, but it won't end there. Very soon the nationals will be onto it and before you know it film crews will be cluttering up the village. The publicity will be very damaging.'

'If only they had listened to me.' Jason interjected. 'This whole thing could have been avoided. We could have found a way through it. Kept the spring going. Done a few things just to show willing. I don't know, maybe cleaned the pipes or something. It would have been okay.'

This was too much for Jim. 'You're forgetting nearly two dozen of your volunteer testers got infected, clearing out a few pipes won't cure the problem, it goes far deeper than that.'

'Okay let's not get into an argument about any supposed deficiency in the pipes. There are far more important things to discuss.' Jason took a moment to take a slurp of coffee while weighing upon the best way to present his proposal. 'We had a film crew here recently – and before you say it, I accept we didn't part on the best of terms. The film they were making was about, what was his name?'

'Isaac Stein, Jason, the man who carved the statue in the Memorial Park.'

'Yes, Jim thank you for reminding me. I believe the film is due to be shown on television very shortly.'

'To celebrate the anniversary of his birth, one-hundred years ago.'

'Again, thank you for that piece of information.' He paused and choosing his words carefully. 'I'm suggesting that we commemorate the occasion here in the village, where the great man was born and spent his formative

'What do you say?'

'What *did* you say?'

I nearly fell off my seat,' Jim replied later in the day when Audrey, Les and Philippa were gathered at his cottage to consider Jason's proposal.

Philippa leant forward in her seat. So, Jim what exactly is the deal Jason's offering?'

'I'm not sure I can believe it, given what a lying, devious bastard he has been in the past, but he says we should celebrate the hundredth anniversary of the birth of Isaac.'

'You mean the village?'

'Yes, and he wants us to take the lead in organising it. But wait, there's more. He says the Pump Room will be closed, and those infected will be offered compensation. After the events of last weekend – those are his words, not mine – it's tainted and will be boycotted by all the tours companies and can never be a major attraction again. Hang on, I can see you're all dying to come in, but I've left the best bit until last.'

'Well, go on, don't keep us in suspense,' they cried in unison.

'The hotel will be closed for a couple of weeks and re-open as the Dancing Couple Hotel and Restaurant.'

This announcement took a moment to sink in. Les was the first to speak. 'I don't believe it. Jason never does anything without a motive, and you can bet your life this is all about looking after number one.'

'You're right to be cynical about his motives, but it's nothing more than a rat jumping a sinking ship. He knows with a couple of dozen of the testers getting their hands infected by the spring water, the whole Pump Room operation is - excuse the pun - dead in the water. For his hotel to survive, he needs – what's the word he would use?'

'An alternative income stream,' Les suggested.

'Yes, an alternative income stream. That's why he has latched onto the whole Isaac anniversary thing. It has nothing to do with the Dancing Couple, it's about saving his hotel. In other words, it's good for business.'

'That's an interesting analysis Audrey,' Philippa replied. 'If you're right, it means we are in a position to demand concessions from him, but what?'

The discussion continued for another hour, as they veered between one idea and another, before finally agreeing on what they should demand in return for their co-operation.

***

The scene when Jim arrived at the High Street the following day took him completely by surprise. The banners were gone, and there was no sign of the bucket collectors. Situated prominently in the path was a large poster announcing the closure of the Pump Room, and referring all enquiries to a local number, which Jim assumed was the hotel. Does this mean Jason has apologised and offered compensation to all those infected, he wondered?

It was a bright, sunny day and yet the building that once had been the lifeblood of the village – and whatever he might think of the rabid commercialism behind it –had brought pleasure and comfort to many locals and visitors, Now, it stood desolate and forlorn. 'Not for long,' he whispered.

He rang Jason that morning and said he and his friends had considered his proposal and were ready to talk. When arrived at the hotel, Jason was seated at the same table on the terrace alone.

'Jim, welcome. Do have a seat. Katie will be joining us shortly. She was called to the reception to deal with a guest who was querying their bill. Ah, here she is.'

'Jim, good of you to come back so quickly, we're very grateful.' Katie said, slipping into the seat next to Jason.

There was no coffee pot on the table nor any offer of refreshments. This was going to be strictly a business meeting Jim presumed, settling into his seat.

'I suggest on this occasion it's for you to share your thoughts with us,' Jason suggested.

'I notice the Pump Room is all locked up, is that right?'

'Yes, Katie's doing' he said squeezing her hand. 'That particular venture had run its course and it was the right moment to bring it to an end. If there is nothing there to see, there's nothing for the media to get excited about. So, I ate humble pie, apologised to all those who had suffered and offered to meet any reasonable out-of-pocket expenses.'

'Good for you.' Jim paused, savouring the anxious look on Jason face as he waited for a response to his proposal. 'As to your offer to celebrate the birth of Isaac Stein, in principle, we are prepared to take the lead in organising the event. We would have to consult the Stein Foundation to ensure we are not over-lapping with anything they have planned, but…'

'I don't think there will be any problem with the Stein Foundation, do you Katie dear,' he said giving her a knowing look.

'Neither do I, but we must have their approval for anything we are proposing.'

'Yes, of course. Anything else?'

'Yes, Jason. We would like the Pump Room to be transformed into a Visitor's Centre, under a Charitable Trust, and for you to meet the cost of the conversion,' he paused waiting for a reaction. Jason stared at him for several moments, before Katie nudged him. 'Okay, yes we will meet the cost of the conversion. Anything else?'

'Yes, Brenda and the other two ladies to be paid while the Pump Room is being converted and employed in the Visitor's Centre once it is up and running.'

'Do you think I', made of money.' Jason's went red and his hands made a tight fist on the table.

But it was Katie who spoke next. 'That's only fair. After all none of this was their fault and they shouldn't be expected to be penalised for what happened. Their wages will be paid while the Pump Room is being converted plus suitable jobs once the Visitor Centre is up and running. How's that?'

'Good, thank you. I leave you to tell Brenda and team the good news.'

'Is that all?' Jason asked through gritted teeth.

'We'll need to discuss the details, once we have formulated our plans for the celebration – how the Trust is to be managed, how we promote the village as the birthplace of Isaac Stein. That sort of thing, but for now, that's all. I think we can shake on it.'

'Yes, let's do that,' Jason said rising from his seat and extending his hand. Katie came around the table, gave him a hug and whispered in his ear, 'Just friends, okay?'

'We should seal the deal with a glass of champagne, but it's a bit early. Maybe next time when we are all together and finalised the details.'

'Yes, Jason we will look forward to working in partnership with you.'

With the formalities settled, Jim got up from the table and headed for the hotel lobby. As he moved out of earshot, Jason turned to Katie. 'I think he is in for a surprise.'

'Let's hope it goes well. Our future depends on it.'

After the bright sunshine of the terrace, it took a moment for Jim to adjust to the relative gloom of the lobby. When he could see clearly, he became aware of a familiar figure hanging around the reception. 'They told me you might be here,' Robin said moving away from the desk and facing him.

'This is a surprise,' Jim replied. 'I wasn't expecting to see you here. I thought...'

'Well, yes. I've booked into the hotel for a couple of days.'

'Oh, right.' Jim replied, not sure why Robin was here unless Jason had invited her, confident of what his response would be, and knowing he and Robin would need to talk about the celebration they were planning.

'Can we talk Jim?' Robin asked.

'Yes, we need to. I've just come from discussing with Jason an idea to celebrate Isaac's...'

'If that's all you want to talk about.'

Yes, no...'

'You left several messages on my phone saying we should talk.'

'Yes, did... I do.'

'I'm and ready to talk if you are. So, why don't we go up to my room and... well, you know.'

Jim needed no further bidding, taking her outstretched hand, he could hear *There's No Land Like Dixieland For Me* from Bix ringing in his ear.

Acknowledgements

There have been many friends and family
involved in bringing this story to
to a successful conclusion
if there are errors, they
are mine and
a mine only

But to all
Thank you

Printed in Poland
by Amazon Fulfillment
Poland Sp. z o.o., Wrocław

60266342R00176